DEATH ON THE SAPPHIRE

DEATH ON THE SAPPHIRE

A LADY FRANCES FFOLKES MYSTERY

R. J. Koreto

CROOKED
LANE

NEW YORK

Published in the United States by Crooked Lane Books, an imprint of The Quick Brown Fox & Company LLC.

Crooked Lane Books and its logo are trademarks of The Quick Brown Fox & Company LLC.

Library of Congress Catalog-in-Publication data available upon request.

ISBN (hardcover): 978-1-62953-590-6
ISBN (paperback): 978-1-62953-591-3
ISBN (ePub): 978-1-62953-592-0
ISBN (Kindle): 978-1-62953-663-7
ISBN (ePDF): 978-1-62953-674-3

Cover design by Andy Ruggirello
Book design by Jennifer Canzone

Printed in the United States.

www.crookedlanebooks.com

Crooked Lane Books
2 Park Avenue, 10th Floor
New York, NY 10016

First Edition: June 2016

10 9 8 7 6 5 4 3 2 1

To my daughters, Katie and Sophie, who
are as good and brave as Lady Frances

ACKNOWLEDGMENTS

I am fortunate in having been able to work with an excellent team, without whom there would be no book. Many thanks are due to my indefatigable agent, Cynthia Zigmund, for her perseverance and wise suggestions over the years. And no writer has been luckier with his publisher: thanks to the wonderful people at Crooked Lane Books—Matt Martz, Dan Weiss, Sarah Poppe, and Lindsey Rose—for their editing acumen, patience, and humor throughout the process.

And finally, thanks also to my family for their unwavering support as I sat on the couch night after night writing away. Most of all, thanks to my wife, Elizabeth, for years of support and never doubting that my novel would be published.

CHAPTER 1

London, 1906

The surprising coda to the tragic death of Major Daniel "Danny" Colcombe, a restless war hero, capped what was already an especially busy day for Lady Frances Ffolkes. The morning had been taken up writing a speech on women's suffrage in her capacity as chair of the outreach committee of the League for Women's Political Equality. Next was following up on arrangements for the Ladies' Christian Relief Guild soup kitchen in the East End. She had also made an appointment for what would no doubt be a tedious meeting with Henry Wheaton, the family solicitor—ever since moving out of the family home and into Miss Plimsoll's Residence Hotel for Ladies, she had started taking care of her own finances. A dull task, but rather liberating nonetheless for an independent woman.

But moving out hadn't meant cutting ties, and she had just finished dining with her brother and sister-in-law. The three were relaxing in the drawing room of the Ffolkes house in London. Cook had made several dishes Lady Frances especially favored in honor of her visit, and now Frances sipped a little port, feeling good about all she had accomplished that day and well rewarded to be lounging in comfort with close family.

It was so delightful to see Charles and Mary exchanging fond looks three months after their wedding. That Frances had introduced them to each other pleased her on several levels: a loving wife for her dear brother, a devoted husband for her great friend Mary—plus the fact that Frances was now able to resign her job of running the family household. She had done it with great efficiency, as she did all her tasks, but did not particularly like it. Mary, by contrast, stepped cheerfully into the role of marchioness, happily managing the Seaforth estate with both pleasure and competence. As Charles, the consummate diplomat, would put it, everyone won.

Charles was talking enthusiastically about politics, as his father used to before him. His marriage wasn't the only thing making him happy—with the twentieth century barely begun, the Liberals were back in power in Parliament, and the new prime minister had given him the much-coveted position as Undersecretary for European Affairs.

Cumberland, the butler, entered the room. No doubt he'd start clearing, and soon Frances would collect her maid from downstairs and head to her rooms at Miss Plimsoll's.

"I beg your pardon, my lord, my ladies," he said. "But Miss Colcombe has called."

"Miss Colcombe? Kat Colcombe? She's downstairs—at this hour?" asked Charles.

"Yes, my lord. She indicated it was a matter of great urgency."

"It must be. Show her up at once."

"Very good, my lord."

Mary and Frances looked at each other. Kat's older brother, Daniel, had been one of Charles's closest friends. They had served together in the Boer War in South Africa, and he had died about two months ago in what was officially listed as an "accident" but some called suicide—although Charles refused to hear of that possibility.

Cumberland ushered Kat into the drawing room. She was still wearing full mourning, an elaborate and awkward black dress, and her hair was in disarray—a striking contrast to Mary and Frances, who were wearing the latest styles in dress and had their long hair done up perfectly by skilled maids.

Kat looked around the room, and before anyone could move, she ran and practically threw herself at Frances, bursting into tears.

"Oh Franny, it's just too awful. It's the final blow."

"Here, my love, have some port. Steady yourself," said Frances. She held the glass while Kat sipped it, as tears poured down her smooth cheeks. The poor girl really was quite young, and it was just her and her mother bearing the brunt as chief mourners.

"You're so kind . . . I feel like such a fool, but there was nowhere else to go, and I couldn't wait until tomorrow."

"Just relax, you're with friends now," said Charles, showing a comforting smile that had charmed everyone from foreign diplomats to young ladies of society. Gradually, Kat calmed down, still holding onto Frances. The eminently practical Mary had realized that the wan Kat probably hadn't eaten recently and asked Cook to send up a tray with toast and butter, plum cake, and tea.

"No man was dearer to me than your brother," said Charles after Kat had eaten a little. "If there is any way I can help, you must let me know. I've always told you that."

"This is going to sound so silly. I don't have to tell you how hard the war hit him, but in recent months—until he died—he had seemed better in many ways. He had been writing a great deal, alone in his study. And one evening just a few weeks before he died, he said to me that if anything happened to him, I was to take the manuscript to you and see about publishing it. It was a war memoir, something he said was important. That scared me, I have to say, but he said it was just a precaution."

Charles nodded. "He hadn't said how far he had gotten, but he had mentioned to me and some of the other lads that he was putting something together."

"Actually, he told me he was almost done," said Kat, "And I agreed to his request, of course, thinking he was being a little dramatic."

Then Danny had died, and in the grief and confusion, she had forgotten. First the police sealed off the study. Then, after they were done, the solicitors had taken over the room to organize the estate's paperwork. It was only then that Kat had remembered the manuscript.

"I knew there had been gossip about my brother's writing, so the police might've been looking for it, but it seems it had already disappeared," she said with a sniffle. "He showed me where it was kept—on a shelf apart from other items. When I went to get it yesterday morning, it wasn't there. There were hundreds of pages—it couldn't be easily missed." She had searched diligently and followed up with the police and solicitors, but they both were clear they had taken nothing.

"He asked me for a promise—and I let him down. I feel like I've lost him again." And out came a fresh wave of tears.

Time to stop this, thought Frances. Kat was too young to be handling this, and her mother, Mrs. Colcombe, was a kind but vague woman who had been taken care of by her father, then her husband, and then her son.

"A fresh pair of eyes will help," said Frances. "Here is what will happen. I will return with you tonight and stay over. And I'll bring my maid Mallow." The Colcombe household might still be in disarray, and an extra servant could be helpful. "Tomorrow we'll have a look at the study together and see what we can find."

Mary looked on with sympathy and Charles with relief. His little sister could be maddeningly unconventional and stubborn, but you could always count on her in a crisis.

"Oh would you, Franny? That would be so wonderful."

Arrangements were quickly made. A footman was sent to inform the Colcombe coachman that they'd be leaving soon. Mallow, who was chatting with her fellow servants downstairs, was recalled, and Mary telephoned the Colcombe household to say Kat would be returning with a friend and maid.

Frances kissed Charles and Mary good-bye and promised to keep them informed, and then they were on their way. Kat and Frances sat next to each other in the coach, and Mallow sat opposite. Emotional exhaustion quickly hit Kat, who fell asleep on Frances's shoulder.

"Mallow, Miss Colcombe has some problems she'd like me to help her with and is not entirely well. We will be spending the night at her house. I've asked the coachman to stop at Miss Plimsoll's so you can pack an overnight bag for both of us."

"Very good, my lady." Perfectly agreeable, even cheerful, in the face of change.

"Did you have a nice evening downstairs with your old friends?"

"Yes, thank you, my lady. It's always pleasant to see them again."

"But they don't call you 'June' anymore, do they? You are now 'Miss Mallow.'"

Mallow preened. "Yes, my lady. It takes a little getting used to."

And you love it, thought Frances. It had been quite a promotion for Mallow when Frances had elevated her from housemaid to lady's maid upon their relocation to Miss Plimsoll's, with an increase in wages to match her new job. Housemaids wore uniforms and were called by their first names. They shared a room with another maid. A lady's maid wore her own plain dress and had her own room. She was called by her last name by her mistress and "Miss" by other servants. Mallow was young for such a promotion, but Frances had wanted someone she could train, as opposed to the "middle-aged dragon" her brother wanted her to hire, to watch over her, almost as a nanny.

"You won't mind sleeping tonight in whatever accommodations they have at Colcombe house?"

"Not at all, my lady." Mallow was affronted that any aspect of serving her ladyship could be a problem. Frances smiled in the dark, and Mallow mentally packed a bag so she could be in and out quickly.

Such last-minute travel changes were not usual among well-bred women. Lady Frances was the daughter of the previous Marquess of Seaforth and sister of the current one. As a young unmarried woman, her life should've been a series of afternoon visits and evening parties, but Lady Frances's life was a little more . . . unpredictable.

Kat didn't wake up even when the carriage stopped at Miss Plimsoll's and Mallow jumped out. It was only a few minutes before Mallow came back down again, and they continued to the Colcombe House.

When they arrived, Frances quickly took charge, entering the house like a bolt of lightning. Her disconcertingly frank eyes took in everything, and a knowing smile played across her sensuous face.

Mrs. Colcombe, also festooned in black, fluttered around like a little bird and was proving incapable of coping with the return of her daughter and a guest. Apparently, she hadn't even known Kat was gone until Mary had called the house. Of course, the Colcombe house, like most of the wealthy London homes, had recently installed a telephone, but women of Mrs. Colcombe's generation tended to forget about it. The call had been a shock, and she had had to get smelling salts from her maid.

Frances ordered one maid to see the sleepy Kat to bed. Then she greeted Mrs. Colcombe. "Kat was visiting and became a little unwell. I'm sure she'll be fine after some bed rest. You have been so overwhelmed, Mrs. Colcombe, I will stay the night to help in the morning."

Briskly, she gave orders to make up the little settee in Kat's room so she could spend the night with her.

"But the settee is so short, my lady," said a maid.

"So am I," said Frances with a smile.

***

A spare bed was found for Mallow with a pair of maids who, rather than being disturbed, were excited about the upheaval and curious about Mallow and her mistress. Mallow was scarcely older than they were but at a higher station—and working for the daughter of a marquess, no less.

"Rather nice of her ladyship to assist Miss Katherine like this when she's so upset," ventured one, hoping for some gossip and juicy details.

"Her ladyship's brother, the marquess, was a close friend of the late Major Colcombe. It was only natural she should come to help Mr. Colcombe's sister when she is . . . distraught."

"I'd think a nurse of some kind would be better. I mean, what good can a marquess's daughter do?"

Mallow glared at her. "Lady Frances knows many things. She has been to university," she said grandly. A lady's maid did not gossip about her mistress, but Lady Frances was proud of her education and didn't mind who knew it.

"Go on!" said the other maid. "Ladies don't go to university."

Mallow glared again. *Who do you think you are?* her eyes said. The maid turned away. "I'm sure I'm sorry, Miss Mallow," she said.

Mallow took off her dress, climbed into the makeshift bed, and extinguished the light. Tomorrow would be a busy day, if she knew anything about Lady Frances.

She remembered being like those girls when she first went to work for the old lord and lady, the parents of Lady Frances and her brother Charles. Mallow's mother had sent her into service young, noticing that her eldest daughter was quick-witted and didn't need anything explained twice. And June—Mallow was still known by her Christian name then—found herself placed in a doctor's house, thanks to a family friend who was a cook there.

The work was dull, and the small household had no other servants her age, but it was delightful to finally be always warm and well fed. Unfortunately, after a year, the doctor suddenly died and the household was to be broken up, with his widow planning to move back with her people in the country.

She had held Mallow to high standards but was not unkind. "Let's see what we can do about getting you a new place. You've been a good, hard worker and progressed very nicely here." She looked at Mallow speculatively. "You have a pretty face, and the really fine houses like a handsome housemaid. My cousin owns a coal delivery company that serves the better neighborhoods, and sometimes word about open positions in the great households gets back to him . . . I will ask and provide you with a reference."

Mallow hadn't dared hope to work in a great house! But a week later, her mistress told her there was an opening at the household of the Marquess of Seaforth and that she had already written a letter of recommendation. So Mallow ironed her one good dress and, with equal parts fear and excitement, presented herself at the servants' entrance at the Seaforth home.

She remembered the day still. The servants' hall seemed enormous, and the butler, Mr. Cumberland, was so grand and imposing, Mallow first thought he was the marquess himself.

He turned a critical eye on Mallow, and she thought he could see every small sin she had ever committed. Then he frowned and said, "Come." He led her into his private pantry while the other servants looked on curiously. Mr. Cumberland sat but left Mallow standing, and he proceeded to ask her questions about her duties. He frowned again, and Mallow thought she hadn't passed. But then he said, "Follow me."

They went up the stairs into the main foyer and then into the drawing room. The opulence astonished her; it was like something out of a fairy tale from an old illustrated book that belonged to Mallow's mother.

Mallow focused on the handsome, middle-aged woman sitting at a small desk. She was reading a sheet of paper.

"I have your reference here. Your mistress says you work hard, are of sober temperament, are careful with fine items, and learn new tasks quickly. You apparently are also talented with needle and thread. Is all this true?"

"Y-yes, my lady."

An elegant eyebrow arched up. "Why did you call me 'my lady,' child? Weren't you trained to call women of my age 'madam?'"

Mallow was dumbstruck. Had she somehow gotten it wrong and ruined her chance? "I . . . I heard the kitchen maid say she was getting the tea tray ready for 'her ladyship' and so I thought you would be 'my lady . . .'" Her voice trailed off lamely.

The marchioness gave a small smile. Mallow had first thought her eyes were hard, but now they seemed warmer, softer.

"Clever child. You are engaged. You will learn your duties from Agnes, the head housemaid. Cumberland, please explain the house rules and terms to June."

"Thank you, my lady." She had not realized she was grinning in a most inappropriate way, but it only charmed Lady Seaforth, who smiled again.

"This is your place of employment, June, but it is also your home. I wish you a long and happy stay here."

She took tea in the servants' hall that afternoon, and although Mr. Cumberland was severe, the younger servants were welcoming and even chatty. They told her the marchioness was strict but not cruel, and the marquess was very busy and took no notice of the servants, except the butler and his valet. The young lordship, Charles, was away in the army, and then there was the daughter of the house, Lady Frances, about whom everyone was a little quiet.

Indeed, the only confusing moment was when Agnes, the older maid who was to train her, asked Mr. Cumberland if June would be taking care of Lady Frances, who still lived at home.

"Why do you ask, Agnes? Is your work so onerous you are already pushing your assigned tasks onto your new junior? You will continue to care for Lady Frances as head housemaid. Is that clear?"

"Yes, Mr. Cumberland," she said. And then she muttered, "Lucky me."

Mallow didn't understand. She knew it was a mark of distinction to care for the young lady of a noble house. Why didn't Agnes want that job?

The next few weeks were spent learning her job and getting used to the pattern of life in a great house. The other maids shared gossip when Mr. Cumberland was out of earshot. She heard the young lordship, who only visited occasionally, was handsome and charming.

"But he doesn't . . . I mean . . ." Mallow had enquired. She had heard about households where young men took advantage of servant girls.

"Oh no, never here. Lord Charles is the perfect gentleman."

"Worse luck," said another, and they laughed.

"And what about Lady Frances?" That didn't get an immediate response.

"She's not your typical young lady," said one maid finally. "Runs around a lot, God knows where, and God knows with whom." Indeed, Mallow had only caught sight of her a few times, briskly walking in or out of the house. "She argues with her parents a lot."

"She argues with everyone a lot," said another.

That made Mallow curious. The other maids may indulge in impossible daydreams about marrying the young lord and becoming the next Lady Seaforth, but Mallow wanted to meet Lady Frances.

And so she did.

Late one evening Mallow was the last one in the servants' hall. Being the junior maid, she had the job of tidying everything before morning. She heard scratching outside the servants' entrance, and thinking the noise came from stray cats, she unbolted the door to reveal Lady Frances trying with little success to draw the bolt from the outside with a hatpin.

"Oh!" they both said, staring at each other.

"You must be the new girl—June, isn't it?"

"Yes, June Mallow, my lady."

"This probably seems rather odd to you." She didn't wait for an answer, which was just as well, as Mallow had no idea how to respond. "You see, I was out with friends for dinner, and we were going to see some works by an artist someone knew and hear a poet. Mother said I had to be home after dinner, but the evening was so interesting. I thought I could slip back in unnoticed." She sighed. "Cumberland will see how late I came in and tell my mother. I'll never hear the end of it. My spending allowance will be cut off for a month." She looked forlorn. "Well, there's no helping it. I'll go upstairs and see if I can talk my way out of it. Anyway, thank you, June."

She took a few steps into the servants' hall, past an astonished Mallow, then turned. "June, you know what the other servants are doing now. Could you sneak me past them into my bedroom?"

Now Mallow realized why the other maids were a little leery of Lady Frances.

"I . . . I suppose, my lady. But you can just stay here, my lady. In a little while, Mr. Cumberland and the rest will go to bed and you can slip upstairs."

"But before that happens, my mother will knock on my door. If I'm already there, I can say that I let myself in earlier through the front door and no one saw me. But if I'm not there . . . couldn't you help?"

Later, Mallow couldn't say exactly why she did it, but Lady Frances had such a pleading look, and the sense of adventure tickled her. Also, she was curious about this young lady who visited artists and poets. It had been Mallow's understanding that young ladies did nothing more than attend well-supervised parties until they found a husband.

"Just follow me, my lady."

It was indeed a bit of an adventure. Mallow told Lady Frances when to make a run for it when Cumberland's back was turned as he checked the hall clock and then when to slip past the footman the second he went into the morning room to make sure the lights were extinguished. Once upstairs, Frances thought she was clear, but before she could reach her room, Mallow suddenly grabbed her and dragged her into an unused guest bedroom.

It was hard to tell who was more surprised—Lady Frances that a servant had laid hands on her or Mallow that she had shoved a lady of the house.

In the dark room, they heard the purposeful tread of a woman leaving the room of Lady Seaforth—it was Pritchard, maid to Frances's mother.

"The tigress always lays out your mother's night clothes at this time," said Mallow.

"The tigress?" asked Frances.

Mallow flamed in embarrassment. "I beg your pardon, my lady. It is Miss Pritchard's nickname among the maids. Please don't tell—"

But Lady Frances was desperately trying to stifle her laughter. "June, that is too funny. Yes, she is as fierce and sleek as a tigress. It is perfectly fitting. But don't worry—your secret is safe."

When Pritchard was safely out of the way, the two women made a final dash for Frances's room. Clothes went flying, and Mallow quickly found a nightgown for Frances, so when her mother looked in a few minutes later, she found her daughter in her night clothes, with Mallow brushing out Frances's hair.

"Franny, why isn't Agnes tending you? And this should've been done more than an hour ago."

"I'm sorry, Mother. I was so busy writing letters I lost track of time. Then I saw June on the stairs, and she offered to help."

Lady Seaforth raised an eyebrow. There was something wrong here, but she couldn't tell what. Mallow hid her surprise that Lady Frances could lie so fluidly.

"June, I've heard good reports of you from Cumberland."

"Thank you, my lady."

"But don't let my daughter take advantage of your good nature. Good night to both of you."

Both girls went limp with relief when Lady Seaforth left.

"June, you are priceless. Now go to bed, I'll brush my own hair—although you do a fine job."

"It's quite all right, my lady. It needs a good brushing."

"I always get too bored to let Agnes finish. So never mind, it's late."

"When I'm done, my lady."

Frances spun around. She wasn't used to being thwarted, especially by a servant.

"The sooner you turn back, my lady, the sooner I'll be done and the sooner you can go to bed."

Frances started to say something—then stopped, smiled, and obeyed the maid. The brushing finished in silence.

"Thank you. You were quite right." Her copper hair gleamed as it hadn't for a while. "Thank you again—for everything. Good night."

All pink and feeling pleased with herself, Mallow went to bed. She thought that was the end of it. She didn't see Lady Frances for a few days, except coming and going. But one evening, while she was putting her clothes away in her little dresser, she found the drawer jammed, thanks to a large bag someone had stuffed in it. Astonished, she pulled out skeins of the finest wool, which she never could've afforded.

A note fluttered to the floor, and Mallow picked it up.

June,

I am sorry for involving you and thank you most deeply. I inquired with Agnes, who mentioned you enjoy knitting. I was told this is the very best wool and enough for mittens and a muf-fler to keep you warm this winter.

With thanks,
Lady F

It was a final bit of wonder. If a few coins had been left for her, that would've been kind, thought Mallow. But that Lady Frances had taken the trouble to find out what she liked and to shop for her—Mallow was inclined to believe Lady Frances was a rare one indeed.

That night had eventually led to her current position as lady's maid. She thought about Miss Garritty, lady's maid to Mary, the current Marchioness of Seaforth—Frances's friend and sister-in-law. When Mallow was promoted, Garritty had congratulated her but warned her life would not be predictable working for Lady Frances—something Mallow had already realized. Lady Frances was going to live in a sort of hotel, and everyone heard his lordship express reservation about some of the organizations Lady Frances was involved with. And not to criticize, but it seemed to Miss Garritty that Lady Frances had picked up some strange ideas and manners during her years in America. Well, America—what could you expect? "I wish you success, June, and I will say your promotion was well-deserved, but I wouldn't have your job if they doubled my pay."

Kat and Frances slept through the night. In the morning, Frances was pleased to see Kat looked refreshed.

"Thank you so much, Franny, for last night. I still feel like such a fool."

"Nonsense. Let's get dressed, have a solid breakfast, and tackle the study."

Kat smiled a little uncertainly. Frances reflected that she didn't really know her all that well. Although her brother Charles and Danny had been close, Kat was several years younger than Frances, just a girl when Frances went off to school. She hadn't realized how Kat looked up to her, so pleased to see her the next morning, giving her a hug.

Mallow came in to help Frances get dressed, and a Colcombe maid started to help Kat get into the black monstrosity that was the mourning wear.

"Miss Colcombe will not be needing that today," said Frances. "Find something simpler, in a muted color; she and I have work to do today, and she can hardly move in that garment." The maid looked a little shocked—full mourning was still indicated. She turned to Kat, who just shrugged. "Very good, my lady," said the maid with a sigh.

It was just the two of them for breakfast; Mrs. Colcombe was having hers on a tray in her room. Eggs, sausage, and toast, washed down with a lot of sugared tea, put some color into Kat's face. As they finished, Mallow, who had breakfasted in the servants' hall, joined them in the dining room.

"Ready to help, my lady," she said. It was likely no other lady's maid helped her mistress with paperwork, but this was Lady Frances.

"Very good, Mallow. Kat, lead us to the study." It was an old-fashioned room. Unlike other rooms, which had largely been changed to reflect more modern tastes, this one didn't seem to have been updated since Danny's late father had been a young man. The furniture was dark and heavy, including a large desk and cabinets and shelves that ran from floor to ceiling around most of the room.

Kat explained the organization of the room. "My brother was very particular and explained it to me the week before he . . ." She took a breath and then described the layout: Business files and correspondences were in the desk and filing cabinets right next to it. The solicitors took most of that away. Personal items, such as letters from friends and many other manuscripts, were opposite the desk.

"It was right here," said Kat, showing her a blank space.

"Are you sure? There seem to be so many manuscripts on the shelf."

"Yes. It was that spot, set a little aside. As for the rest of these—" She laughed lightly. "In recent months, he had the idea of getting involved in theater, perhaps producing plays. He had friends who were writers and artists, and he was collecting plays to see if something amused him. Mother was horrified."

"I'm sure she was," said Frances. It was fine to attend plays, but theatrical work was not quite respectable. "I know Charles mentioned it to me, and he encouraged it. He was pleased to see Danny take an interest in something. Anyway, we have our work cut out for us. We're going to search every inch of this office. Kat, look at that side. Mallow, over there. I'll look here." The three women began, sorting through whatever papers were still in the office.

"You sound so . . . organized," said Kat admiringly.

"I've pored over manuscripts in libraries and sought out obscure books on shelves when I was at college," she said. Kat looked even more impressed.

They worked in silence for a while, carefully reviewing each sheet of paper but not finding any sign of the missing manuscript. However, at one point, Mallow came over to Frances.

"I found something, my lady, stuck between what seems to be a pile of statements from Major Colcombe's wine merchant."

She paused, to make sure Kat was absorbed in her own papers and not paying attention. "There were a lot of them, my lady." Mallow came from a family that frowned on drink, but Frances was aware that Danny, like his father before him, appreciated fine wine.

Frances looked over the torn scrap of paper Mallow handed her. It was clearly not a liquor bill—perhaps it had been shoved into the untidy pile by accident. The heavy ecru paper was commonly used in law offices, Frances knew from her own dealings with solicitors. And the beautiful, masculine handwriting could only have come from a well-trained clerk: "Confirmation of transfer of £500 from the account of Daniel Colcombe to the account of D. Trega—"

It was a pity that so much had been torn away—it might've had the solicitors' name and address and the rest of the payee's name. Danny probably had meant to just read the confirmation and then throw it out after tearing it up. But one part got shuffled into his wine merchant accounts instead of the wastepaper basket.

"Good find, Mallow. If we hadn't searched, it would've been disposed of with these old bills." She stepped over to where Kat was working. "I found a mention here of someone who may have been a friend of your brother's, D. Trega. Maybe 'Tregallis,' an old Cornish name."

"Danny had a lot of friends," she said, and then turned a little pink. "A lot of lady friends." He certainly did, thought Frances. "There was also Captain Dennis, but his surname was Burden. And when he came back from South Africa, he had a nurse named Dorothy. Nurse Dot, we called her. But her surname was Jones, not Tregallis. And neither was Cornish."

Frances decided to keep the paper for now. The office search yielded nothing else. Frances then marched everyone up to Charles's bedroom, but it was very spare, and a search there showed nothing either.

"I'm so sorry to have put you to all this trouble," said Kat.

"I didn't expect to find anything," said Frances. "I just wanted to be sure." Frances had wanted to assume that Kat had simply been confused, but the manuscript was quite obviously gone.

"We are going to sit and be logical," said Frances, and the two women followed her lead and took a chair. Mallow was used to that expression from Lady Frances, which Frances had picked up from a philosophy professor at college.

"We can conclude the manuscript did not disappear while Daniel was still alive, or he would've said something. So it disappeared after his death. But how soon? Kat, when was the last time we are sure the manuscript was seen? I know this brings back unpleasant memories, but we need to establish that."

Kat thought silently, and Frances was grateful she was mastering herself and not getting upset.

"I never went into the study after that day when Charles showed me the manuscript."

"Very well. Have you spoken to any of the servants—to your butler, Bellman?"

"Bellman? No. You mean he might—?"

"Servants know all kinds of things. Could you ring for him?"

Bellman had been in Colcombe service for a long time. Too long. He walked slowly and a little stiffly. But his back was straight and his eyes still seemed sharp. The master's violent death had probably hit him very hard. Frances wondered if it might be time for a dignified and pleasant retirement—perhaps a cottage in the country on Colcombe land.

"Bellman, Lady Frances is helping me find Mr. Daniel's manuscript. As I mentioned yesterday, it has gone missing."

"And I am very sorry for that, miss."

"Oh, no one blames you. But you can help."

But there was no need for a crowd, concluded Frances. "Mallow, why don't you take Miss Colcombe back to her room? Go through her clothes with her and choose several sober outfits for around the house. Then call my dressmaker and arrange for her to come here so she can measure Miss Colcombe for a new black outfit, dignified but simple and suitable to receive callers in."

Kat looked a little surprised but said nothing.

"Yes, my lady," said Mallow.

"I will speak with Bellman."

Mallow and Kat left, and then Frances caused another shock by asking the elderly man to sit. Servants did not sit in the presence of their employers or their employers' guests.

"But, Bellman, as you see, I am rather short, and it is difficult to talk up to you," she said with what she hoped was a welcoming smile. Bellman rewarded her with a ghost of a smile too and then perched on a chair, trying not to make himself too comfortable.

There was nothing wrong with the man's memory. After the police were done, he had taken a look around the room and had particularly noted the manuscript. He was sure, because Major Daniel had made it clear that the maids were not to touch anything on the "personal" shelves, not even to dust. Major Daniel said he didn't want those papers disturbed, and at the time, Bellman had made a particular note of the manuscript.

"And my eye went to it, my lady, I am sure of that. Usually, Major Daniel only had a few letters there. But that large manuscript could not be missed."

"When was the last time you saw it?"

"May fifteenth, my lady."

"How can you be so sure of the date?"

"The solicitors were very formal, my lady. They needed Mrs. Colcombe to sign papers acknowledging that they were done with Major Daniel's room. Two witnesses were needed, and Mrs. Habbers—our cook—and I served in that capacity."

Poor Kat. It hadn't occurred to her to ask Bellman, who could've reassured her that neither the police nor solicitors had removed it. The advantages of a college education—Frances hadn't been allowed to say, "I don't know." She was sent to the college library until she did know.

Bellman had made sure the manuscript was still in the personal section when the solicitors had left. He had locked the door and told both Mrs. Colcombe and Miss Katherine he had the key should they ever want access to the room. The key was kept in his pantry, but no one asked for it until earlier in the week, when Miss Katherine requested it and, as he found later, the manuscript was missing.

"What did you think happened to it?"

"I couldn't say, my lady. A professional thief, perhaps, though nothing of value was removed from this house at any time."

"Could one of the servants have taken it?"

Bellman seemed a little ruffled at that, thought a moment, and said, "They have all been with us some years and have good characters. Besides, my lady, the manuscript had no financial value. Its loss only disturbs the family." He paused. "We are all very fond of them, my lady."

It was a matter of reasoning. Danny's writings disappeared between May 15 and June 20, when Kat walked into the room. It was possible someone from the outside had broken into the house and then into the study, but breaking into an occupied house was no easy feat. And Frances had noticed that the study windows were well bolted. She always saw things like that. The way her eyes would dart around had driven her nannies and governesses mad, but for Frances, it had just been a way to relieve boredom. Her mother had once cheerfully asked her father, "Dear, you're in the Foreign Office, and as Frances seems to notice everything, couldn't you get her a job as a spy?"

So if servants and burglars were ruled out, that meant the manuscript was taken by someone who had been admitted to the house. Frances had no illusions about that study door lock. It was a worn, old-fashioned piece of hardware, like one she remembered in her grandfather's house. At age fifteen, her cousin

Stephen had managed to pick it and sample the good brandy. For the boy's sake, Frances had hoped it had been worth the beating grandfather had administered. No, a lock like that would keep out someone casual, but not someone determined.

"Just one more thing, Bellman. Would it be possible to assemble a list of people who visited the house during this period? That is, after the master's death but before Miss Katherine noted it missing?"

Bellman sighed. "I'm afraid, my lady, that that the house was in something of a turmoil in the days and weeks following the master's death. Large numbers of people came and went, often to pay their respects to Miss Katherine or the mistress, and it was hard to keep track of everyone. At times, things were a little more . . . informal than expected." He thought for a minute. "Major Daniel led a somewhat unceremonious life, my lady, and we adjusted accordingly. Indeed, it was the master's practice to receive late-night visitors by opening the door himself, and I'm afraid that set a certain tone." He sounded a little aggrieved that things should be so. No doubt when Danny's father had been alive, it had not been so.

Frances saw her nice system crumbling. There was no telling who came and went. Frances had long known Danny Colcombe—this casual life was not all that surprising and no doubt had put its stamp on the way the house was run. She imagined a steady stream of people coming in and out of the house, with Kat letting people in herself, or more likely guests themselves letting other guests come and go, with the aged Bellman unable to keep up or even keep track. It would be easy for someone to sneak away, pick the lock quickly, and grab the manuscript.

She stood, and Bellman creakily stood too. "Thank you, Bellman. You have been very helpful."

"I am glad to be of service, my lady. And if I may be so bold, thank you, on behalf of the staff, for helping Miss Katherine in these difficult times."

Bellman went about his duties elsewhere in the house, and Frances stayed a while longer in the room. Very well, a little setback, but not a fatal one. She closed her eyes and found herself back in her old dormitory room. *It could be anyone, couldn't it? No, it would have to be someone who knew the house and where to find the manuscript, not a casual thief. Someone who knew the family, a friend, or at least an acquaintance. Someone who had been there before . . .*

Upstairs, Kat and Mallow had made great progress in the brief time. Mallow had identified three outfits that, while not actually passing a test for "mourning," were somber enough for wearing around the house. And her ladyship's dressmaker would be coming around tomorrow. God knows what ancient and unfashionable establishment Mrs. Colcombe patronized for herself and her daughter. Kat seemed at peace.

"Your butler was of great help, and now I just need a few more things from you."

"Do you think you can find it?"

"I will have to do a little research." She saw pen and paper on a small desk in the bedroom. "Kat, you and I are going to make a list of everyone who came to the funeral."

It took about an hour, recalling names. It became a sort of game, because Frances's sharp eyes had taken in faces, which she described to Kat, who often could put a name to them, such as brother officers, old school friends, more Bohemian types, and so on. It wasn't absolutely complete, of course, but very good. Kat had fully cooperated but seemed rather mystified. No matter, thought Frances.

One man stood out in particular in Frances's memory, a middle-aged man in a somewhat wrinkled suit that no decent valet would've let out of the house. Frances had assumed he was one of Danny's friends from a less fashionable part of town, but although the man watched everyone keenly, besides a quick murmur of sympathy, he had seemingly spoken to no one. Kat remembered him too but had no idea who he was.

"We'll put him down as Mr. Rumpled for now," said Frances, and Kat giggled. They finished the list, then made an extra copy—Kat didn't ask why and Frances didn't explain.

"And now, Kat, we're going to take our leave. But I'll keep you informed." Kat showered Frances with gratitude, and Frances realized it was as much for the companionship as for the help with the manuscript. She resolved to visit again soon and knew that Mary would be pleased to come as well.

"I am glad we can help, Kat. Your brother . . . well, Danny was special to all of us." She paused. "He was special to me."

Then she turned to her maid. "Come, Mallow. Time for more research." She was full of energy. Yes, she'd need help, but she knew the right direction.

Bellman had found them a hansom cab and helped the women into it.

"Please take us to Scotland Yard," she said to the driver.

"I beg your pardon, miss?"

"Scotland Yard, the headquarters of the Metropolitan Police Service," she said. "Surely you know where that is?"

"Yes, of course, Miss. Straightaway." Fancy that, this young woman, a real lady, he could tell, asking to go to Scotland Yard. Wait till he told the missus tonight . . .

As the cab started up, Lady Frances leaned back and smiled at Mallow. "We did a good morning's work. And won't Superintendent Maples be delighted to see me again."

CHAPTER 2

Unaware that Lady Frances was about to descend on him, Superintendent Maples was feeling rather satisfied. A sharp-eyed constable had stopped a burglary in progress overnight, leading to the arrest of a gang of thieves that had been plaguing small shopkeepers. The assistant commissioner had gone more than twenty-four hours without sending him one of his vague, rambling memorandums. And he was drinking a very nice cup of tea and eating a fresh bun.

Sergeant Cardiff knocked and entered. "Those statistics that you wanted, sir."

"Thank you, Sergeant."

"Also, sir, Lady Frances Ffolkes is in the outer office. She would like a word with you, if it is convenient."

The superintendent choked on his bun. He looked up at Cardiff—was that a smile? No, Cardiff had no sense of humor, at least none Maples could detect. But the morning had collapsed now, his tea-and-bun break in ruins.

"And her maid, sir."

"What about her maid?"

"She's accompanied by her maid, sir."

"That's a new one. Did she favor you with the reason she's come here?"

"She told me it was to report a crime, sir."

"Really? Does she seem upset?"

"No, sir."

Further questioning revealed that Sergeant Cardiff had advised Lady Frances to report any alleged crime to the appropriate station. Indeed, he had promised to look up the address for her, even see her into a hansom so she could go there herself. But nothing would do except a conversation with the superintendent in person. Maples sighed. He could say he was busy, but she was patient and persistent. She'd wait. She'd come back. She'd go to the assistant commissioner, the commissioner himself— even the home secretary, the cabinet minister who oversaw all police functions.

Might as well get it over with. "Here—get rid of this damn tea and bun." He shoved them at his sergeant. He stood up, brushed the crumbs off his uniform, and straightened his jacket and tie. "And show her in."

In the outer office, Frances and Mallow sat on unpadded wooden chairs. Frances didn't mind waiting; it was interesting being in a bustling office, men running around, the clacking sound of typewriting machines. They were most interesting devices; Frances considered buying one and seeing if she could engage a professional typist to teach her how to use it. Telephones would ring, and men would shout into them. A few glanced her way; she was not the typical Scotland Yard visitor.

Mallow, on the other hand, was deeply unhappy. Where she came from, no good ever came from police involvement. Respectable people never had anything to do with the police, except maybe a brief greeting to the "bobby" on the corner. She'd done and seen a lot of things with her ladyship, but to be in a police station . . . She was sure his lordship, her ladyship's brother, would be very displeased with this.

But then again, trying to enter into Lady Frances's enthusiasm, she did reason that this wasn't a common police station.

This was the headquarters of all the police, her ladyship had explained. And they were seeing someone very important—a superintendent, her ladyship had said, not a common bobby. He might even be a gentleman. Less a policeman, in fact, than "someone in government." Mallow had only a vague idea of what it meant to be "in government," except that Lord Seaforth was in government, and he was a marquess—perfectly respectable. So this might be acceptable. But she still hoped to leave as soon as possible.

The sergeant with the pleasant face came back to tell Frances that Superintendent Maples would see her now. He asked if he could get her a cup of tea, but she graciously declined. He turned to Mallow. "And you, miss? Would you like a cuppa while you wait?" Mallow was surprised and flattered that she was noticed and said yes, thank you, that would be very nice.

Maples forced a smile on his face and greeted Lady Frances as Cardiff showed her to a chair and then left, quietly closing the door behind him.

"A pleasure as always, Lady Frances."

"My pleasure, too, Superintendent. You have been so helpful in the past, I knew I had to see you again." She remembered the first time she had argued her way into his office: The streets around the mission where they set up their soup kitchen were so dangerous, some people were afraid to come. Couldn't additional officers be deployed? A few weeks later, emboldened, Frances had returned. While organizing a peaceful political meeting in the park, she and her friends had been heckled and jeered. Couldn't the superintendent read them the Riot Act? The third time she came, it was to complain that his officers were harassing beggars who had drifted too close to well-heeled areas looking for richer handouts.

"I'm not a lawyer, Superintendent, but I do not think it is actually a crime to be poor."

And now she was back again—regarding a crime, it seemed.

"I understand you are here about a crime. I hope your ladyship has not been a victim."

"Not at all, but thank you for your concern." She smiled. "I
am here about a family friend, Major Daniel Colcombe, who
died in an accident about two months back. It seems an important manuscript of his was stolen from his house shortly after
his death."

So that's what this was. And next, he'd be asked to help find
the Duchess of Something's lost lap dog. He vaguely recalled the
Colcombe case—not something he was directly involved with,
but a minor scandal nonetheless. Colcombe was a war hero, a
member of Society. But it was just some clumsiness with firearms.

"It's probably just missing," he said. "After his family gets
around to fully cleaning out his rooms, I'm sure it will turn up."

"And that is exactly what I thought," said Lady Frances
brightly. She knew this was going to be an uphill battle, and
on the way over, she had rehearsed in her mind exactly what to
say to the superintendent, who could be, she had found, a little
resistant to change.

She quickly launched into a description of the search they had
conducted, the security situation at the house, the unlikelihood
the manuscript had casually disappeared, and her theory that the
thief had been someone who had shown up at the funeral. She
produced a list. She was brief and to the point. "We put marks
next to names of people we didn't know very well. I wrote out
two copies, one for me to hold and one for you."

Maples looked at the list and frowned. This was not what
he expected from a civilian. Lady Frances's account was organized and coherent, and her procedure for looking for the
manuscript and conclusions made a lot of sense. He reviewed
the names.

"So you see, Superintendent, I believe that the manuscript was
stolen and wish to pursue the theft with the correct authorities."

There. She had made a clear, concise case, and she flattered herself that Maples had been impressed.

"Have you thought about why someone would steal such a manuscript?"

"Perhaps he discussed things that other people did not want made public? But without seeing the manuscript, it's just a guess."

This was a more complicated problem than it had initially appeared—Lady Frances, he had to admit, had made a very good start. Fortunately, although it was a difficult problem to solve, it was also easy to get rid of. He could simply send her to the officer who was handling that case.

"Would you like to speak with the inspector who investigated the accident? He'd be the best person."

"Yes, that would be very helpful, thank you." Frances felt very pleased with herself. She could see that Maples, in the course of their professional relationship, was beginning to respect her. As they had discussed in their suffragist meetings, many men would learn to respect women once they saw they could act reasonably, as opposed to the way so many men falsely assumed—merely emotional creatures, slaves of their whims.

Maples rang for Sergeant Cardiff and then told him to call the relevant station and find the inspector who had handled the Colcombe accident. When he left, Maples leaned back, feeling generous and expansive. No reason not to be complimentary and build some good feeling, especially as she deserved it.

"Your account and handling of the problem was very good, Lady Frances. Clean and organized." Then he overdid it, to his regret. "I wish all my men were so well organized."

"Really? How kind of you to say. I had wondered if perhaps there might be a place for women in the Metropolitan Police Service." What an exciting concept! Imagine that—women police constables. "Can I make a formal proposal to open the police force to women?"

Oh God. "Actually, that's out of my hands. Only the commissioner or even the home secretary can make such a radical change."

"Of course, Superintendent. I will write them—and will be sure to mention your support." Frances smiled at him—and rather enjoyed the look of horror on his face. "But then again, it might be best if I approached the officials on my own."

Sergeant Cardiff returned again, clutching a piece of paper. If Maples didn't know better, however, he'd have said that Cardiff was showing emotion again—he looked confused.

"Sir, I have the name of the inspector in charge."

"Just give it to Lady Frances, then. I'm sure she's quite busy and will want to be on her way." This conversation had gone on long enough and was getting dangerous.

"I'd like you to look first, sir," he said. He glanced quickly at Frances, then placed the paper in front of the superintendent. There was no missing the shock on Maples's face. He mastered it in seconds, but too late for Frances's quick eye.

"Are you sure about this, Cardiff?"

"Yes, sir. I called again to confirm."

He was stunned. Could this manuscript theft be really serious? Or was there something else? Yes, Lady Frances had made a good report, but could she really have stumbled on . . .

Anyway, not his problem. Cardiff's information made that much clear. The sergeant cleared his throat. "They did say, sir, that if Lady Frances would leave her card, they would contact her."

Frances took in every word of the exchange and the tone. She would've given a lot to know what was written on the paper Cardiff had passed to the superintendent. But she knew it was time to take what she had and leave. She could always come back, and she told Maples she would, if the inspector proved unable to contact her. Maples, for his part, pretended the oddness hadn't happened, and Frances let him pretend.

"I'm sure you'll hear shortly. A pleasure, as always, Lady Frances. Cardiff, please see them out and help them into a hansom."

Fancy that, thought Maples, when the women had left. No doubt they'd contact her. That amused him to no end. The thought of Lady Frances and that bunch . . . he chuckled himself back into good humor.

When Cardiff returned from seeing the women on their way, Maples had him fetch another cup of tea and a fresh bun.

<hr />

"I think we've made very good progress," said Frances on the ride home. "We should hear from the inspector in charge soon. I'm sure, with the resources of Scotland Yard, he'll be able to track down whoever took it." Of course, whoever took it might've destroyed it, but she was staying positive—perhaps they took it to blackmail someone or to study it in detail.

That last exchange between Superintendent Maples and Sargent Cardiff at the end of her meeting had been awfully strange. There was an odd secretiveness and confusion surrounding a seemingly simple process—looking up the inspector in charge. But the explanation would make itself clear later, no doubt.

"Will you still be going to the soup kitchen this evening, my lady?"

"Yes. It's been a long day, but I don't want to let them down. I promised."

Miss Plimsoll's had a phone in a small private parlor for residents' use. She called Mary to tell her what had happened. Mary agreed poor Kat could use some companionship and said she would visit. Then Frances called Charles at his office and told him as well. He was a little alarmed that she had descended on a senior Scotland Yard official.

"Oh, we're old friends, the superintendent and I," said Frances. "He has been most helpful when I've called on him in the past."

"I'm sure," said Charles dryly. "But do remember that this is now a police matter, and they don't appreciate amateur inter- ference." Then he laughed. "Consider how Inspector Lestrade resents Sherlock Holmes's interference."

"Very funny, dear brother."

"I thought so. Now, before this happened, I asked you to come to the party at Sir Lytton Moore's. Lady Moore always asks after you; she's known you since you were in short dresses. I know it's not your favorite type of event, but do say you'll come."

"Very well," she said. It would please Charles and Mary, and Lady Moore was a good soul. Also London Society was really quite small, and this would be a political event. Frances assumed she would speak with the mysterious inspector before the party and that she could convince him to share some names of those possibly involved in the Colcombe case. One or more of those "names" might be at the party. She'd reach into the back of the closet with Mallow and pick out a suitable evening dress.

But for now, she had Mallow lay out her plainest dress and a pair of solid shoes that were unfashionable but comfortable. She'd be on her feet most of the evening. They had lunch at Miss Plimsoll's—Mallow in the servants' hall and Frances in the dining room. Mallow had told Frances that the food was not quite as good as at the Seaforth house, but it was acceptable. And better yet, servants sat according to the rank of their mis- tresses, and as Lady Frances was a marquess's daughter, that gave Mallow a perk downstairs, which pleased her immensely. As Frances's mother had said, no one was more snobbish than a superior servant.

In the main room, Frances sat at a table for one and had brought a novel, as she always did when dining alone. After- ward, she took a little nap; it was going to be an active night.

The East End after dark was no place for a woman to walk alone, especially one who wasn't raised to be aware of the grim neighborhood's many dangers. So she met her friend Eleanor, and they shared a hansom together to the mission.

The mission soup kitchen had been the first charity she had become involved with after returning from America. It was a typical choice for progressive-minded young women, and she had originally joined because her mother's friend had been involved with the charity. But the first time she had gone, she barely finished the evening. The lines of sick, hungry people in their ragged clothes both frightened and disgusted her. She had been put right on table duty, and with a trembling arm, she served bowls of stew from a cauldron in the mission hall. The steam soaked her face and sweat poured down from her brow, stinging her eyes. After half an hour, the smell of the greasy food began to sicken her, and the lines never seemed to end.

But she had finished the evening before collapsing on a wooden bench, and Mrs. Ellwood, who ran the mission, put a comforting arm around her.

"You did well this evening," she said.

"How can . . . I never knew . . ." Frances responded.

"It's a hard question. And I stopped asking it long ago. It happens, and that's all I need to know. All we can do is try to make it better."

Mrs. Ellwood didn't expect her to return again—and in fact, she almost didn't. She sat in her room, thinking about that hall and the sounds and smells of desperation. All your lofty ideas, she thought bitterly, just that. Just ideas. Ring for the maid, put on a better dress, and let her brother find her a husband. And that's really what had done it in the end. The only thing she wanted to do less than go back to that soup kitchen was to live with the idea that she couldn't stomach the thought of the soup kitchen.

So she went back. And each time, it was a little easier. That was a lesson, she told herself with no small satisfaction. Everything gets easier the more frequently you do it.

The people were no longer an endless line of misery to her, and she was ashamed of herself for having seen them like that. An old charwoman with no family who was too infirm to work. A woman whose husband had died young, leaving her with three small children. A middle-aged man who had lost his job to a younger, fitter one. She could see the hunger and fear in all of them.

But some were so afraid that they found it hard to even get in the line, pacing in the shadows in the back, until they could bear it no longer. Frances wiped her forehead on her sleeve, as unladylike a gesture as she had ever made, and scanned the rear of the room for these most fearful. Sometimes, she could take a break and talk with them; she was getting better at that, guiding them to a hot meal with a gentle hand on an arm.

From time to time, they got old soldiers in worn-out remnants of their uniforms. Sometimes they carried obvious wounds, limps, or hands that couldn't hold anything. Frances found others with wounds in their minds, injuries that were less obvious but worse than the physical ones.

The old man who was presently last in line was one of the latter, with deep-set eyes that seemed to look without seeing.

"Where did you serve?" asked Frances.

He smiled gently. "India. The Mutiny." That would be 1857. The so-called Sepoy Mutiny, which had resulted in unparalleled savagery on both sides. Frances had heard about it, as she had heard about so many other things deemed "inappropriate" for young girls, by eavesdropping when her father was speaking to friends.

"I'm sorry I reminded you," said Frances.

"That's the thing, miss. I can't forget. Our sergeant, our captain, our colonel. Every man, every minute burned into me forever."

That was nearly fifty years ago, Frances realized. And he was still haunted.

"You may have served in India, but your accent is Manchester."

He grinned. "Right you are. Born and raised, but things, well . . ." He shrugged. "I thought I'd try my luck here."

Frances produced a card from a pocket in her dress. "Here's a card for the Soldiers and Sailors Club. Perhaps they can help you find some work and a room." Although, she sadly thought, not many would hire a man of his age.

"Thanks, miss. You have a good evening." And he took his plate to a table.

Then another wave of the hungry came in, so Frances tucked a damp strand of copper hair behind her ear and started serving again.

By the time they packed up, Frances was exhausted. The day had started early, and the settee in Kat's room had not been an ideal bed. But dear Mallow was waiting for her, sewing in their little sitting room. She helped Frances undress and get into her nightgown.

"Do you know any soldiers, Mallow?"

"Certainly not, my lady," she replied, a little affronted. Soldiers were just out to take liberties with innocent serving girls, Mallow well knew.

"I don't mean out walking with them, Mallow—maybe a servant who had been a soldier."

"I see, my lady. Yes, I know a footman who was in the Royal Navy and a valet who was a soldier-servant in the Coldstream Guards. They don't much like to talk about it."

"But I imagine they don't forget. It's just that I met an old soldier at the soup kitchen tonight, and he said he remembered everything from half a century ago. I wish I could meet a soldier from Major Colcombe's company. He might know something that can help us. Of course, I sent the old soldier to the Soldier and Sailors Club. We'll put a notice up there."

"Very good, my lady. Shall I hand you your book?" Mallow looked at the title: *Kim* by Rudyard Kipling. Mallow didn't read much, but she knew Kipling was very famous, and her mistress once had dinner with Mr. Kipling and his family. Lady Frances knew everyone.

"Yes, thank you." But she said it absently, staring out the window, looking sad.

"Is anything wrong, my lady?"

"I miss him, Mallow. Danny Colcombe. He was so much fun. He was in school with my brother and from time to time would spend school holidays with us. He called me Ursula."

"I beg your pardon, my lady? Ursula?"

Frances blushed. "It means 'little she-bear.' I was always chasing after the boys, demanding they let me play with them. Danny said I was like a little bear cub, small and fierce."

Mallow laughed, imagining her mistress as an angry little girl.

"Yes, it was funny, I'm sure. But oh, when I made my debut, Danny led me out for my first dance. He was in his uniform—a lieutenant in the 17th Lancers. All the other girls were so jealous that I was partnered with a handsome cavalry officer, and he was such a marvelous dancer. He leaned down to me and said, 'You're the most beautiful girl here, little Ursula.'"

It was a side of Lady Frances that Mallow didn't see often, dreamy and sentimental.

"We have a busy day tomorrow and should get some sleep. Good night, Mallow."

"Good night, my lady."

With the lights out, Frances forced herself to think of the future: she was a daughter of the House of Seaforth, and Seaforths didn't wallow in sentiment. Not even the women.

Especially not the women.

CHAPTER 3

Frances and Mallow started the next morning with a typical argument. Mallow wanted to discuss clothing while Frances just wanted to throw something on and start the day.

"Whatever is ironed and ready, Mallow."

"The pale pink?"

"That'll be fine."

"The blue brings out your eyes, my lady."

"Also good. Either one."

"Very good, my lady," she said with just the barest hint of disapproval. Lady Frances's mother, it was well-known, could spend a half hour or more discussing a dress, and that was just for the day—never mind a fancy evening party.

The question of dress settled, the two women started their day, and after a quick breakfast, Frances made her way to the Soldier and Sailors Club. The volunteer manageress, Mrs. Halsey, was an old friend and was pleased to let Frances post a handwritten sign next to the job notifications on the bulletin board in the lobby:

Any soldiers who served in South Africa under the late Maj. Daniel Colcombe should call on Frances Ffolkes, Miss Plimsoll's Residence Hotel for Ladies, and they will be paid for their time and trouble.

The South African campaign had only ended a few years ago. There was good chance at least one was living in London and would get the word.

And now it was off to the solicitor's office.

———•◦••◦•———

The office of Caleb Wheaton and Associates, Solicitors, hadn't changed since Mr. Caleb had died several years ago and his son, Mr. Henry, had taken it over. Indeed, reflected Frances, it probably hadn't changed since Caleb had set up the offices half a century before. The office was busy but without the sense of bustle she had seen at Scotland Yard. The furnishings at Wheaton were old and fine—polished wood with brass fittings. The men wore old-fashioned frock coats, and although telephones had been installed as a necessary concession to modernity, the ringings were muted and no one ran to get them—a sedate walk only.

The seats in the outer office were certainly much more comfortable than at Scotland Yard—deep, well made, and padded. But she didn't have to wait long. A deferential clerk showed her into the office of Mr. Henry Wheaton. Wheaton was dressed to go along with the furniture in a cut of jacket that reminded Frances of her late father. He wore gold-rimmed spectacles.

"Good morning, Lady Frances," he said, smiling as he reached over the expanse of polished mahogany to greet her. "It's a pleasure as always to see you. I have your papers right here."

Papers. This was going to take longer than expected. Charles had offered to handle all this, but she knew that being an independent woman meant taking care of her own business affairs.

"Thank you, Mr. Wheaton," she said, forcing a smile.

He leaned back and steepled his fingers, the way men do when delivering important information. Her father had done it, her brother continued to do it, and none of them realized that it made them look a trifle pompous.

Frances's restless eyes darted around and saw an interesting document on his desk. Before Mr. Wheaton could launch into his usual discussion, Frances spoke.

"Do you enjoy music, Mr. Wheaton? I see a concert program on your desk."

He seemed a little discomfited, and it brought out Frances's mischievous side.

"Oh, yes, I was just, ah, referring to it." He quickly picked it up and shoved it into a drawer.

"What was it?"

"Oh, an Edward Elgar concert." He paused and removed his glasses. His eyes, she noticed, were a rather pale green. "I'm rather an admirer of his. It was a treat for my mother. My sister and her husband were visiting, and we made a little party of it." He paused again and, a little hesitatingly, asked, "Do you appreciate Mr. Elgar, Lady Frances?"

"I am somewhat familiar with his music," she said. "Recently, I've been interested in French music, Debussy and Ravel."

"They're rather unconventional," said Mr. Wheaton with a little smile.

"So am I, Mr. Wheaton," said Frances. Wheaton didn't seem to know how to respond to that, so he put on his glasses again and picked up some documents.

He proceeded to explain her financial situation, as he did every month they had this meeting. Lawyers always wanted to make sure you had all the facts, Frances concluded. Her father had left a substantial amount of money to her, out of which she received a generous allowance, but she could not touch the principal until she got married. Or turned thirty-five. At which point, he no doubt reasoned, no one would want to marry her, so she might as well have outright what would've been her dowry. Her father had been considered progressive, but there were limits.

"I'm sorry, Lady Frances, did you say something?"

"Nothing, thank you. Please continue."

"Very well. The funds are invested in . . ." She forced herself to pay attention. Yes, it was tedious, but it occurred to her Mr. Wheaton was doing no less for her than he did for her brother—or any other male client. He had never suggested that she just let her brother handle her finances. When she went out on her own, he simply said, "Please arrange an appointment with my chief clerk, and I will explain your finances to you." And that was something to be grateful for.

He turned around the paper and handed it to her. "So here is what you can continue to expect to receive every week. This shouldn't be a surprise, as it has been almost exactly the same as we discussed when you . . . moved into Miss Plimsoll's hotel." He stumbled over that. Frances expected he had been shocked at the idea of her leaving the family home and protection of her brother.

Most of London Society knew about Miss Plimsoll. When the well-born but impoverished woman could no longer afford to keep up the city mansion she had lived in her entire life or pay servants who had been with her for years and even decades, she turned it into a residence hotel for ladies—expensive and exclusive but much more reasonable than keeping up a household. It looked like a private residence but had many of the trappings of a hotel. Miss Plimsoll rented only to ladies she knew or from whom she had impeccable references, and nevertheless, there was a waiting list to get in.

The final figure was, as Mr. Wheaton said, the same as always. It would nicely cover rent, Mallow's wages, dresses, hansom cabs, and other miscellaneous expenses.

"Now, do you have any questions?"

But before she could speak, the oak door suddenly opened, and in walked an older woman in a dress that was as dated as Mr. Wheaton's suit. Her cheeks and figure were round, and she was smiling. Over her shoulder, Frances could see an unhappy clerk waving his arms and looking forlornly at Mr. Wheaton. Clearly, he had tried—and failed—to stop this woman.

Wheaton stood. "Mother, is anything wrong? I am meeting with a client."

"I know, dear," she said. She closed the door and made her way across the rich carpet. "You had mentioned you were seeing Lady Frances this morning, and it has been such a long time, I wanted to make sure I saw her." She turned to her. "My dear, you look lovely."

With her family's extensive dealings with the Wheatons, father and son, Frances had met Mrs. Wheaton a number of times and always found her cheerful, outgoing manner a pleasant contrast to the more formal Wheaton men.

"Mrs. Wheaton, I am delighted to see you again. I hope you are well." Mrs. Wheaton sat next to Frances while Mr. Wheaton looked a little exasperated. They caught up on family and gossiped for a few moments, until Mr. Wheaton delicately coughed.

"I don't want to interrupt, but this is a business meeting, Mother."

"You young women today, handling your own business," she said to Frances, but admiringly, not critically. "How modern. But I do understand, and I must be off myself." She turned to her son. "Don't forget you promised to take me to the National Gallery tomorrow afternoon."

"I haven't, Mother. It's in my calendar."

Mrs. Wheaton turned brightly to Frances. "Perhaps you would like to join us?"

"Mother." Now she was stepping over the line. "Lady Frances has a very busy schedule, and we don't want to impose." He paused. "Not that you wouldn't be welcome, of course, but I understand you have extensive charitable and educational commitments."

The National Gallery—she had not been there in a while, and although she had a morning meeting of the Belgravia Women's

Social Improvement Club, there was nothing scheduled for the afternoon.

"If I am not interrupting a family event, I'd be delighted," she said. She had studied art at college, and a visit to the National Gallery with Mrs. Wheaton would be fun. Perhaps even Mr. Wheaton would unbend a little, although she doubted it.

"Very good, then," said Mrs. Wheaton. They made arrangements for meeting, and then Mrs. Wheaton left.

"I am sorry about the interruption," said Mr. Wheaton. "It is very kind of you to agree to accompany us, however. Mother will appreciate it."

"No apologies, Mr. Wheaton. I shall enjoy it." She paused. "I gather Mrs. Wheaton misses her daughter?" The young woman had married a rising physician who had been given an excellent position—in Manchester.

"I'm afraid she misses her dreadfully, especially now that my sister and brother-in-law left after their brief visit to London. It's just the two of us at home now," he said, and again smiled shyly.

Frances thanked him and said she looked forward to their outing tomorrow.

<hr />

Her legal and financial business settled, Frances made her way from the old-fashioned elegance of the solicitor's office to a genteel shabby town house in a neighborhood that was perfectly safe and respectable—merely unfashionable.

An elderly butler admitted her, but the usual announcements were dispensed with. Frances saw herself into what had once been a gracious drawing room, but now almost all the furniture had been removed. It was filled with common chairs that looked like they had been taken from a servants' hall, and they were arranged for a lecture. A podium stood at the head against a window covered with faded blue curtains.

Many women had already arrived, and more followed quickly behind. Frances spoke to several while other women gathered and talked in small knots. Some were dressed like Frances, in the latest fashionable clothes. Others wore the simpler, less-expensive dresses of the middle class.

After a few minutes, a tall woman walked quickly into the room. Her dress was good, if a little plain, and her purposeful stride and crown of white hair gave her a natural air of authority. As she entered, talk trailed off, and the women took their seats.

"Good afternoon," she said in a ringing voice. "I see a few new faces here. For those who don't know me—" There was light laughter; everyone knew who she was. "—my name is Winifred Elkhorn, and it is my privilege to be president of the League for Women's Political Equality."

Mrs. Elkhorn didn't say anything new that day, but it didn't matter. She got her audience fired up, and that was the purpose. Her late husband had been Andrew Elkhorn, the distinguished Liberal politician and a colleague of Frances's father. There were many who felt that it was one thing for a political widow to host a salon and organize dinners, but to start a radical movement . . . And yet, she had friends and admirers, and not just women.

Frances sat at the edge of her seat and listened. As usual, she felt her spirits lifting as Mrs. Elkhorn spoke, describing in ringing words how the lack of political power meant the lack of economic power. Indeed, it was not that long ago that the passage of the Married Women's Property Act had given women any financial power at all, for the first time establishing wives as people in their own right and not just their husbands' properties. And women's ability to earn their own living ranged from difficult to impossible. Women's lives would never be their own until they had political equality. The only solution was the vote.

"And above all, my friends, remember this: it's a new age, and this will be our century."

Everyone applauded, and then the room was filled with the scraping of chairs as the women formed themselves into little groups. Mrs. Elkhorn came around to each of them to talk about their work—publishing, speaking, legal research. She came over to Frances, who was talking about speeches with several other women. They were planning another open-air meeting in the park.

"And presumably, we will be better protected this time—thanks to your contacts with the police, Frances?" she asked with a wry smile.

"I had to wait two hours to see him the first time," said Frances. "But in the end, he came through with the extra constables."

"Yes, he did—and good for you!" Frances flushed with the praise. There were few people in London—in England—whose good opinion she valued more that Mrs. Elkhorn's.

With a little hesitancy, she brought up her idea for a future speech. It had been a joke in Superintendent Maples's office, but after she had given it more thought, it made more and more sense.

"I'm thinking about proposing women police constables—especially detective constables. We are every bit as capable of decisive and rational thought as men. We speak here of the importance of women making laws—why not women enforcing them as well?"

Mrs. Elkhorn was quiet for several moments, and Frances held her breath as she watched the wheels turning in the woman's head.

"Where do women have the vote today, Frances?"

"In the empire, women have the vote in Australia and New Zealand . . . and in America, where I studied, some Western states like Colorado have given the vote to women for local elections."

"And what does that tell you?"

Frances certainly knew what it told her brother. Charles said it was easy for these half-wild, out-of-the-way places to give the vote to women for local elections that hardly changed anything anyway. Voting for Parliament or voting for the U.S. Congress—that was a different matter. But as Frances eagerly explained to Mrs. Elkhorn, women got the vote in places at the edge of civilization, where men relied on them for the hard work of farming and ranching, whether in the Pacific or the American West. In London, Manchester, and Liverpool, women—or more properly, wealthy women—could be merely decorative. Poor women had to work for what they got with less opportunity and less money than men.

"So what do you conclude?" asked Mrs. Elkhorn, smiling again.

"With hard work—no, with dangerous hard work—equality can come?" Frances hazarded.

"Perhaps," said Mrs. Elkhorn. "Something for you to think about. Indeed, something for all of us to think about."

———◆◆◆◆◆———

On the ride home, her mind reflected on the intricacies and possibilities of getting women into the police force. They were making inroads into other areas. Nursing had become a very respectable profession for women. Bobbies did more than catch criminals. They helped people after accidents, for example. That was sort of like nursing. Maybe get women into the force that way—as a kind of emergency worker. Of course, once they were in the force, with a foot in the door, they could gradually push their way into other areas.

She paid off the hansom at the front of Miss Plimsoll's and let herself into the house. The foyer of Miss Plimsoll's had been redone on its conversion to a residential hotel. The stairs were now guarded by a desk outside of a little makeshift office. The severe manageress, or one of her minions, was on duty at all times to make sure no men made it to the bedroom floors. What had been a morning room—a reception room less formal than a larger and more elegant drawing room—had been turned into a lounge where residents could receive male guests. Although it was a quiet place to sit in the evenings, it got little use as a reception area. As Frances once reflected, for most of the residents, if there had been men in their lives, they wouldn't be living at Miss Plimsoll's.

"You have visitors, Lady Frances," said the manageress. She was a few degrees cooler than usual. When her brother had visited a few times, there was almost a sense of gratitude that the marquess was gracing their house. These visitors were probably not as illustrious.

"Thank you, Mrs. Beasley." Curious, she headed into the lounge. At first, she saw only one visitor, as he seemed to take up half the space—tall and broad-shouldered, and it didn't help that his obviously cheap suit was much too loud for the room. Like something a low-level clerk might wear to the horse races on his day off. He was looking around the room as if he had never been in a place like that before, which may have been the truth. He reminded Frances of one of the grooms in their country estate, a former prizefighter whose face bore witness to his former profession. But this man was not so marked.

The man gave her a thin smile and then turned to another man she hadn't noticed yet. He was of a slight build and was looking at the books on the shelf, an informal lending library for residents. His suit was the complete opposite, an inconspicuous brown.

"Sir," said the giant, with a cockney accent so strong even that one syllable marked him as born in London's poor East End.

The brown-suited man then turned as well, and Frances recognized him: the odd man from Danny's funeral, the one she and Kat had labeled "Mr. Rumpled." This suit was rumpled as well, and now Frances could take him in more clearly. He didn't have a handsome face, but it was one full of what her mother would have called "character." A small mustache. And eyes that, like hers, darted around. But not exactly like hers—these eyes were hard.

"Smith, you may wait outside," he said, and the large man said, "Sir," again, nodded at Frances, and left the room and the house.

"You are Lady Frances Ffolkes?" asked the man in a quiet, well-modulated voice.

"You have the advantage of me, sir," said Frances. Who was this man who knew her? A man who was not of her class.

"My apologies," he said, and stepped toward her. He reached into his jacket pocket and pulled out a wallet, which he opened to show her a police department warrant card. "My name is Benjamin Eastley. I am an inspector of police. And I was led to understand you had a theft you wanted to report. Shall we sit and discuss it?"

He sat on a chair, and Frances sat on a loveseat opposite him.

"I was not expecting you to call on me. I thought Superintendent Maples or a colleague would give me your name and I would see you at your station."

"Indeed. You have wide familiarity with police procedure then."

He's trying to goad me, she thought. But she wasn't going to let him. "I have many interests and concerns and so have a wide circle of friends and acquaintances," she said a little loftily. "Are you one of Superintendent Maples's men? Or are you local? My family has long been a sponsor of the Police Widows and Orphans Fund, and we know many of the local senior officers." *Take that, Inspector.*

Inspector Eastley studied her. Would she know who he was? Most women would not. But then again, her family was political, and it was his understanding she was well educated.

"Lady Frances, have you ever heard of Special Branch?"

Eastley was right—she had heard of the elite Special Branch. Its responsibilities took in sensitive cases when political issues were involved. They were part of the Metropolitan Police Service, but they had their own command structure. No wonder she didn't know who he was.

And that explained so much else as well. The surprise on Maples's face when he found out who was in charge of the case, the fact that she wasn't immediately given his name but told she would see him later. What wasn't clear was why an apparently simple theft was put in care of Special Branch.

"May I ask what Special Branch's interest is in this case?"

"Since you seem familiar with police procedure, Lady Frances, you should know in police cases, the police ask the questions. Everyone else answers." His voice was soft, even gentle, but the meaning was clear.

Frances flushed at that and was poised to snap back. But that's what he wanted, she suddenly realized. He wanted her to play the grand dame, the arrogant highborn lady who'd insist on her rights, start listing her influential connections, and provide fodder for hours of amusement among his mates.

"I take your point, Inspector," she said. "I reported a crime, and you've apparently come to investigate. I am not quite as familiar with police procedure as you seem to think, so please tell me how I may best help you do your job."

He raised an eyebrow and looked a little surprised. Perhaps, thought Frances, a little disappointed too.

"Thank you. Now why don't you start by telling me how you became involved with the theft of a manuscript from the Colcombe home?"

So Frances told him about Kat's arrival and her own investigations in the Colcombe house. She even produced a copy of the list she and Kat had drawn up of those who had attended the funeral. Inspector Eastley raised an eyebrow at that but said nothing, as he folded it and tucked it into a jacket pocket. He listened to everything Frances had to say without interrupting.

"You say this appears to be a memoir of Mr. Colcombe's war experiences in South Africa?"

"That's what we believe it to be. No one seems to have read it."

The inspector nodded. "Now tell me about the Colcombe family."

That surprised her. What did he want to know? She stated simply that it had consisted of Daniel and his younger sister, Katherine, known as Kat, and their mother. Mr. Colcombe Sr. had died some years ago.

Eastley smiled. "I know that, Lady Frances. What I need to know is more about the family. Are they wealthy? Where do they come from? What kind of people are they? Any scandals? As a close friend of the family, you should know."

Frances glared at him. Such things were known in Society, but one didn't discuss them openly. Certainly not with the police.

"I can't possibly see what any of that has to do with a stolen manuscript," she said.

"You don't see because you are not a trained police officer. You have no idea how family issues can become intertwined with a crime, how even an apparently simple theft may have its roots in family history and character."

That made some sense, Frances had to admit, but she wasn't going down without a fight.

"You're right, Inspector, I don't know. Perhaps if you accepted and trained women as detective constables, more women like me would have a better sense of how procedure worked."

Eastley chuckled at that. "Very good, Lady Frances. Nicely spoken. But as much as I'd like to debate department policy with you, my time is not unlimited. If you want that manuscript found, you will have to be frank. If it helps, I will assure you that I will hold what you say in confidence, as much as possible. I would like you to describe the family, because I sense a certain shrewdness about you and a well-organized mind. I do not think Miss Colcombe or her mother would be as much help as you."

The assurance seemed genuine and the flattery honest, not condescension. Very well, he'd hear about the Colcombes.

"Mr. Colcombe Senior—that is, Daniel Colcombe's father— had come from a distinguished family, if not a noble one, and as with many other old families, the money was just about gone. So he married the daughter of a wealthy, self-made Sheffield ironmonger, whose dowry restored the family fortune. For all that, Inspector, I think the marriage was happy, if not passionate. Mrs. Colcombe has long doted on her children, especially after she became a widow. She is close to her daughter, Kat, and the two ladies are very much alike—sweet, gentle, and not . . . intellectually inclined."

"But Daniel was different?" Eastley prompted.

"Oh, yes. He was something of an adventurer. Indeed, in a previous generation, he would've been empire building in India, and it was his loss that he had been born into a world that has already mostly tamed. Still, he kept on the move, becoming an officer and going to war. He traveled and made friends with everyone from earls to actors." She smiled. "I don't mind telling you that he had many female friends as well but never married and never even had a public engagement."

"But this was before the war?" he asked.

Oh, yes. South Africa—the Boer War—had changed him, as it had changed her brother, Charles, and every man who had gone. "He was quieter when he came back. He had emotional and physical wounds when he returned to the family home. He was thinner and seemed less inclined to travel, although at the time of his death, he apparently had a number of projects going and seemed happy again. There was talk he was writing a memoir of his war experiences, but no one I knew read it."

That was all the detail she could bring herself to discuss. He had seemed older, but sometimes in his eyes, you could still see the old mischief, the old Danny.

Inspector Eastley listened with care and patience. Frances was impressed despite herself at the way he paid such close attention. Few people did, she had noticed. He really wanted to absorb every single word.

When she was done, he nodded thoughtfully.

"Thank you, Lady Frances, for being so frank with me. It is much appreciated. My men and I will look into this, and we'll let you know, as representative of the Colcombe family, of any progress." He stood.

"That sounds very satisfactory, Inspector. May I ask one question?"

"I'm still not going to tell you my department's interest in this case."

She gave him an ingratiating smile. "I understand. But I was hoping you could tell me exactly how Danny Colcombe died. All the local police said it was 'an accident at home.'" This was not a surprise. The word would've come down from senior officers at Scotland Yard to keep tight-lipped and spare the Colcombe ladies from hearing any painful details about any accident.

"That is a fair question, Lady Frances. Mr. Colcombe died from a gunshot wound to the chest, apparently while cleaning or otherwise servicing his revolver."

Frances now saw the full reason for police silence on the matter. Some might conclude that the death had been a suicide—it was easier to simply say it was an accident. A suicide was a horrible scandal.

"I find it hard to believe that such an experienced soldier made a fatal mistake with a firearm." But then again, suicide seemed even less likely.

"You know about firearms?" asked Eastley, looking amused.

"I know something, Inspector."

"I wasn't involved in the original accident investigation, so I'm afraid I have nothing I can add. I must go now, but as I said, I will keep you informed. Thank you again, Lady Frances, for your time and cooperation."

Frances followed him out the door, where Eastley met up with his huge constable-assistant, and they headed down the street together.

It was supposedly just a manuscript, thought Frances, *written by a man who died in an accident. So why is an elite Scotland Yard unit investigating it?*

CHAPTER 4

The next morning started as usual, with Mallow pulling open the curtains and asking, "What shall I lay out for you this morning, my lady?"

"I have a morning meeting, and then I'm going to the National Gallery with friends."

"I see, my lady. May I inquire which friends?"

A lot of meaning in that question, thought Frances. If these friends were other young women from the suffragist club, Mallow would suggest something simple. But if they were family friends of the Seaforths—lords and ladies with distinguished titles—she'd lay out something more elaborate.

"Mr. Wheaton, the family solicitor, and his widowed mother. You've seen Mr. Wheaton, when he dined at my brother's house."

"Very good, my lady," said Mallow as she chose and smoothed out a dress. Frances's sharp ears detected a tone in Mallow's voice—or maybe it was just her imagination.

"Nothing wrong, is there, Mallow?"

"Not at all, my lady," responded the maid, all wide-eyed innocence. But they both knew what the other was thinking. It was one thing for a lord to invite a trusted family solicitor to his table and quite another for his sister to socialize with him and his family out in public.

A few years working for the House of Seaforth had taught Mallow a thing or two about class distinctions. It was true Mr. Wheaton could chat with Lord and Lady Seaforth, and she had heard he had a fine house himself, wore well-tailored clothes, and employed servants. But Mr. Wheaton worked for his money, and Lord Seaforth did not—he just had it. And that made all the difference: Mr. Henry Wheaton was middle class and Lady Frances was of the aristocracy.

Mallow again thought back to her first days as a housemaid at the Seaforth house, when these important class distinctions had been drummed into her. Agnes, the Seaforth head housemaid, had explained it all to Mallow. She had been curious about the important and wealthy people who dined at his lordship's table and one evening asked the more knowledgeable Agnes about Mr. Wheaton.

"Oh, Mr. Wheaton, who's dining here tonight? He's just a solicitor, probably here because they needed an extra man to round out the table. Very nice of his lordship to invite him at all," said Agnes. The emphasis was on "just." The tone was dismissive. "But tomorrow night, you'll see a real gentleman. Lord Bassington. Owns half of Kent, I hear." She looked around to make sure Mr. Cumberland, who tolerated no gossip, was not nearby. "They say he's very interested in Lady Frances. That's why he's here so often. I expect he'll ask for her hand." Agnes got a dreamy look, thinking about how lovely it would be to be married to Lord Bassington.

Mallow brought her down to earth. "But I understand from Cook that Mr. Wheaton also visits frequently, even when there's not a large party. Is he also interested in Lady Frances?"

Agnes threw up her hands in exasperation. "I just told you, Lady Frances is the daughter of a marquess. She has to marry a lord. That's the way it works. Ladies don't marry solicitors. You have to know these things when you work in a great house."

"But Mr. Wheaton was so kind to me. When he arrived this evening, he asked me my name and said he hoped I would be happy here. No other guest ever did that."

Agnes just shook her head.

The next night, Lord Bassington certainly didn't speak to her. And according to downstairs gossip, it became clear that he wouldn't be speaking again with Lady Frances either. Thanks to the young footman who served at the table, Mallow found out exactly what did happen when Lord Bassington tried to court Lady Frances over dinner: she spoke about women's suffrage, reformation of the poor laws, Irish independence, and some art exhibition that Lord Seaforth had pronounced "disgraceful"—a whole host of topics unsuitable for a young lady. Lord Bassington never came back, and it was a minor scandal among the family and the servants.

And now, some years later, here they were again, socializing with Mr. Wheaton, a man who was not of Lady Frances's class but who had bothered to talk to a new servant girl.

As Mallow helped Frances into her dress, Frances decided to address the matter with her maid openly.

"I realize that Mr. Wheaton is not of the nobility, Mallow, but in my dealings with him, he has shown no prejudices against well-educated, independent women. Or do you think, like my brother, I should only associate with others in the nobility?"

Frances smiled, but Mallow was too sharp to get caught in that.

"It's not my place to comment on your ladyship's friends," she said, a little stiffly.

Most other ladies in London would've dropped the subject right then, but Frances persisted. "But I'm asking your opinion, as I would for a dress or hat." The tone was teasing, but Mallow could see that Lady Frances wanted an answer.

"I believe Mr. Wheaton is kind, my lady," said Mallow.

Frances nodded. "That's a very insightful comment, Mallow."

"Yes, my lady," said Mallow.

Frances was still smiling about the exchange as she headed downstairs to breakfast. Then she called Mary to tell her that the police were investigating the manuscript theft. She held back the information that Special Branch was involved—no need to overexcite anyone, she reasoned. Mary said she'd be visiting Kat and Mrs. Colcombe that afternoon and would pass along the good news.

———————

Frances met Henry Wheaton and his mother at the museum's entrance, as agreed. Henry surprised her. Instead of the dated black suit he used for the office, he wore a modern cut in a light shade—something her brother might be seen in. His sandy hair was a little ruffled by the breeze, and he looked no different from a dozen other young gentlemen on the street.

He smiled when he saw her and ushered the women into the gallery. As they walked, Frances received another surprise. She had expected Mrs. Wheaton to appreciate the pictures and Mr. Wheaton to hover in the background, indulging the ladies with their pastime while he wondered about what was happening at the office in his absence.

But that's not what happened. As they started viewing the pictures, Henry Wheaton started talking: "Do you see the brushwork here, Lady Frances? . . . The shadowing here is typical of the early Renaissance. . . . Only the Dutch masters could achieve perspective like this. . . . Aren't those flesh tones astonishing, Lady Frances?" He said he couldn't stop contemplating the coloring. Mrs. Wheaton smiled and nodded, proud of her son's knowledge.

Frances tried to keep up. She had learned a bit about art in college, but nowhere near as much as Mr. Wheaton seemed to know. After about an hour, he suddenly turned to her and said, "Lady Frances, I'm afraid I've spent the last hour being the world's most frightful bore. I am sorry if my enthusiasm got away from me."

She smiled. "Not at all, Mr. Wheaton. I have been honored to have my own private expert guide."

Mrs. Wheaton jumped in. "Perhaps Lady Frances would like to see some of your own paintings. I know I am prejudiced, but I think some of them are good enough to hang here."

Mr. Wheaton blushed. "Mother, really . . ."

"I didn't know you painted in your spare time, Mr. Wheaton."

"It's just a hobby, to relax after a busy week, that's all. I don't exhibit or have any aspirations." His tone was defensive.

"I think it's a fine hobby," said Lady Frances. "A more intellectual and worthwhile one than my brother's obsession with knocking a little ball into a hole in a lawn."

"Thank you," he said, and seemed very grateful.

When they were done, Mr. Wheaton took the ladies out to tea at Claridge's, a hotel where the best people stayed. It was quite lovely; since moving into Miss Plimsoll's, she had rather gotten out of the habit of elaborate teas, just grabbing the occasional cup in between visits and meetings. They spoke about their favorite paintings, but now Mr. Wheaton did more listening than talking. Over his cup, he looked intently at Frances with those attractive green eyes.

Talk of art gave way to talk of books and music too. Mr. Wheaton listened very carefully to what Frances said and seemed to think deeply before making a thoughtful response. Mrs. Wheaton said little, content to listen to the young people.

During a pause, while the waitress served the little cakes that Mrs. Wheaton delighted in, Frances changed the subject.

"I hope you don't mind talking business during such a lovely lunch, but as you're a solicitor, I was hoping that you could throw some light on a particular issue. I was wondering what you knew about the Scotland Yard division called Special Branch."

He laughed. "My goodness, Lady Frances. Don't tell me you've run into them. I've occasionally had to arrange for a barrister to represent one of my clients in a court of law, but never involving Special Branch."

"Not me at all. A friend of mine was the victim of a crime, and it turns out the inspector in charge of the case is with Special Branch. Perhaps because my brother is in government, she thought I might know about it, but he's Foreign Office, of course."

Mr. Wheaton frowned. "Lady Frances, you can tell your friend this is very serious. Special Branch involves itself in the security of the realm. If she was a victim—well, without the details, I can't really give advice. But if you'd like, you can tell your friend to visit me, and I will treat the matter in strictest confidence and without obligation. If Special Branch is involved, there may be serious implications."

"I had no idea," said Lady Frances. She knew Special Branch was serious, but his words almost made her shudder. "That is very kind of you, Mr. Wheaton. I will tell my friend."

"For my part," said Mrs. Wheaton, "I don't think your friend came to you because of your brother. It's probably because she knew you were so well educated. You took a college degree—in America, I believe?"

Some approved, some disapproved, but everyone was curious about Frances's novel education. It was a school founded expressly for the education of women, with a very progressive agenda. After much begging and pleading, and the not inconsiderable support of her mother, her father agreed to send her there. It was a splendid four years.

"My father finally was convinced because the founder was an Englishman who had moved to America. His name was Matthew Vassar, and the school carries his name."

"How exciting for you, Lady Frances," said Mrs. Wheaton. "Henry, don't you think such an educational experience for women is a wonderful thing?"

He put down his cup and spoke slowly and deliberately. "I am not an authority on education, for men or women, but I can say that it would have been a great shame if someone with your aptitude, Lady Frances, had not received an education commensurate with your intelligence."

And Frances was touched.

———◦‣•‣◦———

Mr. Wheaton saw her to her home. She felt good about the afternoon. A professor had once instructed her to turn surprises into lessons, and she had been surprised that a man seemingly as dry as Henry Wheaton could speak of artwork with such knowledge. No, not just with knowledge—with passion. And he spent his free time painting, a hobby usually associated with young women sent to finishing schools in Italy. Perhaps, she thought ruefully, she needed to be less quick about jumping to conclusions about people.

There were no visitors waiting for her, but there was a note. Mrs. Beasley's manner indicated that this was a message from an acceptable person.

Lady Frances,

I understand you have an interest in a missing manuscript written by the late Daniel Colcombe. I have some information that may be helpful to you. I can be reached through the Military Club.

—*Colonel Zachery Mountjoy*

The name was completely unfamiliar to Frances, but the club was not. Only well-born army and navy officers belonged, such as her brother. However, Charles didn't attend much, preferring more political clubs, so he probably wouldn't know this Colonel Mountjoy. But Frances knew who would.

Major Clive Raleigh occupied what he felt was a very pleasant suite at the War Office. His work taxed him enough to keep him from getting bored but not so much that it exhausted him. He had time for theater and dinner parties, as well as overnight house parties in the better homes. His aide, a young lieutenant, knocked and entered.

"Excuse me, sir. Lady Frances Ffolkes wishes to have a few minutes with you."

Unlike Superintendent Maples, Raleigh didn't get at all upset. He had served with Charles Ffolkes and had met Frances several times. Rather pretty girl, he thought, always well turned out. Those big, gray eyes of hers had a way of looking right at you—a little disturbing, but she had some spirit, and those were the girls who were most entertaining, he had found. And as a practical matter, his family was pushing him to get married—having the Marquess of Seaforth as a brother-in-law would be no small advantage, and the dowry was likely to be substantial.

Not being particularly introspective or aware of what others thought about him, Raleigh didn't know that Ffolkes and his friend Colcombe used to joke about him behind his back, saying that the best way for the British to win the war would be to promote Raleigh to general—in the Boer army. For the same reason, it never occurred to Raleigh to wonder why Lady Frances was visiting him in the War Office—it was enough that she was.

"Thank you, Lieutenant. Please show her in."

Frances met Major Raleigh's broad smile with one of her own.

"Dear Frances, it's so good to see you. It's been months since we danced at the Henshaw's house party."

"I remember. It was a very pleasant evening. I was in the area, and I had a question I couldn't answer. I said, 'I know, I'll call on Clive Raleigh.' I heard you had been given a post here. I imagine this is good for your career?"

Raleigh preened a little. Let him, thought Frances. She believed a truly competent officer would be leading troops somewhere, not pushing papers around in a forgotten corner of a government building.

"But you must be very busy, so I'll ask my question, although it seems so silly now. A friend of mine is having a cheery little party and was asked to invite a certain officer, a colonel, but doesn't know anything about him. It will be so embarrassing for her not to know anything about his regiment or experiences, and I said I could help her find out, so, well, you understand, she doesn't look foolish."

Raleigh thought Frances's friend was being a little fussy— there were always a few odd people out there, and half the fun was finding out about them. Probably some old spinster, set in her ways. Anyway, the thing was to oblige Frances.

"What's this man's name? I may be able to check."

"Oh, could you? He's a colonel. Colonel Zachery Mountjoy. I know the officer corps in London was a rather small group, so I'm hoping you may know him, or at least know of him."

She watched Raleigh closely as he leaned back and frowned.

"I, ah, do know him. He has a . . . well, he sort of has a general HQ assignment."

You're a horrible liar, thought Frances.

"Do you know if he served in South Africa? Which regiment was he attached to? I know a little bit about military affairs. My brother and father served in the Life Guards. My ancestors served under Wellington. Even going back to Marlborough."

Raleigh smiled. "Of course. I had forgotten what a distinguished military family you come from. The colonel was attached to the Royal Reconnaissance Battalion." Frances looked at him expectantly, hoping to learn more. "Sort of involved in map making, various charts and so forth, descriptions of the terrain. Important work, if not particularly exciting."

"I see. Well, thank you for your time, Major. Just one more thing—do you know the motto of the Reconnaissance Battalion? Or perhaps its nickname? I'm curious about mottos and look forward to surprising the colonel."

Raleigh looked hard at her, and Frances wondered if she had pushed her luck too far, showing more curiosity than she should.

"I couldn't say, Lady Frances. It's not an especially well-known unit."

"No matter. Thank you again, and I hope to see you at some future house party." She stood, and Raleigh followed suit, opening the door for her.

"Lady Frances, you say you collect regimental mottos. Do you know the motto of your brother's regiment, the Life Guards?"

"Of course. '*Honi soit qui mal y pense.* Evil be to him who evil thinks.' Good day, Major."

Raleigh, alone in his office, composed himself again. He reconsidered a possible alliance with Lady Frances. She asked too many questions, he realized. Lady Frances Ffolkes might be a little too clever to be the wife of an ambitious army officer, he sadly concluded.

Frances was meanwhile feeling rather pleased with herself. She had a name and that was interesting. Something was clearly wrong: well-born gentlemen who managed to get themselves into the distinguished Military Club did not work for obscure map-making units.

One person could help her with the next step, but it was going to cost something.

◆━◆◆◆━◆

Angus McDonald had been with her brother Charles through one posting or another and was now his chief clerk in the Foreign Office. He gave Frances a warm welcome.

"Lady Frances, his lordship didn't tell me you were visiting today, but you're most welcome. May I get you some tea?"

"Thank you, Mr. McDonald, but I'm just making a flying visit to my brother if he's available. Also, if there are any openings, I'd like to apply—yet again—for the job of clerk in the Foreign Office."

McDonald was not a man given to humor. He actually nodded, as if he were considering it. "With your university degree, I daresay you'd do as well as any of the lads," he said.

A darn sight better, thought Frances.

"But you take a seat here, Lady Frances. His lordship doesn't have a meeting for another hour, so I'll see if he can see you now." And a few minutes later, she was ushered into her brother's office, large and elegantly appointed, as befitted an undersecretary in an important department.

"Franny, what a pleasant surprise. Nothing wrong, I hope?"
She sat down on one of the comfortable visitors' chairs.

"Not at all. I was making calls and thought I'd stop to visit."

That was a mistake. Charles's eyes narrowed. "What calls are you making in this neighborhood?" Among these blocks were government offices and other businesses—not fashionable residences.

"Oh, just helping a friend organize a dinner party—looking up some people for her in the War Office."

"Liar. This is about your radical politics, isn't it?" he said, referring to her women's suffrage work. "Although I can't figure out why you'd be calling in at the War Office. Angling for a commission in the Blues? Come to think of it, you'd look awfully fetching in one of those uniforms."

"Very funny, dear brother. You can take your act on the music hall stage. But we're off subject. I heard a phrase that seemed rather odd to me, and you know how I don't like not knowing something. When you were in the army, did you come across a unit called the Reconnaissance Battalion?"

The smile vanished quickly, and he leaned over his desk.

"Frances," he spoke slowly and deliberately, as their father had done when she was up to something she shouldn't be, "what are you up to? I can't think of any reason for you to meet someone from that unit."

"Oh, it was casually mentioned in the hall in the War Office suites." Frances was a much better liar than Major Raleigh, but Charles had known her too long and too well to be taken in. However, no point in challenging her now.

"Very well, don't tell me. You have a name. But don't do . . . whatever it is you're doing. These aren't officers you should be mixing with." Frances knew what her brother meant but didn't openly say. If Frances were to associate with officers, it should be with those from certain distinguished regiments that everyone in Society knew about. "I'll explain it to you if you promise not to follow up on . . . whatever you're doing."

"Don't talk to me as if I were still a child. I am capable of discretion and prudent behavior."

Charles, ever the diplomat, just smiled. "I stand rebuked. I just need to impress upon you the seriousness of this. And I will extract your promise not to use this phrase in discussion?" Frances nodded. "Very well. Do you know what the Secret Service is?"

"I've heard the term. They're spies, right?"

"Yes. But there's been a change in how they're organized recently. Out of the Boer War, what had been a casually organized network of agents gathering intelligence was turned into a formal government department designed to protect the security of the realm by uncovering foreign designs against Britain and preventing other nations from doing the same within Britain. Many of the men had been recruited from the ranks of officers in the army and navy. To hide their real purpose, they were given the obscure name of Reconnaissance Battalion. Within the army, because they work in the dark, they're called the Shadow Boys.

But that's just used quietly in certain government bureaus. It's not for drawing room gossip. I'm trusting you, Franny. I'm giving you this information in return for which you won't get involved in something you shouldn't. Now does that satisfy your curiosity?"

It did, actually, for the most part. But Frances had more questions.

"You said they protect our security. Doesn't that overlap with Scotland Yard's Special Branch?"

"In God's name, what do you know about Special Branch?"

"I'm taking an interest in government. It is the family profession, after all."

"Oh, very well. Again, for your ears only, Special Branch and the Secret Service are supposed to work together, with one supplying intelligence information and the other providing security and policing functions. In practice, there is considerable rivalry. The Secret Service has political ties because of the nature of the men who run it. Special Branch comes out of Scotland Yard, which is more civil service—men who have come up from the ranks, so to speak. And that's enough information for you, dear sister."

Frances nodded, and Charles watched her. Then everything started to come together.

"Wait—this isn't a suffrage issue. This is about the Colcombe manuscript, isn't it?"

She had told Charles about reporting the loss to Superintendent Maples, but Charles had assumed Maples would indulge her and then forget all about it. Then, a month or so from now, the manuscript would turn up in a forgotten drawer somewhere. That an inspector was looking into it, someone from Special Branch no less, was beyond belief. What exactly had Danny been writing about?

As children, Frances and Charles could read each other's minds. And so it was no surprise when Frances leaned over, put her hand on Charles's, and said, "Yes, that's what it's about. And so I need to know, what happened in South Africa?"

She knew the basics. The Boers were farmers of Dutch descent, tough and strong, who chaffed under increasing British influence. The professional British army had fought a bitter war against something they were not used to: a citizen army where every able-bodied man could take to the field with a rifle in a strange landscape the enemy troops knew far better than their opponents from Britain.

"South Africa was nothing like the war we were used to, lines of men in uniform across an open field. Battles were sudden and chaotic, with attacks coming out of nowhere, and nothing we had been trained for prepared us. But the British can learn quickly." He smiled grimly.

General Audendale, their commanding officer, had an idea for a different kind of company. As an extraordinary horseman, Danny was selected as one of the leaders for a new independent unit comprising the best English riders and hard-bitten Australians from the colonial force, men who had grown up in a land as unforgiving as the African veldt. The Empire Light Horse, they called themselves.

Danny took to it well. They were effective, brutally so, copying their enemy's tactics while armed with the very latest European firearms, and they gave the Boer many a surprise. The war was already winding down, with the Boers mostly in retreat, when disaster struck.

They were ordered into a battle along the Sapphire River. Danny wanted to wait until night, but a day raid was ordered. The company was split up as night fell, and the casualties were terrific. Danny had been wounded, and after the battle of Sapphire River, the Empire Light Horse was disbanded.

"You say you can be discreet," said Charles, "so I'll tell you that although Danny never spoke about it, there were rumors that the mission had been badly planned—not by Danny, but by someone above him. They took a unit that was lightly armed for fast travel and set them up for a traditional battle with a line of men. Some imbecile somewhere wanted to show that the English could still win in a traditional formation.

"It was foolish—no, beyond that. It was criminally stupid. But there was no stomach for an investigation. Everyone was sick of the war by that point. The men were pensioned off, and soon it was over. Perhaps Danny was writing about that—I could see how that could ruffle a few feathers."

"But after all this time? The war ended several years ago. And we won—that should've settled everything."

But Charles shook his head. "There had been too much embarrassment, too many ill-planned ventures, too much confusion in learning a new kind of warfare. Even years later, the Sapphire River debacle remains a sensitive point. That whole wretched war. Know this, dear sister, and never forget: we didn't win that war. The Boers lost, but we didn't win." He gave his sister a look. "I know you want to help the Colcombe family. For their sake, for Danny's memory. But do be careful, Franny."

She prepared a smart response to tell him to stop being so overprotective, but then she saw real concern and bit back her remark.

"I promise to be careful. But surely there's no danger in speaking with some old government hands, those who were in power back then. Someone with stories to tell."

Charles laughed. "And they're just going to admit to you that they were authors of a military disaster."

"It's been some years. Someone may give up some information, let something slip, give up another name. As you know, I can be very persuasive."

"No, Franny. You're not going to march through Whitehall making a spectacle of yourself."

"Oh yes I will. But Charles," she sweetened her voice, "you know everyone, you and Father. There was someone in the government who knew. And if you give me a name, I won't have to march all over Whitehall."

Charles sighed. "Oh, very well. Do you know Lord Ashton Crossley?"

"I know the name, but nothing about him. Was he in the War Office?"

"He had no position. But he wielded great power behind the scenes. If anyone knows, he does, and because he was unofficial, no personal embarrassment would attach to him. But I don't even know why I tell you. He won't see you."

"He will if you write me an introduction."

Charles laughed again. "Franny, use your head. He's a staunch Conservative, and we're Seaforths. An introduction from us? He'd toss it in the fire. But if anyone can get past his front door, you can. Now that's all, Franny. Go embarrass yourself if you want, but don't blame me."

Frances just gave her brother a kiss on his cheek. "Don't worry. As the phrase goes, there's more than one way to skin a cat."

Mr. McDonald knocked on the door to remind his lordship that it was time to prepare for the meeting. Charles told his sister to be good as she took her leave, and she found herself lost in thought about tight-lipped police officers, secret service agents operating in the dark, and soldiers killing and dying in the African heat.

CHAPTER 5

Frances made the next day fun for Mallow. That evening was the Moore dinner party, and Mallow was delighted to dress her ladyship up. Frances rarely attended formal events, so Mallow hardly ever got to help Frances get into an elaborate ball gown and choose jewelry.

For Mallow, the day started early, choosing the right dress and thinking about her ladyship's hair, which was enough to drive Frances to distraction.

"It isn't until evening, and we haven't even had breakfast yet." Mallow looked so disappointed, Frances took pity on her. "How about this? I have another committee meeting this morning and then—" and then a meeting with the mysterious Colonel Mountjoy, but no need to tell Mallow that. "And then I'll be home. So go through all my clothes. Consider jewelry. And we'll have all afternoon to choose." And happily, Mallow agreed.

———◦━◦◦━◦———

That morning's meeting with the Ladies' Educational Improvement Club focused on trying to increase opportunities for education and training for poor youth in London. Frances remembered her cousin Susan had married a man "in trade," to the family's shock. He was a builder and had made lots of money. Perhaps he could be persuaded to lend some of his carpenters and bricklayers to teach the unfortunates? Frances reasoned he'd want to oblige his noble-born in-laws. After some discussion, of course.

"Oh really, do you think he'd listen to you?" asked the committee chairwoman, Lady Anthea Trent.

"Yes," said Frances, thinking of Superintendent Maples. "In the end, people usually do." She wrote it down in her notebook and then, with the meeting adjourned, left for the Military Club.

The club porter gave her full deference, or as much deference as even a well-born woman would ever get at a gentleman's club. She asked for Colonel Mountjoy. The porter said he would check if the colonel was present and then showed her into a room for visitors. It was comfortable but separate from the main rooms. *Now here was something to change*, thought Frances. *These clubs, as much as Parliament—perhaps even more—served as seats of power. How about opening these clubs to women?*

Parliament would probably be easier. She reflected on when Charles would talk about the Crimean War, a war fought before high-powered rifles in the days of cavalry charges. But there were old officers in this club who fought in that war, and they would not change easily.

The door opened to admit an impeccable man. His suit was beautifully cut for his large frame. He sported a neatly trimmed military-style mustache that partially covered a generous smile, and when he spoke, his voice was a warm baritone.

"Lady Frances? I am Colonel Zachery Mountjoy. Thank you so much for coming. But first I owe you apologies for dragging you here. For propriety's sake, I thought this would be better than your residence or mine." The colonel knew his manners. "Your brother is also a member here, although I know his government duties spare him little time. I only know him by sight, but he enjoys a reputation here as a fine officer and a highly effective member of the government."

The words poured out smoothly. Frances thought to match them. "How kind of you, Colonel. Actually, although we haven't met, your face is familiar. I recall that you attended Daniel's funeral." He had been noted as an "unidentified officer" because of his bearing—Kat hadn't been able to remember his name.

He seemed surprised, but only for a moment. "Very good, Lady Frances. You have a good eye for faces. Yes, I believe the military fraternity should turn out when a brother officer passes, especially when he was a hero like Colcombe. I paid a condolence call later as well to Mrs. Colcombe." His name had probably gone in one of Mrs. Colcombe's ears and out the other.

"All that does you credit. Thank you for attending, on behalf of the Colcombes. But I admit I was a little surprised to get your note, and I look forward to hearing what you have to say."

"To start with, I just want to say, on behalf of so many soldiers, thank you for all the help you've given the Colcombe family. I'm afraid I knew Colcombe only by reputation, but I was aware of his exploits in South Africa. His family deserves well. I am glad they have friends like you. I understand you've been helping them with a manuscript Colcombe lost?"

"Did you speak with the Colcombes? I didn't know anyone else was aware I was helping them."

Mountjoy smiled, a little paternally, which irritated Frances.

"It's very hard to keep secrets in as tight a community as London. I've heard a certain Inspector Eastley has been searching for it."

"I hadn't realized that. Would it be rude for me to ask what your interest is?"

Mountjoy laughed. "A perfectly fair question. My interest is purely philanthropic. As an old soldier myself, I keep an open ear and open eye for any of the King's men who have run into difficulties. There was much talk about poor Colcombe. I made a few inquiries, quietly, of course, to make sure he hadn't left them in financial trouble and that they were being well advised."

Charles had done that, Frances knew. He went over family affairs in their solicitors' offices. It was interesting that Mountjoy had looked into it as well. Purely out of goodness? He was in the Secret Service after all.

"But about the manuscript. Frankly, I don't know what happened to it. But Colcombe had been talking about war memoirs, and that doesn't always please everyone. Many things didn't go well in South Africa. I don't need to tell you, Lady Frances, that by the end, the public was disgusted with the war, with its cost not only in money but in soldiers' lives and the devastation it had wreaked in that country."

"The Seaforths have always been in public service. I remember the talk in our house."

The colonel nodded. "Men in the government saw careers damaged or ruined. And no one wanted to be reminded of what had happened. And perhaps, if Colcombe's manuscript came out, it would cause more damage. No telling what was in it, and no telling whom it would upset."

"Are you warning me to stop looking for it, Colonel? To not cooperate with the police?"

Mountjoy threw up his hands and laughed again. "Warning you? This is England, my lady, not some mythic land in a gothic novel. Of course not. It's really just a matter of tactics. Personally, I don't think it was destroyed—it's too valuable. Someone may want to read it—and then return it or even publicize it. If you chase it, and they know you're chasing it, it becomes more valuable. Someone may hold onto it longer, thinking he can make even greater use of it for political purposes, sale, or even blackmail. When I was a boy, my lady, my grandmother had a ginger tabby. When I chased him, he ran. But when I sat quietly, he'd come and crawl into my lap."

Frances nodded.

"So that is my advice—and not my warning—Lady Frances. You called in Scotland Yard, and while in retrospect that might not have been the most strategic move, what's done is done. There's no point, however, in encouraging them, if you get my drift."

"So you're saying that the sooner this calms down, the sooner the manuscript might make its way back?"

Again, Mountjoy threw up his hands. "I couldn't phrase it better myself, my lady. I am so pleased that we understand each other." He stood to indicate the discussion was over. "I won't keep you any longer. But if you or the Colcombes have any questions, here is my card. It has just my club address, since this is where I can usually be found, but I wrote my home address on the back, just in case you need to reach me urgently. And one more thing—if you do hear anything, just let me know, without acting first, of course, and I'll have a discreet word around town."

Frances pasted a smile on her face and gave Colonel Mountjoy her hand. "You've been too kind," she said.

"Please, let me see you into a hansom," said Mountjoy.

"That's quite all right. I'm sure the club porter can get me one."

"The pleasure is all mine, Lady Frances. Your brother is a fellow club member—I can do no less."

He indeed hailed a cab for her. The door slammed, and she was off, back to Miss Plimsoll's. The exchange played again and again in her head. He was Secret Service. But that didn't mean he wasn't genuinely being thoughtful. Two serious agencies—the Secret Service and Special Branch—with interest in the same manuscript. But unlike Inspector Eastley, Colonel Mountjoy didn't question her. He didn't seem to care about finding it, so maybe he really did want to help out.

Part of her confusion centered on social class, she realized, thinking now about what her brother said about agency rivalry. Men like Mountjoy, the officer class, in the same club as her brother. It wouldn't be a surprise to see him at a social event.

Should she tell Eastley about Mountjoy's interest? Or would that make it worse?

Frances wasn't sure why, but she found it irritating that Mountjoy had sought her out to discuss the manuscript. He seemed to know a lot and was vague on how he came by this knowledge. Simple kindness didn't seem sufficient for his interest, but maybe she was being cynical.

Once home, Frances forced herself to put the Colcombe manuscript out of her mind and catch up on both her personal correspondences and letters on behalf of various clubs and committees. After lunch, she took a nap; these parties lasted well into the night, and she wanted to be fresh. Mallow gently woke her in plenty of time and then helped her into the waiting dress and did her hair. Mallow had a lot of opinions on what would best work for her ladyship's complexion, hair color, and face shape and wasn't shy about vocalizing them.

"Oh, my lady, you do look grand, if I say so myself. You'll turn all the heads."

"It's your work, Mallow. Nicely done."

"Thank you, my lady," said Mallow. Frances glanced at her maid—she was all pink, the way she was when she was pleased with herself. Why shouldn't she be pleased—she had done her mistress proud.

"I will admit that every once in a while, it is fun to get you truly dressed up, my lady."

"And I admit, every once in a while, I like getting dressed up. I am sorry I don't give you a chance to dress me up more often. If you worked for another lady, you'd have more of an opportunity."

"That's quite all right, my lady. There's plenty to keep me busy."

Frances laughed. "But what if I meet a duke tonight, Mallow, and because I behave myself, for once, he proposes. I become mistress of a great house, and you become lady's maid to a duchess. A huge town house and a country estate instead of a little hotel suite and balls every week. Oh, but I'm just being silly. Now what about a hat . . . ?"

But she had put some ideas into Mallow's head. She enjoyed the prestige of being a maid to an aristocratic lady, but it might be nice to be in a great house. What if Lady Frances did marry well? Mallow imagined herself in a London town house, full of junior maids who had to defer to her. Maybe someday she would even become a housekeeper, the highest rank a female servant could aspire to. She'd be Mrs. Mallow then—housekeepers were always called "Mrs." as a mark of great respect. A housekeeper in a ducal household—then maids in the house would have to serve her tea while she sat . . .

"Lost in thought, Mallow?" said Frances with a smile.

"I'm very sorry, my lady," said Mallow. It didn't do to daydream.

"Not at all, it was entirely my fault for starting it. Yes, that goes nicely with my dress. Good choice." Frances glanced at herself in the mirror again. Then she sighed.

"Remember when we went to my cousin's country party in Lincolnshire last summer?" she said. "It was so hot, and I persuaded you slip outside with me so we could cool our feet in the pond late at night."

Mallow remembered. She had been afraid at first. A city girl born and bred, she found the country so dark and too quiet. She imagined wolves hiding behind every tree. But oh, it was so delicious in the pond, and she followed her ladyship's example, lifting her skirts and slipping into the water up to her knees. Lady Frances had gossiped to her maid about the other guests, and Mallow had giggled as Lady Frances mimicked them.

"Oh, go on, my lady," she had laughed.

"It's true, Mallow, every word."

Frances looked at her maid and brought her back to the present. "You do know, Mallow, that if I became a duchess, you and I could never cool our feet in a pond again."

Now Mallow sighed, too. "Yes, my lady."

A cab dropped Frances at the elegant Moore home, and the butler announced her. Lady Moore found her quickly, and the two women caught up with each other. Lady Moore was delighted to hear about all of Frances's achievements and the committees she worked on. She seemed shocked when Frances mentioned her suffrage work, but Frances guessed she was more titillated than upset.

"Maybe it was the old Queen's death," said Lady Moore, "but things seem to have changed so much. Women especially seem to have more . . . well, more choices today. But some things haven't changed." She smiled. "People still get married. Have you met the Honorable George Ralston? He's the eldest son of Viscount Wellchester . . ."

Frances had no interest in meeting the Hon. George Ralston. "Not yet. I really must meet him. Meanwhile, I seem to have lost sight of my brother and sister-in-law. I'll call on you very soon, Lady Moore . . ."

Charles and Mary were part of a knot of other Foreign Office couples. They welcomed her, but Frances quickly snatched her sister-in-law away "for sister gossip," she told the group, to much amusement.

"Thank you so much," said Mary when they were by themselves. "I do accept the responsibilities of being a political wife, but it's getting so tiring hearing about the kaiser in Germany, the emperor in Austria, and the sultan in the Ottoman Empire. But enough—you look lovely tonight."

"As do you, dear sister." They giggled. "Now tell me," said Frances, "I've not been as closely tied to Society as you these past months—even these past years. Tell me who is who."

Mary pointed out the bishop's nephew (who was engaged to the second daughter of a baron), the grandson of a duke (who was being sent to India until that mess in Oxford blew over), and the young earl (who was engaged to an American woman, but the money was needed and Americans seemed to have so much of it).

They weren't alone long. First Charles found them, and then another man about Charles's age sauntered over. He had a handsome face—no, more than that, decided Frances. He had a face out of another era, from the regency at the beginning of the nineteenth century, not the beginning of the twentieth. His eyes showed some merriment, as if from an earlier, wilder London, and his suit was a little livelier than what most of the other men were wearing.

"Seaforth, don't you think you're being just a little bit selfish, keeping the two loveliest women here to yourself?"

It was a signal for Charles to introduce them, but he hesitated for a few seconds, and his smile seemed artificial. *How odd*, thought Frances. *No man had better manners than Charles.*

"Allow me," he finally said, introducing his wife and sister to Lord Gareth Blaine in a toneless voice. "You're something in the Home Office, right, Blaine?"

"Yes—something," said Blaine with a grin. "A pleasure to meet both of you."

The Home Office. It was the ministry that had overall authority over policing functions and security of the realm. Her decision to attend this party was already paying off.

"I imagine your work must be very interesting," said Frances.

"My sister would like to be a police inspector," said Charles.

Blaine laughed. "If it were in my power to do so, I would appoint you today. Unfortunately, supervision of Scotland Yard is not in my remit. But your name is familiar to me—tell me, Lady Frances, do you know my cousin, Genevieve Ballentine?"

"Of course. She is a very active member of the women's suffrage committee."

Mary grinned, and Charles rolled his eyes.

"I imagine you don't share your cousin's views," said Frances with a hint of challenge in her voice.

Charles interrupted at that point, saying he would happily leave them to their political discussion, and he wanted to introduce Mary to some people from the Exchequer. Mary gave Frances a quick wink as she left with her husband.

"If I may say, you imagine a lot," Lord Gareth said when they were alone. "But regarding my politics, you imagine wrong. Please ask Genevieve about me, and you will find I am one of the few members of our family talking to her. Because of her stance, her mother is beyond furious. But I still visit with her. Indeed, I have great sympathy for your cause, and I support universal suffrage."

"Do you really, Lord Gareth?" So many men said so just to make fun of her. Others tended to hedge so as not to offend her. It was rare to find an outspoken supporter like Lord Gareth.

"Again, Genevieve will happily confirm my views."

"May I ask what convinced you?"

"I like to think I am well read. Certain philosophical writings . . ." And that led to a discussion of favorite authors and favorite philosophers. Lord Gareth had taken a degree at Cambridge, and Frances lost no opportunity in telling him about her unusual education in America. Lord Gareth was curious and asked many questions. The conversation was a challenge—and although Frances worked at it, she had a sense Lord Gareth had to work at it too.

"So tell me, do you really want to be a police inspector?"

"I think I'd be very good at it. Are you sure you don't have anything to do with the police at the Home Office?" she said with a smile.

"My dear lady, if it were up to me, to please you, I'd appoint you commissioner. But my work is so dull, I can't tell you about it, as it would spoil your good opinion of me."

"Isn't it rather arrogant of you to assume you already have my good opinion?" But her tone was mocking, not serious.

He mimicked her. "I'd be very wounded if I did not."

Frances eyed him. "But I don't think you have my brother's good opinion."

"So you noticed," he said dryly. "My politics and beliefs sometimes upset even my progressive colleagues among the Liberals. And as a second son, I don't have expectations of becoming a duke like my father and influencing the world that way. But don't think the feeling is mutual between me and your brother. I admire your brother as a man of principle and intelligence, even if we disagree sometimes."

Blaine then waved his hand as if to clear the air. "As entertaining as this has been, I'm in danger of monopolizing your evening and causing a dreadful scandal. But I wonder . . . are you familiar with Lord and Lady Heathcote?"

Even people who didn't know the Heathcotes—and their circle of intimates—knew of them. They held fashionable parties where the liveliest members of Society mingled with poets and artists. Perhaps too fashionable: Frances had never been to a Heathcote event but had heard the rumors of behaviors that were never discussed in polite drawing rooms . . .

"They are quite notorious. I did not know you were a member," said Frances.

"A member? You make it sound like being a member of a political party. It isn't that formal. One simply shows up."

"My brother and late father said they weren't to be trusted." There had been whispers of papers stolen, secrets passed, scandals hushed up . . .

"We're just a lively group of friends assembling a little theater party with a reception beforehand. Don't believe society gossip. Care to join us? Unless you're afraid." His eyes were inviting, but there was also a challenge.

"I never said I was afraid," she snapped back. She was not subject to her brother's approval. "It sounds pleasant. I love the theater. I saw one of Mr. Shaw's latest plays, *Major Barbara*. Very thought provoking."

"I agree . . . and I look forward to discussing it with you when next we meet. But I should tell you that this evening of theater will be a little different. May I reach you at your brother's house?"

"Actually, I now reside at Miss Plimsoll's Residence Hotel for Ladies." She tripped it off proudly. Lord Gareth raised an eyebrow.

"How independent of you. This has been very interesting. Good evening, Lady Frances."

Frances made the rounds for the rest of the evening, catching up on gossip and enduring comments, sarcastic and otherwise, about her work with the suffrage movement. She found Mary as the party wound down. Charles was just finishing a conversation in another room.

Mary smiled slyly. "You seem to have made quite a conquest this evening."

"I don't know what you mean. Lord Gareth and I were talking politics." But she reddened nonetheless.

Coaches waited outside, but not for the Seaforths. Charles had traded in the family coach for a motorcar. Frances had never thought about the sound of iron-shod horses on pavement, but now it was startling to hear the hum of a precision engine instead of the clop of hoof beats. It was very smooth. Charles said that in twenty years, there wouldn't be a horse left in London. It made Frances feel very modern to be in an automobile. She was sure the Heathcotes would approve. She suppressed a shiver at the thought of being at a Heathcote event. She felt guilty at not telling Mary, fearing her sensible friend would try to talk her out of it.

They drove to Miss Plimsoll's, and Charles got out with Frances, waiting until the night porter came to open the door. The porter grumbled as usual, and Charles gave his sister a kiss on the cheek and told her not to run herself down with committee work.

The porter bolted the door behind her. Frances was looking forward to bed. She had told Mallow not to bother waiting up, but the loyal maid was knitting in the lounge and rose to greet her mistress as soon as she came in.

"A good evening, my lady?"

"Yes, thank you. By the way, would you like to live in Norfolk? Lady Moore seems determined that I become the next Viscountess Wellchester."

Before Mallow could respond, they heard the knocker on the door. Another resident at a late-night party? Through the heavy door, they heard a muffled voice. "It's the chauffeur. Left something in the car, my lady." Frances was surprised. She had her wrap and her little bag—there was nothing else.

But the porter was already opening the door before Frances and Mallow could stop him, and it was barely cracked before a man pushed himself inside. He was tall and lean with an outdoor complexion.

The women and the porter froze. The porter was neither young nor fit, and there was no one in easy call.

The man gently closed the door. Then he grinned. He pulled himself up and gave a mock salute. "Private Alfred Barnstable, late of his majesty's colonial force and the Empire Light Horse." The twang was unmistakable—he was an Australian. Frances had never actually spoken with an Australian but had heard the accent, often mocked by Englishmen.

"Sorry, ladies. Would you be Frances Ffolkes? Or know where she is? This is Miss Plimsoll's, isn't it? She left a note that she'd like to speak with anyone who had served under Major Colcombe."

Frances gathered her wits. "I'm Frances Ffolkes. And your entrance here is rather abrupt and unusual. How do I know you are who you say you are?"

The soldier considered that. "How about this? The major had a scar on his left hand—a fencing accident, he said."

"That's true," said Frances.

Then the soldier grinned. "I have one more. He liked to talk about his women. And if you're Frances Ffolkes, he called you 'Ursula.' I got that right, didn't I?"

Frances was speechless, but Mallow jumped in.

"Mr. Barnstable, this is Lady Frances Ffolkes. She is not anyone's 'woman.' And when you address her, you will call her 'my lady.' Is that clear?"

He didn't look at all abashed. "Sorry about that. Now what might you be called?"

"Miss Mallow to you. I am her ladyship's personal maid."

"You have a pretty face, Miss Mallow. Would you be interested—?"

"Mr. Barnstable," jumped in Frances, "flirt with my maid on your own time. It's late, and I sense we have a lot to discuss. Go sit in the lounge, and I'll be along shortly."

"Right you are, my lady." He bowed and headed into the lounge.

"Well," said Frances.

"Well indeed, my lady," said Mallow. "He's Australian." That explained everything.

Frances turned back to the porter, who was looking a little stunned himself. "This man fought with my brother in South Africa. I don't suppose you have any beer I could buy off you? I'll pay you double what it cost."

A rare smile lit up his craggy face. "Quite all right, my lady. You can have them at cost."

"Thank you, that would be lovely." She drank very little during the evening, but the thought of a beer was suddenly welcome. The porter said he'd bring along the bottles while she saw to her guest.

Private Barnstable had made himself very comfortable in the best chair. She doubted his lodgings had overstuffed leather chairs.

"I am glad to see you settled here," she said with a wry smile. "I thank you for responding to my note. But it is a little surprising to see you sneaking in like this at such a late hour."

"I'm sorry I startled you, my lady. And this one here, too." He winked at Mallow, who did not give him the pleasure of a response. "But being in the war, being in *that* war, has made me a very cautious man, and when I tell you what I have to tell you, maybe you'll see why. I'll give it to you straight. Daniel Colcombe was the finest man I knew, and when I heard he died, I almost died myself—but what's this?"

The porter carried a tray with three bottles of beer and three glasses. He placed them on the little table between Barnstable and the women and made as if to pour.

"You looked thirsty," said Frances.

"Well you're a lady, no mistake—but don't pour that out, man. No need to get a glass dirty." He snapped the top off and drank from the bottle. "That's good. But don't mind me, ladies, go ahead and use your glasses."

And then, to Mallow's astonishment, Frances snapped the top off her beer and took a drink. What would Frances's mother have thought? But then, feeling there was nothing to do but follow suit, Mallow sighed, opened her own bottle, and took a sip herself.

The porter shook his head and left. Barnstable took another swig and told his story.

He had grown up in Australia and said he had learned to ride before he could even walk. Enlisting in the army was a way to get some adventure before settling down, and he found himself in South Africa. His skill on horseback had landed him in the newly formed Empire Light Horse under Colcombe.

"I won't bore you ladies with the details, but we raised some hell, I can tell you, pardon my language."

"But it ended badly," Frances prompted.

Barnstable nodded. "And that's what this is about, my lady, what I wanted to talk to you about. But now I don't know if I should tell women—"

"Oh, for goodness sake, Mr. Barnstable, you're keeping me up after a long day. I've not been as sheltered as you think, and Mallow grew up in one of London's livelier neighborhoods. Get on with it."

He grinned. "That I will." He took another long drink. "We'd been harrying Brother Boer and were heading out for another patrol when some red-tabbed officers from HQ showed up. The major received them in his tent, but the discussion became an argument, and although we couldn't hear all the words, it was clear they wanted the major to do something with us he didn't want to do. We kept hearing references to the War Office, but that was all we could make out. Still, we found out what happened soon enough."

Barnstable's cheerful face suddenly looked grim, and his eyes lost focus as he went back to the African veldt. Frances was reminded of the older soldier at the soup kitchen, the veteran of the Sepoy Mutiny.

"On that last day, we didn't do what we had been doing. We didn't attack the way Major Colcombe had us do in the past. We bit off more than we could chew, and that's a fact, and we got hit hard. As the sun fell, a couple dozen of us found ourselves stuck between an exposed ridge and a Boer force twice our size by the Sapphire River. Our lieutenant was killed.

"We dug in, but it was only a matter of time. Night fell, but that meant nothing to the Boer. Ammo almost gone and worse yet, water gone. You don't want to be without water in Africa. The full moon rose, men said their prayers, and we fixed bayonets and prepared for one last charge. But we heard some

Boer shots just to the left of us. They were shooting at Major Colcombe, half-running, half-crawling in the dark and carrying canteens and ammo. Two trips he made, a quarter mile each way, dodging bullets and carrying water and ammo. He even carried a wounded man on his back to bring him to the field hospital. On his second trip back, he was shot in the shoulder but made it anyway."

"Oh! May God bless him!" cried out Mallow.

Barnstable just smiled sadly at her. "Yes, Miss Mallow. May God bless him indeed."

Frances was lost for words, however. She tried to imagine the horror, with bullets in the dark, an unseen enemy, and a score of men whose lives depended on him.

"We thought we were dead men, but with water and enough bullets, we held them off. The major had sent the fastest rider with two horses to bring back reinforcements, and shortly after dawn, a score of mounted troopers appeared on the ridge to pin down the Boers long enough for us to escape. I'm not what you'd call a religious man, but whatever Major Colcombe did in life, his sins were wiped clean by what he did that night. And I take some comfort from knowing that he's in a better place."

Barnstable leaned back to finish his beer while Frances and Mallow contemplated the story. No one had ever doubted Colcombe's physical courage, Frances knew well, but this seemed beyond comprehension. Two trips, a mile under fire.

"But why didn't anyone know about this? My brother? The general staff?"

"Well, that was the thing. The senior officers came back and told them that because of extensive casualties, and with the Boers on the run anyway, we were being disbanded. Everyone was given an honorable discharge. We got what they called a bonus, and they told us not to discuss what had happened. We could be prosecuted, they said, for causing a loss of morale. Well I was having none of that. Major Colcombe was the only officer left who knew what had really happened. So I told him, and not just me, all of us who owed our lives, we said that we'd throw away the money and go to prison, but the major ordered us to keep quiet. He said someday, when things had quieted down, he'd tell the story and told us not to hurt ourselves by disobeying his orders. So we left, back to England or Australia. A few stayed to make new lives in Africa."

That explained a lot—the book was no doubt about that tragic battle, which was apparently covered up. It was a travesty, and she felt herself getting angry. Danny couldn't even tell his friends, and he should've received the Victoria Cross, the highest decoration in the army.

"Tell me why you're in London—and why you seem so cautious."

"Well, I wanted to see the home country after I was mustered out, and the major said to come back to London with him and he'd find me work, and so he did; he was that kind of man. I wasn't really cut out for city life, but the major wrote a friend and found me work handling sheep up in Scotland. It was good, but I decided it was time to go home, look up my brothers, and think about getting a place of my own. I thought to look up the major but then heard he was dead and how it happened. I was going crazy trying to figure out who could help me. And then I see your note, my lady, and it was a godsend. The major could disassemble and reassemble a firearm in absolute darkness. He never would've had an accident like that. And any man who tells me he killed himself is a damn liar. Again, pardon my language."

He started asking around—other veterans he had known all expected the major to tell the full story eventually, and Barnstable didn't want the major's death to silence the truth about the Empire Light Horse forever. From his time in London, he had become friends with a Colcombe footman. He said the staff knew that the master had been writing something but that the manuscript had disappeared sometime after the master's death.

This footman had said a family friend was helping them look for it—and when he heard who it was and then saw the notice in the club, that decided things for him.

"The major was an easygoing sort, my lady. I remembered your name from talks around evening fires. And he said how your brother was a mate of his. I never served under your brother, but I knew many who did, and there was no one to say anything against Major Ffolkes. He was a right good man and officer. I figured if you were a Ffolkes, I could speak with you. But like I said, South Africa made me a cautious man, and I wasn't taking any chances I didn't need to. Especially with the way the major died."

"You mean you thought Major Colcombe was murdered?" Frances spoke quietly, almost afraid of the words.

"I'm saying that an accident was impossible, and he never would've killed himself. If you have another choice, my lady, then I'd like to hear it."

Frances leaned back in her chair and contemplated Barnstable. He was a frank man, and she sensed no dishonesty there.

"Thank you for your kind words about my brother and for trusting me. I am trying to find the manuscript. Can you tell me if Major Colcombe ever said anything to you about it?"

"Not in England. But we were laid up together in a field hospital in South Africa right after we were relieved. He told me again not to worry. He wanted to give things a chance to calm down and then he'd tell the whole story, the truth, for all our sakes. 'All of it,' said the major, 'more than you men know. But not now—later, when feelings aren't running so high. And I promise the bastards who sent us to be slaughtered on the Sapphire River will pay.'"

Barnstable finished his beer.

"That was all the major told me," said Barnstable. "But I'm glad I could pass the story on to you. I know I promised the major I'd be quiet about this, but now he's gone, and I don't care what they do to me. I've been shooting my mouth off all over London. If they want to find me in Australia, good luck to them. Now you're titled, my lady, you and your brother. I hear he's a marquess. You know the right sort. Maybe you could talk to your brother—"

"Thank you for the suggestion, Mr. Barnstable, but I think I'm capable of doing what needs to be done."

Barnstable wasn't offended. He grinned.

"You sound just like my mother, God rest her soul. She was a fine woman and did not take well to being crossed."

"I'm sorry I never met her," said Frances.

Barnstable stood. "I think I told you all that I could, my lady, and feel better for getting it off my chest. But I'll tell you to watch your back, if I may be so bold. There's a lot of talk about this. As for myself, I'll probably be in London another month, then off to Australia. But I'll call in again if I think of anything else before I go. I'm staying with a mate in Rotherhithe, and I wouldn't send a lady there."

"What you did tonight was good and brave and a testament to Major Colcombe," said Frances. Barnstable just blushed and stammered. Frances pulled out one of her calling cards and gave it to him in case he needed to write or even telephone her. "I just want to make sure you're settled. Now, my note said any veteran who came to be would be rewarded." She reached for her bag, but Barnstable just got annoyed.

"No need for that. I came here out of duty and respect, not for a handout. I took your beer as you're my hostess. Visit me in Australia and I'll make you welcome and serve you one in return. But no money."

Embarrassed, Frances apologized.

"You have a good heart, and I know you meant no harm. Thanks for listening, and for the beer, and God be with you." Barnstable stood and made for the door, but Mallow suddenly stood up.

"It was wicked, Mr. Barnstable. Wicked what they did to you and the major. My lady and I won't let this go."

Frances was astonished. She had never seen Mallow angry like that, but it made a certain amount of sense. People like Barnstable and Mallow served people of quality, gave them loyalty, and in return received care and protection. It's the way Mallow believed the world worked. And when the system didn't work, when loyal men like Barnstable were abandoned and great men like Major Colcombe had to give so much to save them and then die, what hope was there?

"I'm sure you won't, Miss Mallow," he said, and then he was gone.

Mallow took a moment to control herself. "My lady, I apologize most deeply. I spoke without thinking, and I assure you it will not happen again."

"Don't apologize, Mallow. You were completely right. It was wicked, from beginning to end. Why were those men sent to their deaths? Who sent them and why? Forget propriety, Mallow. Take a seat and let's work this out."

"Thank you, my lady."

"So Danny—that is, Major Colcombe—knew what had happened and why. But he wanted to wait for the right time, when passions had cooled. He was too thoughtful to even tell my brother, because Danny didn't want let Charles hurt his own political career doing the noble thing."

"Mr. Barnstable said they were talking about the War Office, my lady. You must know people there."

"You're right, Mallow. I do. Let's start with General Audendale. He was Major Colcombe's and my brother's superior in South Africa. Charles always spoke of him as a man of honor—one of the old school, he had said. He now lives in family manse about a two-hour train ride outside of London. I'll write to him and ask for a visit. If the War Office had interfered in South Africa, Audendale would know."

"Very good, my lady."

"And we'll just hope my brother doesn't find out what we're up to. Come Mallow. It's time for bed. We'll take a fresh look at this in the morning. We have a lot to do and think about."

Frances quickly got into bed. She was exhausted but couldn't stop thinking about Danny. His death was tragic, but she thought of the men he had saved, and no one could have a better epitaph. Tomorrow was soon enough to plan.

She forced herself to stop focusing on South Africa and instead thought about the party. Frances had enjoyed it more than she had expected. The conversation with Lord Gareth had been entertaining . . . no, make that stimulating. He'd be introducing her to Lord and Lady Heathcote and their lively set! And feeling rather warm inside, she fell asleep.

CHAPTER 6

Frances didn't sleep quite as late as she expected but felt refreshed and went downstairs to call General Audendale.

"Hello, General Audendale? This is Lady Frances Ffolkes. My brother, Charles Ffolkes, served under you in South Africa."

"Of course, my dear. Very nice to speak with you."

"I was hoping to visit you in the near future. I know Danny Colcombe was working on a manuscript. I had some questions about it and hoped you could help me. Would it be acceptable for me to visit you?"

"Poor Colcombe. Tragic end. But of course. Let's set a date and you can come down by train. Don't get many visitors and would like to see you, my dear . . ."

Frances stepped out of the phone closet and saw two notices waiting for her—unusual for early in the day.

"Both delivered by hand," said Mrs. Beasley, who approved of old-fashioned ways.

The first was from Henry Wheaton:

Dear Lady Frances,

I very much enjoyed our visit to the National Gallery, and mother was pleased to have another woman to speak with. On

Saturday, if your schedule allows, we would be pleased to have you join us for a brief excursion in the park.

Hoping to see you then.

That sounded most pleasant.
The next was from Lord Gareth:

My Dear Lady Frances,

I know it is short notice, but we're going to have our little theater party tomorrow evening. I will pick you up in my motorcar, and then it's off to the Heathcotes' followed by a performance.

Luncheon was the annual planning meeting of the Greater London Library Guild. The goal was to improve literacy by giving greater access to books for the less fortunate. Then it was back to her flat at Miss Plimsoll's to get ready for dinner at her friend Thomasina's house. Thomasina—"Tommie" to her friends—was a fellow suffragist, and their good friend Gwendolyn would also be joining them. Tommie lived in a drafty old place with her bedridden mother, who ran their few servants ragged keeping up with her demands.

Frances brought along a bag full of suffragist papers—pamphlets and speeches she wanted to go over with the other women. They spent an hour reviewing them but gave over the rest of the evening to fun. Tommie had given the cook the night off after she served Tommie's mother an early dinner, and the three women had great fun making toast and cheese in the kitchen along with baked beans. Frances had also brought some fine apple cider, and they stayed up late talking about childhood days.

Gwen had already said she would stay the night, and Tommie offered to put Frances up for the night as well, but Frances gracefully declined, saying it was just a ten-minute walk home, and it was a pleasant night. She had worn shoes that were comfortable, if unfashionable. Also, she was able to take a shortcut by passing through the mews behind some fashionable homes instead of the busy main street that was well lit. Frances wasn't nervous; her neighborhood wasn't dangerous, and she had done this walk plenty of times.

When she first heard the footsteps in the dark, she assumed it was a groom seeing to horses. But the footsteps kept coming. She stopped to listen more closely, and the footsteps stopped too. She told herself she was being ridiculous. She picked up her pace and heard the stranger following her more quickly as well.

Her heart pounded and throat got dry. She thought of running, but even in a simple dress and good shoes, she knew that she was unlikely to outpace her pursuer. She was stupid—she had just learned that Danny Colcombe had been killed. She had stepped into Special Branch and Secret Service territory; Lord only knew what she had stirred up.

There was only one thing to do—scream. Maybe a servant at the back of the house would hear her. She took a deep breath, but then she heard a shout: "You there, stop! Police!" Then more footfalls and the sound of an ash can being overturned.

She knew the sensible thing would be to race home, but she was too curious. "Constable?" she called into the darkness. She saw the glint off a helmet.

"Are you all right, my lady?"

"Yes, Constable, thank you. But I think that I was being followed."

"Yes, my lady. I saw a lurking figure and gave chase, but there are several exits for grooms along the way, and he disappeared into the night. But if I may, you shouldn't be walking home alone this late. I'll see you the rest of the way."

"Thank you, Constable. I'm just around the next corner, at Miss Plimsoll's." They walked in companionable silence the short way along the rest of the mews and then onto the street again. By the front door, Frances turned to him, her mind work-ing furiously.

"You were both diligent and kind, Constable. I would like your name so I can commend you to your superiors."

"Thank you, my lady, but that's not necessary. Just glad I could help. They wouldn't know me here anyway—a couple of the local lads were sick, so I'm filling in from another station. Good night, my lady."

And before she could ask another question, the constable dis-appeared into the dark.

Mallow was waiting for her upstairs, and Frances told her the story. Mallow was horrified and asked for a promise that her ladyship would never again take a shortcut or walk alone after dark.

"There is great wickedness in this city, my lady. Begging your pardon, you have no idea."

Frances was going to argue with her but stopped. She saw a little piece of London's grimmer parts while working in the soup kitchen, but that was relatively safe. Mallow had grown up in the East End, seeing horrors Frances could only imagine.

"You're right," said Frances. "I will be more careful."

Mallow shook her head as she tidied up. "I don't know what I'd do if something happened to you, my lady."

"Nothing will happen. And even if it did, Lord and Lady Seaforth would take care of you and see you into a new position."

"Very nice, I'm sure, my lady. But . . ." Mallow struggled to find the words, and Frances sat patiently. "But I would like to keep working for you, my lady." She blushed and turned to cover it.

Frances was touched. "Let's not worry. Nothing really hap-pened. It was probably just a thief after my bag—oh, that's it!" Frances grabbed her bag, which was full of suffragist club papers. "What if someone thought my bag contained Danny Colcombe's manuscript and that's why I was followed?"

"You mean, my lady, someone else wants it too—and thinks you have it?"

"Exactly—but who? And there's something else I can't figure out." She frowned.

Mallow was used to her mistress's reflective moods. It was something she learned in university, she said, a way of looking at the details of a problem. "Going to the text," she called it.

"The constable called me 'my lady.' He shouldn't have made that assumption. 'Miss' or possibly 'Madam.' Unless he knew me—but I certainly didn't know him. Now that, Mallow, is the most interesting thing about the whole affair."

—◆—

Frances woke up the next morning feeling frustrated. She could go to the local station, but she'd look a fool, talking about a constable whose name she didn't know on the suspicion he apparently knew her. She was sure she hadn't seen him before.

She could go to Colonel Mountjoy with her thoughts, but he hadn't wanted her further involved, that much was clear. And there was nothing connecting this with the Colcombe manuscript except coincidence. He'd give her a pat on the head and send her on her way. Inspector Eastley? If there was something funny with the police, he'd already know it and wouldn't discuss it.

Perhaps it was a lucky guess on the constable's part—or maybe it had something to do with Barnstable's recent visit. No telling now, but it would bear consideration for later.

Meanwhile, she focused on the night. Lord Gareth would be picking her up for the theatrical evening with the Heathcote set. She wondered what he had meant when he had said that it would not be a typical evening of theater.

"I'll be going out this evening. Find something smart in the closet—drinks first, then the theater."

Mallow went through Frances's closet and produced a dress Frances had almost forgotten about, something unusual she had had made a couple of years ago, elaborate and elegant and entirely in black and white.

"At the time, my lady, I recall you saying the simplicity of the color scheme didn't suit you, but perhaps a second look. I really think you'll find it a flattering cut."

Frances agreed, and Mallow helped her get into it. Once it was all buttoned up, she gave her mistress a critical look as Frances reviewed herself in the mirror. Mallow had learned a thing or two about women's clothes and how they change or flatter the ladies who wore them. The severity of the cut and the black and white scheme exaggerated Lady Frances's hourglass figure. The copper hair stood out in sharp relief, and even her ladyship's cheekbones seemed more prominent. The gray eyes appeared deeper, and the overall effect was to make her a little older. A little worldlier. So different from the soft and romantic styles she had for eveningwear or the brisk and cheerful outfits she favored for daytime.

Mallow hid a smile. Her ladyship rarely took a real look at herself in the mirror, but she was doing so today. Was it an important evening to her ladyship?

"Very well. Run an iron over it and I'll wear it tonight."

―――•❀•―――

Lord Gareth was in the guest lounge when she came down that evening. She watched his eyes closely and was pleased to see his approval at her outfit. Mallow really did know best, she concluded.

Her escort's evening clothes were splendidly tailored for his slim form. And again, she imagined him in something from the last century, from the lively days of Beau Brummel, the arbiter of fashion in the early 1800s, who strode through society like a peacock.

"You look lovely, Lady Frances," he said.

She curtsied. "Thank you, my lord."

He had a little two-seater car, smaller and more nimble than her brother's. "We're meeting at the Heathcote house, then we're going in a group to the theater. It will be an evening of music and dance. Do you like dance, my lady?" She liked the way the slightly mocking "my lady" rolled off his tongue.

"I haven't been to the ballet recently, but I do like it."

"Tell me what you like about it," he said with a smile.

"I like the elegance of the French dancers. I am less interested in technical proficiency than in emotional engagement."

"So you are less interested in the Russian dancers?" he asked, and she sensed a challenge. It was like the conversation the other night, almost a fencing match, and they went back and forth.

"I've actually seen the dancers in Russia," he said. "Perhaps some of the finest dancing in the world can be found in St. Petersburg."

"You've been to Russia?" she said. She had never met anyone who had visited Russia, and Lord Gareth launched into several anecdotes, amusing and illustrative, populated with fatalistic peasants and talented but dark-humored musicians.

"May I ask what you were doing there? Merely to entertain yourself?"

"No, I was carrying on an affair with a married Russian countess, a cousin of the czar, no less."

"You're making fun of me," she said. She watched him closely, trying to get to know him completely, but new facets kept appearing.

"You don't think I'd be so bold as to have an affair with a woman whose husband could have me executed?"

"I still believe you're teasing me, and you think very well of yourself if you think a Russian countess would have you." And Lord Gareth laughed again.

They pulled in front of the Heathcote house, a handsome well-kept building whose location cleverly, like the Heathcotes themselves, straddled a line between aristocratic elegance and artistic fashion.

Lord Gareth parked the car and turned to Frances.

"Tell me, my lady, do suffragists believe in marriage?"

Frances opened her mouth in astonishment and then brought her hand to cheek. "Lord Gareth—this is so sudden! I had no idea you were so overcome. But I can't bring myself to refuse you. We will visit my brother at once to ask his permission."

She had the pleasure of seeing Lord Gareth deeply discomforted for several long moments before he grinned and wagged his finger at her.

"See—I can tease, too," she said. "Anyway, suffragists believe in the marriage of true equals. And when you are ready to propose, you may ask my brother for his blessing but not his permission. Now do lead me inside."

Other guests were already gathered in the drawing room, which was dimly lit. The dresses were ornate and perhaps too lavishly trimmed for the most proper society events. She saw Lord and Lady Heathcote themselves in clothes so beautiful and well-tailored that they almost succeeded in covering up their dissipation with elegance. She waited for Gareth to introduce her to them, but he whispered. "This is not your typical gathering. If they wish to meet you, they will say so. But probably not tonight." He smiled and shrugged, trying to excuse this strange breech of etiquette. "They only talk to people after they've been to several of their gatherings. It is the way of things here."

Frances recognized a few people, although knew none of them well. But she could attach at least a minor scandal to them—Lord M., who had once left London very quickly after a card scandal at the Wentworth Club, and Mrs. J., whose attachment to her husband's cousin had set all the tongues wagging last season. These were people who had come from aristocratic families—nevertheless, Frances knew her mother would never have admitted any of them to her home.

No servants were evident. Gareth saw her to a drinks table, where Frances couldn't recognize half the bottles: odd-colored liquors with labels in foreign languages.

"Will you allow me to choose for you?" he asked.

"Thank you. But a sherry will be satisfactory." She wanted her wits about her, and there was no telling what some of those drinks might do to her senses. Frances wondered if that would disappoint Gareth, if she would appear unsophisticated. But she was pleased when her choice had the opposite effect.

"Interesting, Lady Frances. You are a progressive, even revolutionary, but you turn away from novelties. That shows a nicely balanced mind."

Frances blushed at the compliment and simply said, "Thank you."

Apparently, although everyone knew it was a theater party, the location was kept secret until whispers began to permeate the room, and Gareth said it was time to be off. They didn't drive to the West End theaters but to a slightly shabby bohemian neighborhood that she rarely had occasion to visit. She probably would've walked right by the theater had Lord Gareth not pointed it out to her. It could've been a warehouse. He drove the auto through a narrow alley into what had once been a stable and parked it. The rest of the party soon followed in their own vehicles, and Lord Gareth tipped a half-asleep porter to watch them.

"While you were on the other side of the Atlantic, did you manage to make it to South America?" asked Lord Gareth.

"You're still teasing me. South America is as far from New York as New York is from London. But I bet you have."

He just gave her a mysterious smile. "What we're seeing tonight is a sort of circus, a troupe from Argentina. There will be singing and dancing and other acts. It will be rather unusual."

The Heathcote party entered the theater and milled about with the other patrons, who ranged from ladies and gentlemen in eveningwear to artistic types in worn tweeds flecked with paint. Everyone rubbed shoulders without a fuss; no one seemed to resent sharing the lobby with those much richer or poorer.

As she took in the crowd, she heard a familiar voice address her from behind. "Lady Frances, what an unexpected pleasure." It was Colonel Mountjoy.

"Colonel, I didn't take you for a lover of theater. Especially rather obscure entertainments like this."

"As a retired bachelor, I find time for many interests." She saw his eyes light on Lord and Lady Heathcote. "But I never took you for a member of the Heathcote set."

"I am not a member of any 'set,' Colonel. My friend, Lord Gareth, invited me to join some friends of his in a theater party." She found the colonel's assumption a little bold, as if he were cataloguing her.

Frances introduced the two gentlemen—the colonel as belonging to her brother's club and Lord Gareth as a government colleague of her brother's. This was all completely respectable.

"It's a trifle warm in here, Lady Frances. May I get you a glass of water?"

"Thank you, Lord Gareth." His meaning was clear. He was going to give the colonel a few moments alone with her out of politeness, but he was her escort for this evening, so it would be just a few moments. The colonel understood this too. He leaned in close to Frances when they were alone.

"It is not my place to comment on your choice of friends, my lady, but you should know that no one is invited to a Heathcote party unless the Heathcotes want something from them. Whispers about the Colcombe manuscript, and your interest in it, have made their way around Society. I advise you to think carefully before becoming too deeply involved in them."

"I assure you, I have no intention of being taken in by anyone," said Frances coldly. "Maybe you're right. But they don't seem to want to speak with me at the moment. I am really here at the invitation of Lord Gareth," she said.

"Yes—I haven't met him. I only know of him as the second son of the Duke of Carrolton. Perhaps you should ask what the Heathcotes want from him, as well."

At that, Lord Gareth returned with the water. The colonel told them to enjoy the show and bowed out. A few minutes later, Lord and Lady Heathcote led the way into the small theater.

"Unusual" didn't begin to describe the evening. First some vocalists sang a tune accompanied by the strums of a guitar. She listened to the lovely songs in Spanish, which she didn't understand, but the emotion in the singers' voices affected her powerfully. There were dances that Lord Gareth told her were from native tribes, older than any European influence. Some juggling acts appeared as well, and everyone was dressed in bright lavish clothes. They reminded her of the ornately colored parrots and other tropical birds she knew only from pictures.

At the end, the small band began playing a seductive piece with a strong beat—alien, as much of the music had been that evening. A man and woman appeared on the stage. He was slim and wore tight black pants and a red shirt. The woman was stunningly beautiful and wore a dress of the same color as the shirt that shockingly left much of her leg visible. And then they danced to the music, a ballroom dance, but like nothing Frances had ever seen. They flowed with each other—it was almost indecent, she thought—and yet it made even the most graceful waltz in her memory seem awkward.

The couple went through several numbers, and at the end the applause was enthusiastic.

"It's called the tango," said Lord Gareth. "It came out of the slums of Buenos Aires, where the Catholic Church has spoken out against it."

"If they continue to perform it here, I'm sure the Anglicans will follow suit," said Frances.

"Come with me," said Lord Gareth. He took Frances's hand in his own. His hand was much larger than hers, cool and strong. Lord Gareth led her through a door near the stage, and they found themselves backstage. Dancers and singers were in a state of half-dress, and only the fear of looking unsophisticated in front of Lord Gareth kept her going. He knocked on the door of a dressing room. Frances heard Spanish, and Lord Gareth opened the door.

The tango dancers were the only occupants. The man was lounging against the wall and smoking a cigarette that filled the room with a blue haze. The woman was taking off her makeup. Up close, she was even more exquisite. Lord Gareth surprised Frances again by speaking to them in Spanish. They both answered, and the man laughed while the woman smiled.

"They are Matias and Dolores. I told them that you found their dancing both magnificent and shocking. Did I tell them right?" Frances just nodded. She had Lord Gareth tell them she had never seen anything like that, and words couldn't describe . . . When he translated, the two dancers briefly bowed in acknowledgement of the compliment. Matias said something to Lord Gareth and laughed again.

"He said he will give the pretty English girl tango lessons, if she would like."

Frances rallied. She wasn't going to come off as cowed in this exotic setting.

"Ask them how much would it cost."

"He says, for the beautiful señorita, there would be no cost."

"Tell him he's a flatterer," said Frances.

But Dolores didn't like the exchange. She frowned at Matias, and the Spanish between them was so fast, even Lord Gareth had trouble following. But then they stopped. Dolores rolled her eyes, and Matias shrugged. He thanked them for coming, but it was late and they had to go to their rooming house . . .

Frances managed a simple "adios" and let Lord Gareth lead her out again. The audience was almost gone from the theater. She saw Colonel Mountjoy exiting and fancied he looked at her before heading out of the door, but she couldn't read his expression. It suddenly felt very warm in the room, and Lord Gareth seemed so close. It was delicious to step outside again into the cool evening air.

For the moment, they had the empty stables to themselves. Frances was still flushed from the tightly packed theater, and all the evening's memories came together: bandying words with Lord Gareth in his car, laughing over his "marriage proposal," the achingly beautiful melodies, the tango dancers with their legs weaving in and out . . . and now he bent down and kissed her, and she kissed back. Frances almost forgot how to breathe; she held him tightly, with her arms around him, and they kissed again. He kissed her neck. "Franny, Franny, Franny," she heard him say and wanted to say something back, but her voice was gone.

She didn't know if thirty seconds or thirty minutes had passed, but then others came looking for their rides home, and without realizing how it happened, Frances was back in the two-seater, and they were driving through dark London streets in absolute silence.

Lord Gareth drove the car directly to Miss Plimsoll's. He hopped out and walked around to help Frances out, which was just as well, as her legs were weak. She was about to thank him for the evening, as a proper young lady should, but under the light of the doorway, he silenced her with another kiss, this time much more tender.

"Good night, dearest Franny," he said. Once more she was left speechless.

She vaguely remembered walking upstairs and letting Mallow help her get ready for bed. Mallow, for her part, at first wondered if her mistress had perhaps taken a little too much drink, which would've surprised her greatly, as her ladyship never had more than a drop, just to be sociable. No, Mallow had seen plenty of those who had overindulged, from kitchen maids to dukes, and this wasn't it. Overtired perhaps? Her ladyship could hardly focus on what Mallow said or asked, and her eyes seemed to be looking at something else.

And another thing: her hair was a mess. That was from the motorcar. Never mind what her ladyship's brother did—a lady should be in a hansom cab or better yet a carriage.

"Good night, Mallow," said Frances absently as she slipped into bed, and Mallow turned off her light.

"Good night, my lady," said Mallow. By that point, Mallow had figured out what had happened. She was young and naïve in many ways, but between the crowded boisterous neighborhood she had grown up in and her days as a servant in a great house, she had seen many things. She didn't blame Lady Frances at all—Mallow had watched when Lord Gareth had picked her up, and he was awfully handsome. Would Lady Frances become Lady Gareth?

One thing was certain: Lord Gareth had kissed her ladyship that evening. And from the look on her ladyship's face and the state of her mind, he had done a proper job of it.

CHAPTER 7

The next morning all Frances wanted to do was to lie in bed and think about Gareth, close her eyes and imagine his face, listen to his voice call her Franny . . . but the Seaforth women were not expected to wallow in emotion, good or bad. She had calls to make and a walk in the park with Mr. Wheaton and his mother.

"A pleasant evening, my lady?" asked Mallow.

"Very, thank you," said Frances. "Didn't I tell you last night?"

"You seemed especially tired, my lady, and not inclined to conversation," said Mallow. Frances studied her maid as she quickly and efficiently laid out Frances's clothes. The trouble with maids, her mother had always said, was that the good ones always knew what was occurring in your life. There was no keeping secrets from them.

After breakfast, Frances caught herself a hansom and mixed business with pleasure, calling on friends who belonged to various groups and committees to both socialize and get some work done.

Her calls complete, she headed to the Wheaton house and reflected on what a fine day it was for a walk, not too warm. The Wheatons lived in a sober mid-Victorian town house, a model of respectability. Mr. Wheaton was wearing his modern light suit again and smiled at her arrival.

"My mother will be down in a moment. You know, Lady Frances, your visits mean a lot to her."

"I am glad, but you make it sound like some sort of charitable service I'm providing. I enjoy your company, you and your mother. But as we've established that this is a social event, you must call me 'Franny,' like all my friends."

He gave her his shy smile again, which she found disarming. "Then you will call me 'Hal.' Outside of the office, ever since my school days, everyone calls me 'Hal.'"

"Like Prince Hal?" asked Frances. She referred to the medieval prince, a pleasure-seeking wastrel who came into his own on his father's death, becoming England's great warrior king, Henry V.

"Hardly," said Wheaton with a slight blush, and then Mrs. Wheaton came down.

The Wheatons still had a coach, not a car, which carried them to the park. At that time of day, the park walks were almost crowded with people enjoying one of London's clear days. Mrs. Wheaton leaned on her son's arm and asked Frances about her college experience and the United States in general. She was astonished to hear that Frances had actually met and spoken with Red Indians in New York.

"Just like in James Fenimore Cooper's *The Last of the Mohicans*," said Hal.

A cry from a park bench snapped them out of their discussion of America. A woman of about Mrs. Wheaton's age, sitting next to a maid, called out to her.

"Delia, I had no idea you were out again," said Mrs. Wheaton.

"My physician has ordered plenty of fresh air," she said.

"I'm glad we met. Let us talk a while." The maid pulled out some knitting as Mrs. Wheaton sat down to talk to her friend. "You young people take a walk while I talk with Delia and collect me later."

"If you're sure, Mother," said Hal. Reassured, he and Frances continued walking. But after a few steps, Hal stopped and, a little self-consciously, offered Frances his arm, which she took.

"You seem very interested in America, Hal. I hope you make some time to visit someday."

"Yes, I hope to. But if I may be so bold, it's less America that I'm interested in than, I should say, the idea of you there. The sense of independence you show. I am acquainted with Miss Plimsoll's Hotel, of course, but if you will pardon my curiosity, why have you chosen to live there when you could live with your brother and sister-in-law, who is your great friend?"

"I don't mind talking about it," she said. "It is modeled on a ladies-only hotel in New York called the Barbizon, where ladies can stay without having their virtue questioned." She explained that she loved her family, but she had become too used to the freedom of college, of being on her own. She could never give up those freedoms.

"That is remarkable," said Hal. "You are still so young, if I may make an observation, and to have done so much—to be so, well, different. I'm rather awestruck."

"I am flattered you think so." They walked along, and Frances could see he was lost in thought, as if he were trying to formulate what to say next—or wondering what she would say. "I will say that it is I who should be impressed by you. My brother is a fine judge of character, and he has often mentioned that there is no better solicitor in London, that you took over the practice at your father's untimely death and not only kept the practice but increased it. You take care of your mother. You saw your sister properly married. I'm sure it was most trying and exhausting, but you persevered. I find you admirable, Hal." He looked at her and smiled, but then she added one more thing. "But must you wear that old-fashioned black coat in your office? It doesn't become you at all."

Then Hal laughed, and it all came spilling out. He told Franny she was the first person who seemed to understand, the doubts he had had, the late nights poring over books, the nerve-racking meetings with lords and merchant princes. He had to remain confident in front of his mother and sister and set a strong example for the juniors and clerks.

"And as for the black coat . . . never mind the fashions of the last era; I have clients born during the reign of William IV, who remember Queen Victoria's coronation. They wouldn't trust me in anything else."

"Then concerns of business must take precedence over sartorial matters. But the suit you have today works well for you."

"Thank you for listening," he said softly. And Frances gave his arm a squeeze and told him that as his friend, she was pleased to. Now, she knew, was the time to ask him a question she was very curious to know the answer to.

"Tell me, Hal, what are your views on giving women the vote?"

Agree or disagree, Gareth would've answered right away. But Hal took a moment to think first. It was his way, she saw, planning each word of each sentence.

"My feeling had long been that the vote for women was not necessary or even advisable. But then you and I spoke during our business meetings in my office and now at social events. You discussed your education with me. I heard about all the fine charitable enterprises you work so hard at. Your good sense, sensitivity, and intellect show through in everything you say and do. And although you mentioned nothing to me about suffrage until today, I cannot see how someone like you could support something that wasn't fair and right. Without regard to your intention or mine, I have been convinced."

He stopped talking, and they walked in silence for a while. Frances did not know how to react immediately but finally told

Hal she did not think she had ever been complimented so nicely. Perhaps a little embarrassed, Hal changed the subject.

"Are you familiar with the American novelist Mark Twain? It was a revelation to me. I never thought I knew anything about America until I read it. I was also appalled by it."

"Appalled? Why?"

"A society built on two classes of citizens separated by race. I admire America and Americans, but to think they thought it was morally and practically possible to proceed indefinitely with such a system." He shook his head.

"You are more progressive than I expected," said Frances. Then she heard what she said. "I am sorry. I came across as patronizing. I, who get so offended when men do that to me. Forgive me?"

"Nothing to forgive, Franny. Your assumption was natural. Look whom I spend my days with: the cream of London society, the wealthy and socially prominent. There are exceptions, but as a group, they're not inclined to push for social change."

"I have to agree," said Frances. "Apologies again, this time on behalf of the nobility."

Hal laughed, but meanwhile, something tickled Frances's mind. She was thinking of this amiable man as a pleasant companion for a walk around the park, but she had just been reminded he was also one of the most distinguished solicitors in London. As he said, he served the cream of London Society, families like the House of Seaforth. Did he serve the Colcombes too? She remembered the scrap of paper from Danny's study, the legal paper with the name of an unknown person.

"Hal, does the name 'D. Tregallis' mean anything to you?"

She expected a denial, even confusion. After all, there were lots of solicitors in London. But he smiled and shook his head. "I knew it. Your brother told me you were helping the Colcombes. And you would be too thorough, and Major Colcombe too careless, for you not to come across that name. But I'm afraid my hands are tied by the rules of my profession."

"I'm not a solicitor, but I thought that privacy rules were no longer in effect after death?"

"You're absolutely right," he said, surprised a layperson knew that. "But this is not only about Major Colcombe's privacy. Other peoples' lives and reputations are at stake."

"I understand. But I can't just give up. I'll ask and ask. I will find them and figure out why Danny paid them such a large sum. Maybe it has nothing to do with his book. But I have to see." Her chin was held high, and her mouth was set.

"Of course. I understand." He paused. "Very well. I may be able to help you, but I have to consult someone else first. Call my chief clerk in a few days. And please don't mention D. Tregallis to anyone meanwhile."

It seemed like a very nice coincidence—but maybe not, thought Frances. If Danny had a secret, whether or not it was connected with his manuscript, then he'd share it with Charles if he shared it with anyone. And if legal or financial advice was needed, Hal was the obvious choice.

Hal broke into her thoughts. "Our cook does a very nice tea, so shall we collect my mother and head home?"

Mrs. Wheaton had had a good time catching up with her friend, and soon they were back in the coach heading home. "The workmen are probably there, so you will excuse some noise," said Mrs. Wheaton.

"You'll be interested to know, Franny, that I'm adding a small annex to the back of the house to serve as a studio for my painting. There is some hammering and sawing going on."

"But how marvelous. I am pleased to see you taking your painting so seriously," said Franny.

Once inside, Mrs. Wheaton said she was quite tired from all the fresh air and would lie down for a bit. But the young people should have tea without her. She headed upstairs, and then the housekeeper came into the drawing room to say tea would be ready presently.

"Now that I have again heard about your painting, Hal, I insist on seeing some of them."

"Franny, they are hardly fit for public exhibition."

"I'm not the public. I'm your friend."

"Well if you must—I have three in my private office here in the house. Come, but you've been warned."

He led her into an office that was a miniature version of the office at his firm, expensively furnished and old-fashioned.

"These three are mine," he said.

Her first reaction was that Hal had made the right decision in choosing the law as a career rather than art. It's not that he didn't have talent. They were technically well executed, but there was no excitement, nothing to raise them from merely competent to inspirational.

Two were still lives: one with a bowl of fruit, bread loaf, and a bottle of wine. The second had the same fruit bowl, now accompanied by a candle and a dead pheasant, ready for plucking and roasting. The third was the best: a seascape. He had done a good job of capturing the texture of the waves and the battered wood of the fishing boat plunging between them.

"You like the seascape best, don't you? It's my favorite of what I've done. We take a house there for a holiday, and always as a boy, even now, I dream . . ." and perhaps feeling he had said too much, he stopped. Well, maybe, thought Franny, he was a better artist than she thought. He just needed the right emotional push.

"And meanwhile, I do fruit," he said with a self-deprecating laugh. "There is always fruit around."

She asked if he ever did portraits, and he quickly shook his head—much too difficult, plus all the problems and expenses of hiring models.

The housekeeper interrupted them to say that tea was almost ready, but she was afraid the master had received a call, and the man was most insistent. Hal rolled his eyes.

"A client. Somehow they always find me. I am terribly sorry, Franny. I won't be more than a moment. I know who it is, and I just need to reassure him."

"The Seaforth motto is 'My duty is my life.' Take your call, by all means."

Hal picked up the extension in the office, and the housekeeper showed Frances back to the drawing room.

"Excuse any noise, my lady, from the workmen. They're building a new, ah, work area for the master." The housekeeper no doubt felt it was not her place to comment on the master's pastime.

"Mr. Wheaton has told me it was an art studio," said Frances. "I encouraged him to continue his work."

"Very good, my lady," said the housekeeper, relaxing now that this titled lady had given her blessing to the master's artistic pursuits. "He has been talking about this for some months. He previously used a sort of little studio right off of this room," she said, pointing to a side door. "But he said it was too small and the light not very good. Now, I'll see about tea. The master should only be a few moments."

She left, and Frances found herself alone. There was nothing in the room to hold her attention, just some old-fashioned furniture and indifferent landscapes you might find in dozens of similar London town houses. But there was that door . . . the door to Hal's little studio. Frances knew she should leave well enough alone, but curiosity won out. She turned the doorknob and entered.

She had been in artists' studios before in bohemian neighborhoods, and this gentleman's studio looked much the same: an easel, tubes of paint, boxes of brushes, and a stack of unframed canvases against the wall. Frances kept her ears open for footsteps and began looking through them: Another still life, this one with stilton cheese and a silver knife. A country scene, woods bordering on a summer field, with a farmhouse in the distance. Then the third canvas . . . she was stunned and felt the heat rise to her face. She didn't know what to think.

But then she heard footsteps and just had a moment to leave, close the door behind her, and compose herself before Hal entered.

"Sorry again. But now we're ready, and I gave my housekeeper strict instructions we're not to be disturbed again."

"Oh good, because I'm absolutely parched." They had a lovely afternoon, talking more about literature, and then he saw her into a hansom cab. But Frances didn't head back to Miss Plimsoll's. Rather, she went to her family home. She very much wanted to talk to Mary.

———◆•◈•◆———

The butler greeted her warmly and told her that Lady Seaforth was home and alone—a visitor had left a little while ago, and she was writing letters.

"Frances, what a nice surprise. Mavis, bring some more tea for Lady Frances."

They gathered around the little table in the morning room and caught up on each other's lives since the party at the Moores'.

"Oh my—you've been out with the Heathcote set? What was that like? I hear they can be quite notorious," said Mary.

"And that is why I'm here. It was quite an evening with the Heathcotes. We went to a very unusual theatrical performance with a dance that was almost obscene." She watched her friend's eyes get wider. "And then, as we were leaving, Lord Gareth kissed me. Again and again."

Mary nearly spilled her tea. "Good Lord, my dear, I can't imagine . . . that boldness . . . I mean . . ." She seemed astonished. Then she gathered herself and said, "Are you very happy at his . . . courtship of you?"

And Frances nodded. "It is a beginning, I know, and I won't be foolish. But I am very happy. I have never met a man so forward, so progressive and intelligent. A man who treated me as an equal."

"Then I am delighted for you." She dropped her voice to a dramatic whisper. "But we'll keep this from Charles a while, shall we?" And Frances giggled. Mary studied her friend. *She is so intelligent, normally so full of good sense. Oh please, Lord, keep her from getting hurt.*

"But there's more. I've had a rather busy week. I just came back from a walk in the park with Henry Wheaton and his mother—"

"You mean the family solicitor?"

"Any reason I shouldn't?" asked Frances.

"Not at all," said Mary calmly. "As you know, Charles thinks the world of him."

"It was really a matter of kindness. He's so busy and can't properly watch over his mother, who's perhaps a little too solicitous of her health, although rather nice. It was a surprise, really. He has more of an intellectual and artistic sensibility than you'd expect from a solicitor, and he works so hard, I don't think he gets to socialize very much. He seemed pleased to have someone to talk to about books and music. Did you know that he paints as a hobby?" Mary hid a smile as Frances talked.

"But then when we got to his house for tea, I'm afraid I did something I rather shouldn't have. His mother was upstairs and he had to speak on the telephone, so I sneaked into his art studio."

"Oh, Franny . . ."

"You know curiosity is my besetting sin. And now I've been punished for it. The first two paintings I saw were just a landscape and a still life, but the third one—was a portrait of me."

"Oh my." Mary smiled wryly. "You've made two conquests this week, my dear. You're in danger of becoming notorious."

"What do you mean 'conquests'? Hal and I are friends—intellectual companions, that's all."

"Hal?" asked Mary with an arch of her eyebrow. "Mr. Wheaton is now 'Hal'?" Frances reddened. "It could be Mr. Wheaton is too shy to engage a model, dear Franny, but I don't think gentlemen paint portraits of women who are just intellectual companions. But was it any good?"

Frances blinked. "I don't look at myself in the mirror much, but I found it . . . more flattering than I deserve."

"What were you wearing? I mean, you weren't, well, like what some painters . . ." Now Mary reddened, and then Frances caught her meaning.

"Mary! Do you think he'd go that far? I was in my blue dress, you know the one. Can you imagine if he had painted me . . . undressed?"

They both broke into helpless laughter at the thought. "My dear, I'd give a year's dress allowance to buy such a portrait and put it over the mantle. Think of your aunts coming into the house and seeing that . . . and after they pass out, telling them it was painted by the family solicitor." And they laughed so hard they could hardly catch their breath.

"Sweet Franny, in all seriousness, the man has developed feelings for you. I will tell you to be careful all around and leave it at that. Now, any progress with the Colcombe manuscript?"

"Following leads, as the detectives say. I have hopes, if nothing solid yet."

"You worry your brother."

"Then reassure him I am staying safe. In fact, there may be certain aspects of today's conversation that might be best to omit from Charles."

"Franny, as far as your brother is concerned, I think this entire day's conversation never happened."

CHAPTER 8

Frances caught an early morning train to Grenville. She did enjoy train travel, watching the world pass by and wondering about the other passengers. Were they going home or visiting friends and relations? On business or on holiday? What were they hoping to find at the other end?

She was the only one who got off the train at Grenville, a sleepy village that probably saw more freight than passenger traffic from the neighboring farms. With her small bag, she found herself alone in the empty station, but then an older man, heavily bearded, approached her. He wore rustic clothes and walked with a slight limp.

"Lady Frances Ffolkes? I'm Tredwell, the general's manservant. He sent me to fetch you. I'm afraid there's no car or coach here, just a simple pony cart, if you don't mind. It's about five miles to the house."

"Thank you, Tredwell. I am sure your cart will be most acceptable." He easily helped her onto the seat next to him and cracked the reins. The horse ambled on, clearly in no hurry. Frances truly didn't mind. They had had such a cart in their country place. When they were children, Charles would take the reins, but if she pleaded enough, he'd give her a turn.

"My brother served under General Audendale. Perhaps you knew him—Major Charles Ffolkes—and his great friend, Major Daniel Colcombe?"

"That I did, my lady. A fine man, your brother, by all accounts. An important figure in London, the general says. And I knew Major Colcombe, too, my lady." He scowled, and his face grew black. "That was a hard day for the general. He doesn't like to travel much anymore, but he came up to London for his funeral. He had too much respect not to. That's the way he's always been, my lady. He has always put duty and honor first." Frances remembered the general at the funeral, walking with a cane and looking frail.

He stopped speaking, and Frances was sorry she had led him into such a painful subject. But Tredwell brightened when she asked him if he had been with the general long.

"I was a green recruit, and if you can keep a secret, my lady, the general was a young lieutenant who didn't know one end of a rifle from another." They both laughed at that. "Eventually, he took me on as his soldier-servant, my lady, what we in the army call a 'batman.'"

They had been together ever since, more than forty years, through transfers and promotions and wars. A bullet in India had ended Sergeant Tredwell's military career, but General Audendale kept him on as a sort of assistant/valet. They traveled together to South Africa for what would be the aging general's last command.

"I have been blessed to have such a good master all these years," said Tredwell. "It's rare in this world to meet such a gentleman, my lady. I would do anything for him."

"From what I see, he has also been blessed to have you."

"That is very kind of you to say, my lady."

As they approached Egdon Hall, the seat of the Audendale family, Frances thought back to what she knew of architectural history. The main section had gone up during the Stuart era, she guessed, in the seventeenth century, but the family had added on sections during the Georgian period that followed. Frances imagined a large central hall that had once held elaborate balls. She thought of the shocking tango—this house had no doubt held dances when even the waltz was considered risqué. But now, the house looked dark and a little unloved. The grounds were barely tended, the minimum done, with no flowers. Tredwell noticed her look.

"Yes, there are only a few servants left now. The general is alone here. Most of the house is closed up."

Frances knew General Audendale had been a widower for a long time. He had one daughter, but she lived in India with her husband, who had a government appointment in Bombay. She was glad he and Tredwell had each other. They probably played cards and drank whiskey in the evening and relived battles past.

The main hall was indeed splendid, with some good oil paintings that could've used a cleaning. Sheets kept the furniture free from dust.

"Just follow me, my lady. We've set the general up right nice in a little apartment on the second floor." The staircase was grand, but the carpet was getting worn. They walked along a hallway past closed doors before stopping at one. Tredwell knocked, then walked in without waiting for an answer.

They had done the general nice, as Tredwell had said. Here, at least, it was cheerful. The general had a little sitting room with a bedroom beyond. It reminded her of her own suite at Miss Plimsoll's. It was well lit, and the walls were covered with framed pictures and photos, memorabilia of people and places in the far corners of the empire. She saw more photos and knickknacks on the table, including some exotic pieces. But despite the number of items, Frances was glad to see the room was clean and tidy.

General Audendale himself seemed to have become even more frail than she had remembered him from the funeral. He sat in a large comfortable chair and seemed to disappear into it.

He wore a smoking jacket, and his legs were covered with blankets. He had become quite thin.

Still, he seemed to recognize her at once and smiled.

"You bring me a visitor, Tredwell, good man!" His voice was weak but still audible. "Lady Frances, I remember you as a little girl. I knew your father and commanded your brother. But you know that. Come, sit near me. Tredwell, be a good lad and see about getting this young lady some refreshment."

But a maid had been alerted when they arrived and a moment later came in carrying a tray with a large pot of tea and some tempting baked goods. The maid and Tredwell set it up. Tredwell leaned over and whispered to Frances, "We'd all be most grateful, my lady, if you could get the general to eat something," he said. Then louder, he said, "General, sir, we'll leave you with your guest. We'll be close at hand if you need anything." And he and the maid left.

Frances poured for the general and herself, giving him plenty of sugar.

"My staff has outdone themselves today, dear lady. Please have something."

"Only if you do first," said Frances with a sweet smile. "Come, these buns look divine." The general said he could refuse her nothing and joined her.

"So a young girl like you comes all the way here for a book poor Colcombe was writing?" asked the general. He closed his eyes, but just for a moment or two. "That was such a sad day. Funerals are always sad, but his . . . Anyway, as you can see, I don't know how much use I can be. It's just me and my memories."

"But it's your memories I want, General." She gave him more details, telling him that Colcombe had written something but it had been stolen.

"Indeed. I am sorry to hear that. He was an intelligent man, as well as being a brave and resourceful officer. I am sure that book would've been a fine addition to military literature."

"I think we may still find it, General. But that means figuring out why it was stolen. I think someone doesn't want what Major Colcombe wrote to be publicly known. And that may refer to something that happened in South Africa."

The general was looking at her intently. Even when sipping his tea, his eyes never left her.

"I think it may refer to Sapphire River, the last battle of the Empire Light Horse."

"My God, dear Lady Frances. How did you ever hear about that? It seems like ages ago. Tell me, my dear, what do you know about the Crimean War?"

"We were talking about South Africa," said Frances. Was the general's mind getting frail? He smiled gently at her.

"Don't worry, my dear. My mind is not that far gone." She was a little embarrassed. "But you need to know. Back then, my man, Tredwell, was then a private under my command—I was a newly minted lieutenant. You see him as an old man with a limp, but I can tell you, he was the fiercest, most loyal man in our regiment. Crimea is ancient history to you, already old when you were born. Did you learn anything about it?"

"A bit. I come from a military and diplomatic family." The conflict had been complex: England, France, and the Ottoman Empire trying to contain Russia. The politics had been a muddle; the battles had been horrific.

"Of course. Back then, things, and by that I mean battles, were done a certain kind of way. But we were already in the middle of change—the cavalry charge had passed its day. By the time South Africa came around, you see, war had taken on a different kind of cast. It's odd talking to a woman about this," he said.

"I heard enough from my brother," she said, hoping he wasn't going to become too old-fashioned to discuss it with her.

"I suppose so. You girls are so modern today. Where was I? Yes, back in South Africa. No worse than Crimea, you see, but different. We didn't understand . . ." His eyes stopped looking at her and lost their focus.

"But you did understand, General. The Empire Light Horse was your idea, your plan for a different war. Charles said so."

The general smiled, but now it was mirthless. "My idea. We thought it was good, but it was too good. We couldn't understand that battle lines were gone, that everything we knew about war was over. That we were no longer necessary."

"'We,' General? Who is 'we'?" She felt on the cusp of something, even closer to finding out what had happened in South Africa—more than what Charles knew, what Private Barnstable knew. Frances felt her heart pounding. She felt she was getting close to those who wanted the manuscript stolen, people who didn't want anyone to know what Danny was writing about.

"'We,' Lady Frances? It was all of us. Men in the government halls, men in Parliament, men from the War Office, the general staff. No one likes change. Why do you think I live here?" He raised an arm and waved it to show the entire house, with its dozens of unused rooms.

Frances didn't want to get off the topic. "But one man, General. One man ordered the Empire Light Horse to change its tactics, to meet the enemy in a battle it couldn't win." One man who didn't want that manuscript to come to light.

"One man? That man was me, Lady Frances. But you knew that. I was the commanding officer. I gave the order."

Frances didn't know much about how the army was organized, but she knew everyone answered to someone. Danny Colcombe had never said a bad word about the general. Someone had ordered the general to give new instructions to the Empire Light Horse. She thought of what Barnstable had overheard: "War Office." The government department that supervised the army. She felt a chill. She had been so sure she could find one man who was responsible. But was it some shadowy committee? Was it some group who stole the manuscript and killed Danny?

All the men with a stake in a concealment? She thought of Colonel Mountjoy and Inspector Eastley, servants of the government. What were their motives? Who were their masters? But she refused to despair. There must be an answer.

"But there was another man, General. Someone who gave you the order?"

He smiled at her again, this time warmly. "Like all the Seaforths, my dear—both men and women—you are interested in politics, but you are young and have much to learn. When you are older, you will understand how foolish that question is."

He wasn't unkind, and because of his age, Frances was prepared to forgive his patronizing tone—it was because she was young, not because she was a woman. She thought about what he really said: there were byways in London's political circles, and somewhere there was an answer.

After a few moments, he spoke again. "As for me, if you find that manuscript and publish it, I will buy the first copy that comes off the press. For reasons I can't discuss and don't even agree with, Colcombe never got the recognition he deserved for his heroism. If he gets it posthumously, I'll die a happy man."

And Frances had to be content with that. She smiled at the elderly officer. "Then I shall redouble my efforts. You have provided an education to me, sir, and I thank you. Now, as I am here, you might like to ask me questions in return."

He laughed. "Yes. That is kind of you. Except for the sad occasion of Colcombe's funeral, I haven't been to London in years. The pretty young girls—are they all wearing dresses like yours? I remember the ladies from the Queen's Golden Jubilee, back in eighty-seven. How are they dancing today?"

She wondered what General Audendale would think of the tango.

"I will tell you all about it. But first, I will make you another cup of tea, and you will have one of these delicious cakes."

The general was beginning to look tired. Tredwell reappeared as if he knew how the general was feeling—of course he would have a good sense of how long the general could last.

"I know I speak for the general when I say you are more than welcome, but we need to leave in the next thirty minutes to make the next train, and there's not another for some hours afterward, if you have evening engagements, my lady."

Frances thanked the general for the conversation. He replied he was sorry he couldn't be of more help.

"Oh, but you have helped, General," she said, and he seemed surprised. She bid him farewell and followed Tredwell out the door.

Frances wanted to think on what the general had said but decided to postpone reflection until later. Once more sitting in the pony cart, she decided to see if she could get anything out of Tredwell. He started the conversation by thanking her for her visit—not many stopped by nowadays.

"I'm glad I could. He seemed pleased when I told him the late Major Colcombe had been writing a book. He said he'd be interested in reading it, if it ever came to be published."

"I'm not sure it would've made good reading, if you'll pardon me, my lady. Nothing against the major, but South Africa was a mess, and I'm not sure we all want reminding. Things happen on the battlefield, and those who haven't served might take it the wrong way. I know what happened at the Sapphire River, my lady. And it's best left there. Let the dead rest. And the living."

It was curious way of putting it, Frances thought. "I take your point. And I am not at all offended. You were there and I was not. But it was my understanding that Major Colcombe performed an act of extraordinary heroism. Don't you think it should be recognized?"

Tredwell didn't speak for a few moments and got that brooding look on his face again. "May I ask your ladyship how she heard of what Major Colcombe did there? It wasn't supposed to be public."

"I heard it from one of the soldiers the major had saved. He felt the major deserved recognition for his heroism. The general seemed to agree."

Tredwell sighed. "The general is an old man, and I hope I don't sound disrespectful, but he has been in odd humors. Perhaps you've had elderly relations, my lady, and when they reach a certain age, they don't know what's good for them anymore. But I will tell you this, sometimes things happen in battle, and you don't tell anyone what happened later. It's understood. I don't know what Major Colcombe was putting in his writing. Maybe it was just for himself, not to be shared. But the soldier you spoke with shouldn't have said anything to you, my lady. He had been ordered not to. And in the army, there are severe penalties for disobeying orders. Very severe. There are reasons things are kept secret."

They drove in silence for a bit. Frances didn't feel she could say anything more. But as they approached the station, Tredwell shook off his gloom and smiled. "But I'll say this, my lady. He enjoyed your visit, and thank you for getting him to eat a little."

On the way back, she mused over General Audendale's cryptic remarks and Tredwell's protectiveness. Considering that the general has probably spent more time over the years with Tredwell than his own wife, it was almost like a marriage. It was true that she had no idea what men in battle were like. She wondered if Colcombe had broken some sort of officer's code. It wasn't like him to do that; he was a man of honor, everyone said. She knew Charles wouldn't talk more about it.

Time to put into effect another college technique: when an assignment wasn't going well, put it away and approach it with fresh eyes later. Tomorrow she'd see about contacts in the War Office. Someone higher up than Major Raleigh.

The train made good time; it wasn't even dinnertime when she arrived back at Miss Plimsoll's to find a note waiting for her. Her heart fluttered when she recognized the crest on the heavy cream stationary.

Dear Franny,

Your most excellent maid told me you were expected home later today. I should've asked further in advance, but I would very much like to have dinner with you this evening. I was going to wait a decent interval, but I couldn't bear it. Please say your evening is open.

She read it three times. He had enclosed his card with his telephone number. How convenient that was not to have to send servants running back and forth with responses. She went into the telephone parlor, and a few moments later she was talking to Gareth.

"That is very presumptuous of you," she said. She lied and told him she had made plans to visit one of her tedious aunts, but that could be postponed, since Gareth had written such a nice note. But he wasn't to do that again. He said he would come by at seven o'clock and begged her forgiveness.

Frances left the telephone room feeling a little light-headed. Then she remembered her conversation with Hal. *Pull yourself together,* she told herself. *You have work to do.* She called his offices, and the clerk said for her to come back at ten o'clock the following morning—Mr. Wheaton had something to say to her. She then walked briskly upstairs—just enough time to write a few letters and pick out a dress before dinner.

Mallow was determined the make the most of her mistress's social life. "This dress, my lady? I thought it would go well with the hat with the feather . . ."

"That'll work nicely, Mallow. I'm sure you know best."

"It's just that I'm not sure where you're going this evening?" asked Mallow, making it half a statement, half a question.

"I don't know either," said Frances with a smile, hoping that would end discussion of clothing.

"Very good, my lady," said Mallow in a very cool tone that was as close as she ever came to voicing disapproval. *Imagine going out but not knowing where!* "I just want to add that in my experience, gentlemen like seeing a well-turned-out lady."

"Do they indeed? We'll see what Lord Gareth says then," said Frances with a wry smile.

Gareth arrived not in his car but in a hansom. "It's not easy to bring a car where we're going," he said.

She had assumed they'd go to one of the fashionable restaurants but should've known better. Gareth guided the driver to another unfamiliar street, to a restaurant with a simple sign announcing its unpronounceable name. "This is a secret, dear Franny. Englishmen who have spent so much time in India that they have become Indian dine here when in London."

Frances had expected something modest, based on the plain exterior, but inside the decorations were lavish, upholstery in red and gold and colored silks on the wall. The other diners wore dinner clothes like themselves, but the staff members were all from the subcontinent, with turbans and fierce-looking mustaches.

The headwaiter greeted them. Gareth pressed his palms together, bowed, and said a few words in a foreign tongue. The man smiled and led them to a table.

"Don't tell me you know Hindi, too," she asked.

"Just a few words in order to amaze impressionable young girls," he said.

"I'm not all that impressionable," she said with mock severity. She had thought herself worldly with her travels to America, her education, and her politics. But keeping up with Gareth was a challenge—exciting, but a challenge. Gareth started by apologizing for offering no wine with dinner. "The proprietor is a good Hindu and so will sell no wine or spirits. You can discreetly bring your own, but as for me, you are intoxicating enough."

Frances blushed and was annoyed at herself for it. She quickly spoke. "Flatterer. But why does the Hindu not drink? I don't believe the Muslim does either. I knew some Jewish girls in college, and they didn't drink much, but wine was important in certain rituals." And that led to a religious discussion. Frances had taken a basic theology course at Vassar, but Gareth was at least her equal.

They continued their talk over the food—strange, highly spiced concoctions she couldn't identify, cooked with herbs not found in England, using methods unfamiliar to Western chefs. All the items were delicious, and in between their discussions, Frances caught Gareth looking at her as if he expected her to turn up her nose at the unusual delicacies. If so, she disappointed him.

During a break in their talk, Frances changed the subject. "Gareth, I was wondering about other evening. Don't misunderstand me; it was delightful. But I have heard stories about the Heathcote set, that aside from your motives, their motives for inviting me to the event may have been more . . . commercial. I was wondering if it was in connection with a favor I am doing for a friend. I think you know what I'm referring to."

Gareth usually responded to any comment or question quickly, but now he just toyed with his water glass for a few moments.

"I won't deny it, Franny. There is a great deal of interest in the Colcombe manuscript. You may not realize just how important that manuscript is to some people. I mean politically."

"Why shouldn't I know it? Because I'm a woman and therefore must know nothing of politics?" She felt her anger rise—this is not what she expected from Gareth.

But he shook his head. "No, Franny. Of course not. It's because you are good. You want to do good. But other people have other motives."

"Like the Heathcotes?" asked Frances.

"They are powerful people, Frances. They have powerful friends. You want the manuscript to bring justice to the men who died at the Sapphire River."

"You seem to know a lot," said Frances.

"You've been in Society long enough to know how hard it is to keep secrets. There were plenty of men who knew what happened in South Africa. They talked no matter how many threats and incentives they were given to be quiet. But we need something like the manuscript to really make a change. You could make a difference."

Frances looked at the earnestness in his eyes. He seemed very sincere, but Frances was from a political family. People rarely worked for free.

"And what do the Heathcotes want out of this?" she asked.

"A chance to do some political housekeeping before publication."

Of course. The Heathcotes had favors to grant and return. The manuscript would allow them to do that before its content became public. Merely the threat of what it contained, of the political mistakes that led to the carnage, would be effective.

"And what do you want, Gareth? Are you merely a Heathcote agent?" She was sure Gareth could see how hard her heart was beating.

"I am merely a messenger. If you want to work with them, they can be powerful allies." He shrugged. "But my commission is over. It is up to you to decide if you want to join them or play a lone hand, as they say."

"And what do you want?"

He answered by leaning over the table and kissing her on the cheek. "Only what you want."

Then all thoughts of the Colcombe manuscript went out of her head. Gareth signaled their waiter and paid. It was a nice evening, and Gareth suggested walking. Frances was unfamiliar with the neighborhood but felt safe with Gareth. She was realizing how little she really knew London—just the fashionable areas where she and her friends and family lived and the one grim corner of the East End where she worked at the soup kitchen.

Other couples and some young families, taking advantage of the evening, were walking on the sidewalks as well. Frances held onto Gareth's arm. After the chatty dinner, they were silent now, and she concentrated on feeling him next to her.

The sun was setting as they turned onto a wide commercial street, where Gareth hailed a hansom cab. Frances was a little disappointed; she wasn't ready for the evening to end. But her spirits soared when Gareth announced grandly to the driver, "Into the park and round and round until I tell you otherwise."

As they entered the park, Gareth kissed her again, first soft, then insistent, and Frances found herself half-delighted and half-fearful, so overwhelmed by emotion and so unused to the delicious loss of control.

Gareth stopped and put his lips next to her ear. "I do so love you, sweet Franny."

But she wasn't completely gone—not yet. She pulled back. "Do you really?" She looked as serious as she felt. "Do not say that unless you mean it."

He took her chin in his hand. "Are you now an old-fashioned maid, pretending you had no idea?"

"I knew you desired me. I didn't know you loved me," she said, trying to keep her voice from shaking.

"How stupid of me to forget how shrewd you are," he said. "But how do you feel about me?"

She started to answer, but he quickly put a finger to her lips.

"No, don't answer. I may be stupid—but I am smart enough to know you are too young and too inexperienced to know your own feelings." He smiled to take away the sting, as if he were just teasing her, challenging her. And then he kissed her again, and it was divine. Eventually, the evening had to come to an end, and Gareth left her at the door of Miss Plimsoll's, happy, dazed, and more than a little confused.

CHAPTER 9

The next morning, Frances studied her maid for any kind of a smile, but Mallow was her usual brisk and efficient self. Frances decided to draw her out.

"Has there been any mention downstairs about Lord Gareth?" asked Frances, trying to sound very offhand about it.

"My lady, I do not gossip about you, your friends, or the family." Mallow was deeply affronted.

"Of course not, Mallow." You could never be too direct with Mallow. She had been too well trained. "But I am sure you have seen Lord Gareth call for me, and I wondered what you thought of him."

"You are asking for my opinion, my lady?" It was like their discussion about Mr. Wheaton. Again, any lady would ask for an opinion about clothes, but Lady Frances wanted insights on people. About someone she seemed to be falling in love with, if Mallow was any judge of her ladyship's behavior.

"Yes, Mallow. Your frank opinion."

"Then I would say, my lady . . ." Frances watched her look for the right words. "I would say that Lord Gareth cuts a fine figure, my lady."

Frances laughed. "Well said, Mallow." But she wondered what Mallow would've thought of Gareth's manners last evening.

Mallow busied herself brushing Lady Frances's hair and fixing it up for the day.

"I forgot to ask, Mallow. On your recent afternoon off, did you have a nice tea at the Ansons' next door?" Mallow had been invited to take tea in the servant's hall in the neighboring town house. More specifically, she had been invited—with the butler's permission—by Mr. Gregmon, valet to Sir Simon Anson.

"Very nice, thank you, my lady. Cook baked a cake and scones, and there was marmalade sent up from the country."

Frances turned and smiled. "And Mr. Gregmon? He was pleased to introduce you to his friends?"

Mallow blushed, and Frances turned away.

"I am sorry, Mallow. I was prying." Mallow's mother insisted that servants were allowed their privacy. Whatever they did on their own time was their business, as long as their behavior brought no disgrace to the household. One may show some guidance for an inexperienced and young maid or footman, but a senior servant like a lady's maid would be allowed wide latitude.

"Quite all right, my lady," said Mallow cheerfully. Indeed, she would welcome Lady Frances's opinion. "Mr. Gregmon and I have enjoyed walks in the park. Only very respectable outings, my lady. But he is looking for a new position." Mallow sighed.

"Sir Simon always seemed like a good master," said Frances.

"Oh, yes, my lady. Mr. Gregmon much admires him. But he would like to be a butler. He says he may find such a position in the country. And butlers—especially in the country—well, my lady, they can get married. Valets are expected to remain unmarried." Just like maids.

Frances felt a pang. Would she lose Mallow? "Has he made you an offer of marriage?"

"No, my lady." Mallow began pinning up Frances's hair, and they were silent for a few moments. "And I would not say yes if he did. He is very nice and will make his way in the world. But I do not love him."

Now it was Mallow's turn to feel anxious. Would Lady Frances tell her she was a fool not to even consider a man who would make a good husband?

Frances turned and looked her in her eye. "Then if he asks, you should not marry him, Mallow."

"That is what I thought, my lady."

Mallow was glad to hear Lady Frances agree with her. Frances was pleased her maid was being sensible—and relieved she would not lose her, even though she was honest enough to admit that was a selfish thought.

"Marriage is a noble institution, Mallow, but it changes many things, and I am very satisfied with my lot in life right now."

Mallow thought about being married to a butler in the country. It would not be very interesting, stuck in an estate miles from anywhere, and she would lack the prestige that came from being a lady's maid to an aristocrat.

"I am satisfied with my lot as well, my lady. Now would your ladyship be so good as to hand me more of those pins?"

Mallow chose something brisk and businesslike for Frances's trip to Hal's law office. She had been consumed with curiosity about what he could tell her about the Colcombe manuscript.

It would be odd seeing him in his office—the first business visit after their friendship had developed. If it was just a friendship. She thought about the secret portrait and was sorry she had pried. But it could have been perfectly innocent: he wanted to paint a young woman and had no idea how to hire a model or maybe felt it wouldn't be respectable. So he painted a woman he knew from memory. She was merely convenient.

But his sister was attractive. Hal knew her even better and had photographs to work from—why not paint her? Frances frowned and shook her head. This would bear watching.

She arrived a few minutes early, but a clerk quickly showed her into Hal's office.

Hal stood up and walked around his desk, smiling at her as he folded his gold spectacles and put them away. He signaled over her shoulder, and an office boy came in with a tray of tea and biscuits, which he put down on a small table. Then the boy shifted two chairs around the table and left. The clerk began to leave as well, and Hal called to him, "Mr. Waller—"

"Yes, Mr. Wheaton?"

"We are not to be disturbed or interrupted for any reason. Is that clear?"

"Absolutely, sir." He left, closing the door quietly behind him.

When they were alone, Hal showed Frances into a seat. With mock annoyance, she said, "I thought that you had serious business for us to discuss. But this was just an excuse to have tea with me."

"Tea with you would always be a delight, but as what I have to discuss with you is not only serious and legal but also very personal, I thought this would be best." He paused and smiled again, this time wryly. "But I'm still wearing my black coat."

"I owe you so many apologies. That was very childish and unkind of me to tease you." She felt silly for having spoken like that. Hal just waved it away. "But I will still call you Hal, and you will still call me Franny, even in this office, as long as your staff isn't within hearing distance. Very well . . . now I shall pour."

She filled their cups, each sipped, and then Hal leaned back as he ordered his words in his head—Frances was sure he had rehearsed it. And then he began to speak.

"I wasn't going to say anything. But I know you would keep going until you found her. So I communicated with a woman who lived in the south, on the coast. It was Major Colcombe's secret, but hers too. She gave me permission. And so I have a story to tell you."

Hal explained that his firm had never acted for the Colcombe family, but he had known the name because Lord Seaforth had mentioned his close friend Daniel to Hal on several occasions.

One day, Daniel Colcombe showed up in the office on Lord Seaforth's recommendation. Colcombe needed some special legal work done, and he wanted it done apart from, and unknown to, his old family firm.

Frances realized she was about to learn something significant, even shocking, and had to hold her tongue and not ask him to hurry up with the story. She had to let Hal tell it in his own way, in his own time.

It seemed that Colcombe was not in the best condition when he came home from South Africa. The bullet wound wasn't healing as fast as the doctors would like, but more than that, his nerves were shot and his health was broken. Something happened out there—he had done something rather extraordinary, although Hal never knew what, and it had taken its toll.

Frances knew the details about Danny's great heroism, of course, but she didn't want to interrupt.

The family hired a nurse to take care of him. Colcombe's physician recommended Nurse Dorothy Jones—they called her Nurse Dot—most highly. She had experience tending wounded soldiers and was trained in the tradition of Florence Nightingale. "You are aware of Nightingale, of course?" asked Hal.

Naturally, Frances knew of her. Another Crimean War reference: Nightingale had been the heroine of that war, her nursing saving countless men, and she had professionalized nursing. She was still alive, and Frances had even been introduced to her once.

Well, from the first day, Nurse Dot was a credit to her mentor and to her training, according to all accounts. Gradually, Colcombe improved. The wound healed. He could sleep again, and his mood improved. He had been skeletally thin when he returned, but now he was eating well and putting on some badly needed pounds. And then he showed up at the Wheaton offices.

Hal now looked very uncomfortable. He finished his tea and looked away. "This is a hard story to tell to anyone. Especially to a lady. Especially to a lady who is my friend. You see, Franny,

Daniel Colcombe came to me to help him set up some financial arrangements, take care of the complex paperwork under the required laws . . ."

He's spinning this out, trying to avoid getting to the point, Frances realized.

"In short, Franny . . . in short, Nurse Dot was carrying Daniel Colcombe's child."

And then Hal quickly poured himself another cup of tea to cover up his embarrassment while Frances tried to sort out her emotions. Handsome, outgoing, and flirtatious, Danny had been linked with any number of women over the years. But it had never occurred to Frances things would've gone that far with any of them. He must've been . . . broken. There was no other explanation for Danny doing something so brazen. She badly wanted to think this wasn't really Danny, that something had unhinged his mind in South Africa . . .

"It must be upsetting to hear something like this about a close friend," Hal said softly, and Frances nodded.

He continued the story. Colcombe said he had offered the young woman marriage, but she had refused. Now he wanted to make sure financial provisions were made for Dorothy and their child. Hal told him he would draw up papers, but he had to bring her as well. He returned a week later with Dorothy. She seemed to be a smart, sensible woman—but you'd have to be to have been a military nurse, Hal said. Colcombe pressed her to marry him again, in Hal's presence, but she wouldn't discuss it.

"That would've been the easiest solution. Certainly the most common one," said Hal.

"And Lord knows that wouldn't be the first time a marriage started this way," said Frances. Hal looked up, and she was afraid she had embarrassed him by mentioning that. But he looked at her quizzically for just a moment and then relaxed. *You did not talk about such things with a typical lady. But Frances, he had realized, was not a typical lady.*

"Would it shock and appall you if I said a substantial part of my practice is handling problems like that? Mostly wretched servant girls in households with persistent young lords, but a fair number of well-born women too."

"I am not shocked, Hal. Merely saddened."

"At any rate, I helped them make the necessary arrangements. Nurse Dorothy didn't much care about herself but didn't want the shame of illegitimacy to touch her child, so she changed her name to her mother's maiden name, Tregallis, in order to start a new life."

"That's a Cornish name. But Kat Colcombe said she knew no one from Cornwall."

"Good detective work," said Hal. "Her father was from the Lake District, and that's where she was raised, so no one would've known her Cornish ancestry from her accent."

"She had no family left in Cornwall? Or among her father's people?"

"She told me she had no close family left. So Colcombe bought her a cottage by the sea in the south and arranged for a regular income as well as help for the birth and support afterward. She told everyone she was the widow of an officer on a merchant ship."

She gave birth to a healthy boy, and Colcombe came down regularly to see his son, saying he was a cousin looking out for her. He always stayed in the inn and never visited with her after dark, so no one suspected anything odd.

"And here's the point. Mrs. Tregallis, as she now called herself, and Colcombe got on rather well. My understanding was that there was no romance anymore but a comfortable friendship and a mutual delight in their child. Colcombe shared many things with Mrs. Tregallis. He found her easy to talk to, probably one of the things that made her such a good nurse. And apparently, he hoped one day to be able to openly claim parentage of the child."

Frances wanted to cry at that, the thought that Danny could have a family and his mother a grandchild to remember him by.

Hal was put in a terrible position when he found out Colcombe had died. Dorothy wrote to him saying she didn't believe he had had an accident and suicide was unthinkable for him—he had been happy. She wrote that she thought he must've been murdered based on things he had told her, but it was just supposition. Hal had nothing to take to the police. But then he had heard about Frances's interest and suggested to Dorothy that the two meet and that Dorothy share her suspicions based on her talks with Colcombe. Dorothy was very enthusiastic—especially as she already knew Lord Seaforth.

"My brother knows about this? But of course Danny wouldn't have kept it from him. I wish he had told me."

Hal smiled. "Of course. In fact, with Colcombe's death, he became the trustee of the inheritance for Mrs. Tregallis and her son. But the secret was never his to tell. Indeed, Franny, it isn't yours either."

She nodded. "But may I tell my brother I know?"

"Yes. But it wouldn't make him happy. He'd be embarrassed you knew. Annoyed at Mrs. Tregallis for dragging you into this. He might even be upset I told you, even though I had Mrs. Tregallis's permission."

"Then I won't, of course. Charles doesn't like my involvement in the manuscript search anyway. He's very worried about my safety."

"An older brother's prerogative," said Hal.

"I am surprised you have suggested this. Aren't you worried about me?" She said it teasingly, but Hal frowned.

"Of course I'm worried. I almost didn't tell you or communicate with Dorothy Tregallis. But you are . . . you are my friend, Franny. A woman of intelligence and good sense. It would've been unfair, even disloyal, of me to assume I know what is good for you better than you do yourself."

Hal was surprisingly good at giving very sincere compliments. "Thank you," she said.

"I have the particulars here for you. You can take an early morning train and leave that evening. Mrs. Tregallis said she is always available and eager to speak with you. If you wish to stay overnight, she has a spare room and is happy to put you up."

Frances had one more question: could she assume that Danny's mother and sister knew nothing of this?

"Nothing at all. Apparently, they don't have a very suspicious nature."

"It didn't excite any comment when the nurse departed? I imagine she left rather quickly."

"She did, but I don't believe it caused undue commotion." He paused. "It was clear Major Colcombe was back to perfect health."

Frances looked at Hal closely—was that a thin smile? Was that last comment a bit of dry lawyerly humor? She wouldn't have thought it of Hal, but he was full of surprises . . .

"I will wire Mrs. Tregallis and arrange to visit as soon as possible." She reached over and put her hand on Hal's. "I owe you many thanks for this. I will be off now, but we'll speak soon. Meanwhile, please give my regards to Mrs. Wheaton."

"I will—when I next speak with her. My sister and brother-in-law have invited her for a stay, and she will be leaving in the morning. She and Edwina—my sister—have always been especially close, and both are looking forward to it."

"I am glad for them, but you'll be all alone in that big house."

"Yes. It will seem odd dining by myself at the dining room table. Perhaps . . . might you be free to join me one evening?"

And Frances said she would.

She had time to go home before her next meeting but instead went directly to Mrs. Elkhorn's house. She'd be early for the league meeting, but she wanted to request Mrs. Elkhorn's help.

"Frances, happy to help, of course. You can help me arrange the chairs while we talk."

She briefly outlined the search for the Colcombe manuscript and its background with the Boer War. It had become a bigger problem than she expected, and she needed allies, especially those with connections.

"My brother gave me a name, but I think it was just to tease me. This man could potentially help me, but Charles said he'd never let me over his threshold. However, you know everyone, even members of the Conservative Party."

"Even them," she said with a wry smile. "I've tried to build bridges everywhere. And if that wasn't possible, there was at least some advantage in knowing one's enemies. But whom do you want to meet?"

"Lord Ashton Crossley."

"Oh my. Your brother did set you a challenge. He's a man of great power, although largely retired now. He's . . . he hasn't been well. But we do know each other. And I will write you a letter of introduction."

"So you're friends?" asked Frances.

"Oh no. We loathe each other. But there's a mutual respect. And he may see you, if for no other reason than he'll be curious as to why I am recommending you. But I warn you, Frances. Even sick, he's a very cunning man. Give him your respect but not your trust."

Frances nodded.

"That's an enormous help. Thank you so much," she said. *Ha*, she thought. *Charles challenged me and I beat him.* Thoughts chased themselves around her mind as she helped Mrs. Elkhorn set up.

"There's more, isn't there?" asked Mrs. Elkhorn. "You're not just interested in your late friend?"

"It may sound foolish, but I keep thinking of those men who died on the South African veldt, sacrificed for the stupidity and selfishness of the men in power."

"Is that all?" asked Mrs. Elkhorn. "No wonder you do so well here. Nothing seems to daunt you."

Frances glowed with the praise. "You're the one who keeps telling us that this will be our century."

"And it will be."

The other women showed up, and the meeting began. Through Mrs. Elkhorn's introduction and the committee sessions that followed, Frances felt strong and optimistic thanks to her mentor's help and enthusiasm. Afterward, she went home and caught up on correspondences and other club and committee commitments. She wired Dorothy Tregallis, asking which day would be good to visit.

And before she knew it, it was time to for her and Mallow to head to the Seaforth home. One generally didn't take a maid for just a dinner visit, but Mallow enjoyed a chance to visit her old friends from her days as a housemaid.

As Frances expected, Charles questioned her about the Colcombe manuscript over dinner, concerned that she was involving herself in something dangerous, or at least unwise. Frances had to deflect him with half-truths about mild inquiries among old civil servants to see if anyone knew anything. Charles felt that the manuscript was still in some drawer somewhere, or perhaps Danny had destroyed it before he died, and his sister Kat had just become confused.

Over port in the drawing room after dinner, Charles moved to another topic.

"I hope you two ladies can help me. I ran into Aubrey Laverton today. He's member of Parliament for some district down in Suffolk and asked me if I could help get his niece involved in various activities, political teas, volunteer committees, and so forth."

"Of course," said Mary. "Who is his niece?"

"I think you know her—I saw you talking to her the other night at the Moores'. The Honorable Miss Claire Chillingford . . ."

Both Mary and Frances giggled.

"What's so funny?" he asked.

"I'm sorry," said Mary. "Of course we'll help. It's just that Miss Chillingford, well she isn't—we know her somewhat, and I didn't think that she would find such activities to her taste."

"You mean she's rather dim?" asked Charles ruefully. "That's what Laverton indicated. But perhaps there is something that she could do?"

Mary said she would certainly extend an invitation to next week's luncheon—several other political wives would be coming, and even if Miss Chillingford could not contribute much, she'd learn something by listening. Charles thought that a splendid idea.

Meanwhile, Frances offered a place in the London Children's Improvement Society. "We arrange wholesome trips for poor children into the country. Healthful meals and country air. I think helping pick sites for day trips from London should be well within Miss Chillingford's ability."

And Charles said if Frances could arrange that—without the sarcastic comments—he would be most grateful.

"Why the sudden interest in improving Miss Chillingford?" asked Mary.

Charles looked very self-satisfied. "It seems I have a piece of society gossip that even my wife has failed to pick up. It's not official and still very secret, but according to Laverton, it seems Miss Chillingford is to be married and so will enter political circles. And this will entertain you particularly, Franny. Remember at the Moores', you spent most of the evening with Lord Gareth Blaine? I've always found him too outrageous, but he seemed to amuse you."

Mary closed her eyes, but Frances didn't get it right away.

"What does Lord Gareth have to do with Miss Chillingford's future husband?"

"That's whom she's marrying—Lord Gareth. I wonder if she'll be as sympathetic a listener as you were, Franny."

Frances felt herself getting dizzy and thought she'd faint. It couldn't possibly . . . it was too ridiculous. All she knew right then was that she had to be alone. "Will you excuse me? I over-indulged in the venison. Aunt Felicity always said game meats were unwholesome for young women. Just let me lie down for a few moments."

As Charles looked on with concern, Mary practically carried Frances to the room that was still kept as her bedroom for when she stayed over. Frances managed to make it to the bed and wait until the door was closed before bursting into tears.

"How could he have . . . the things he said and promised and told me . . ." It seemed like some great cosmic joke that she had met the only person in London who she felt could fully appreciate her, only to have that dream yanked away by Claire Chillingford.

"What he did was unspeakable," said Mary. "Charles said he never quite trusted Lord Gareth, and now we know why. To do that to anyone, but especially you, dear Franny . . ."

Every conversation, every word they had exchanged, was nothing but a temporary amusement for him, and the kisses were just base lust, Frances realized. She was disgusted with herself for not seeing through the charade.

Charles rapped on the door.

"I'll be fine. Tell him it's just a woman's problem." She smiled through her tears. "Men never want to hear about that."

Mary slipped out the door and tried to keep her voice down, but Frances could still hear them. It wouldn't take Charles long to figure out that this wasn't about eating too much venison.

"It's that Lord Gareth, isn't it? He played with Franny's heart. As soon as I mentioned his name—"

"Charles, Franny may have become emotionally tangled with him. The man is charming. Don't overreact. I'm sure Franny will recover in a day or two."

"Did he make promises to her? Because I will publicly horse-whip him." Then the old argument started. "If Frances lived at home, like a young woman should, I would've seen this coming and headed it off. There are jokes around the club about all the ladies he's romanced. What could anyone expect? If I had been around while this developed—"

But Mary broke in, unusually sharply for her. "Frances has made the decision to lead her own life, with the triumphs and defeats that come with such a choice. And so far, the former far outnumber the latter. And if I know Franny, she'll turn this defeat into a victory too. The last thing a girl wants right now is a brother saying, 'I told you so.' Go back downstairs and have another glass of port and a cigar."

And with that, Mary turned away from her astonished husband and reentered the room.

"I'm afraid you heard all that," she said.

"If you can give speeches like that, you should be in Parliament," said Frances. "Thank you."

"You flatter me. Would you like to spend the night here?"

"That's sweet of you. But I have plenty to keep me busy tomorrow. It's another soup kitchen tomorrow night."

"Can't someone else take your place? Give you a quiet evening?"

At that, color came into Frances's cheeks. She felt something else pushing away the hurt, at least for now. The Seaforths didn't wallow in emotion, she remembered. "It will do me good. Down at the hall, everyone's heart is broken. Perhaps I need reminding there are worse things in life than being courted by a cad."

At that, Mary hugged Frances. "You really are the best person I know."

Mallow was summoned from downstairs to help her mistress rearrange herself before leaving. Seeing the remnants of tear tracks, Mallow guessed what had happened but said nothing direct.

"I am sorry you are unwell, my lady."

"It's not really that. I had some bad news about Lord Gareth Blaine."

"I hope he has not come to any harm, my lady."

"I hope he has," said Frances with some warmth. "He was toying with me. That's all I have to say about that."

Mallow was upset for Lady Frances, but she had always thought there was something a little too cocksure about him. At any rate, there was only one thing to say.

"Yes, my lady."

Charles dispatched a footman to fetch a hansom after Frances refused his offer of the family car and chauffeur to take her and Mallow home. Frances just tucked herself into a corner of the cab and said nothing. Mallow considered some advice Miss Garritty had given her about taking care of one's lady during "emotional disturbances." The ability to soothe a mistress in trying times was what separated the merely competent lady's maid from the superior lady's maid.

Mallow cleared her throat, and Frances opened her eyes. "If I may suggest, my lady, you might feel better if we didn't go directly home."

"Where do you suggest we go at this hour? Tell the driver to take us round and round London?" Lady Frances had never been impatient with her like that.

"I have an idea, my lady."

Frances's eyes got wider, but she said nothing. Her ladyship was too curious to say no. Mallow stuck her head out. "Driver, I have a new address for you." And she rattled it off.

"Very good, miss," said the driver.

"Soho," said Frances. "That address you gave is in Soho, isn't it? I've been there, and I can't imagine what I would like to see at this hour."

Of course Lady Frances had been there. It was the raffish haunt of writers and artists, and Mallow was sure her ladyship had met with residents there who would never be admitted to the drawing rooms in Belgravia and Mayfair.

But she was equally sure her ladyship had not been where they were going tonight.

"I trust you will find our trip entertaining, my lady," said Mallow, and Frances smiled despite her sad feelings. She had sprung enough surprises on Mallow; she would be inclined to allow a surprise in return.

Mallow had some reservations about what she was doing. It was taking a bit of a liberty for a lady's maid. She felt even more nervous when the cab stopped, at her direction, in front of a rather seedy-looking tea shop. It had seemed so fine when she was a little girl, before she had taken up residence in one of London's great houses.

"Mallow—"

"Please, my lady, I am sure you will like it," she said, forcing confidence into her voice. She watched Frances climb out of the hansom, her face full of curiosity. Mallow peered in through the shop window and rapped sharply on the door.

"We're closed," came the muffled reply.

She rapped again, and now the door opened to reveal a plump, older man, who was already speaking as he opened it. ". . . and if you bother me again I'll have the police . . ." Then he peered into the dark street and broke into a smile. Mallow answered him with a smile of her own. The shop hadn't changed over the years, and neither had Mr. Pennystone.

"Bless me, it's little Junie. What are you doing here? But come on in, you're always welcome."

"I brought someone with me," she said. "My lady, this is Mr. Abel Pennystone, manager of Ely Street Tea Shop and great friend to my late father. Mr. Pennystone, please meet my mistress, Lady Frances Ffolkes."

"Well, don't stand in the street. Junie—and my lady," the man gave a brief bow, "I am pleased to welcome you."

Mallow felt a shiver of delight in seeing the wonder on her ladyship's face as they entered. The tea shop was indeed closed, with chairs put up on the table and the floor a little damp after a mopping. But two men in waiters' uniforms, half undone, stood up and, at Mr. Pennystone's direction, placed two chairs at table. They smiled briefly but said nothing. The tea shop often employed immigrant waiters, Mallow remembered.

"Now what can I get you, my lady, Miss Mallow?" said Mr. Pennystone grinning.

"Don't tease me. You know very well," said Mallow a little coyly. "And you of all people may call me Junie."

"You're maid to a lady," he said. "And so I will call you Miss Mallow." She felt herself turn pink as Mr. Pennystone headed behind the counter.

"Mallow, what is this place?" asked Frances.

"Just a tea shop, my lady. Mr. Pennystone was an old friend of my father's and helped out after he died. He's managed this shop as long as anyone can remember, and for special days, there were special treats here for me and my sisters. As you will see."

One of the waiters deposited a plate with plain biscuits, and a moment after that, Mr. Pennystone came around with two frothy pink drinks in tall glasses.

"Pink lemonade," said Frances.

"The very best in London, my lady. In all of England," said Mallow. Now was the test. Had she judged right? Her ladyship was used to the very best wines and sherries. Mallow took a sip and felt her body practically dissolve in bliss as the sweet-tangy taste slid down her throat and spread throughout her body. But her eyes never left her ladyship's face.

Frances took a long drink and then leaned back.

"I have never tasted anything like this," said Frances. "Do you share the recipe?"

"An absolute secret, my lady, but I thank you for the compliment and for taking on little Junie here. We were so thrilled when we heard, back in the neighborhood, that our June Mallow was maid to a titled lady. She's done us proud."

"She has done herself proud indeed, Mr. Pennystone. A fine maid . . . and, apparently, full of surprises." Mallow felt transported at the compliments from Mr. Pennystone and Lady Frances.

"Well, the lads and I will finish tidying up. No rush. Enjoy your drinks."

Mallow now saw the Ely Street Tea Shop as her mistress must have as she watched her ladyship's eyes dart all around. The English pastoral scenes she adored as a child were nothing like the oil paintings in great houses. The glassware and china that seemed so elegant back then were chipped. The chairs rocked. Lady Frances liked the drink, that was clear, but what would she think of this place so dear in Mallow's childhood memories?

"When I was ten, our cook made me the loveliest walnut cake for nursery tea. That was the last time I felt like I do right now."

Mallow completely relaxed. "Do you feel better, my lady?"

"Oddly, I do." She toyed with the spoon in her glass. "Do you know, Mallow, he used me—that is, Lord Gareth. His true affections were engaged elsewhere."

"He was a cad, my lady. He was not worthy of you," said Mallow. *Just let Lord Gareth call on my lady again*, thought Mallow. *He'd better pray I'm not around to receive him.*

"It was more than that. You know I've been working to find the manuscript for the Colcombe family. You helped me at the Colcombe's house. Lord Gareth is part of a group of friends, and they want the manuscript, too. Lord Gareth clearly had other motives. It is very dark, Mallow. I do believe Major Colcombe was killed because of what he wrote."

Wide-eyed, Mallow just nodded. She had seen a bit of life since going into service, courtships and infidelities, tenderness and fights, protestations of friendship and nasty wit. But at the end of the day, she thought of Society—with a capital *S*—as one group. They would sleep with each other's wives—that she knew. But such sordid crimes as theft and murder . . .

They sat in silence for a while, quietly finishing their pink lemonade. The only sounds came from Mr. Pennystone and the waiters cleaning up.

"You look very thoughtful, Mallow." Her ladyship raised an eyebrow.

"I can't understand why the major was killed, my lady. Whatever he wrote, why would anyone care?"

"It's not about money. It's probably power. People want to be in charge. What was in that manuscript would end someone's political career. Maybe a lot of people's political careers."

Mallow frowned. She wasn't sure what a "political career" was. These were men who already had houses and servants and all the food they could ever want.

Her ladyship broke into her thoughts. That was a spooky thing about her—she seemed to know what people were thinking. "You're wondering, what is a political career, and why is it worth so much? It's not worth a man's life. Indeed, it may not be worth anything at all."

"Yes, my lady." Her mistress now looked restored. The pink lemonade would do that. She looked full of purpose again.

"Do you remember the reception for the French ambassador—when I was home from college? I slipped out to go to my very first suffragist meeting, counting on my mother to not notice among all the people that I had gone. But she did. What did you do, Mallow? You were still just a housemaid then, but what did you do?"

"I lied, my lady," said Mallow quietly. She remembered. She had never been so scared. "I lied to your mother, Dowager Marchioness of Seaforth, and told her you were in bed with a headache and didn't want to be disturbed." It had hurt to do it. She had kept secrets from Lady Frances's mother before, but this was the first time she had told her a bald-faced lie. The marchioness had been good to her, but Mallow, for reasons she could not articulate, had developed a closer loyalty to her daughter, Lady Frances.

"You weren't concerned that I was doing something foolish, even dangerous, and that my mother and brother should know about it?"

"I trusted you, my lady."

"Yes, Mallow. Trust and loyalty. I believe I will need all of your trust and loyalty in the days to come."

"Yes, my lady."

Seeing they were done, Mr. Pennystone came back. Frances realized they were there as guests, not customers, so did not insult him by offering to pay. Mallow was glad Frances had accepted the lemonade as a guest.

"I cannot thank you enough, Mr. Pennystone. This has been delightful."

"You're welcome anytime, my lady. A friend of Junie's is a friend of mine." He then realized his gaff—Lady Frances was not June's friend but her mistress. He frowned and said, "Beg pardon, my lady, I only meant—"

Frances felt terrible for Mr. Pennystone, who seemed so embarrassed at his error.

"I know what you meant. And there is nothing to apologize for. Thank you again."

And that was worth everything to Mallow.

Smiling again, Mr. Pennystone dispatched one of the waiters to walk them to a cabstand. He was from somewhere in East Europe—Poland, perhaps—as were so many of the workers in Soho. But his lack of English skills didn't prevent him from being respectful and attentive, and he saw them into a hansom on the main road.

"Thank you, Mallow. You anticipated my needs, and only the very best lady's maids can do that."

"I do my best, my lady," she said. And then Lady Frances started to laugh out of nowhere.

"Remember Miss Pritchard, my mother's maid, the one you called the tigress? Can you imagine her bringing my mother to Mr. Pennystone's for a pink lemonade?"

Mallow knew a proper maid did not show undue emotion in front of her mistress. But there was no helping it—a moment later she was laughing too.

CHAPTER 10

When Frances awoke the next morning, the pain of what Gareth had done to her came rushing back. But she had been soothed by her late-night Soho visit, and she was determined to pour all her energies into the tasks at hand. She swung her legs out of bed: time for tea and eggs and toast and a visit with Mrs. Elkhorn's—well, "friend" probably wasn't the best word. "Colleague," perhaps: Lord Ashton Crossley, the retired War Office powerbroker.

Social calls weren't properly made until later in the day, but this wasn't really a social call yet perhaps was something less than a business visit. Most of the political figures Frances knew were members of the Liberal Party, friends and associates of her brother's and their father before him. Except for brief pleasantries at large events, she had never spoken with a Conservative politician.

Frances had Mallow dress her in the same severe dress she used for the Wheaton law office. The thought of Hal picked her up a bit. She hadn't bothered to even open it last night, but a message from him had been waiting for her when she got home, fixing a time for the promised dinner at his house.

Well-breakfasted, Frances assigned Mallow some tasks for the day and then made her way to Lord Crossley's town house.

His house was small but well appointed on the outside. The brass shone and the windows were clean. Frances knew the signs of a house that was owned by someone who cared for it and had money to spend.

A butler answered the door and accepted Lady Frances's card. He showed her into the morning room and said Lord Crossley would see her shortly. It would seem Mrs. Elkhorn's letter of introduction had done its work.

The room was perfectly decorated. Not an item was out of place, and there were enough interesting objects to keep visitors entertained. A maid had cleaned it carefully. It was almost like a stage set—Frances wondered if she was the first person to visit the room in more than a month. She was there for a fair amount of time. Usually, people of their class saw you right away or not at all.

But eventually the butler returned and said Lord Crossley would see her if she would follow him. Frances was a little surprised, believing that this little room would be perfect for a two-person meeting. Of course, if Lord Crossley was old-fashioned, he might want to receive her in a more formal drawing room.

But the butler didn't lead her upstairs to where a drawing room would be. Rather, he led her across the hall to what was no doubt a study. He entered without knocking.

"Lady Frances Ffolkes," he announced.

The study had the same particular smell of polished wood and old paper as Hal's study. The furniture too was a little old-fashioned. But everything fell into the background at the site of the man behind the desk. His hair was completely white and brushed straight back to reveal a high forehead. Dark eyes took in Frances very quickly, and she felt as if he could see right through her. His face was lined, and his mouth was formed into a sarcastic smile. *He's already decided to laugh at me*, concluded Frances.

She was shown to a large, comfortable chair facing the desk. But it was low, and because Frances was short to begin with, she had to look up to Lord Crossley. She felt like she did as a child, when she was allowed into her father's office at Whitehall as a special treat.

The butler left and closed the door behind him.

"Please excuse my not standing, Lady Frances. It is a little difficult. My apologies." He gestured to a silver-topped cane leaning against the desk. His voice was smooth and precise. Frances decided to match him for courtesy.

"Do not apologize, my lord. I should be thanking you for taking the time to see me at Mrs. Elkhorn's request."

"Dear Winifred. Do you know we see each other every Sunday? We both worship at St. Edmund's. We have almost nothing in common politically, but the Church of England is one commitment we share. And barely that. I pray to God to release me from my pain. And she prays that God keeps me on earth until I can personally witness women get the vote. We view it as a popularity contest with the Almighty as judge. He's the only authority Winifred respects. And some days, perhaps not even Him."

Frances didn't know what to say to that. But she realized Lord Crossley's expression was not designed to mock her. It was a grimace of pain. This was not the comfortably tired old age of General Audendale. This man was in agony, with a body rebelling against a mind that she could tell was still sharp.

"Like Mrs. Elkhorn, I'm sure I would relish political debate with you. But I respect your time and come only to see if you can help me." When he didn't respond, she added. "This is a matter that goes beyond party politics."

"Indeed. How unusual. But I knew your father somewhat and your brother by reputation, so perhaps reasonableness is a family trait." Frances thanked him. "Now tell me, and I'll see if I can help. No, I misspoke. I'm sure I can help. The question is whether I want to. Are you going to behave like Winifred, racing around like a bull in a china shop, wrecking beautiful things in your zeal for a better world and leaving men like me to clean up the mess? Or can I count on you to show some moderation?"

Frances wanted to argue with him but stopped herself. It would be neither prudent nor profitable. She took his warning to heart and began. She spoke clearly and succinctly: "As you may remember, my lord, there was a war scandal involving the Empire Light Horse and the battle of Sapphire River. An officer, a man who led the troops in the battle, was writing a book about it. Now he is dead, and we don't know how. His manuscript was taken. I want to find out who took it. And I want it back."

"Talk of the Colcombe manuscript has reached even me in my solitude here. So if I understand you correctly, you want justice, my lady?"

Frances started to answer yes but stopped. He was looking so closely at her. He didn't want that pat answer. That would be a naïve response, and Lord Crossley was not going to help an idealistic child in an unwinnable crusade.

"Justice is always a goal," she said carefully. "But neither you nor I are in a position to dispense it. For now, I will settle for the manuscript."

Frances met his eyes and realized she had answered correctly.

"Fools tire me. Winifred said you weren't a fool, and I see she was right. I remember the scandal of the Empire Light Horse very well. Believe it or not, Lady Frances, I was too high up to know exactly what happened. As a member of a political family, you may know that men of power don't always know what's going on under them. I cannot tell you who was responsible for that debacle or who covered it up. Do you believe me?"

He flashed her that sardonic smile again, a mix of amusement and pain.

"Mrs. Elkhorn told me you might help me but that I couldn't trust you."

Lord Crossley allowed himself a laugh at that.

"Then you and I shall prove her wrong, and I cannot tell you how much satisfaction that would give me," he said. "I no longer possess political power, and I am facing a meeting with my maker. The politics of yesteryear seemed petty. If I can help you, I will. Even my political colleagues deserve what they get, Conservatives, Liberals . . . we all do. But tell me, if this manuscript is so important, why would someone not have destroyed it?"

Another test, thought Frances. "Because possession of the manuscript is power. This is all about power, I am sure of it. To destroy the manuscript is to lose that control." She gazed at Crossley, hoping for his approval.

He nodded and reached for paper and pen on his desk and started to write, consulting a small leather notebook as he did. When he was done, he folded it carefully, put it into an envelope, and then held it out to her. Frances stood to take it from him.

"I have written a name on that piece of paper. Many are responsible for the Sapphire River debacle, but more than anyone, he was the architect. Did he steal the manuscript to protect himself or destroy his enemies? I have no idea. But more than any man, he has the most to lose from its publication."

Frances thought again about the mysterious fight she had witnessed in the mews and the police constable who wouldn't give his name. She thought about Danny, who was no doubt murdered. She was getting close to some powerful people who were not used to be being casually thwarted.

"Mr. Davis Bramwell, member of Parliament." Frances raised an eyebrow, and Lord Crossley smiled. "I see his name is known to you."

"Yes. He attended Major Colcombe's funeral. His name was on the list Kat Colcombe and I compiled."

"Indeed," said Lord Crossley dryly. "That is interesting. Mr. Bramwell was Parliament's de facto policy liaison with the general staff during the war. He is a member of Parliament still, ambitious and obsessed with power, chaffing until the Conservatives are back in control and he can resume what he no doubt believes is his rightful place in the world."

He leaned back in his chair, and his face was looking a little ashen. "You look concerned for me. I think Mrs. Elkhorn is concerned, too, but perhaps she is a better actress. Don't worry. My butler will be in shortly with some relief. But since I've helped you, please indulge me and answer one question. What led you to the War Office?"

Frances told him she had concluded someone well placed was behind the theft because there were whispers among the aristocracy. She told Lord Crossley that she had been invited to a Heathcote event because, she suspected, someone in the group was curious about her and her connection to the manuscript.

"In your sojourns with that august company," he said, "did you come across Lord Gareth Blaine? He's deeply involved with them. Too deeply."

Frances tried to control her reactions but felt her face grow red anyway. Crossley chuckled. "The answer is yes, I see. Don't be ashamed of your feelings. He's had the devil's own charm since boyhood."

"I take it you know him then?"

Crossley leaned back. "You are very bright, my lady. You are well suited to be Winifred's protégé. But you are still a student and have made a mistake she wouldn't have. Winifred would've checked connections beforehand. Lord Gareth is my nephew, son of my sister, the Duchess of Carrolton. He was in this very room just days ago asking what I knew about the Sapphire River debacle."

Equal parts embarrassment and rage surged through Frances. Crossley was right—she should've done more research. Her favorite professor at Vassar would've roasted her over the coals for that omission. And Gareth should've told her his uncle was a powerful man in possession of key information. He was more deeply involved than he had indicated.

"That is very interesting, my lord. I have to say . . . I don't know what to believe."

"You must believe what you think is right, Lady Frances. And now, my lady, we really are done."

There were beads of sweat on his brow, and Frances noted his hands were shaking. She was about to ask if she could ring for a servant when the butler entered with a tall glass. With great care and patience, he helped his master drink.

"Momentarily, I will become useless. If I did not inspire trust, I hope you can say at least I gave you something to think about."

Frances stood. "You helped me immensely, Lord Crossley. I shall pray for your relief and that it should be immediate."

"Not even a wait for suffrage?" he said.

"Oh no, my lord. I pray that will be immediate as well."

And she heard him chuckling as the butler showed her out the door.

Back on the street, Frances breathed deeply. That beautiful, much-loved house had been filled with pain, both physical and emotional, and it had gotten into her too. She felt guilty for feeling relief to be away from it, because she knew what it had cost him to receive her, to talk with her. She hoped the morphine solution—for that is no doubt what he had been served—would provide him at least a little peace. Frances was not particularly religious, but she hoped the Almighty would take into account the good work Lord Crossley had done that morning.

She opened the envelope and looked at the address. Mr. Bramwell was just a short walk away. As an old governess had said, "No time like the present." Parliament was not currently in session, which meant Bramwell might be working out of an office at home.

His town house was somewhat larger than Crossley's and well kept, but without the elegance that came from someone who cared deeply about his house. The butler received her with more casualness.

"Do you have an appointment?" he asked. Frances raised an eyebrow and produced a calling card.

"No, but I was hoping Mr. Bramwell could spare a few moments. Lord Crossley, his colleague in the party, suggested it. And my brother, you may want to remind him, is the current undersecretary for European Affairs."

This butler clearly wanted her to establish her bona fides, and this seemed to do it.

"Very good, my lady." He showed her into a morning room, and again she saw the difference. This room was used heavily—furniture was not aligned and items were disarranged. Frances didn't know if there was a Mrs. Bramwell, but at any rate, the house wasn't being properly supervised. The morning room should look better, and as Frances knew, she looked every inch a lady; the butler should not have questioned her on the doorstep.

Maybe this said something about Mr. Bramwell.

The door opened, and a young man, neatly dressed, walked in. He looked not unkind but a little harried.

"I am sorry you were sent here to wait, my lady. Mr. Bramwell has been in the middle of important parliamentary business. I'm Arthur Appledore, Mr. Bramwell's secretary." He then apologetically asked if Lady Frances could describe the reason for her call.

She thought for a moment and decided to be oblique to keep Bramwell guessing and encourage him to see her in person.

"I am helping some friends named Colcombe. Daniel Colcombe, who was a major during the Boer War, died recently, and I am researching some actions that occurred toward the end of that war with his command, the Empire Light Horse." She added that Lord Crossley had particularly recommended she speak with Mr. Bramwell.

It was only a few sentences, but by the time she was done, the secretary had gone from harried to deeply anxious. It seemed way of out proportion to her story. Unless, of course, Mr. Bramwell had already had words with him about this manuscript.

"Yes . . . ah . . . thank you, my lady. Let me just discuss this and see if . . . if this is something he can address right now." He almost stumbled out of the room, closing the door behind him. Frances's curiosity was roused beyond control. She gave Appledore a few seconds to return to his master, then she left the morning room herself. Sounds from a door along the hall gave away the location of the office. No servants were in view, so she decided a bit of eavesdropping was not amiss. One voice rose to the point where there was no need to put her ear to the door—and she guessed that was Bramwell having a talk with his soft-spoken secretary.

". . . Well why didn't you just get rid of her . . . Yes, I am very much aware she's the sister of a marquess . . . I don't bloody well care; that's the last thing I want to get involved with . . . Look, Appledore, maybe I'm not making myself clear. I have no intention of addressing this with one of Winifred Elkhorn's lapdogs. Now get the Seaforth bitch out of here."

Frances felt the two red spots on her cheek that she always knew appeared when she was infuriated. She beat a retreat to the morning room so Appledore wouldn't find her outside the door. Frances had composed herself when the secretary returned, but he looked somewhat the worse for wear.

"You must excuse me, Lady Frances, for the delay. Something . . . rather urgent came up."

"I'm sure," she said coldly.

"Another time, perhaps, he may be more, ah, available," he said. He escorted her out of the room and toward the door. They were in the middle of the foyer when Appledore said, "Meanwhile, he assures me he will give the problem his full attention." That final ridiculous lie was too much. Before Appledore knew what was happening, Frances spun on her heels and was striding down the hall to the office. Without knocking, she entered.

"Did you get rid of her?" said Bramwell without looking up. He was tucked into his desk, absorbed in his papers. He was only of middle years, saw Frances, but already portly and jowly. He enjoyed food and drink.

"He did not," said Frances. A few seconds later, a terrified Appledore followed her into the room.

"What the devil—" said Bramwell.

"During my demonstrations in the park, I've been called bitch. And worse. But at least those men had the courage to say that to my face. I came here to discuss a heroic British soldier. Now are you going to help me?"

With some effort, Bramwell stood, his face drained of color. "You forget yourself, Lady Frances. You'll play no games with me. Appledore, get her out of here at once."

"Don't you dare touch me, Appledore," said Frances. She had learned that being imperious was a powerful technique in situations like this. It only postponed the inevitable, it was true, but sometimes a postponement was all that was necessary. "I want to let you know I will see to it the Colcombe manuscript is published—and don't insult me by pretending you don't know what I'm talking about. You will regret your behavior."

"I have nothing to say except that there are libel laws in this country, even for the aristocracy. Now you will leave or I'll have my servants remove you."

"With men like you in Parliament, is it any wonder that women want the vote? Good day to you, sir. I will see myself out."

And feeling triumphant, she left the office and the house. She had hoped to get more out of him, but what she had learned was actually very helpful. Mr. Bramwell was beyond angry. The tone of last sentence wasn't rage—it was fear. Mr. Bramwell was frightened when she mentioned the manuscript, and Frances found that enlightening.

It wasn't even lunchtime—it had been a very profitable morning.

Back at Miss Plimsoll's, she looked at the rack of letters and messages, half-hoping and half-fearing one from Gareth, but there was nothing. She shook her head as if to clear it. No point in brooding, she reminded herself. Meanwhile, she had some time to change before another committee luncheon, then she'd be able to rest in the afternoon until it was time to go to the soup kitchen.

She found herself looking forward to the evening. The hard, difficult work would be a refreshing change from the intellectual complexities of government ministers and, yes, from lingering thoughts of Gareth.

———◆◆◆———

Indeed, as the crowds of the hungry flowed through the door that night, all other thoughts left her. By the end of the evening, she was weary in body but at peace in mind. She bid good night to Eleanor at her house and then continued in the cab to Miss Plimsoll's, looking forward to her bed. The night porter let her in, and usually he said nothing more than "Good evening," but tonight he said, "A visitor, my lady."

"At this hour?" No one would call unless it was an emergency—something about her family? The porter jabbed a thumb at the lounge. As tired as she was, Frances suddenly felt awake and practically ran into the room. But it wasn't family or one of their servants: it was a large figure in a loud, checked suit—Constable Smith, Inspector Eastley's right-hand man. As before, he was looking around the room in wonderment but focused on Frances as soon as she entered.

He bowed to her and, in his heavy East End accent, said, "Good evening, my lady. The inspector requests your immediate presence. I am to take you there."

"Why? What has happened? It can't wait until tomorrow?"

"The inspector wants to see you tonight, my lady. He will explain."

Curiosity won out over fear.

"Very well, if he insists. Let me tell my maid, and I will be back down in one minute." She raced up the stairs, her mind spinning. Inspector Eastley hadn't seemed to want to see her again, but now he was asking for her at night.

Mallow was stalking the small sitting room in high indignation.

"Good evening, my lady, I am very glad you're back. I must tell you that a police constable had the nerve to call on you and demand your presence. He actually asked where you were. Of course, I told him nothing except that you were expected tonight."

"Thank you, Mallow." Frances hid a smile. "I saw him downstairs in the visitor's lounge."

"He was bold enough to wait here, my lady?" Mallow couldn't believe it—the lounge was for *gentlemen* visitors.

"I'm afraid the police don't observe typical proprieties, Mallow. But thank you for handling this. Now, I will be going off with him—I am sure I will be fine, but I wanted to tell you so you wouldn't worry."

"Very good, my lady. I shall wait up for you."

"Thank you, Mallow."

Back downstairs, she told the constable she was ready, and they headed out the door. Smith said there was a cab waiting just around the corner. He helped her in graciously but said nothing to her or to the driver, who clearly had already been given his orders. The whip cracked and the horse took off.

As she watched the neighborhoods pass by, she realized they were headed back to the East End. Indeed, when they finally stopped, she figured they were no more than a ten-minute walk from her soup kitchen.

The street, like so many in that area, was narrow and dimly lit. Frances made a mental note to find out which London bureau handled street lighting and make a case for more illumination. As they stepped out of the cab, Frances saw a knot of men gathered on the sidewalk. One of them separated from the group and walked over to her—Inspector Eastley, again in a suit in need of an ironing.

"Your man practically kidnapped me. Do you care to tell me why?" she asked.

Eastley raised an eyebrow. "Constable, did you kidnap Lady Frances?"

"No, sir. I told her you requested her presence, as you said, sir."

"I'm glad we cleared that up," he said. "But I do owe you an explanation. A man was murdered here this evening, my lady. There were no witnesses, but he was identified by an acquaintance."

Frances knew it was a dangerous neighborhood. She was determined to not appear shaken and then faint, as might be expected of a woman, and she told the inspector she was not surprised there was a murder here.

"No surprise at all, my lady. Except for this." He produced a card from his pocket. "Not many men in this neighborhood carry with them the calling card of Lady Frances Ffolkes, sister of the Marquess of Seaforth."

At that, Frances paled. She looked over the inspector's shoulder to where uniformed constables were guarding what she could now see was a body covered by a sheet. She knew who it must be: Private Alfred Barnstable, formerly of the Empire Light Horse, to whom she had given a card at their meeting.

When the local inspector saw a lady's calling card in the dead man's pocket, he had brought in Special Branch. Inspector Eastley told Frances he thought it too much of a coincidence: Lady Frances Ffolkes's card in possession of a man soon identified as having served under the late Daniel Colcombe. He had been found near a bar owned by an Australian and frequented by his countrymen—the Red Kangaroo.

"If he had your card, I assume you met. I'd like to know about it." His voice was silky, but Frances sensed the command, and she instinctively fought against it.

"Mr. Barnstable seemed to me to be a fine man in our short acquaintanceship. I shall mourn him. But surely this is just a simple robbery. I can't see what it has to do with our talk."

"You have an unpleasant habit of questioning police methods, Lady Frances." He was more menacing now. "You haven't asked how Mr. Barnstable died. I will tell you. It was a gunshot to the chest at close range, just like Major Colcombe, but he wasn't cleaning a weapon here." He went on to list a range of ghastly ways violence was meted out in the East End—knives, clubs, garrotes—and Frances strove not to look queasy.

"But the local criminals and gang members generally don't use guns. They're expensive, heavy, and make a lot of noise. So we don't think he was killed by a common robber. And in the police, we don't trust coincidences. Tell me what you discussed and don't make me ask you again."

"Very well. It is late, and I am tired too. However, there's no need for discourtesy. Mr. Barnstable came to me because I had posted a note at the Soldiers and Sailors Club asking to speak to anyone under Colcombe. He told me the major had been a great hero but that the debacle had been covered up by politicians and War Office bureaucrats."

Inspector Eastley was a careful listener, she'd give him that.

"But no names came up?"

"None. He had no idea, and Major Colcombe would hardly confide something that important to a private soldier."

"Of course," he murmured. "But tell me, my lady, have you made any progress in your quest for the manuscript?"

She could tell the inspector about the attack in the mews, the mysterious constable, and her connection with Lord Crossley. But she hesitated.

"Do you ask out of curiosity? Or is that the subject of your investigation?"

He smiled. "I do apologize, Lady Frances, but as I said, the police don't answer questions. They just ask them."

"Of course," she said and smiled back. "But perhaps one specific question. How close was the man who shot him? You can tell that, can't you, by looking at the wound, at least approximately?"

He looked surprised. "I can tell you that, Lady Frances. The shooter was no more than a foot or two away."

"Thank you, Inspector. And now, I will be frank with you. Private Barnstable was a very cautious man who stayed alive in a difficult war. He would not have let someone he didn't know get that close to him."

Before the inspector could comment, they both turned at the sound of a hansom arriving on the quiet street.

It stopped, and a well-dressed man alighted. Colonel Zachery Mountjoy. He walked as quickly as he could without losing dignity. The hard set of his mouth, clear under his mustache, showed he was angry. The inspector greeted him with a thin smile, and Constable Smith stepped back to let the colonel into their little circle—but never took his eyes off him.

"You are most welcome, Colonel. Did you hear about this particular incident? Or do you just frequent this part of London?"

"I have no use for your impertinence," said Mountjoy. "I heard about this the same way you did. What I couldn't believe is that you dragged Lady Frances down here. Her brother is a marquess—a crown minister and a member of several prestigious clubs. Have you completely lost your senses?"

"Lady Frances is here voluntarily. We uncovered a connection between her ladyship and the victim. I wanted to discuss it with her as soon as possible." His voice was crisp and level but in no way apologetic.

The colonel turned to Frances. "Were you able to help, Lady Frances? Or was your unfortunate trip here a waste of your time?"

"Thank you for your concern. Only the inspector knows if it was worthwhile, but I don't think we have anything further to discuss."

Inspector Eastley sighed. "No, Lady Frances, I think not. I was hoping for a name . . ." He glanced at the colonel. "But we will proceed without it."

A uniformed constable approached and saluted. "We spoke to the customers at the Red Kangaroo, sir. Except for the man who found the body, no one saw or heard anything."

"Thank you, Constable. No one in this neighborhood ever has anything to tell the police, it seems."

"If you're done, Inspector, I'd like to take Lady Frances home," said the colonel. "With your permission, my lady."

"Or I can send you back with one of my constables," said Inspector Eastley.

Frances considered the two offers. Both were acceptable, but she wanted to talk to the colonel. She thanked Inspector Eastley but said she didn't want to take any of the constables away from their duties and would accept the colonel's offer. The colonel looked triumphant.

"Just one favor, Inspector," said Frances. Eastley raised an eyebrow. "I do not know what happens with such men who die so far from home with little money and no family. I would be in your debt if you would tell whatever authorities are responsible that the Seaforths will see Mr. Barnstable gets a proper Christian burial."

The colonel and the inspector both were temporarily rendered speechless by Frances's observation that Barnstable was more than a police case—he had been a person.

"Thank you, Lady Frances," said Eastley eventually. "I give you my solemn promise the body will be released to you."

And with that, Frances let Colonel Mountjoy lead her away.

"That was a very kind gesture," he said as he helped her into the cab. "If I may say, typical of the very best women. Men don't think along those lines, and I mean that as a compliment."

"I take it as such," said Frances. She had the ride back to Miss Plimsoll's to see what she could get out of the colonel and was determined to get off on the right foot. "I am grateful for your arrival, but I can't imagine how you knew."

Mountjoy stroked his mustache. "Well, I do have contacts in the Home Office," he said. "And we'll leave it at that."

"What a coincidence. Lord Gareth Blaine, whom you met earlier at the theater, has a position in the Home Office."

At that mention, Mountjoy frowned. "It would be most bold for me to tell you how to choose your friends, Lady Frances, but I think it only fair to warn you that the Heathcotes—and their circle—can be a rather dangerous lot. Involved in things that are, well, not quite nice." He made it sound as if nothing could be worse than "not quite nice."

"Thank you for your warning," she said, fighting the urge to tell him to mind his own business.

"My, ah, contacts at the Home Office mentioned you were brought there because the deceased had your calling card. Is that correct?"

"Yes," said Frances, planning her response carefully. "The man had heard my name in the soup kitchen when he was looking for a friend down on his luck. He asked if I was related to an officer he knew in South Africa, Major Charles Ffolkes. I told him he was my brother and gave him my card so he could find me again and perhaps even meet my brother before going back to Australia."

The story seemed plausible to the colonel.

"Did he mention anything about the manuscript, Lady Frances?" He looked at her closely. "If he knew your brother, he might well have known Major Colcombe too."

"Very likely. But it didn't come up. I think he was homesick and was tickled to find someone he knew—or the member of a family he knew."

"So nothing about the manuscript came up when you spoke with Barnstable? Don't be alarmed if you didn't tell the inspector. He can be rather—official. But with me, since I'm not official, it might be easier to talk." He looked closely at her.

"I very much appreciate the distinction. But at your advice, I have not been seeking the manuscript actively and did not discuss it with Barnstable."

The colonel frowned again. "I don't want to seem forward, but this could well have to do with the manuscript, even though you didn't discuss it with him. Please be careful. Don't even mention it. There are people in government—but I don't want to say too much or scare you. Again, it may eventually surface, but meanwhile, you don't want to upset people."

"Of course not."

"For now, we'll keep this among ourselves, but let's be a little more circumspect in the future, shall we?"

"An excellent suggestion. But just one question. Can you tell me why Inspector Eastley has been so unpleasant? I've known so many men in government, and all of them have been polite."

The colonel gave her a condescending look, which made her blood boil, but she had asked for it, and it was for a purpose.

"Policemen are not gentlemen. Oh, in the very senior ranks, yes, but a mere inspector—certainly not. Did you know that many hadn't even wanted England to have a professional police force, and they have only been around for less than a century? There was a feeling that it was giving too much power to the wrong sort—men who had different allegiances from the aristocrats and military elite who had run the country for centuries—like your family, Lady Frances. They could easily become tools of grasping men, would-be despots who needed a force to bring them to power. In France, Napoleon had used a secret, national police force to stay in power—what more proof do you need?"

The neighborhoods got better until they were on familiar streets and pulling up to Miss Plimsoll's.

"Thank you so much, Colonel, for both your rescue and your information."

She made her way upstairs to a very relieved Mallow, who helped her change into her nightgown. She gratefully slipped into bed—but not before saying a prayer for a soldier who had died far from home.

CHAPTER 11

It had been a while since Frances had been to the shore. She had always liked what the waterfront did for her senses—the slap of water against wooden boats and the rattle of anchor chains, the smell of the salt air and the taste of fresh fish. As Frances alighted from the train, she turned her face to the sea and closed her eyes, feeling the damp breeze on her cheek.

Mallow was very skeptical, however. She liked the train trip, but the smells and sights were unfamiliar, and there was nothing like a London hansom cab in sight.

"I'll see what I can do about some sort of transportation, my lady." At an inn by the station, a serving girl told her that for a modest fee, a local deliveryman would take Mallow and her mistress to wherever they needed to go in the village.

"I'm sorry, my lady. It's the best I could arrange."

"Quite all right, Mallow. When we were young, Charles and I would grab rides from farmers and fishmongers all the time near our country estate. It'll be fun."

"If you say so, my lady."

The driver was polite and welcoming and helped the ladies onto the seat beside him. Then, whipping his team, he headed to Bluefin Cottage on the Rye Road, where Mrs. Tregallis lived. They passed through the village proper, where almost every house sported nets in various states of repair and the smell of fish was so pervasive, the residents probably didn't notice it anymore.

Bluefin Cottage was small and neat. Frances thought it looked like an oversized dollhouse. It was well lined with flowers and the house itself had been painted recently, white with blue trim. The whimsical brass door knocker was shaped like a clam.

"Charming, isn't it, Mallow?"

"Yes, my lady." Charm was well and good, thought Mallow, but she couldn't imagine living in a town so small that it lacked a music hall.

As they watched the door, a little boy in a sailor suit ran out and stopped, looking at the women curiously.

"Hello. My name is Lady Frances. This is Miss Mallow. What is your name?"

"Crispin. Crispin Tregallis, ma'am."

"Good day to you, Master Tregallis. Is your mother at home?"

Frances looked up and saw the answer to her question—Dorothy Tregallis was standing in the doorway.

Danny Colcombe favored a certain type of woman, as Franny knew, because she would quietly listen to the men talk when they didn't know she was around, laughing about the women they fancied. His type was a dark-haired woman who had a generous mouth and full figure and who viewed the world with what Franny's mother had disparagingly called "a bold eye."

But Dorothy didn't fit that at all. She was a tall, spare woman with soft, brown hair. She wasn't what men would call a pretty girl, but her face was welcoming and full of good humor. It seemed a surprise, but on second thought, the recuperating Danny hadn't wanted a beautiful or charming woman; he had wanted a sympathetic one.

"You must be Lady Frances Ffolkes. Please come in."

"Yes," said the boy. And he reached up to take her hand in his and bring her inside, with Mallow following.

"Your son is quite the gentleman." Frances looked at him to see if she could find anything of Danny in him, but no, at least not yet.

"Thank you. I can't help but be proud of him."

Inside, the cottage was simple, and its cleanliness was a testament to Dorothy's profession.

"Please, both of you sit. You must be weary from your long train journey."

"We are weary—weary of sitting. Anyway, the sea air is invigorating. I suppose that's why you nurses are always telling us to recuperate by the sea." Dorothy laughed as Frances began slicing bread and Mallow filled a kettle.

"There's no need to do that—you're my guests."

"Oh, but we can't just sit and watch and let you do all the work. When I was in college, I learned how to make and serve a very nice English tea for my American friends, and very impressed they were."

Dorothy laughed again. "You are just as Danny described you. Cheerful, brisk, and kind—Danny said no one would guess you were the daughter of a marquess, and he meant that as a compliment. Now let's all of us have some tea, and then— and then we'll talk."

Dorothy talked about the village over bread and jam, and young Master Crispin proudly showed his shell collection to Mallow, who wondered how clean they were.

"Mrs. Tregallis," said Mallow, "if you would like, I will take Crispin for a walk around the harbor so you and my lady can talk in peace."

"That would be lovely, Mallow. Thank you. Do go to the coast guard station—you can't miss it. The district officer is an old Royal Navy hand, and when Danny came for visits—" Her voice broke for a second. "—he'd take Crispin there. The men would chat, and he'd let Danny play with his telescope."

A quick cleanup and Mallow and Crispin were ready to go. But before they left, Frances quickly whispered in Mallow's ear. "The coast guardsman knew Danny. See if you can draw him out." And Mallow nodded.

The two women sat again at the table with their cups of tea. "You're like your brother. I could see right away when you looked at me. He was so kind to me, both before and after Danny died. Most men would see me as no better than a tart. But not your brother. And I see the way you look at me—not you either. You must be a remarkable family."

Frances was full of pride at her brother—she so wished they could talk about this together.

"We try," she said modestly.

"I know Mr. Wheaton told you the full story at my insistence. Although you don't judge me for what happened, do you think me a fool for not accepting his marriage offer? We could never have made each other happy, not over the years, as husband and wife." She paused. "Danny was always seeking something. Even after the war, once he recovered, he was talking about everything from running his own theater to returning to Africa and farming to setting up a tea plantation in India. I wanted a more settled life—I am not looking for more adventures. We'd only end up with resentments. Danny was not meant to marry me. Perhaps he was not meant to marry anyone. You probably think me ridiculous, however, to turn down such a good man, so well set up."

But Frances shook her head. "I don't think you're a fool. I do think you are very brave." She thought about Gareth, and Dorothy's eyes were so inviting. She was so full of sympathy, she could see what had attracted Danny. Dorothy would understand.

"I loved a man. And had he . . . had things been just a little different, I might've. But I won't pretend that I would've refused a marriage proposal from a man who I now know could not have made me happy. I don't know if I would've had that much courage."

Dorothy looked at her with understanding and nodded.

"I don't want you to think I put all the blame on Danny," said Dorothy. "I don't want to cast him as the evil, lecherous master and me the innocent, young girl." She smiled wryly. "I'm a nurse. I know where babies come from."

Frances laughed, and Dorothy joined her. "I accept your reasons for not marrying Danny, but you would've been very good for him. You are remarkable, Mrs. Tregallis."

Dorothy smiled. "Thank you, but since Tregallis isn't really my name, please just call me 'Dorothy.'" In Society, it was a little early in their relationship to call each other by their Christian names, but with Dorothy, it seemed a genuine invitation to friendship.

"Very well. But you must call me Franny."

Now that they knew something about each other, Dorothy felt she could come to the reason Frances was there: Although there was no more passion between them, Danny had visited frequently and seemed genuinely pleased with his son. It had been awkward at first, but they did enjoy each other's company, and they gradually fell into the roles they had made up for themselves, friendly cousins. She looked forward to his visits . . . and when she heard he had died, under those strange circumstances, it was devastating. There was no one she could talk to about it and tell the whole story, no practical way to go up to London, nothing to tell Crispin.

"So when Mr. Wheaton told me about you, that you had made it your business to find out the truth, it seemed like a godsend. He was too careful to die by accident, and suicide was unthinkable from the Danny I knew."

"What did he tell you about a book he was writing, war memoirs?"

"Not much more than that. I gathered from his tone there was something secret, but he didn't discuss it much."

"Then I have a story to tell you," said Frances. She summarized the mystery of the manuscript, the idea that it threatened powerful figures and caught the attention of an elite Scotland Yard inspector and men like Colonel Mountjoy, a keeper of secrets. Dorothy's eyes got wider and wider, and she almost cried when Frances told the story about Danny's heroism.

"That explains so much," she said.

"So you see, this is about a concealment, a conspiracy. And I will find out why and who is involved and where the manuscript is."

"If you can—and I do think you will. As I said, it seems that you're the remarkable one, Franny." She leaned over the table—the sadness was gone and she seemed eager. "Now tell me how I can help."

Dorothy provided details about Danny's unguarded moments, when he had first become her patient. He had been moody and feverish and hadn't slept well. The shoulder wound wasn't healing and gave him continual pain.

"At night, in his dreams, he'd call out for the 'men who rode by night.' I guess those were references to battles, to the men he commanded. From what you say, they traveled and fought at night."

They weren't the only ones. The Secret Service, the "Shadow Boys," also worked at night.

"What about General Audendale, his commanding officer? Did he discuss him at all?"

"Yes, he mentioned him a couple of times, that they had visited several times after the war." Dorothy paused to gather her thoughts. "I got the sense that Danny liked and admired him but felt sorry for him. There was a sadness when he spoke of him—but not anger."

Frances found that interesting. "But was he angry with anyone?"

"The fools at Whitehall," said Dorothy, referring to the warren of government offices in London. That had become a favorite expression of Danny's, she said. He had contempt for all of them—except for Frances's brother, Charles. And that's why he didn't share certain things with Charles, Frances realized yet again. He knew Charles would do what was right and didn't want him to damage a promising political career. Charles would've done anything for Danny—and Danny knew it.

Frances mentioned Lord Crossley and the reference he had given her, Mr. Bramwell—but neither Crossley nor Bramwell were familiar to Dorothy. She even took out the list of funeral attendees she and Kat had drawn up—again, Dorothy recognized none of them except for a few brother officers he had mentioned.

"But I can tell you this. Danny visited us a month before he died. He was in excellent spirits and seemed hopeful. He told me he was finishing the book and eventually would see about publication."

"Was he fearful?"

Dorothy vehemently shook her head. "Not at all. He didn't feel threatened by anyone. He was excited. He did say his book would 'stir the pot in Whitehall.' That was his expression. But he wasn't frightened. He said the War Office could be damned. He didn't care what they did."

Frances couldn't think of anything else to ask, but their talk had been useful. Danny had known something about the manuscript's importance to men of power in London—he was not naïve.

The coast guard ran its operations out of a shingled cottage right on the water. Crispin was clearly thrilled at visiting and ran ahead to knock on the door. It was opened by a man in a half-buttoned uniform, who grinned widely when he saw who was calling.

"Well, if it isn't young Admiral Crispin. Do come in. And who's this? Don't tell me you're old enough for a governess already?"

"I'm Miss Mallow. I'm personal maid to Lady Frances Ffolkes, a friend of Mrs. Tregallis. I'm serving as a nanny so my mistress and her friend can have a visit."

"You are more than welcome, too, Miss Mallow. Come in. District Officer Faroe at your service."

Mallow couldn't judge the man's age. He was in good shape, but his face was so heavily weathered, he could be anywhere from thirty to fifty. But one thing was certain—the cottage was so clean and neat that the strictest housekeeper in London couldn't have found fault.

Faroe noticed her look. "You're impressed, Miss Mallow? I was navy trained. Everything in its place and a place for everything. I'm glad I meet the approval of a personal maid to a titled lady."

"You do indeed, Mr. Faroe," said Mallow, and he laughed. He gave some brass instruments, including a compass and telescope, to the delighted Crispin and then made some tea for Mallow in a mug that was cheap but clean.

"If I may, I want to say how glad I am that a friend is visiting Mrs. Tregallis. So tragic, first losing her husband, and then we hear that nice cousin of hers who used to visit, Major Colcombe, dying like that."

How would my lady draw him out? wondered Mallow. *It shouldn't be too hard. This man obviously likes to talk.* "Lady Frances knew Major Colcombe in London and was also upset at his death."

"He was a fine man. We had some very good talks. Glad to have another military man here."

"What kinds of things did you talk about?" she asked, and Faroe gave her a curious look. What could a lady's maid want to know about two veterans' conversation? She realized she had gone too far. "It's just that if there were any talk about my lady, it would be a comfort for her to know."

"Oh I see," said Faroe with a knowing look and winked at her. "Your mistress wants to know if the major spoke about her. She was sweet on him. Don't worry—I won't tell a soul. But I'm afraid we didn't talk much about the ladies." Mallow felt her heart sink. That's not what she meant to indicate. And she had so wanted to help her ladyship. Then he grinned. "Except for one girl, a real live one, he said, name of Ursula. Said he wanted to see her again, had some things to tell her."

Oh! That was the nickname Major Colcombe gave her ladyship.

"She was a friend of my lady's," said Mallow. "If he told you, and you told me, I could have Lady Frances pass on the words."

"A friend, was she?" asked Faroe, and he gave Mallow a shrewd look. "Very well then, something for your lady, a *friend* of Ursula's. Now I can't remember the exact words, you know, but we were talking about men of honor, and he said, 'I'll tell you, Mr. Faroe, they're the worst. The greedy, selfish, and cowardly, you can see through them. But those obsessed with honor are the most frightening and dangerous of all. There's no one like a fanatic, Mr. Faroe. Men like you and me, we fought with them and against them.' He shuddered at that and then suddenly laughed. 'My dear Ursula has her causes, but she'll never be a fanatic; she has too much humanity in her.' Well, that's the long and short of it, Miss Mallow."

"Thank you, Mr. Faroe," said Mallow.

"If you want, I can give you paper and pen to write this all down."

"I'm a lady's maid," said Mallow. "We don't forget things. Now, thank you for your hospitality, but I should be getting this young man back to his mother."

❖

As expected, there was fresh fish for supper, and Frances found it delightful that they shared the table with Crispin. In better

London homes, children were not welcome at the table until they were much older.

"He's a bright lad," said Frances afterward as she prepared to leave.

"I'm pleased you think so. I agree—but I'm his mother. I am fortunate: Mr. Wheaton explained that Danny left sufficient money for us in his will. I haven't had much experience with lawyers, but Mr. Wheaton seemed, well, kinder than one expected."

"Yes, very much so," said Frances with more enthusiasm than she intended, and Dorothy gave her a moment's look before continuing.

"It seems there is enough money to either set up Crispin in business someday or to be trained in a profession, as a physician or for the law. I would be so pleased to see him as a local doctor in a town like this."

"Oh—a boy that bright should be a specialist in Harley Street," said Frances, referring to the neighborhood where the very best London doctors had their practices. Dorothy laughed.

A neighbor said he'd drive Frances and Mallow to the station, but before they departed, Frances promised to write often and keep Dorothy fully posted on her investigations.

"You've given me hope," Dorothy said, and she gave her new friend a hug before waving her off.

"That was very enlightening," said Frances when they were on the train. "Did you get anything from the coast guardsman?"

"Yes I did, my lady," said Mallow, full of pride. She repeated the conversation Mr. Faroe had with Major Colcombe. Frances listened closely without interrupting.

"Well done, Mallow. This shows us something new. We haven't seen much in the way of honor so far, outside of the major himself. Unless . . . there seems to be multiple motives at work. I'll have to think that over. But good work."

"Thank you, my lady. But just one more thing. I am afraid that District Officer Faroe may have realized that you are the 'Ursula' the major talked about. And, well, he thought that you and the major were . . . involved." She was affronted.

"Oh dear," said Frances. "But no matter. Major Colcombe is dead, and who is Mr. Faroe going to share any gossip with anyway?" She sighed. "I'll tell you a secret, Mallow, when I was a girl, Danny Colcombe quite stole my heart."

"Oh, go on, my lady!"

"He was quite dashing. He never did anything improper, of course. He was my brother's best friend. And I was just seventeen. My mother and I had just convinced my father to let me study in America, and Danny was devoted to the army. Also, he was not the kind of man, especially then, who was looking to settle down . . ." She shook her head and didn't speak for the rest of the ride.

CHAPTER 12

Although she got back late, Frances woke up early the next morning, full of purpose. She was feeling that as complicated as this problem seemed, everyone was giving her a piece of the puzzle. The confusing part was that even though the manuscript put some politicians in a bad light, she couldn't see how murder entered into it. If there was a murder every time a politician faced a scandal, the London streets would be littered with corpses. But her professors would have told her to keep asking questions, and so she would.

However, academia went out of her head when she left the dining room after breakfast—Gareth was waiting for her. He was in the process of leaving a note for her with Mrs. Beasley, and when he noticed her, he greeted her with a smile that hinted of shared secrets. Desire and anger welled up together in an unpleasant mix.

"Franny! I was just leaving you a note. It's been too long, but this time I'm giving you fair notice. The day after tomorrow, I thought—"

"Perhaps we should discuss this in the lounge," she said, fighting to keep her voice steady. Gareth seemed to sense something in her tone and frowned as he followed her into the room, where she closed the door behind him.

"Dinner? Are you planning to take me out to dinner?"

"A late supper . . . Franny—"

"Because we'll need a table for three—you, me, and your fiancée, Miss Chillingford."

Frances expected, almost hoped, that Gareth would glibly deny the whole thing. But he said nothing, just sat down and put his head in his hands. Frances sat opposite him and waited.

"It's not exactly . . . you see, Miss Chillingford and I have known each other since we were children. Her father's estate borders our lands, and we saw quite a bit of each other when we were young. It was hoped, even assumed, that someday . . . and without even realizing it . . ." He realized how weak that sounded and let his voice trail off. "But I swear to you I never made a formal offer of marriage to her or asked her father for her hand."

Disappointment replaced anger for a moment. "A man of your education and experience, with Claire Chillingford, who can barely tie her own bootlaces . . ."

"No, she is not intellectually inclined, I admit, but she has other qualities."

Frances gave him a cold look that spoke volumes.

"I don't mean her physical beauty. She is gentle and sweet and patient, and I thought that would complement my own personality, and I'd have other outlets for intellectual pursuits. But then I met you. I never thought that a woman like you existed; you have everything: charm, wit, intelligence—and, yes, beauty." He peered at her to see if this was making an impression. It wasn't.

"How fortunate for you to find the one person who could keep you entertained in your drawing room, dining room, and bedroom."

"Franny—"

How nice, she thought, to be able to actually embarrass him.

"I never expected, when I sought you out at the Moore party . . ."

"Before you lie to me again, know that I had a very fruitful meeting with your uncle, Lord Crossley. He told me you had seen him about the Sapphire River days before. Why didn't you tell me? I also got the impression from him that you were deeply involved with the Heathcotes, not a casual messenger as you implied. You went to a lot of trouble to sound me out about the Colcombe manuscript. I might forgive you if I found out you were courting two women at once. But to lie to me about the manuscript is appalling. Tell me the truth."

Gareth smiled sadly and shook his head. "Uncle Ashton sees almost no one anymore. I had to push to get him to see me. God knows what you did to get into his study, but if there was one woman—no, one person—in all of London who could do it, it would be you."

Frances felt a small stab of excitement at the compliment. But then she squashed it. She wasn't going to let him flatter his way back into her good graces.

"Understand, Franny, I am a second son. I was expected to make my own way in the world. I know the Heathcotes have a certain dark reputation, but they merely make deals and alliances the same way government ministers do. It's not a criminal gang. It's a chance for ambitious men—and women—to create a place in the world. The Seaforths have long been in government. The Heathcotes and those in their circle do nothing worse than anyone in government."

"Even if I believed that, they seem to have gone to an awful lot of trouble to make my acquaintance, sending you into the fray to pursue me. I'm just a fellow searcher."

Gareth sighed deeply and paused, as if to gather his courage to say something important. "No, Franny. The Heathcotes didn't think you were looking. They thought you had the manuscript and that everything you were doing was jockeying to make the most use of it. Maybe blackmail a politician or two to support women's suffrage and get justice for the men of the Empire Light Horse. It's known Colcombe was a Seaforth friend, that you were a guest in their house, and that . . . when you were younger, there was talk he might even have made an offer of marriage to you. I'll tell the truth now—they wanted to be your partner, to give you the resources you don't have in order to fully exploit it."

Frances thought about that while Gareth searched her face for signs of a reaction. "You are all wrong. I don't have the manuscript. I really am just looking. And someone made a foolish mistake if they thought my childhood infatuation with a handsome cavalry officer was anything close to an engagement."

Gareth closed his eyes for a moment. "We were wrong. I don't think any of us are any closer to knowing where it is. My part in this, as far as the Heathcotes are concerned, is done. But know two things are real: I have not made an offer of marriage to Miss Chillingford or anyone else. And however we met, the point is now I really do love you. Surely you saw that. How can you really think me such a good actor?"

"There are those who say you've courted every available lady you've come across. I thought I was special, but apparently I'm just the latest in a series."

"I thought you of all people would refrain from basing judgment on Society gossip."

She sat there feeling her heart pound and looking into the saddest eyes she had ever seen. It was a rare occasion for her—struggling to find something to say.

"I have a lot to think about," she eventually said. "We will talk later. Much later. For now, I think you should go. When this is all over, we will talk again."

Then a sound distracted her. She turned to see the door open—and Henry Wheaton walked in. He was in his black lawyer suit, and she could see his gold spectacles peeking out from the pocket. His eyes took in the scene.

Gareth stood. "Good day to you, Mr. Wheaton."

"You as well, Lord Gareth."

Suddenly, Gareth seemed his usual self, with his slightly amused look. "Mr. Wheaton has long been employed by my father to handle our family's affairs. I assume he does the same for the Seaforths?"

"Yes, since my own father's day," said Frances.

"I didn't know you made house calls, Mr. Wheaton. My father has always called upon you at your offices."

"When circumstances dictate. Indeed, I am coming from a client now whose great age has made it unwise for him to leave his house."

"An affliction that fortunately does not affect my father," said Gareth. "Or Lady Frances."

It was an awkward moment, and Frances wished Gareth didn't seem to enjoy it so much.

Hal turned from Gareth to address Lady Frances directly. "I was passing by and thought, as you are dining at my house tonight, I can send my carriage for you." From the corner of her eye, Frances could see Gareth's surprise.

"That is very kind. But there's always a cab available at the corner."

"Very good, Lady Frances. I'll leave then, and my apologies for interrupting."

"You weren't interrupting. Lord Gareth was just leaving."

Hal brightened at that news, and Gareth accepted defeat gracefully. "Yes. But I am sure we can continue this conversation at another time."

Both men said gracious good-byes and then proceeded to try to outdo each other in politeness in letting the other one exit first, and Frances almost laughed.

"It just occurred to me, Lord Gareth. My coach is outside. It would be a pleasure to take you to your next destination."

"That is most kind of you, Mr. Wheaton, but it's a fine day, so I think I'll walk."

Finally, Frances had the lounge to herself. She felt limp and didn't think she could make it up the stairs. Competing emotions chased themselves around her mind. What was needed was a strong cup of tea, she decided, and with renewed vigor at the thought of it, she headed to her rooms.

———•❖•———

After tea and some rest, Frances had to face Mallow, who sought yet another lengthy discussion about dress for the evening.

"Mr. Wheaton is not of the aristocracy, Mallow. They may not dress as elaborately as lords and ladies, but he may feel insulted if I'm not dressed to the highest standards. The same dress I wore to Lady Moore's should do fine."

"And we'll have to do your hair up proper, my lady."

Frances sighed. "Of course, Mallow."

It was odd really, Frances reflected as Mallow got her ready—Hal Wheaton was technically middle class, but with the size and success of his firm, he probably had more money than many noble London families whose farmlands could no longer support their lifestyles. When Hal married, he would doubtless be able to afford to send his wife to the finest dressmakers in London, even as many noble ladies wondered if they could make their current outfits serve another season.

As it turned out, when Hal met her at the door that evening, she was glad she had made the decision she had. Hal wore a perfect evening suit, classic and well-tailored. He seemed a little self-conscious.

"You look lovely, Franny. Thank you so much for coming." He led her into the drawing room, decorated at the height of style of some forty years ago but in good condition. Frances had been in that room once before, after the funeral for Hal's father. She had thought the room was used only for very special occasions—funerals, visits of great men, and apparently, dinners with Lady Frances Ffolkes.

"Dinner will be ready shortly. I'm afraid our cook is rather limited—plain English cooking. But she's been with us more than twenty years, and it pleased my parents well enough."

"I have great respect for plain English cooking," she said. "Indeed, I had a delightful meal of simple fish at Mrs. Tregallis's house."

"I am glad you got on. She sent me a brief note thanking me for effecting the introduction but gave me no details. But no—" He stopped Franny from speaking. "—you have no legal or, if I may say, moral responsibility to tell me."

"Oh, but I'd like to tell you. I'd like your legal insights," she said and thought it very sweet the way Hal cocked his head and steepled his fingers in that way of his. She summarized their talk and what Daniel Colcombe had hinted at. She also told him about her meeting with Lord Crossley and discussed the death of Private Barnstable. He listened closely and then he frowned.

"I don't want to sound melodramatic, but it sounds like you're involving yourself with some powerful and connected people." He smiled wryly.

"And yet there is something so . . . sordid about these murders. Daniel Colcombe was killed because his manuscript threatened someone. Perhaps many people. But a simple Australian private? Was he truly a threat to the great men in Whitehall?"

"And what do you deduce, my lady?"

"That perhaps . . . there are multiple motives here," she said slowly. "One manuscript, but different people searching it for different reasons?"

"You're thinking like a lawyer now," he said. And Frances laughed.

"Thank you," she said. "I'll have to mull that over. Meanwhile, Dorothy—Mrs. Tregallis—and I have agreed to start a correspondence. So at the very least, I have made a new friend."

"A new friend is always a cause for rejoicing," said Hal. "And speaking of friends . . . I am sorry for interrupting your conversation with Gareth Blaine." He was looking closely at her. He wanted to know how deep their friendship went.

"Not at all. We were just finishing. But tell me, do you know him well?"

"Not very well. As he said, we've acted for his family for years, as we've done for the Seaforths. And he does something in the Home Office."

Frances suspected Hal knew more—a lot more. She had noted how stiffly the two men had greeted each other. Had Hal extricated him from a romantic entanglement in the past?

"I don't know him well myself. We only met briefly at a reception full of government people. There were hints he rather has something of a reputation." She made it almost a question.

"Lady Frances," said Hal with mock severity, "do you really expect me to gossip about my clients?"

And she was saved from having to answer by the announcement that dinner was served. They rose, and Hal gave her his arm.

"We're not going to our dining room. It's a bit large for just two. We have a small library, and as someone who likes books so much, Franny, I thought you'd like to dine there." Hal made it sound more informal than it was. The table was elegantly set. The butler poured the wine, and a footman placed the roast in front of Hal and then served the potatoes and vegetables. Then they both bowed out.

With a flourish, Hal began to carve.

"My maternal grandfather felt carving was an art," said Frances. "He'd be pleased at how well you do it."

Hal gave a mock bow. "No less a personage than Sir Hubert Salisbury, chief of surgery at Guy's Hospital, admired my carving." *You keep surprising, Mr. Wheaton,* thought Frances.

Hal began by asking Frances what cities besides New York she had visited in America. The only other big cities she had been to were Boston and Philadelphia, both of them wonderful in their way, but she wanted to know more about Hal—what had he done? What were his schooldays like?

Gradually, he shared with her, a little shyly. Perhaps he thought with her travels and aristocratic upbringing, she wouldn't be interested. But Franny, who had been educated by tutors until she went to college, loved hearing about life in a boy's boarding school—Charles hadn't ever discussed it with her, as if it were a secret club.

"I was quiet and studious, I suppose," he said. "My scholastic highlight was a series of unauthorized drawings I made one evening in the dorm, caricatures of some of the masters. My schoolmates roared with laughter, and I attained great popularity as a result. But I got careless and was found out. I was brought before the headmaster—I'll just say I couldn't sit for a week."

Frances laughed at his story but turned serious at the conclusion. "Outrageous. I know most people would disagree with me, but I can't see how corporal punishment helps the learning process."

Hal laughed in return. "I wish you had been there to defend me. I've heard you have to suffer for your art, and I certainly did. But it sounds like you have strong opinions on education. So tell me what theories you subscribe to."

"I do have strong opinions." Then, feeling a little priggish at what she had said, she smiled. "One of my governesses said, 'Frances, you have strong opinions on everything.' She did not mean it as a compliment."

"I'll bet she didn't," said Hal. "There is nothing wrong with knowing your own mind—indeed, it's quite admirable. As long as you can be flexible in the face of new facts." And Frances agreed.

Cook had made a tart for dessert, and after, Hal said there was a pleasant little garden in the back, and as the night was mild, perhaps they could sit outside for a while. Frances thought that a fine idea, and soon they were outside on wrought iron chairs with pillows for comfort. The only light came from the windows in the house, and Frances could just barely see Hal.

Sitting in the dark and quiet, Frances thought again about Hal. He was correct: strong opinions were all right, but, yes, one needed to be flexible. She had always thought of Hal as limited in his point of view, but that wasn't true, she was realizing. He liked music and art. He painted. He wanted to travel. But there was more.

"I want to thank you," she said.

"For dinner? My pleasure."

"No—although dinner was lovely. I meant for all those times we met in your office and you explained things so clearly and fully. You never condescended to me because I was a woman. You never suggested I just let my brother handle it. And Dorothy told me how well you treated her. It was her good fortune to be in the care of you and my brother, probably the only two men in England who wouldn't look at her with contempt because of what she had done. These sound like small things, but they're not. And for them I owe you great thanks. You think I am unusual because of my education and travels. But you're the unusual one."

He was so quiet, she wondered if he had heard. No—he was thinking carefully before he spoke.

"You may be the only one who thinks me unusual."

"That's not true. My brother, your distinguished clientele, they think you're a wizard at the law."

"At the law, Franny. But you think I'm an unusual *person*—not merely a man of law." The next words flowed out quickly, as if he were afraid that by thinking on them, he'd lose courage. "It's true that my life has been usual—and until recently, that was satisfactory. But since our first meeting, that changed, and now my life is defined by the memory of our most recent meeting and anticipation of our next one."

So Mary had been right—men didn't paint portraits of women who were just friends of the mind.

"I know this is very forward of me, but I had no illusions I could hide my feelings from someone as sensitive as you. So I bring this up now to assure you that despite my feelings, I shall never behave improperly."

Frances peered into the darkness. Was Hal trying to make a joke? But no, his face was serious.

"Hal, do you think I'd be afraid that you'd lose control and ravish me here in your mother's garden?"

"No, of course not. I don't mean improper in that sense. I meant that I wouldn't presume."

Now Frances was lost. Was this more confusing lawyer talk? "Presume what?"

Hal stammered again, and she was reminded of when he was trying to tell her about Danny Colcombe and his illegitimate son.

"Well, naturally, that as deep as our friendship could be, that it could be nothing beyond, that it couldn't progress—that it would only be a friendship."

What was he getting at? Oh—was it just like with Gareth? He was promised to another? It had never occurred to her, but why shouldn't a well-set-up solicitor have a young woman eager to become his wife?

"You're engaged?" she asked softly.

"Engaged? What—of course not." He laughed. "Whatever gave you that idea? My mother throws me in the way of eligible women, whether I like it or not, but there has never been anything close to an offer of marriage. Franny, you're the daughter of a marquess. I'm the family solicitor. I'm not such a fool as to forget that."

Ah, now everything was clear, and Frances felt in control again. "Hal, maybe our friendship will continue to grow. My feelings for you continue to deepen. And if they do reach a certain point, I assure you, your status as the family solicitor will be irrelevant."

"Irrelevant to you, Franny. Not to your brother—Lord Seaforth—or the rest of your family, I'm sure."

"You do me an injustice. And my brother. When I choose to marry, I am independent of my family, both socially and, as you well know, financially. And as for Charles, he's more open-minded than you give him credit for. Anyway, Charles and the rest of the family have already glumly concluded that my progressive opinions and radical politics had ruined any chances of an aristocratic marriage. A solicitor would come as a relief." Even in the dim light, she could see him smile when she said Charles would probably expect a discount on fees from a brother-in-law.

"But understand me, Hal. I want to continue our friendship. I want to continue to spend time with you. But there are still things I want to do before I move on to the next stage of my life."

"Franny, I have never been so pleased to be wrong and that our different positions will not be a barrier. I respect your feelings without reservation. And if I can keep spending time with you, I will be a happy man."

And Frances felt happy too and pleased at the way she handled it. Hal . . . could she possibly? Perhaps someday. And meanwhile, time spent with him was pleasant indeed.

Nevertheless, when Hal said he would accompany her in a cab home, she became prickly and said she was perfectly capable of riding in a hansom by herself.

"It's not to protect you, Franny. It's to extend the evening with you." And Frances had to apologize. There were assumptions you just couldn't make when conducting a love affair, she concluded.

The ride home went quickly, and she let Hal give her a gentle kiss on her cheek when they arrived at the hotel. *Imagine that,* she thought, *wanting to kiss me but holding back because of my family.* He really was an old-fashioned man, but she had already changed his mind on universal suffrage, women's education, and class differences. Yes, she reflected, Lord Gareth was more progressive already, but there was something delicious about influencing the wonderfully kind Hal to her way of thinking.

"We are allowed to invite guests to dine with us at Miss Plimsoll's. Even men. May I play hostess to you one night?" Hal said he'd be delighted, and they fixed a day.

Mallow was waiting for her upstairs and helped her get ready for bed. Again, Mallow found her mistress a little distracted. *Could it be . . . ? Well, Mr. Wheaton is not titled, but he is better behaved,* Mallow imagined, *than Lord Gareth.*

"A pleasant evening, my lady?"

"Yes, very, thank you, Mallow." Mallow helped her out of her elaborate evening dress. "Mallow, men can be rather funny, don't you think?"

For questions like that, the all-purpose answer was best: "Yes, my lady."

Frances had various committee meetings the next day and tried to put the manuscript out of her mind for a while. Why did anyone think she had it? What gave anyone that idea? She tried to organize her thoughts over dinner, filling pages in her notebook. She was vaguely aware of the other ladies, most of whom tended to older widows and spinsters, looking at her and shaking their heads.

Frances and Mallow sat in companionable silence in the sitting room. It had started to rain, and as the drops beat against the dark windows, there was no other sound but the turning of the pages and the click of Mallow's knitting needles. When they had moved into Miss Plimsoll's, Mallow would typically retire to her room after dinner until it was time to get Lady Frances ready for bed. But one night, after several weeks, Frances had knocked on Mallow's door.

"How can I help you, my lady? Are you ready for bed?" It seemed early for Lady Frances.

"No, I was just thinking that your room—well, it's a little dark and small to properly knit. The choice is yours, but you may join me in the sitting room, if you'd like. I just read and write letters."

"If you don't mind, my lady, it would be rather nice," she said. And so it became their custom. Mallow decided it was very thoughtful of her ladyship. Frances never admitted, even to herself, that after growing up with her family, then living in a busy college dormitory, she rather missed company in the evening.

Frances noted how nimble Mallow's fingers were; whether it was sewing, knitting, or even lace making, Mallow excelled. Would she leave Frances's service when she got older and work for one of the fine London dressmakers? She was a pretty girl—would some man claim her one day? Perhaps not the neighboring valet she had been walking with on her day off, but someone else.

Or maybe they'd grow old together in this flat? No—Henry Wheaton would press his suit. Did she want him? Keep him waiting long enough and she'd likely lose him. Men won't wait forever.

A firm knock on the door roused her, startling both women. It was rare to be disturbed this late.

"Let me see, my lady," said Mallow. She opened the door to admit one of the household maids.

"Ever so sorry to disturb you, my lady. But a gentleman downstairs says he's most eager to see you this evening." She handed Frances a card—Mr. Davis Bramwell, member of Parliament.

"Come to apologize, I hope," said Frances. "Very well. Thank you, Mabel. Mallow, I will see what this gentleman has to say."

Bramwell was pacing in the lobby.

"Lady Frances, I am glad I found you in. We have much to discuss."

"First, you have much to apologize for," she said.

"Yes. I can waste time begging your forgiveness for my language. And you can beg my forgiveness for eavesdropping and invading my office unannounced. Or we can get down to business. My coach is outside."

"You want to meet in your coach? Where are we going?"

"We'll just ride around. It's private."

Frances felt a momentary fear—but this was a member of Parliament. He may be selfish and untrustworthy, but he'd have to be a madman to lay hands on the daughter of a marquess.

Frances excused herself to go upstairs to get a cloak. She told Mallow not to worry and gave her Mr. Bramwell's card. "He's a member of Parliament," she said, trying to calm her dubious maid.

It was still raining, but Bramwell had an umbrella and showed her into his coach. He told his driver to just keep going—a stopped coach could catch someone's attention, and he clearly didn't want that.

"I ask you again, Lady Frances. Why do you seek me out?"

"I told you. I am looking for Daniel Colcombe's manuscript." She thought to challenge him. "As are you—I believe you were at the Colcombe funeral?"

"As a member of Parliament, it behooves me to attend funerals of many leading citizens. Your brother no doubt attends many as well. But back to our subject: it may interest you to know that I've heard about this manuscript for weeks. And since we last met, I made some inquiries and have given the matter more thought. You're an intimate of the Heathcote set. Have they made you an offer? I'll give you a better price."

Frances was astounded. How had Bramwell gotten the story so wrong?

"Sir, what possibly makes you think I have the manuscript? If I did have it, why would I have shown up at your house? I assure you it is not in my possession, and I have only the barest acquaintanceship with the so-called Heathcote set. Indeed, I wasn't even introduced to the Heathcotes."

But he was already shaking his head. "Don't waste your time or mine. Rumors about that book have been flying around London since Colcombe died, and I wanted to distance myself from it as much as possible. But old Crossley knew. He must've known you had the manuscript. I know you visited him. And I know your suitor, Lord Gareth Blaine, is his nephew. You were just using them to see who'd be interested in it and how much you could get."

Frances just stared for a moment at Bramwell and his grim smile. She was so surprised at how utterly wrong Bramwell was. It was both frightening and fascinating to see how much of her actions had become public. Who was uncovering her secrets like that—and grafting on falsehoods like her possession of the manuscript? She doubted Bramwell had the skills to orchestrate this himself. Who else could be doing this?

"I went to Lord Crossley looking for the manuscript. I'm *looking* for it. I don't *have* it. I'm not trying to sell it. I want it so I can publish it." Did Bramwell really believe her showing up at his office and talking about the manuscript was just some genteel blackmail? "Seriously, Mr. Bramwell, tell me who told you I have the manuscript."

He stared at her, incomprehension all over his face. "People who know, Lady Frances. I am going to pay you an honest compliment. I know you are both bright and shrewd—yes, I've asked about you, and even those who dislike you respect you. Indeed, you are too sharp to be unaware of men in London who make it their business to know things. And as a member of Parliament, even in a party not in power, I know these men. And they know me."

"Again, all I can say is that I don't have it. I thought you had it." He started to protest, but she cut him off. "Don't bother. I now know I was wrong. You don't have it. I saw you weren't just angry when I brought it up; you were afraid."

He sighed. "I have to make a lot of decisions in my official life. I have to decide who is lying to me. I'll pay you another compliment, my lady. I think your brother may be using you as his agent. He's one of the most promising men in the Liberal Party, and I'm willing to wager the two of you are in this together to make the Conservatives look bad."

He pulled an envelope from his jacket. "Keep pretending. Inside is a very substantial bank draft. I know that despite your many faults, your charitable work is genuine." He flashed her what he obviously thought was an ingratiating smile. "How does this sound: as a member of a political family, you will do me a favor and not publish anything that would embarrass me. You will edit the manuscript accordingly—when you find it, of course." He winked at her. "And as a favor to you, one of the leading philanthropic women in society, I will give you this bank draft. Turn it over to the soup kitchen. You give them dinner? Start giving them lunch as well. Do we understand each other?"

The only word for this was *bizarre*. That Bramwell was so convinced she had it and that she would be receptive to a bribe was beyond all reasoning. When she refused the offered envelope, he grabbed her wrist with one hand and thrust the envelope into her hand with another.

"How dare you?" she said. Frances pulled away. This stupid man was not a genuine threat, but his insults were not to be borne.

"You suffragists want to be treated like men. This, Lady Frances, is how unreasonable men are treated. Now take the damn money. It's all you'll get."

"Tell your coachman to stop. I'm getting out." She started to open the door, but Bramwell reached across her and shut it again.

"Don't be a fool. Know when to stop. Now for the last time . . ."

On a warm Sunday afternoon at Vassar, one of Frances's lady friends had proposed a small picnic in a remote part of campus. Just her, Frances, her young man, who had traveled from New York City, and a friend of his. It started well, but the men had brought a flask, which Frances found somewhat objectionable, and then the "gentlemen" started getting amorous with the ladies, which Frances found very objectionable, and finally she had cooled the man's ardor with a sharp smack across the cheek.

It also cooled Mr. Bramwell.

"Now tell your coachman to stop and let me out. Or by God, I will make you sorry you ever met me."

"I'm already sorry," he snapped, rubbing his cheek. But he didn't have to give any orders because the coachman brought the carriage to such a sharp halt, they were both almost thrown out of their seats. The horses reared and whinnied in protest.

"What the devil—"

"I am very sorry, sir," called down the coachman, "but a hansom pulled out in front suddenly. He must be mad to drive like that."

Curious, Frances leaned out of the window and into the drizzly weather. The coach had stopped on a quiet corner, and the hansom was blocking the intersection. Its door opened and a figure got out. Frances couldn't make out the features at all; the street was poorly lit and the man was wearing a wide-brimmed hat. He walked purposefully toward the carriage.

"See here—" cried the coachman, but before anything could happen, the man yanked open the door on Bramwell's side. Frances could see now—the man wore a wool scarf that left only his eyes visible. *A highwayman,* thought Frances, the romanticized robbers that used to inhabit the countryside. But they had been stamped out more than a century ago—was this some sort of joke? It was true that cutthroats roamed dangerous neighborhoods, but such criminals did not wander on respectable quiet streets, and the criminal classes did not travel by hansom cab.

Bramwell had gone pale. He tried to talk, but nothing came out. The stranger grabbed him by the lapels of his jacket and pulled him out of the coach. Frances heard his body hit the pavement with a thump. She and the assailant then met each other's eyes for one moment. Neither spoke, but then Frances remembered that two men had been shot over the Colcombe manuscript. She opened the door on her side and jumped out. She heard the coachman yell something, but she just ran, and in a moment was lost in a dark street in the London rain.

Frances didn't even look where she was going, running past dark buildings and trying to stay away from streetlights. This was even worse than the mews, because all the nearby windows were closed tight against the weather; no one would hear her scream. And now there was more than just a vague fear of some stranger following her—a large, violent man had actually attacked the coach she was in. The search for the manuscript had become desperate. She thought she could hear the large man's heavy footfall and expected his huge hand to land on her shoulder.

Her breathing came so ragged that her throat hurt, and then she tripped and fell, scraping her hands. Righting herself, she turned to see what had caused her fall—it was a short, stout piece of lumber, probably left by a workman. Frances grabbed it and stood up, staring into the night. She would go down fighting.

But nothing. No one was following her; no one was on the street. Frances looked around. With relief, she recognized a storefront and knew where she was—not so very far from home. The coachman had been driving around local streets. A brisk fifteen-minute walk and she was at the door of Miss Plimsoll's.

Mallow was horrified at Frances's condition, and Frances smiled ruefully.

"My lady, what happened? Are you hurt?"

"I am unhurt, just some minors scrapes, but it has not been the best of evenings. Put on a kettle and get me into something dry."

She told her story while Mallow fussed over her, getting her undressed and tending to her minor wounds. Thoughts chased themselves around her mind. Who could've attacked them? The Heathcote set or someone whose life could be ruined by what was in the manuscript?

It took her a while to get over the terror of being attacked and think about what was actually the most unusual aspect of the evening: Bramwell's absolute conviction that she had the manuscript. He was too stupid to have worked out any conclusion himself. Someone whispered the idea in his ear. Was it whoever told Lord Gareth and the Heathcotes? Someone was trying to put the focus on her—and away from himself.

Was Bramwell the real object of the attack—was she just someone who got in the way? And what happened to Mr. Bramwell after she fled? Well, there was no helping that now. She'd find out in the morning. And, she thought with a little satisfaction, she didn't much care what happened to him.

"Shall I go downstairs and call the police, my lady?" asked Mallow.

"We probably should—but no," said Frances. "I'm not badly hurt . . . and frankly, I think we need to be a little more circumspect about whom we trust. Someone knows too much about what's happening to me, and if we call the police, there will be an official report, which will be shared all over the Home Office—I want to keep a lower profile. And besides that, can you imagine what my brother would say?"

"He would be extremely displeased, my lady."

Despite the warmth of the evening, Mallow got her into a flannel gown and robe and served her a cup of strong tea with sugar. She undid Frances's hair and began brushing it out. Frances would rather have just left it like that for now, but there was no point in complaining. It had to be done now or it would be even worse in the morning.

"I'm sorry you had such a horrifying evening, my lady."

"Thank you, Mallow. It wasn't that awful, really. It was like getting stuck in a play. A poorly written play." She turned to her maid. "We're going to write the next act ourselves."

CHAPTER 13

The next morning, after a good breakfast, the next steps seemed clearer to Frances. She decided another visit to Scotland Yard was in order. It was time to get away from drawing room fencing for now—it all remained a muddle. It was like in school: when one paper wasn't going well, she'd start on another. A break gave fresh perspective, and there were other avenues to explore in the meanwhile.

"Mallow, I have various calls to make this morning, including Scotland Yard." She watched the expression on Mallow's face. "I'll be seeing Inspector Eastley again—it was his constable who brought me out the other night. He lacks good manners, but he's treated me with respect, and I'm inclined to trust him."

"Very good, my lady," she said, indicating it was not "very good" at all. Yes, Lady Frances was unusual, but these continual visits with the police were a bit much. "I do hope they make some progress in finding out who killed poor Mr. Barnstable. He was a good man, my lady."

"Yes, he was, Mallow. And I am confident his killer will be punished."

"I am pleased to hear that, my lady. And may I ask if you have any evening plans? I will help choose and prepare an appropriate dress and jewelry."

Perhaps dinner with Mr. Wheaton again? Or had she made up with Lord Gareth? He had very much upset Lady Frances, so Mallow would be keeping a sharp eye on him.

"Thank you, Mallow. My evening plans are uncertain at this time. But I expect to be back for lunch, and we can discuss evening dress then."

"Very good, my lady."

Outside, she quickly found a hansom.

"Scotland Yard," she said.

"Beg pardon, miss?"

She sighed. Maybe someday a woman wouldn't startle a driver by requesting transportation to Metropolitan Police Headquarters.

Meanwhile, she saw newspaper boys crying the latest headlines: nothing about a member of Parliament being attacked in the street last night. So Bramwell had not reported it. No doubt the circumstances would prove embarrassing: too many things to explain. But why had he been attacked? Someone hadn't wanted him to talk about the Colcombe manuscript. But Frances herself had not been attacked—not now, not in the mews. Was she just lucky? Or was it by design?

There was the usual fuss at the front desk at Scotland Yard. They assumed that as a lady, Frances only wanted to report a crime, probably something very minor, that should be handled by a local station. But Frances was firm.

"I am here to see Inspector Benjamin Eastley with Special Branch. I have information for him and him alone." Her high-class accent and expensive clothes cleared the way, and she was provided an escort to the inspector's office. It proved to be a cramped room, not nearly as large as Maples's office and not as well appointed. Inspector Eastley was sitting behind a battered desk with a wry smile. Frances raised an eyebrow at him.

"Excuse my manners," he said, standing slowly. With an exaggerated flourish, he invited Frances to sit. "That will be all, Constable. Please close the door behind you and see we aren't disturbed."

Frances made herself as comfortable as possible in the hard, wooden chair. It really was too bad—none of Eastley's clothes were in proper condition. There was a light stain on his shirt, and his collar was crooked. His mustache could use a trim. She would love to turn him over to Charles's valet.

"So, my lady, you have some information of use to us?"

"Very much so, Inspector. I have had some thought-provoking discussions recently that may be of interest to you."

"About the death of Private Alfred Barnstable?" he asked.

"And the death of Major Daniel Colcombe," she responded. "Along with the theft of his manuscript."

Eastley leaned back in his chair. "You mention multiple cases," he said.

"I mention one. And if you're going to be silly about this, I'm going to the commissioner. He'll listen."

"Will he now?" asked Eastley.

"He went to school with my cousin Michael, who's now rector of St. Jerome's. He will see me."

Eastley looked amused. "I do believe he would. Very well. We do officially consider those various . . . incidents related. So yes, I am interested in what you have to say."

"I knew you would be." She took a breath. This was the hard part. "But this is something of a trade. I want to know what progress you've made."

"And why do you want to know that?" asked Eastley.

"Because Danny Colcombe was a great friend of my family's. And Private Barnstable—he was of great help to me." Eastley didn't respond. "I can always go to the commissioner," she reminded him. And now he laughed outright.

"I take your point, Lady Frances. Very well. Perhaps an exchange of ideas, a limited exchange of ideas. Now please, as a lady, you may go first."

Unlike with Bramwell, this time Frances paused before talking. She had to trust someone at this point if she wanted to get anywhere, and she wouldn't get anything from Eastley without giving something. And she was inclined to feel differently about him. Perhaps because he was a workingman and had no obvious connections to the men in Society she had spoken to.

Frances took a deep breath and launched into a summary of her meetings with Lord Crossley and Mr. Bramwell, individuals who she knew would never be forthcoming with Scotland Yard.

Inspector Eastley listened carefully and patiently as before, occasionally writing something down in a cheap notebook.

"I am sure all this has been rather prosaic, Inspector. But last evening, things came to a rather startling conclusion." She described what happened in the coach—the attack on Bramwell and her quick retreat.

"You have no idea who it was? The attacker said nothing? Very odd, indeed."

"Apparently, Mr. Bramwell never reported the incident."

"Apparently not. Believe me, Lady Frances, I'd have heard." He didn't seem surprised, however. Had he heard of it unofficially? "I am glad you weren't hurt. I compliment your succinct summary, my lady. Can you answer a question for me: are you really sure that no one to your knowledge has actually read this manuscript?"

"I don't believe Danny—Major Colcombe—showed it to anyone."

"And yet everyone seems to think it has something terrible in it for them. What terrible things did these people do to merit such concern?"

"I couldn't say, Inspector. It may sound silly, but I see a lot of theater. I think I can tell when someone is acting. Someone is pulling the strings of a puppet show."

She expected the inspector to laugh at her, but he just shook his head. "That wasn't silly. You used your experience to draw a conclusion."

"Well, then, thank you. And that's all, Inspector. Perhaps you can now share with me what you know."

"Ah yes, we have a deal. Very well. I can tell some things I know. But I can't tell you why or how."

"I understand procedures, Inspector. And I also understand that what you tell me is in confidence. I am my father's daughter; I can keep a secret."

Eastley nodded. "Thank you."

This was going rather well, Frances thought. The inspector was being both helpful and polite, and she thought maybe she had misjudged him.

"I will tell you what I know and what I have concluded. That manuscript has resonated throughout much of London Society. For a work no one has seemingly read, everyone seems to believe it has something horrible in it about them. The Boer War wasn't that long ago, and it seems many people have something to hide. The two people you told me about were not new to us—but what was interesting was that they clearly don't have the manuscript. We thought someone in government had it— and that would lead us to the murderer. But thanks to your account, that doesn't seem to be the case."

"I am glad I could help. Now let me tell you my conclusion and see if you agree—I am wondering if we're looking for two people. Or even two groups. A murderer and a thief."

"Is that because you can imagine someone high in government stealing a politically sensitive manuscript—but not committing murders?"

Frances frowned.

"You seem doubtful, Lady Frances. You cannot imagine someone wealthy and influential would have reason to commit murder? Don't you think that's rather narrow-minded of you, to think only poor people kill each other?"

He was taunting her, but she refused to get angry. At least not openly. "Your conclusion is wrong, Inspector. Desperate people kill. Well-fed people with warm clothes who live in comfortable houses with plenty of coal are rarely desperate." She thought of the people who came to the soup kitchen. Everyone there was desperate.

"And now you're being naïve. Ask your brother, who occupies the great halls of power, how many times he has seen men desperate for power."

"My brother is a good man, and he knows many other good men." There was as much virtue in the mansions of Belgravia as in the tenements of Rotherhithe. She thought of what Colonel Mountjoy had said about men like Eastley, where they had come from. If there was any prejudice here, it was on his side. But he had a point. "Very well. Men in power kill. But shooting an obscure Australian soldier? Whom did he threaten? And the killing of Major Colcombe, while more understandable, was risky and poorly planned. It was just luck someone got away with that. It's all so . . . sloppy. And I grew up among men of power. They can be selfish and greedy and even vicious. But this lacks their hallmark."

She looked closely at Eastley to see his reaction, but he was unreadable.

"I have more to share with you," he said after a few moments of silence. "With all these happenings, we took a fresh look at the original death. Major Colcombe was not killed with his gun."

"How can you be sure?" she asked. She prepared to listen carefully, making sure the inspector wasn't pulling some kind of trick.

"You may not know this, but different kinds of guns use different kinds of bullets."

"I know a little bit about firearms, and that much is clear," she said.

"Good. This is what we think happened. Someone shot Major Colcombe. Then he took the major's gun, moved a heavy brass decorative urn, fired it into the floor, and covered it by moving the urn back. He assumed no one would look. The police would conclude Major Colcombe committed suicide." But the inspector and his men looked. They found the bullet in the floor and the bullet that killed Danny. The one in the floor was from Danny's revolver, which he kept in his desk drawer. The bullet that killed him was a different kind—it wasn't from his revolver and no other ammunition was found in the office. But it was the same kind that killed Private Barnstable—a somewhat older but still useful type of bullet. "Possibly a coincidence, Lady Frances. But I don't think so. I think someone is killing people connected with the manuscript. Someone was a little more careful than you may have thought. They were hoping there would be a verdict of accidental death. Or suicide. Did one person do that? To me, this looks like a conspiracy."

"I will accept your conclusions on the firearms. Your technical staff is no doubt highly competent. But you're guilty of extrapolation far beyond the facts." She paused. "You may be interested to know that Colonel Mountjoy, your colleague from the other evening, thinks that if there's any conspiracy, it's at your end."

Frances hoped to shake up the inspector a little, and she succeeded. He didn't say anything for a few moments, just studied her, and she almost felt like an animal in a zoo.

"May I ask what your connection is with Colonel Mountjoy?" he asked.

"He and my brother are members of the same club," she said, and realized that sounded a little weak.

"Yes, of course. The colonel is one of you, isn't he?" His sarcastic tone was thick. Frances gave him what she hoped was a haughty look. How does one explain to someone like the inspector what that meant—that the colonel was indeed "one of us"?

"May I ask what Colonel Mountjoy's connection is to you?" asked Frances. "I gather you two know each other but are hardly friends." She was curious what he would say. Inspector Eastley no doubt knew the colonel was in the Secret Service—he didn't know, however, that Frances knew that as well.

"The colonel, as many bachelors of means, has a lot of time on his hands and many connections in government and chooses to involve himself in areas beyond his sphere, to use your language, Lady Frances. He is a keeper of secrets. You must decide whom you trust," he said, looking at her closely. "But you mentioned a conspiracy. Did he say the police were involved in a conspiracy?"

"Colonel Mountjoy seems to believe the interests of the police and the English people are not always aligned."

At that, Inspector Eastley laughed, but there was no humor. "I suppose you will continue to look for the manuscript on your own? That is your right. But murder is police business."

"But aren't you going to warn me to be careful? Men keep telling me to be careful."

"I am busier than the men you usually speak with. I will not waste my time giving you advice you will not take."

She smiled. "I think there is a compliment there somewhere. Despite our disagreements, I thank you for being frank and forthcoming. You've been most helpful. And I forgive your lapses in manners."

Eastley said nothing but gave her his wry smile in return. He stood, opened the door for her, and asked a constable to escort Lady Frances out of the building.

Riding home, she turned over the inspector's information in her mind. The news about the firearms was intriguing—there was perhaps more thought to the killings than she had surmised. The inspector didn't seem too keen on her idea of multiple motives. On the other hand, he had a point about being too trusting. How far would any of them go—including Colonel Mountjoy? Was he just being helpful? What part did the Secret Service play?

Should she entirely trust the inspector, for that matter? You'd think he'd be more concerned about an aristocratic lady who was poking her nose into police business.

Eastley called Mountjoy a "keeper of secrets." And Frances kept running against those secrets, not just the ones being kept, but those being revealed.

He certainly left her with some new avenues to explore. There were too many assumptions about the manuscript, and maybe some other people had an idea of what happened in South Africa—and who was willing to kill for it all these years later.

After lunch, she told Mallow she'd be going out that evening in her soup kitchen dress.

"Very good, my lady, but I hadn't realized it was your turn again tonight."

"Oh, I'm wearing the dress but not going to the soup kitchen."

Mallow froze. There was nothing that dress was suitable for except the soup kitchen.

"I beg your pardon, my lady. Perhaps I can find something more suitable for wherever it is you're going."

"I am going to a rather simple . . . tavern, I guess you could call it. I don't want to call attention to myself." She tried to be offhand about it, but she could tell her maid was about to explode. "I shall be just fine, Mallow."

That was too much. "I beg your pardon, my lady, but you will not be just fine." She bit her own lip, shocked at herself for so openly disagreeing with her mistress. "I know you go to the soup kitchen, my lady, but ladies do that, and I know constables keep watch. Any low tavern is dangerous, my lady. They'll catch you out right away. The only women who go there are . . . I can't even say, my lady . . ." She blushed.

Frances was surprised at the outburst, but then again, Mallow may have had a point. There was a line between brave and foolhardy, and she was about to cross it.

"I thank you for your concern. But it has to do with the Col-combe manuscript, so I simply must go."

"If it's your duty, it's not my place to argue, my lady. But I'm going with you."

"Mallow, I couldn't possibly ask you to do that."

"Nevertheless, my lady, I will go with you. That's a neighborhood I know something about. And if I may be so bold, my lady, as soon as you start to talk, they'll have you down as Belgravia. You can't go alone."

"You do have a point. Oh very well, we'll both go. But you can hardly be my personal maid there. We'll have to be friends. I'll call you June, as I did when you were one of my mother's housemaids. And you will have to call me Franny." She got a mischievous look in her eye. "Let's practice now so we don't slip up. Give it a try—June."

"Very good—Franny." It almost stuck in her throat.

"We'll work on that. Meanwhile, I'll walk to the cab stand and reserve Mr. Tomkinson." He was a cheeky young cockney who was very solicitous of Lady Frances when she was his fare. He appeared to be fit, and Frances had no doubt he'd be ready with his fists if need be. "I'll have him wait for us right outside in case of any problems."

"I heard you asked for me special, my lady," said Mr. Tomkinson. He graciously helped Lady Frances into his cab and then helped Mallow as well. He winked at Mallow, but she studiously ignored him. "Glad to oblige. Now where may I take you two this fine evening?"

"Do you know the Red Kangaroo in the East End?"

"Beg pardon, my lady—you want to go where?"

"A tavern called the Red Kangaroo. I believe it's on Hazlemere Street—"

For once, Mr. Tomkinson was not smiling. "I know the place, my lady; bent my elbow there more than once. Filled with Australians, a good lot, for the most part, but if I may be so bold, I don't know if you'd find the place exactly to your taste."

"Thank you. But I have some business there. You will wait around the corner and keep watch."

He shrugged. "As you wish, my lady." He climbed into his seat and they were off.

"June, what do you have in that bag?"

She pulled out a rolling pin. "Borrowed it from the kitchen. A very effective weapon, if need be."

Frances instantly got a picture of Mallow—scarcely taller than her mistress and weighing about one hundred pounds— swinging the pin like a sword in the hands of an Arthurian knight and wreaking havoc among the hard-drinking colonials in the East End tavern. She coughed to hide her laughter.

There was no problem finding the tavern. Business was brisk and the noise carried down the block. Mr. Tomkinson stopped at the corner. Feeling a little nervous now that they were here, Frances steeled herself and walked down the block to the Red Kangaroo. She and Mallow squared their shoulders, pushed open the door, and entered another world.

The room was full of men talking, laughing, and yelling. They stood in groups or sat around rickety tables. These were working men in rough shirts with sleeves rolled up to reveal muscled arms that frequently were marked with tattoos. The cigar and pipe smoke lent a haze to the already dim room. She saw women, too, dressed in cheap, bright dresses. Most of them paired off with men, curling up comfortably against them or even, in a couple of instances, sitting on their laps.

And there were more than Englishmen and colonials. Two Chinese men, dressed in sailors' clothes, hovered over mysterious drinks, and they also saw a dark man who might've been Indian or Malay.

Frances began to have second thoughts. She felt she might as well have the Seaforth crest emblazoned on her dress. Many were so involved in their talk or so much the worse for drink that they didn't seem to notice her and Mallow. But a few of the women looked at them curiously, and some of the men appraised them.

Frances and Mallow threaded their way to the bar, where a tall, ruddy-faced man was pouring drinks with the aid of a pair of plump barmaids in clean aprons. Indeed, the place was well kept, Frances would allow that. The floor wasn't sticky and there was no smell of stale drink.

The man gave them an amused look. "And what can I pour for you two?" His Australian accent gave him away as the proprietor.

They had agreed to let Mallow start the talk, as her accent fit in better.

"Your beer ain't watered down is it?" she asked. The man just laughed.

"Hand on heart, absolutely not. But try a half pint of cider? It's very good."

One of the barmaids upstaged him by rolling her eyes. The man sensed it and turned around. "Do I pay you for your opinion?" he snapped.

"No, just for my beauty." She winked at them and carried a tray to a table.

"Very well, we will try your cider, Mr.—"

"Davey, miss."

"Mr. Davey."

"No, just 'Davey.' It's what everyone calls me." He poured cider into glasses that seemed clean. Frances reached into her purse, but Davey stopped her. "I'll run a tab. You two look good for it." The cider wasn't bad, and Frances was feeling better about this.

"Davey, I'm actually here to help a friend," said Frances, trying to play down her posh accent. But Davey's eyes narrowed.

"I didn't think you were here for the company," he said, sweeping his arm across the room.

"In a way, we are. I'm hoping you or someone here can give me some information about a man I knew. He died recently, and I believe he came here often. His name was Alfred Barnstable."

Davey turned serious. "Aye, I knew him. A lot of us did. He came here when he first arrived in London, then headed to Scotland, but was back here in the weeks before he died. We drank to his memory." He gave Frances a thoughtful look that made her feel very self-conscious, and then he grinned. "Alfie always had an eye for ladies, but that he'd know someone as presentable as you, miss—well, all I can say was that he was doing even better than we ever thought."

Oh dear God—Davey thought she was Private Barnstable's . . . girl.

"That was not our relationship," she said crisply.

"If you say so," he said, still grinning. *Dear Lord*, thought Frances. *Why is a romantic attachment the only way some people can understand any kind of connection between a man and a woman?*

"I am here because of another man who was killed, Major Daniel Colcombe, who was Private Barnstable's commanding officer in South Africa. Both men are dead. And we have some questions."

Now Davey looked at her with real consideration. She didn't belong here, had a posh accent that spoke of Belgravia or Mayfair, and had some knowledge of murder that no lady should have.

"You're not with the police?" he asked.

Frances gave him a cutting look. "Very well, Davey. My voice gave me away. But do you think Scotland Yard now employs young ladies with finishing school manners to investigate East End murders?"

Davey laughed. "Serves me right for asking such a stupid question. I think I can help you, Miss—I didn't catch your name."

"Miss Franny Ffolkes." She decided to keep it simple. Her class was clear enough without admitting she was the daughter of a lord. "And this is Miss June Mallow."

He reflected on that for a moment. "One moment, Miss Ffolkes, Miss Mallow. I want to make some introductions." He turned to one of the barmaids. "Jock and Andy around?"

"When are they not?" she said. "Over there, at the table in the corner." Frances saw two men in their early thirties amiably chatting over pints of beer and accompanied by a rather blowsy looking woman with a red face. Davey headed over to the table and started to talk to them. The two men looked at Frances with no little surprise, but the woman's look was hostile. She probably wondered if Frances and Mallow were rivals.

Davey waved her over. They picked up their cider and made their way to the table.

"Jock, Andy, this is Miss Ffolkes and Miss Mallow, friends of Alfie's." More knowing looks from the men. Oh well—at least any gossip here was unlikely to make its way back to London Society. "Jock and Andy served with Alfie in South Africa, Miss Ffolkes. And this here is Jewel—did I get that right, sweetie?" Jewel just gave Davey a sour look. "I'll be back at the bar."

"A pleasure to meet you," said Frances, and she and Mallow sat down.

Andy seemed entertained by Frances's presence. His cheerful face took in her dress, which was much simpler but still probably more expensive than what any other woman there wore.

Jock scowled at her, though, as if he expected a trap, and only looked at her furtively.

"Well? Davey said you wanted something. What is it?" said Jock.

"To help find who killed Alfie—that was it, right, miss?" asked Andy.

Jock, however, made it clear he didn't believe that for a moment. Ladies didn't come into taverns like this asking after murder.

"I am a very unusual lady," said Frances.

"We're respectable," said Mallow.

"Are you now?" said Jewel. "Anyway, the red-haired one must've been special to have caught Alfie. He liked the ladies, and they liked him, but you must've been taken bad to try to find out who killed him. Well, I'll say this for you—you have a sweet face and nice figure, Miss Ffolkes, but you don't look like someone who would even know what to do with a man if you got one."

Feeling Jewel's contempt, Frances was about to snap back, but that hardly seemed appropriate and would not do anything to establish herself seriously with Jock and Andy, both of whom were enjoying Jewel's comment.

"You're right about that," said Frances. "I doubt if I have anywhere near your level of expertise and experience with men."

That made both men laugh, but Mallow looked appalled and Jewel got even redder. Frances was suddenly sorry. It was an unfair fight with a woman who had a hard life and would probably find herself taking a bowl of stew from Frances in the soup kitchen, if she hadn't already.

"Be a good girl and take yourself off," said Andy to Jewel. "Men's business."

"These two aren't men," snapped Jewel.

"I don't know what they are," said Andy so cheerfully, it was hard to take offense. "But if it's about Alfie, I'll listen. Oh come on, Jock, it can't hurt us none to listen, and it's better than listening to you complain. It's the least we can do for Alfie's girl—and her friend with the pretty face." He winked at Mallow.

She might as well accept it, thought Frances. It's the only way they could understand who she was.

Jewel took herself off with bad grace. Andy continued to smile and Jock to scowl—but she saw she had his attention too. She didn't know how much Davey had told them, so she explained again how her brother and Major Colcombe served in South Africa together, how Colcombe had apparently been murdered, and how it seems Alfie had been killed the same way.

"I know things went very badly for you men at Sapphire River. And I know Major Colcombe was writing a book to tell what really happened. He was killed for it. Mr. Barnstable knew something about it too—and he was killed. I'm hoping Mr. Barnstable told you men something that you could tell me."

"And you're not with the police?" asked Jock dubiously. It was a shame, but the police were not popular in neighborhoods like this. "And if not, why do you know so much about how people were killed?"

"I'm not with the police, but I know people—important people who can do something. Now, we're wasting time."

Mallow, meanwhile, let her eyes rove over the room. This was not a drawing room. People got angry fast and took offense easily. She saw Jewel talking to a small group of men and women who were now looking at them. She and Lady Frances didn't have many friends in this establishment, and Mallow was thinking it might be prudent to make sure they could make a quick exit before they made any more enemies.

The two men looked at each other, and then Andy spoke. "He was a good man, was Alfie, but a little bit wild. Had trouble settling down to army life, but Major Colcombe, well, he was a little bit wild too. So they took to each other particularly." Indeed, continued Andy, they all took to Major Colcombe, and he looked out for them. "Alfie told you that the major got him a job? He got both of us jobs, too—right, Jock? Good jobs."

And they never forgot what he did to save them.

"But there was a lead-up to your final battle, wasn't there? Mr. Barnstable said there was a fight between Major Colcombe and some generals. Did you hear that too?"

Jock turned his head and spit on the floor.

"For God's sake, Jock," said Andy, "that's an insult to Davey and to the lady."

"No insult to them," he grumbled. "That was for that bastard Audendale."

That was a surprise. Barnstable hadn't said anything to Audendale's discredit.

"Now, Jock, we don't know anything for sure," said Andy.

"The hell we don't. You know damn well it was Audendale. The major was doing fine, and then the bastard Audendale changes everything. You think the major got us into that mess?"

"So you think it was Audendale's fault? Did Mr. Barnstable? He never said anything to me about him. Do you think General Audendale wanted the book stopped?"

"That's a lot of questions," said Andy, laughing. "Anyway, we all thought that maybe Audendale didn't, well, didn't do right by the major and by us. But who knows?" He shrugged and drank some more. "It's all above the heads of a couple of Australian privates. But Major Colcombe said he didn't want anything said against Audendale, so we took that serious. Most of us did, anyway—" He glared at Jock. "Still, if you're thinking General Audendale killed anyone—well, I can't see him doing that."

Jock muttered something.

"Let's think more recently," said Frances. "Did Mr. Barnstable say anything about men he was afraid of? Anyone threatening him or asking him anything about the book?"

"As I said, miss, Alfie was a bit wild, and he and the major took to each other well. So Alfie felt it special when the major died. He knew better than any of us that the major had promised a full accounting, when the time was right, and he wanted it, for the major's sake, for all our sakes, right Jock?"

Jock sighed and began speaking, as if it were an effort. "Alfie told me some men were bothering him, but he wasn't worried."

"Men—you mean more than one?" She leaned over the table, and even the surly Jock seemed startled with this short woman all but grabbing him by his shirt in her excitement.

"Yes, miss. Now how did he put it? 'But I don't care if it's a toff or one of us,' he said, 'they could all go to hell.'"

"By 'one of us,' did he mean another Australian?"

"Could be. Or just any working man—you know, not a toff."

"Toff" was a nickname for anyone from the upper classes. So Private Barnstable was up against both his own kind and a gentleman.

"But no names? No further details?"

"No, miss, no names," said Jock. "But he laughed and said he'd be aware of the men who rode by night."

"It's what we called the Boers—they often traveled after dark," explained Andy. "But who'd be afraid of the Boers in London? Still, after he died, we wondered."

Frances remembered that Dorothy Tregallis had mentioned Danny Colcombe had said it in his sleep—the "men who ride by night." Was it a joke? Or did Colcombe mean something by it, something that Barnstable didn't pick up, at least at first? She felt the hairs rise on the back of her neck. Keepers of secrets. Men who rode by night . . .

The four were lost in their own thoughts for a few moments. Frances caught the eye of one of the barmaids. "Please serve Mr. Jock and Mr. Andy another drink. Davey has a tab for me," she said.

Andy grinned, and even Jock managed a pleased look. When their fresh drinks were served, Frances said she just had a final few questions.

"I want to know about the night Mr. Barnstable died. Was he here drinking with you? Was there anything odd about him that night, anything unusual?"

"Yes, he was drinking here, but no more than usual. He was laughing, talking with everyone—flirting with the ladies.

No offense, miss," continued Andy, still thinking Frances was Alfie's girl.

"Not at all," she said dryly.

But nothing odd that night. They didn't even hear the noise. Someone just stumbled over his body, lying flat on his back, halfway down the block. No one had seen anything. Frances was a little disappointed. She had hoped that someone had knowledge they hadn't wanted to share with the police but would share with her.

"But I will tell you this, miss. Do you know anything about firearms?" asked Andy.

"Just a little."

"I don't want to upset you, but I've seen lots and lots of bodies killed by guns. It looks different when it happens up close. And with Alfie, it was up close. Someone was right near him when he shot him, I'll stake my life on that. This place being loud and all, though, we heard nothing." That was what the inspector had said, too.

They all lapsed into silence again. Frances couldn't think of any additional questions to ask and was about to thank them and take her leave when she became aware that others had joined them. Jewel was standing over them, looking smug, along with another woman and an angry-looking man.

"What the hell do you want, Mickey?" asked Jock. His scowl was worse than ever, and now even Andy lost his smile.

"You and your friends—" He glanced at Frances and Mallow. "—insulted Jewel here. And I think you owe her an apology." The new arrival—Mickey—had an English accent.

Jock told the men to get lost—and did so with language so foul, even Jewel and her friend, who were more used to it than Frances, winced. Mallow glared at him.

"I see you Aussies need to learn some English manners," said Mickey.

"Now see here—" said Andy. He stood up, and Jock stood too.

"This is an Australian bar and you and your English tarts can go elsewhere," said Jock.

And then Mallow stood. "You, Miss Jewel, can watch your mouth and take your friends elsewhere. My—Franny and I are respectable girls and won't be threatened here."

Frances had never seen Mallow like that. There was steel in her eyes, and Frances was reminded again of just how tough Mallow must've been to grow up where she did.

Jewel looked thunderstruck, and even the two men with her looked a little stunned. Then Jewel suddenly turned to Frances, maybe seeing an easier target, and as if in a dream, Frances saw the woman's arm go back. *My God. She's going to hit me.*

Mallow quickly grabbed a glass and threw the beer into Jewel's face. She shouted, and the Australians stood to face the Englishmen. Voices fell, replaced by the sound of chairs pushed back violently as Englishmen and Australians squared off.

But Mallow had bought them some time. As quickly as everything came to a boil, it ended. Davey, who was several inches taller than Mickey, suddenly showed up to grab him by his shirt collar. "This is the last problem you're causing for me," said Davey, and he quickly dragged the protesting man across the floor, finally flinging him out the door. Anger dissipated in laughter, but Mickey had the last word.

"You can go to hell! To take the side of some stuck-up lady from Belgravia."

His words sent a chill down her. It was time to go before something else blew up.

Andy looked hard at Frances. "Miss, I don't know what this is all about, but if you can help find what happened, you'll have my gratitude. And Jock's too—right, Jock?"

"Yes, miss," he said, still a little sullenly.

Frances stood, thanked the men for their trouble, and headed to the bar, while Mallow scowled at anyone who dared look at them.

"Thank you for standing up for me, Davey. I'll pay my tab now."

"Not at all, miss. I hope we could help—but as pleasurable as it was to see you, you and your friend might want to do your drinking elsewhere." He said it with a smile, but the meaning was clear.

"Davey, does Jewel have a tab here?"

Davey sighed. "She does. She used to have men pay it, but that doesn't happen so much anymore."

"I will pay it in full. On one condition—you tell her some man paid it."

Davey said nothing, just nodded and presented the total bill. Frances pulled out her coin purse and settled, adding gratuities for the barmaids.

"God bless you, my lady. Can you see yourself home safely?"

"A hansom cab with a driver known to me is around the corner—thank you. And good fortune follow you, Davey."

While she had been paying and talking to Davey, a couple of men had left—and now one came rushing back in, shouting.

"Davey, it's Mickey, who you just threw out. He's been worked over real good."

Davey swore, and after telling the barmaids to keep an eye on the place, he raced out with Frances, Mallow, and several other patrons right behind. Not far from the entrance, they saw Mickey laid out flat. For a few sick moments, Frances thought he had been killed like Alfie, but then the man sat up, groaning. He was bruised and would have a black eye in the morning, but he didn't seem seriously hurt.

"A great big bloke," said one witness. "Only saw him from the back. Did it for no reason."

Frances heard horse hooves and saw Mr. Tomkinson's cab approaching. He must've seen the commotion and become concerned. His arrival was most welcome; Frances didn't want to stay around and see if she and Mallow, as strangers, somehow took any blame for the attack. The cab barely stopped—Mallow opened the door and the two women jumped in. Before they even sat, Mr. Tomkinson cracked the whip, and they headed home at a brisk pace.

Frances gathered her thoughts. It had been a frightening experience, but she had learned something.

"Mallow, I'm sure you noted that Private Barnstable had been talking about the major and manuscript. And he said two men had been bothering him—a toff and another, probably a fellow enlisted man. I told Inspector Eastley that I thought we might be faced with both a thief and a murderer."

"Do you think they are working together, my lady?"

"Not if they want different things," said Frances.

CHAPTER 14

Frances hadn't realized how tightly wound she had been in the Red Kangaroo. The unfamiliar place and people, the disagreements, and the violence had taken their toll, and she was suddenly limp.

"Are you all right, my lady?"

"Just exhausted. It wasn't a bad place, but I have no wish to return," said Frances.

"Of course not, my lady," said Mallow, and Frances smiled. She longed for a cup of tea and her bed.

Back in the welcoming familiarity of Miss Plimsoll's, Frances paid off Mr. Tomkinson with a generous gratuity and her thanks and headed inside, where the night porter let them in. There were two letters waiting for her.

The first letter was from Hal, in his neat lawyerly hand, confirming he'd be at dinner the night after, as they had discussed, and that he was looking forward to it.

The second had a crest, and Frances recognized it. But she'd open it later.

"You're back late," she heard and looked up to see Charles coming out of the lounge.

"Charles, what are you doing here so late? You're well? And Mary?"

"We're well. I was reading, waiting for you to return." He looked at her dress. "At the soup kitchen?"

"Where else would I be in this outfit?" said Frances.

"And, Mallow, you are now accompanying your mistress to the soup kitchen? Very noble of you."

Mallow hated lying to his lordship. He was a marquess and was very important in government. He even knew the King! But that didn't mean she couldn't do it.

"Thank you, my lord. I frequently meet her ladyship there to escort her home."

"Commendable. I just came by to give you a piece of news before you heard it elsewhere—and started drawing wrong conclusions. General Audendale died earlier today. Franny—" he said, forestalling her protests, "he was an old man and went peacefully in his sleep, tended by the local doctor and loyal servants. I know how busy you've been, looking for the Colcombe manuscript, but don't start reading anything into this. Now, it's late. I'll just grab a hansom at the corner." He gave his sister a kiss on her cheek, then turned to Mallow.

"I trust you will take good care of my sister?" he said.

"Of course, my lord," said Mallow.

"Excellent," he said and quickly headed for the door. But not quickly enough.

"Charles, just a few questions."

He turned back and sighed. "I knew I wouldn't get out of here without your making an issue out of this. What?"

Frances felt sad about the general but also a surge of excitement. This was too much to be a coincidence, no matter what Charles said. And it was an opportunity. "Who is settling the general's estate? He has that large house and must have a vast accumulation of papers and other items from his long life and career to sort through."

"His only close family is a married daughter in India. The local solicitor will be settling everything, probably selling the house, putting anything his daughter wants into storage, and paying off the remaining servants. Why do you ask?"

"I thought I could help. There's no one to oversee the servants properly. A village solicitor is not going to know how to supervise them."

"Franny, did you become a solicitor all of a sudden?" He smiled.

"Of course not. I can't do that work. But I can make sure valuable items are handled properly and everything else is sold, donated, or thrown out. I can box up confidential family papers. You will admit that I learned from our mother how a great house should be run. Servants will give me respect as the daughter of a marquess that they will not give to some local solicitor. And I'll have Mallow with me as well."

Charles gave that some thought. "Franny, is this some sort of trick?"

"What trick? You always tell me to do something useful and not poke my nose where it doesn't belong. What is more respectable than helping sort through the effects of a late family friend—a brother officer?"

Charles pursed his lips. "You make a lot of sense. I have to agree with you." Then he grinned. "And you won't be making trouble in London for a few days. Good idea. We'll have to run it by the solicitor, but I'm sure he'll be thrilled not to have to take on that work. I'll send a telegram in the morning. Good night again."

He saw himself out, and upstairs Mallow made some tea while Frances put biscuits on a plate.

"A very long evening, Mallow. And I should say, you handled yourself with remarkable grace."

"Thank you, my lady." She poured tea for both of them. "I wouldn't want you to think that I was used to such establishments, however. Except as part of your work, my lady, I would never enter a place like that."

"Of course not, Mallow. I never thought you would. Oh—tomorrow night, Mr. Wheaton will be dining here."

"We must think of your outfit then, my lady."

"It's just the dining room downstairs, Mallow. We don't have to do anything fancy."

"As I've said before, gentlemen like to see ladies well turned out."

Frances raised an eyebrow. "Who told you that?"

"Your late mother, the marchioness, God rest her soul, my lady. More tea? Or are you ready for bed?"

Relaxed and comfortable in her favorite nightgown and tucked in nicely in bed, Frances toyed with her unopened letter. Fear and excitement went through her in equal parts. She slit it open to read the note in Gareth's elegant hand.

Dearest Franny,

I was speaking with my cousin Genevieve, your colleague in the suffragist movement. She is quite an admirer of yours. Not only do you give your all to that group, but Genevieve tells me you provided great assistance in Rev. Joseph Ollivet's excellent work in rehabilitating members of the criminal class who are trying to forge a new life. And I ask you this: if robbers and thieves are worthy of a second chance, why not me? Think on that, dear girl, and then think on our kiss outside the theater, and tell me—no, tell yourself—honestly if you can truly say you will never see me again.

Yours till next we meet,
Gareth

Frances read it several times but couldn't make up her mind what to do. Why did he have to bring up that kiss? She had so wanted to forget it but knew she never would.

Finally, irritated at herself, she decided to think about it tomorrow. She folded the letter carefully and put it on her night table before turning off the light. Frances then tried to think about General Audendale. Yes, he had been sick, but it was quite a coincidence. Soon, however, she was thinking of nothing, fast asleep in her bed.

✦•❈•✦

The next morning, Frances had a good breakfast and then reviewed her list of meetings planned and calls to make. She had been giving some thought on whom she should approach next about the manuscript, but now, on further reflection, that didn't seem necessary. She recalled the past days: violence seemed to trail her in the mews, in Mr. Bramwell's carriage, outside the Red Kangaroo. But oddly, it didn't touch her directly. And she thought she knew why.

However, all this did indicate that others had some interest, some very serious interest, in the manuscript. Jock and Andy had some definite thoughts on the matter, and so did some of the highest in the land. She bet the protective Colonel Mountjoy of His Majesty's Secret Service would have something to say. The keeper of secrets would no doubt visit her again. And this time, she would press him as she had pressed Inspector Eastley. Audendale's death meant something, she was sure of it, and if nothing else, it would be a catalyst. Although Frances liked to forge ahead, she counseled herself to be patient and see if anything she had said would set others in motion first.

✦•❈•✦

In deference to the hotel's somewhat more casual atmosphere, Mallow eventually decided on something less ornate than Frances had worn when dining at the Wheaton house. Frances had explained this to Hal. Still, he showed up dressed elegantly in a new waistcoat.

"We'll make a dandy out of you yet," said Frances. The women gathered in the hallway to enter the dining room as the gong was rung. Tonight, Hal was the only male guest, and Frances had to make many introductions to satisfy everyone's curiosity. It wasn't that men were completely uncommon; for example, once a week, the son of old Lady Comstock joined her for dinner. Ideally, she should be living with him, but she and her daughter-in-law detested each other. And about once a month, the Bishop of Somerset came to town and dined with his sister, Mrs. Jasper. But to have a young man, unrelated to anyone, as a guest was a cause for excitement. Hal handled it with aplomb, Frances was pleased to see.

After they were seated, Hal said, "Your brother told me this morning that you'll be helping settle the Audendale estate. I had told him and his local solicitors that I was prepared to step in if they needed any help at the London end. But that won't be necessary with Franny on the job."

Frances laughed, and Hal enjoyed the way her eyes crinkled up.

"I told Charles I was just trying to be helpful. But I sensed there was some things left unsaid. And servants always know more than they admit. With their master gone, Mallow and I might be able to get them to talk."

"But please be careful," said Hal. Hal's eyes were usually a sharp green, but now they seemed softer, like the color of a new leaf.

She reached over and squeezed his hand. "I certainly will," she said. "And now you can help me with strategy."

"Ah, you want me to help you think like a lawyer. Actually, I could travel down to Egdon Hall with you if you'd like."

"I would love to have you there—but as a London lawyer, you'd make the servants nervous. They won't suspect anything from a young lady who came just to pay off the servants, make sure accounts are up to date, and see the rugs get rolled up carefully. But teach me how to be clever like a lawyer."

And Hal did. He explained about what to look for in bank books—were there inexplicable transfers of money? That might be a signal to casually ask servants about any changes around the same time. Bills for private messenger services may indicate something important and secret being shipped. Were typists or secretaries hired at any time? There was no telling what exactly Audendale's connection with the manuscript might have been, but his paperwork could provide clues. Perhaps there were even old diaries that could help answer the question about why the Australians—at least some of them—detested him, although Colcombe and Charles both held him in esteem.

"It seems like such a muddle. Violence is following this manuscript, but I can't see who's pulling the strings. People seem to think I may have it, but whatever gave them that idea?"

"Did you study Latin at Vassar?" asked Hal.

"Yes, a little. Caesar marching through Gaul and Virgil going on and on about shepherds."

Hal laughed. "Exactly. I ask because lawyers love Latin. And there's one phrase in particular we like: *cui bono?*"

"'To whose benefit?'" said Frances.

"Yes. Why should someone want the manuscript published? Why should someone want it hidden?"

"But we don't even know what's in it. No one seems to know," said Frances.

"Yes. I find that very interesting," said Hal. "Don't you?"

Frances sliced another bite of chicken. "It doesn't seem to matter with the fear it has created. Men are dead because of it."

"Men? I know of Daniel Colcombe. But who else?"

Of course, she hadn't told him about Barnstable. Frances told him quickly about their meeting and how she was summoned to the site of his death.

"I didn't realize quite how deeply you were committed to this, Franny. Multiple murders and Scotland Yard inspectors. You've stirred up a hornet's nest."

"I should be frightened, I know. But I do believe I have a guardian angel."

"That's a little fanciful for you," said Hal.

She told him everything and was touched to see how concerned he was. "So you see, I was stalked in the mews—but my pursuer was knocked out before he could reach me. Then a man attacked Mr. Bramwell, and I escaped. But the attack was well planned. If they had wanted to get me, I think they could've. Why didn't they? And after a man threatened me in the Red Kangaroo, he was given a thorough beating just moments later. I'm surrounded by violence—but it hasn't really touched me."

"And what do you conclude?"

"Nothing—yet. But I have some ideas. And don't worry. Mallow is prepared to defend me with a fearsome rolling pin."

Hal laughed. And it was time to change the subject, Frances concluded. The man was courting her, and she was talking about murder. Also, even with his liberal outlook, he'd eventually try to talk her out of any further involvement.

"But enough of this. You have been very helpful, and now I want to hear about you. Tell me about your next painting project. You do marvelously with seascapes; why not try outdoors in London? Landscapes in the park?"

Hal looked a little uncomfortable. "You don't think it would seem a somewhat . . . foolish pastime if a business acquaintance saw me?"

Frances shook her head. "As I said, my brother plays golf. Badly. And there are men who stand in cold water trying to catch trout. Why is painting in oils foolish? Perhaps if you were forthright about it, you would change the opinions of others. You would be a leader—start a fashion."

Hal cocked his head and thought about it. "Lady Frances, I love the way you look at the world."

"Mr. Wheaton, you do give the nicest compliments."

After dinner, Hal and Frances had brandy in the lounge along with a few residents who were reading a novel or a lady's magazine or busying themselves with embroidery. She could sense his disappointment they didn't have the room to themselves. However, they didn't have to wait long—soon the other women said good night. And Frances was sure at least one of them flashed a knowing smile.

"Franny—" he said, and he had that look about him she recognized, that he was about to say something important, something he had thought about. "There is no one like you. I realize that more and more. Still, I knew your father. I can't imagine that you—even you—were able to persuade him to let you study in America."

Hal wanted to know more about her. Well, she'd tell him.

"Yes, 'even me.' It was my mother in the end. Father was convinced I'd do something to embarrass the family horribly if I wasn't watched every moment. My mother told him that I'd embarrass the family right here in London. If I were in America, my antics would occur among people who didn't know us. The logic was inescapable."

She had expected that would make Hal laugh or at least smile, but he looked serious.

"I can't imagine you doing anything to embarrass your family," he said.

Oh really? thought Frances. "When I was twelve, at our country estate, I was so furious I had to ride sidesaddle that I dressed myself in one of Charles's outgrown pairs of pants and sneaked onto his already saddled horse. I scandalized half the county before they caught up with me.

"Then my debutante year, going out of my mind with boredom at the so distinguished Brantley House ball, I convinced half a dozen other young ladies to abandon their chaperones and join me in a champagne-drenched carriage ride through the park in the middle of the night. It took a long time for my father to forgive that particular escapade.

"And," she continued, "all of that paled in comparison with the time—the first time—my family found out I not only had visited Scotland Yard but had done so alone. At least my father had been somewhat amused when his assistant at the Foreign Office had nervously told him that the newest applicant for a junior clerk position in his department was his own daughter— but for a lady to involve herself with the police!

"And finally, dear Hal, do you want to hear about my speaking in the park about universal suffrage? That was more outrageous than anything previous, as far as the family was concerned. Have you really given any thought to the fact that I've actually involved myself in a murder investigation? And it would take another evening just to take in my American antics. If my parents knew half of what I did . . ."

Frances hadn't realized at first what she was doing. An amusing story had become an outpouring, and now she just sat there watching Hal, unable to read his placid face. He, in turn, looked at her, defiance all over her face—but did he see a little fear there too?

After a few moments, Hal put the palm of his hand on her cheek, then he leaned in and, as she closed her eyes, gave her an unbearably sweet kiss.

"I know your feelings about me and about marriage. But I will tell you now, I don't see how I could go back to a life without you. Have a good journey and know that I will come at a moment's notice if you want me. Thank you for dinner and good night."

She walked him to the door and said a final good-night. When he was gone, her first thought was that, once more, a man had left her speechless. She was certainly learning a thing or two, including the extent of her own ignorance. Frances was pleased she had not disenchanted Hal. And he never told her to stop what she was doing. He kept surprising her.

After the carriage stunt with the other debutantes, her father had threatened to send her to live at a grimly austere Spanish convent he knew of—never mind that the Seaforths were solid members of the Church of England. Now, as she tried to sort out her feelings for Hal and Gareth, Frances realized that there was no doubt nunnery life would've simplified many things.

CHAPTER 15

Frances and Mallow left the hotel before breakfast the next morning to catch an early train. Mallow had packed fully but efficiently, and the cab brought them in plenty of time to the station. As usual, Frances had purchased two round-trip, first-class tickets. It was more practical—as well as more fun—to have Mallow with her on the train trip than by herself in a third-class car.

The trip to the coast to visit Dorothy had been pleasant, but this was a much more elegant train, which served a full breakfast. It was a pleasure seeing how much Mallow enjoyed herself, taking such a childlike delight in watching the world go by. For all her maid had picked up from the duties, routines, and manners of London's high society, Frances realized she was barely twenty and had seen little of the world.

"Although it's a large house, the staff is small," said Frances. "Only one man, practically bedridden, lived there. We are to start the process of shutting up the house, although most of it is already closed up, and seeing the servants understand the terms of the master's will. I heard from the lawyers that General Audendale left them well-provided for."

"That's very kind of him, my lady," said Mallow emphatically. Of course, realized Frances, Mallow would think that. Some were nicer than others to servants who couldn't work anymore or who were left unemployed by death after decades of serving one family. Did Mallow, even at her young age, think about what would happen when she couldn't work anymore? Would the Seaforths take care of her? Would the Seaforths still be around? Perhaps marriage and the security that comes from a man with a good job and children to take care of her would be better for her.

Of course, the Seaforths always took care of their servants, but it wasn't right that servants had to be dependent on good graces. *That is yet one more thing that needs to be changed*, thought Frances.

"I know it really isn't your place, but would you help with beds and other domestic activities?"

"Of course, my lady."

Frances knew Mallow would be agreeable, but it was wise to acknowledge that she was being asked to perform duties beneath those of a lady's maid. "And there may be a bit of a treasure hunt, going through the papers, as we did at the Colcombe house. But even more complicated."

"Very good, my lady. May I pour you some more tea?"

"Yes, thank you. And I'll be counting on you to talk to the servants, pick up gossip, and so forth. They may not even know what they know, if you get my meaning. The general's manservant, Tredwell, was almost slavishly loyal. A rather odd man. We'll see if we can draw him out."

"Of course, my lady. Remember old Sir Joshua Fleet, my lady? Had the same valet for forty years, and when Sir Joshua died, the valet's mind just slipped away. That's what they said. The family had to put him in a sort of home."

"Yes, Mallow. I think we may be seeing something similar here."

After breakfast, there was time for reading and knitting and watching the villages pass by. As before, they were the only ones alighting at Grenville, and Tredwell was there to greet them. He looked somber and wore a black armband.

"Very good to see you again, my lady, although I wish it were in better circumstances."

"Thank you. Mallow, this is Mr. Tredwell, the late general's manservant. Tredwell, this is Miss Mallow, my personal maid, who will be assisting me over the next few days."

"Yes, my lady. We have rooms prepared . . . and that's all right, Miss Mallow, I can take the bags. My leg's a bit crooked, gives me some pain in the wet weather, but not weak for all that."

Mallow reluctantly gave up the bags to Tredwell and approached the cart with a little trepidation—this was no elegant carriage, London hansom, or even his lordship's motorcar. It was little better than the delivery cart when they visited Mrs. Tregallis. But Tredwell treated Mallow the same as he treated Lady Frances, helping both up.

"I hear the funeral was yesterday," said Frances, once they were on their way.

"Yes, my lady, and there will be a memorial service in London in the coming days, so all who served under him can pay their respects."

Charles would take his uniform out of the back of his closet and attend, Frances knew. She did not expect the regulars at the Red Kangaroo, however.

"If I may be so bold, my lady, and speaking on behalf of the rest of the staff, we're pleased you're coming to help us get settled, as it were. That is, a friend of the family's."

"Thank you, Tredwell. And I am sure I can count on the staff's full cooperation." There was a hint of steel in her voice. Frances recalled her mother's words: "You may learn history and literature and math from your tutors, dear daughter, but from me, you will learn how to run a household."

"Of course, my lady. Mrs. Scotley, who's a sort of cook/housekeeper, has had Gladys, who is a sort of maid of all work, prepare rooms."

Mallow looked a little surprised. In her experience, maids had very specific jobs, and no one would confuse a housekeeper with a cook. Apologetically—and more to Mallow than to Lady Frances—Tredwell said, "It wasn't always this way. The house used to be better staffed. Then Mrs. Audendale passed on and his daughter got married and moved away. He got old and tired, and servants died or moved on. I was all that was left from the old days. Just the two of us. As God is my witness, I would've given my life for my master." He went into a brooding stare at that, and Mallow and Frances met each other's eyes.

When they arrived at Egdon Hall, Tredwell said he'd see to the horse and would make himself available whenever her ladyship wanted. He passed the women on to Gladys, the maid Frances remembered from last time, who was waiting to greet them.

"We have prepared food and drink for you, my lady. I will bring a tray to you in the master's sitting room. And you, Miss . . ."

"This is Miss June Mallow, my personal maid."

"You are most welcome to join us in the servants' hall, Miss Mallow."

"Thank you," said Frances. "But you have plenty do, and we don't want to make additional work for you. I need a look at the whole house anyway, so rather than have you carry trays upstairs, Mallow and I will both join you in the servants' hall." Frances wanted to see what was happening with the household.

"Oh, yes, if you wish, my lady."

The kitchen and the accompanying servants' hall were clean and orderly, a sign that someone cared. That person seemed to be Mrs. Scotley, the so-called cook/housekeeper who was having a cup of tea herself. She was a spare woman in her sixties with iron-gray hair slipping out from her cap. She stood quickly, surprised, when Frances and Mallow entered.

"Oh, my lady. I didn't expect you." She shot a sharp look at the Gladys. "You were supposed to be shown to the master's sitting room."

"Don't blame Gladys," said Frances cheerfully. "I wanted to see the kitchen and meet you and didn't want to make work carrying trays."

"Very good, my lady. Please have a seat." Introductions were made, and Gladys served tea along with scones and cakes. "Hired as a cook, I was, some twenty years ago," said Mrs. Scotley. "I'm a good plain cook, none of your fancy French food, but I can do solid English cooking."

"And a fine baker," said Frances. "I had these cakes when I last visited the general. I assume they are yours?"

Mrs. Scotley smiled briefly. "Thank you, my lady. I always did have a deft hand with cakes, if I may say so. Not that there's been much call now. Things changed over the years. I became more of a housekeeper. Not that there's much of a house to keep anymore." She grimaced and drank her tea.

"No visitors to cook for? The general didn't entertain?"

"No, my lady. He had spent so much time away, he didn't know many of the people thereabouts anymore. They had died, moved away—"

"Oh, but remember, Mrs. Scotley—" Gladys broke in.

"Yes, the vicar once or twice for tea and the solicitor for lunch, that hardly counts," said Mrs. Scotley, and she gave Gladys another sharp look. That was interesting, thought Frances. They had been here only a few minutes, and already Mrs. Scotley was lying to her. Something to come back to later. Meanwhile, Mrs. Scotley quickly changed the subject.

"You'll be wanting a full account, my lady. I've kept the books accounting for every penny." She almost dared anyone to disagree.

"I have no doubt, Mrs. Scotley," said Frances.

"I also have the key to the master's suite. In the final days, he had a nurse with him at all times, and when the end came, the doctor came, and the local solicitor, too. The room was locked, and I was given the key. I have it still, my lady."

"Have the solicitors been back?"

"They said they had the papers they needed and would send what was necessary to the general's daughter in India."

"Thank you for being so strict in your duties. But why was the key not given to Tredwell, as the master's manservant?"

"My lady, if I am to take on the duties of housekeeper, I will accept the responsibilities. I don't know what Tredwell has said, but it would've been inappropriate for anyone but me to have charge. Anyway, Tredwell has his own cottage on the estate and so is not around all the time except when the general is doing poorly."

"Did Mr. Tredwell help the general with his papers at all?"

"Hardly, my lady. Tredwell was not very comfortable with his letters."

Ah, he is illiterate.

Then, perhaps feeling she had been overly critical of Tredwell, Mrs. Scotley added, "Tredwell may not complain—he's a good, hard worker—but his leg has been giving him trouble of late. The general sent him to doctors in London. He's been away some."

"That's kind of the general, and of course, you were right to take charge," said Frances soothingly. "But all this can wait until later. Let us finish this lovely tea, and then, Gladys, you can show me and Mallow to our rooms."

So Tredwell couldn't read. Illiterate men would have a hard time with any task involving a manuscript, Frances mused.

A house of that size should've housed servants in their own section, but because much of the house was closed up, Mrs. Scotley placed both Frances and Mallow next to each other. "This was Miss Audendale's nursery when she was a girl, and the nanny was next door. I trust this will do, my lady?"

"Very nice, Mrs. Scotley. Mallow and I will change from our trip, and then I'll go over your accounts later today—which I'm sure are excellent. Also, if you give me the key to the general's suite, I'll go through his papers later."

"Very good, my lady."

"I understand that the general kindly included the staff in his will. Did the solicitors explain the terms clearly?"

"The master was very generous, my lady. He left me a nice sum, and the young man from the solicitor's office explained it clearly. I will be staying on for the next few weeks, then will move in with a married niece and her husband and their children. We will expand the house, of course."

A pleasant arrangement all around, thought Frances. "Thank you for your assistance, Mrs. Scotley. We'll talk again later, no doubt."

"Very good, my lady," she said. She handed Frances the key to the general's suite and departed.

"She's a closed one," said Frances. "Again, Mallow, keep your ears open during dinner in the servants' hall. And see if you can pick up any gossip from Gladys. I imagine she'd like to talk. I'm hoping to find out something about Major Colcombe's manuscript. But don't say anything about it to anyone."

"Very good, my lady," she said.

Mallow left to join the other servants, and Frances made her way to the general's suite. It was much as she had seen it last time. The plaid blanket was thrown over the good chair, and a clean cup and saucer waited on the side table, as if the general had just stepped outside for some fresh air and a cigar. The local solicitor and doctor must've bundled everyone out quickly. Frances wandered through the sitting room to the bedroom. Except for a couple of prints of military scenes, the room was almost bare—this was little more than a chamber for sleeping. A double silver frame on the night table held the only personal items: photographs of two women, no doubt his wife and daughter.

It was in the closet off the bedroom that Frances came across what she was hoping to find but not daring to expect: an accumulation of papers testifying to decades as a military commander. Hal had told her she would find financial papers, but this was more than she had dared hope: not only a treasure trove, but a well-organized treasure trove. General Audendale, like most career officers, had been orderly and tidy and had stacked his closet shelves with dispatch boxes, clearly labeled by year.

Frances had the fanciful notion that the general had kept his papers neat not just as a matter of habit but because he knew—he even hoped—someone would dip into them after he was gone.

At least she could be certain that the boxes contained military-related papers: the most recent box was labeled with the final year of the Boer War, the general's last command. He had collected nothing afterward.

This was going to be interesting. Frances had another flash-back to college, poring over books, looking for the few nuggets of gold she could add to a paper or incorporate into a presentation. She carried the dispatch box and diaries into the sitting room and placed them on the table among the knickknacks. Looking around vainly for a cloth, she ended up using her handkerchief as a duster; Mallow would have something to say about that later.

Inside the box, she found a miscellaneous collection. Some were just forms dealing with the purchase of supplies. Hadn't Napoleon said an army moves on its stomach? She saw refer-ences to ammunition and rifles. Neither her tutors nor Vassar had thought military matters necessary for a young woman's education, but she had picked up bits and pieces from her brother and father.

The box held various notes on battle plans that meant little to her along with rosters of men. And then a photograph. At first she thought it was a picture of the Boers, not that she had ever met any of these rough-living farmer-soldiers, but she had heard enough about them. The men in this portrait wore scruffy jack-ets and pants that could barely be called a uniform and slouched wide-brimmed hats that didn't come from any official quarter-master's storehouse. All of them badly needed a shave.

The men had clearly posed for the photograph, but casually: rifles were balanced lazily over knees or draped over shoulders. But there was one man who seemed somehow familiar . . .

My God. It was Danny Colcombe. These weren't Boers; they were the men of the Empire Light Horse. After she got over her shock, Frances grinned. No British soldier ever looked like that. She was so used to well-tailored officers in red coats. And Danny—he had always been such a dandy.

Beneath the photo was a letter from Davis Bramwell, member of Parliament, who had practically attacked her in his carriage. It was dated two months before the Sapphire River debacle.

Dear General,

Not being a military man, I seem to be unable to appreciate a soldier's humor. I asked for a photograph of men under your command in order to share it with my constituents via the illustrated press and give heart to civilians that our brave boys were carrying the standards of the home country to other lands. That British soldiers dress like that is appalling. That they posed for a portrait in such disarray is inexcusable. That you thought it appropriate to send this to me is disgraceful. If it isn't too much trouble, please send me a photograph of properly dressed and groomed soldiers in full dress on parade ground.

Emissaries from my office are on their way with new orders for a new deployment of troops under your command.

Yours,

So General Audendale had a lively sense of humor. It no doubt greatly amused Danny to have his men sit for a portrait looking like a band of brigands, and it would be just like him to send a print to his commanding officer. But she wouldn't have expected Audendale to send it to a member of Parliament. Good for him.

Farther down in the box she found more invoices, requisitions for everything from marmalade to bayonets to bandages. And then another letter from Bramwell, dated some weeks after the battle of Sapphire River:

Dear General Audendale,

We are in receipt of your letter of last month recommending the Victoria Cross for Major Daniel Colcombe, commander of a unit of His Majesty's forces known as the Empire Light Horse. I regret to inform you that it has been decided not to grant any decorations for that particular engagement. The memorialization of that battle is not in the best interests of the War Office or the general public. The nontraditional nature of the Empire Light Horse would best remain a secret. I remind you again of your orders not to discuss its engagements.

Yours,

Frances was furious. Danny deserved the Victoria Cross, the nation's highest military honor, given for gallantry above and beyond the call of duty. She remembered what Private Barnstable had said: the Empire Light horsemen were forced into a traditional engagement. From Bramwell's letter about parade-ground soldiers, it was clearly to satisfy the War Office's desire for an image of a line of soldiers in red coats, not a band of rough-living horsemen fighting a new kind of war they couldn't understand in London.

It was monstrous. Mr. Bramwell and men like him needed to sell the war to the public as empire building. Well-dressed soldiers in the now-obsolete "British square" formation were what people expected, not unshaven soldiers dressed like bushrangers. How could you promote a war when the British looked no better than the men they were fighting? Bramwell didn't care about those who fought and died, even when they were successful. He cared about how they looked.

Was Danny to be forgotten because of the stupidity of men in Whitehall, who even now weren't brave enough to admit their mistakes?

It was obvious from the letters that Bramwell bore heavy responsibility for both the planning and the concealment. He had been careful; there's wasn't enough information in the letters to make his role completely clear. But Danny knew. And if the English public found out about the lies and concealments, careers would be destroyed and reputations left in tatters.

It was the emissaries from Bramwell and his cronies that Private Barnstable heard in the tent. Poor Audendale had said that he was looking forward to Danny's book, even though it would've tarnished his reputation, too. Was he not the commanding officer, even if Bramwell was the true cause of the defeat? A lifetime of obeying orders had prevented the general from revealing the depth of the scandal, but he would rejoice if Danny had done so.

Honor again, thought Frances. Audendale following orders to the end, if reluctantly.

She emptied the box, but there was nothing else of interest. Frances had seen enough, though.

Mrs. Scotley broke into her thoughts by knocking and entering. "I have brought the cash boxes and my account books. The general also entrusted me with certain banking transactions in Blackburn, the nearest large town, and I brought those records as well."

"Thank you, Mrs. Scotley. I will look them over presently." She was still almost dizzy from the revelations among the general's military papers that Bramwell was so directly involved in the mistake and concealment. For now, the relatively simple task of reviewing the financials would be welcome . . . unless there were more surprises there. Frances watched Mrs. Scotley glance over the general's private dispatch boxes. Her look said, *If her ladyship wants to amuse herself with the late master's papers, that's her affair.*

"Tell me, has Mallow been making herself useful?"

"Very much so, my lady. If I may be so bold, it's a pleasure to see a young woman properly trained for service nowadays."

"Thank you. I'll review the accounts now and see you this evening."

After the earlier revelations, the finances were rather ordinary. The general had substantial means but very few expenses: wages for the small staff and their board and upkeep of the house. The only large expenditures were regular payments to his daughter—no reason to wait until his death to make her life more comfortable. Frances saw no large, unexplained expenses or income. The bills from the local wine and spirits merchant were a bit more substantial than she would've thought, and again she had visions of Audendale and Tredwell spending evenings by the fire downing glasses.

As she mused over the revelations, Mallow showed up with fortifying tea and biscuits.

"Thank you. Most welcome. I understand you're making yourself very useful."

"Thank you, my lady." She sighed. "Things are not up to our standards here, I'm afraid. They may have been once, but not now."

Frances nodded. "I agree, Mallow. But I have found some very useful items among the general's papers. Tell me, is Tredwell nearby?"

"He doesn't seem to have anything to do, my lady. He's been pacing outside these rooms like a cat." Mallow sounded very disapproving.

"It must gall him to have a stranger, even the sister of his master's fellow officer, going through his master's effects—maybe he thought they'd just be boxed up and put into storage. Very well, we will give him something to do. I haven't heard any suitable explanation for the general's death, other than he was old. I want to talk to the doctor. Find the pacing Mr. Tredwell and see if he can bring the doctor back. And ask Mrs. Scotley to have some sandwiches waiting for him."

"Very good, my lady."

Mallow left and found Tredwell moodily polishing some swords hanging on the hallway walls, souvenirs of some old campaign.

"Mr. Tredwell, it is her ladyship's wish that you go into the village at once and see if you can fetch the doctor, the one who treated your late master."

He just stared at Mallow. "Why does she want to see him? Is it about the general?" he finally said.

"It's not your place to question her ladyship's orders. She runs this household for now." Tredwell winced at that. "It is just for you to obey."

"I served the general for half a century. I think if there are queries about him, I have a right to know."

Mallow glared right back. "Maybe out here it is the fashion to question your betters. But in London, when we are given an order, we say, 'Yes, my lady,' and do it. I suggest you head downstairs right now, get into your pony cart, and set about bringing the doctor back here." Mallow turned quickly and headed back to linen closet where she was sorting out sheets. Tredwell said nothing else, but she had the satisfaction of hearing his boots on the stairs behind her.

CHAPTER 16

The old morning room, where visitors would've been received when the house was fully occupied, was not usable. Sheets covered all the furniture, and heavy curtains, which had been collecting dust for years, closed off the windows, so Frances said she'd see the doctor in the general's suite.

When Mrs. Scotley brought him into the room and made introductions, Frances upbraided herself for having assumed the local medico would be as old as the general, someone who had been in the village forever, with a spinster sister who kept house for him.

But Dr. Mallory was only in his thirties. He wore fashionable clothes and had a quick step, although it was clear he was tired. In a rural district, he may have spent his day traveling widely to patients who couldn't make it to his surgery.

However, his eyes lit up when Gladys appeared with a plate of beef and cheese sandwiches. And instead of tea, she had provided a glass of beer. The cook knew her customers.

"Dr. Mallory, thank you so much for coming. Please sit down and help yourself. I don't know what you heard, but I'm a family friend of General Audendale, helping close up the house."

"Anything to help, Lady Frances. I moved here two years ago, after my predecessor retired, and I spent a lot of time with the general. A fine man, and I was deeply sorry at his passing."

"I'm sure you were," said Frances. "But were you surprised?" She looked at him closely, and he looked right back at her. And then chuckled.

"I saw the look on your face. You thought I'd be older. And forgive me, I thought you'd be older, too. When I was told I had been summoned by Lady Frances Ffolkes, I was thinking I'd be meeting with someone like Lady Catherine de Bourgh from *Pride and Prejudice*, who would upbraid me for not giving the general some useless patent medicine she was devoted to."

Now it was Frances's turn to laugh. "But you came anyway. You're brave."

He shook his head. "No, actually, I'm a coward. A young doctor like me can't afford to offend the nobility." Frances nodded. She knew well that aristocratic families held sway throughout England, but in rural districts, deference to the old families was practically feudal. "But you clearly aren't here to talk to me about patent medicines."

"No, I'm not. And don't worry," she said with a smile. "I'm not easily offended. In fact, the franker you can be, the better. Believe me, I am in no way criticizing your medical skills. But the general's death came at an interesting time. There are . . . investigations into certain occurrences in his past, having to do with some old associates of his. His death was fortuitous for some. I know I'm sounding very melodramatic, but I want to know if his death was unexpected. I will be discreet, on my word of honor."

Dr. Mallory nodded. He was looking better, fortified by the sandwiches and beer. "Mrs. Mallory enjoys the Society pages in the papers and knew your name. She wondered if you were related to Charles Ffolkes, the Marquess of Seaforth, a government minister."

"My older brother."

"Then keeping secrets runs in your family." He paused for a moment to think, and then Frances saw he had reached a decision. "Yes, Lady Frances, I was surprised. He was old and had various ailments, but nothing immediately life threatening. And he was cheerful and feisty. I'd tell him to ease up on the port, and he'd pour me a glass, tell me to mind my own damn business—pardon my language—and say he'd live long enough to attend my funeral. But then, some weeks before he died, he suddenly seemed to just give up. He didn't want to live anymore."

"Were there any changes before he died?"

"Nothing I could tell. He had gone up to London some time ago for a funeral of an officer who served under him and was sad when he came back but bounced back. However, I saw him frequently. There were a number of conditions I had to monitor. He started to brood. And then—all of a sudden, Tredwell, his manservant, called me late one night. And that was the beginning of the end. The man was a wreck, not even aware, hallucinating."

Frances tried to control herself. The pieces were falling into place. "About what?"

"You are frightening me, Lady Frances. What is this about?" He gave her a wry look. "Or shouldn't I ask?" He pulled a leather-bound notebook from his coat pocket and thumbed through it until he found the right page.

He handed it to Frances, who read it out loud. "'The patient was fevered and didn't seem to recognize me or his familiar servants. He spoke incoherently, and the names he mentioned sounded like towns in South Africa. He mentioned sapphires repeatedly.'" Frances looked at the date in the doctor's medical diary: two days after the murder of Private Barnstable. Just enough time for the news to make its way to the general. She handed back the book, trying to keep her hand from shaking.

"Did you ask anyone about the sapphires?"

"Is this a case of jewel theft, my lady? I asked Mrs. Scotley, thinking if I could give him the sapphires he wanted, he'd calm down. But she said any jewelry belonging to the late Mrs. Audendale had long been sent to their daughter. And she remembered no sapphires in particular. Tredwell knew nothing either."

"Really?" said Frances.

"He's an odd one, isn't he?" said Mallory. "Don't laugh, but he almost behaved more like a wife than a servant, so protective he was. Ah well, they'd been together most of their adult lives. Is there anything else? I'm sorry I couldn't be of more help—Lady Frances, are you quite all right?"

Frances blinked. She realized she had slipped away for a moment, completely lost in her thoughts. A murdered private. An obsessively loyal servant. A visitor the housekeeper didn't want anyone to know about.

"My deepest apologies, Dr. Mallory. You have been extremely helpful, more than I can ever tell you. Now I must send you back to your wife; I've kept you late enough. I'll have Tredwell drive you home." And she bid good-bye to a thoroughly bemused Dr. Mallory.

Oh dear, she thought. *They'll be gossiping about me all winter.*

———◆◆◆———

Mrs. Scotley put Gladys to work wrapping up some fine ceramics for storage, with severe warnings about being careful.

"I can help," said Mallow. "I finished with the linens, and from my days as a housemaid to the Marchioness of Seaforth, I learned how to care for fine objects."

"Well then, Miss Mallow, that would be a great help. Gladys, follow Miss Mallow's lead in this."

"Yes, Mrs. Scotley."

And soon the two young women were busy. Mallow saw the inquisitive look in Gladys's eye, and it didn't take long for her to start asking questions.

"It must be very exciting, working in a great house," she said.

"Oh, yes. It was very strict, of course. We had to do every-thing just so. But it was exciting when the King came to dine."

"The King came?" Gladys almost dropped a vase in her astonishment. "Did you serve him at dinner?"

"A maid serving the King? Of course not," she said with a complete air of superiority. "Only footmen served at formal din-ners. But I helped collect the ladies' cloaks. And I was as close to the King as I am to you now. And the Bishop of London and the prime minister also visited."

"I would give anything to work in a house like that, Miss Mallow. Nothing ever happened here. No one ever visited. And now, I'm out of a job," she said with a frown.

Mallow remembered how Gladys had started to gossip when they first arrived, only to have Mrs. Scotley silence her. Lady Frances would want to know what happened—who had come.

"Didn't you say earlier that someone had come? When we first arrived?"

"Mrs. Scotley said we're not to gossip," Gladys said. "And I need her to give me a good reference."

"If it's gossip about your late master, you can say it now. You're allowed to talk about the departed," said Mallow.

"Really?" said Gladys. She wrinkled her nose as she con-templated an apparent loophole she had never heard of. But Miss Mallow was a lady's maid from an aristocratic household, no less. She should know.

"If it turns out to be unimportant, my lady will forget it and tell no one. But it may be something important about the Auden-dale family, and in that case, she needs to know. She's a great lady and knows about things." She tossed her head. "And Mrs. Scotley may be cook and housekeeper, but she's just a servant, too."

Mallow heard the cart outside. Tredwell was bringing the doctor home, and that meant her ladyship was available to hear the story.

"As my mother used to say," said Mallow, "tell the truth and shame the devil." And taking the reluctant housemaid by the hand, she led her to the general's suite.

Frances was still thinking furiously about the doctor's revelations when Mallow entered with a nervous-looking Gladys.

"My lady, Gladys has realized she has something to tell you." And she gave the housemaid a look that was half encouraging, half commanding.

The girl looked so miserable, standing there, Frances felt her heart go out to her. She had been given strict instructions by Mrs. Scotley and now was supposed to disobey them on the words of a titled lady she hardly knew.

"Gladys, you were quite right to listen to Mrs. Scotley. She represented the will of your master. But now, he has gone. And until other arrangements are made, I am the mistress of Egdon Hall. You may tell me anything without any fear of doing wrong."

Gladys relaxed a little. "Well, putting it like that, my lady, I do have something to tell you."

"Good. Now both of you take a seat, and I'll hear your story."

Gladys sat on the edge of one of the chairs and started to talk. "We had a visitor, a soldier, my lady. At least that's what he said. But we've had soldiers here, and he didn't look like one."

"Do you remember his name?"

"Yes, my lady. We have few enough visitors here. Mountjoy. Colonel Mountjoy."

Frances felt herself tense up but tried to act casually so as not to upset Gladys. "Do you know if he was a friend of your master's?"

"I don't know, my lady. The general was a friendly man, but with Colonel Mountjoy, he was just reserved, like one gentleman meeting another. But not angry. Mrs. Scotley brought them some tea, but that's all I know about the meeting."

"Did you see Colonel Mountjoy leave?"

"Oh, yes, my lady. The general came down to say good-bye and seemed cheerful. We liked the master and were glad when he had a visitor. That seemed to perk him up."

There was a hesitancy there. That wasn't the whole story.

"What happened then, Gladys? It's all right. You can tell me."

"You see, my lady, the kitchen is sort of under the front of the house. We were baking a lot that day, and it was very hot, so I stood on a chair and opened the little windows. They're at ground level, my lady; you can hardly see them if you're outside."

Ah. The girl had been eavesdropping on what went on at the front of the house. There were worse sins.

"Of course you did. That was very sensible. And it wasn't your fault if you heard anything outside. It wasn't like you were listening on purpose."

Gladys looked relieved she wouldn't be criticized and then began haltingly. Frances was so frustrated at the hemming and hawing that she wanted to shake the girl. Gradually, it came out. "Mr. Tredwell had seen the master back up to his room, then came down to drive Colonel Mountjoy to the station. And then the two men had words, my lady. It started soft and then it seemed as if Mr. Tredwell was asking the colonel something and didn't like the answer. They got louder, and Tredwell kept using words like 'honor' and 'duty,' and the colonel said 'government' and 'responsibility.'" Frances sensed there was a lot the girl didn't understand. "Oh, and they said something about soldiers—what was it? Yes, the Empire Light Horse. And a man named Major Colcombe. I remember that name special, my lady, because it was just a month later that the general went to his funeral in London, and he rarely left his house."

That was all she could drag out of Gladys, but it was enough.

"Very angry they were at the end. The colonel cursed Mr. Tredwell for his impertinence, and that stopped him. It was so odd; Mr. Tredwell was usually so well spoken. Anyway, they drove off, and Mrs. Scotley told me it would be very embarrassing for Mr. Tredwell if their argument came out—embarrassing for the general, too."

Frances couldn't blame Mrs. Scotley. An old and experienced servant, she wouldn't want the hint of a scandal to mar the family name, and if it got out that Tredwell had argued with a guest . . .

"Thank you, Gladys. We can do what Mrs. Scotley suggested and forget the whole episode now. I shan't discuss it with anyone else, and I see no need to tell Mrs. Scotley that you and I discussed it. Now, I imagine you'll be out of work shortly. Would you be willing to move to London?"

"Oh, yes, my lady. I'll stay with my married sister for now, but I would like to work in a great house. Mr. Tredwell, Mrs. Scotley, and the groundskeeper all received nice remembrances from the general and will retire, but I'm young, and I'll still need to work."

"I have many relations, and there's always someone looking for a housemaid. Leave me your sister's address, and I'll write you. Thank you for telling me the story."

"And thank you, my lady," said a once-again cheerful Gladys, who left to see what other tasks Mrs. Scotley had for her.

"Nicely done, Mallow." It was the last item. Frances could see the whole horrific episode now, with both noble and base motives leading to the same awful place.

"My lady?" asked Mallow, looking concerned.

As with the doctor, Frances had let her mind wander again. "I'm sorry Mallow—I'm being terribly rude today. First to Dr. Mallory and now to you. We're almost done, you and I. Indeed, I was proved right: we have two criminals and two crimes, one of theft and one of murder. And we're about to solve both of them."

She thought of the so-helpful Secret Service colonel, who seemed to know everyone and everything. Everyone wanted something from Lady Frances—but him. He just wanted her to stop investigating, trying to keep her away from the police. But he had overplayed his hand, treating her as a silly girl. She had never liked the colonel, and now she knew why.

He wasn't a murderer, she concluded. That was another story. But he had a lot to answer for nonetheless.

Frances was lost in thought, but when she looked up, Mallow took heart again. This was the lady she knew, with a glint in those gray eyes, her chin up, and a set mouth.

"Enough of this, Mallow. We have work to do. We'll have dinner soon, bundle up the general's papers for the solicitors tomorrow, and catch the last train back home." Frances looked around the suite. "This is a sad house, Mallow. It's been sad for a while, I think. There's no more we can do here. But for General Audendale, for Major Colcombe, for Private Barnstable, there is plenty to do in London."

CHAPTER 17

By afternoon the next day, Frances had bundled up all the documents for the solicitors, who sent a carriage to pick them up. She saw that Mrs. Scotley had everything else well in hand and promised Gladys again she'd find her a place.

Frances asked Mrs. Scotley to find Tredwell and have him drive them to the station, but the housekeeper sighed. "His leg took up with him badly again, my lady. It comes and goes, more and more as he gets on in years. I took the liberty of telling him to lie down in his cottage and arranged for young Ben Hazzlit, from the next farm over, to drive you. He's waiting now."

"Thank you, Mrs. Scotley, for everything."

"A pleasant journey to you, my lady, and you as well, Miss Mallow."

Mr. Hazzlit was clearly tickled at transporting a titled lady and her maid and had given his wagon a good cleaning. He helped them on and off with all the flourish of a Renaissance courtier, which impressed Mallow and amused Frances. They were on the train, even as the sun set.

The dining car served a very nice late supper. Her ladyship ordered wine for both of them. Mallow had firm ideas on the evil of drink, but when people like her ladyship and her family ordered wine—nothing vulgar like gin—it was perfectly respectable with a meal. And Mallow sipped it slowly.

"When we departed London, you left word at Miss Plimsoll's that we would be going to Egdon Hall at Grenville?"

"Yes, my lady, as you told me to."

Very good. The colonel might find this out. And panic.

It was late when they arrived, and Frances longed for her own bed, but she stopped at the small piecrust desk at Miss Plimsoll's. Two letters awaited her. One was from Hal—she would open it upstairs. The other was in the sharp, strong letters of a decisive man.

Dear Lady Frances,

I do not wish to sound melodramatic, but you are in great danger. I am investigating here, but I strongly suggest you leave London for your own safety.

Your servant,
Zachery Mountjoy

Well, men in general and military men in particular did so enjoy protecting women. But she had just come back to London and had no intention of leaving for a while.

Frances smiled wryly. "Sometimes, Mallow, people aren't who you think they are."

Mallow often became confused when her ladyship started talking like that. Was she referring to the old general? A great and good man, his servants seemed to think, but as her ladyship said, you never could tell.

"Yes, my lady," said Mallow.

Once upstairs, they quickly got ready for bed, and when she was finally under the covers, Frances opened Hal's letter.

After such an emotion-filled couple of days, it was absolutely delicious to read a love letter in bed.

Right after breakfast the next morning, she called Hal's office. The deferential clerk told her Mr. Wheaton was in conference with a client, but he took the message that Lady Frances Ffolkes was back in London and would call Mr. Wheaton later. "And please tell Mr. Wheaton it was a very profitable trip."

After the phone call, Frances went back up to her room. Mallow had finished her breakfast and was quietly catching up on her sewing. She sat at her desk and toyed with her pen. She knew now. She knew everything, or close to it. But the next step seemed beyond her abilities. Frances smiled at the thought of Mrs. Elkhorn throwing up her arms and saying, "Lady Frances can't figure something out? To think that I was present for such a historic moment!" She thought and jotted down some notes, then thought some more.

Deciding to take another tack, she turned to her maid. "Mallow, how was Tredwell below stairs? Was he upset, worried? Did he talk about leaving the household? He was ill when we departed, if you remember."

Mallow pursed her lips. "I must say, my lady, that he could be a little sullen and was most impertinent when I sent him to fetch the doctor. He questioned your orders. I couldn't believe my ears. I can't imagine what your late mother would've done with such an impertinent servant."

"Impertinence was the least of his sins," said Frances with a look of deep sadness. "I'm sorry to say, but it seems our Sergeant Tredwell was also a murderer."

"My lady . . . I don't know what to say," said Mallow.

"Neither do I. I have some notes to make and letters to write. And then you and I will talk further."

"Very good, my lady."

Mallow busied herself with domestic duties while Frances wrote away at her desk. A solid plan in motion, Frances wrote a detailed note on her good stationery, emblazoned with the Seaforth coat of arms. It always commanded attention. She addressed it to Inspector Benjamin Eastley, Special Branch, Metropolitan Police Service, and then after a moment's thought, wrote "personal and confidential" on it. She sealed the envelope and headed to the dining room, where the staff was already setting for lunch. She caught the eye of one of the waiters, who supplemented his income as a discreet and reliable messenger. Frances put the letter and some coins into his hand.

"Could you deliver this after you go off duty?" she asked.

He looked at the address and his eyes flickered, but that's all the surprise he showed.

"It would be my pleasure, my lady."

Back upstairs, she put her plan in motion. "Mallow, you know how the shop girls talk in the really fine stores. We've been to such stores dozens of times. Do you think you could imitate one of those girls on the telephone? That is, pretend?"

"I . . . I suppose so my lady." What was this about? Even for Lady Frances, this was unusual.

"Good girl! I knew I could count on you. Now, I'd do this myself, but my accent is wrong. I need to find out when a servant is going to be absent. So here's what you'll have to say . . ."

A few minutes later, Frances and Mallow were downstairs in the phone room, dialing. Frances handed the speaker to Mallow.

"Is this the valet of Colonel Mountjoy? I would like to speak to your master about an important delivery of goods he has purchased," said Mallow. She had it down perfect, the superior tone those shop girls used when speaking to servants.

Frances leaned in so she could hear the response too.

"I am the colonel's valet. The master is not home. I can receive any deliveries. May I inquire where you're calling from?"

Frances had not anticipated that, but Mallow was surprisingly equal to it.

"You may not," she said. "I just need to know when you or your master will be available to receive the package during the day."

"I am home during the day, except for brief periods to run errands for the master," said the manservant a little stiffly. "And I have a half day off, which is tomorrow, so tomorrow afternoon will not be convenient."

"Very good. We will give you some notice," said Mallow, and she rang off.

"Oh, Mallow, that was perfect. Very nice. However, we have to work fast. If tomorrow is his half day, we must proceed now. Back upstairs to pick a dress."

Frances had hoped to have a couple of days to plan, but perhaps it was better like this. If she gave it too much thought, her nerve might break.

"We'll be making a call tomorrow. Take out the dress I wore for the Moores' party again. No, even better, the deep-green one."

Mallow blinked. Her ladyship never cared about dress before. And now, she was making a choice that was . . . inappropriate. "For a daytime call, my lady? If I may say, it's rather ornate. It's more suited to a formal dinner engagement."

"Exactly, Mallow. I want to be a little bit . . . overdressed tomorrow. See that it is looking its best. Also, check on the back stairs, where old delivery boxes are stored until they're hauled away. Grab at least three. We'll want to tie them up as if they were new. That should take care of everything. I have a luncheon meeting today and then another committee before dinner. Then an early night for both of us. Tomorrow is going to be very busy."

"Very good, my lady."

When Lady Frances actually said it was going to be a busy day, it was going to be a very busy day indeed.

Frances walked to her various appointments during the day to make sure she was tired enough to sleep during the night. But she was still troubled by dreams, flickers of faces that kept visiting her: Tredwell, the colonel, Hal, and Danny.

She woke up suddenly and looked at her clock. It was early, but that was good. She'd want Mallow to make her look her absolute best today.

Mystified but pleased that her ladyship was for once giving her time to really do her up right without a fuss, Mallow went to work on Frances's hair.

"I owe you an explanation, Mallow. Because I am doing something rather . . . difficult."

"Very good, my lady." The steady hands didn't falter as they gathered up Frances's copper tendrils.

"Colonel Mountjoy has the manuscript. I can't prove it, but I know it. And we are going to take it back. The colonel is too clever to let us near it. But he spends his days in his club, leaving his flat in the care of his manservant. My mother knew how to cow a servant, as you pointed out. That is why I have to look very much like a grand lady today." She turned to face Mallow. "I think there's a bit of my mother inside me."

"Most definitely, my lady."

"And it will be of great help, Mallow, if you would come with me. I won't think less of you for not going though. These aren't the duties of a lady's maid. And this could be unpleasant."

"However I can be of service, my lady," she said, forcing her voice not to tremble.

"I knew I could count on you," said Frances. She turned back so Mallow could finish her hair, which Mallow did, as soon as took she took a moment to dry her damp palms on her dress.

She finished dressing her mistress, and when she was done, they both had to admit the results were impressive. Frances looked quite grand.

They grabbed the boxes and hailed a hansom to Colonel Mountjoy's residence. He lived in a flat in a block of maisonettes, elegant apartments suitable for bachelors of means who didn't want the trouble of running a household. The street ended in a small park with no outlet, so it was quiet, as there was no reason for anyone to travel there unless they had business in one of the houses.

They walked up the steps. Mallow balanced the boxes, and Frances rang the bell. She heard feet behind the door. No turning back now.

A well-appointed manservant opened the door, and Frances breezed right in.

"Oh thank you so much. We have been so busy in the shops and can't stand on our feet another moment. Come on, Mallow."

"Excuse me—" said the servant, but he was already talking to Frances's back. She and Mallow found themselves in a masculine sitting room. The furniture showed little style; it was good but obviously just pieces that came with the apartment and lacked any sense of individuality. A few nondescript paintings hung on the wall. *Hal could do better*, thought Frances with some amusement. A door led to a bedroom, no doubt, and down the hall was probably a small kitchen with a chamber for the manservant.

Fortunately, the telephone was in the hall, not directly in the apartment, which might make things easier later.

Frances flung herself into a chair and motioned for Mallow to take a seat, too, which she did, but she sat ramrod straight. They had chosen right, Mallow observed. Her ladyship looked like a grand duchess, not someone a mere valet would dare overrule.

"I beg your pardon, miss," said the servant. He was in a terrible position. He had no idea who this woman was, but he took in her dress—this was a person of quality. She had to be handled carefully.

"You will address me as 'my lady.' Lady Caroline Westwood. My husband is a knight commander of the Order of the Bath.

Didn't Colonel Mountjoy tell you to expect me? I'm his cousin, up from Rye, to visit the shops. He didn't mention me? How tiresome of him. But I know what a busy man he is. I assume he'll be along shortly."

The valet appeared dumbstruck. "I believe he is at his club, my lady. He said nothing to me about your arrival."

"I shall upbraid him for that most severely when he arrives. But never mind. You may go about your business, and my maid and I will wait."

"I beg your pardon, but it is my afternoon off. If you could come back later, my lady . . ."

"I have no intention of leaving. My maid and I are exhausted from walking here and there. Mallow, do put those boxes down and see about making some tea so this good man won't miss his afternoon off." She turned to the valet. "Be on your way. Do not let me stop you. I am sure the colonel will be along shortly." She had settled deeply into a big chair and made it clear nothing was going to remove her.

"Very good, my lady," He looked a little uncomfortable, and Frances held her breath, wondering if her ruse would work. But she was right—she knew well-trained servants like the colonel's valet. They read people, put them in categories, and then made decisions on how to behave. Here was a perfectly dressed lady with the right accent and her perfectly dressed maid. The valet would assume that someone like her would never tell a bald-faced lie. He wouldn't dare question her bona fides—as he would with a man. So he left and returned a few moments later, holding his hat.

"If there is nothing I can get you, my lady . . ."

"Nothing. Enjoy your afternoon off. I will wait for my cousin, the colonel, to return."

"Very well, my lady." Still looking reluctant, he bowed out. Frances heard the lock turn, and through the window, she watched the man head down the stairs and along the street.

When he passed out of sight, Frances jumped out of her chair quickly and Mallow followed suit.

"He trusted us this far, but I am sure he is going to leave word with his master, Colonel Mountjoy, at his club. He was too embarrassed to use the telephone to report on us while we were here. But the colonel will rush back as soon as he learns, so we have little time. Your job will be simple. Stay here and let me know if anyone comes to the house. Just sit in the chair and watch the street."

"Very good, my lady." Her voice was steady, Frances noted. She could rely on Mallow.

The only place in the sitting room to hide a manuscript was a small desk. Frances opened the top drawer, which was probably too small to hold the manuscript but might contain a key to a hiding place elsewhere. *My goodness—a service revolver. Just like Danny has. Charles no doubt has one too, somewhere. At any rate, no manuscript or key anywhere else in the desk.*

Frances entered the colonel's bedroom. It was larger than most bedrooms one would find in such a small house and contained a sort of niche that served as an office. The niche was lined with shelves, much like the general's closet. To Frances's dismay, it was filled with papers—bound and unbound, in boxes and loose. Some looked official and some more casual. Frances was sure these would make fascinating reading, but for now, there was only one to locate. One by one, she started to pull them down and see which one was written by Danny Colcombe.

Fortunately, she was familiar with Danny's handwriting, a strong lavish hand she knew well from the letters he always wrote to her on her birthday. Not this one . . . not that one . . . She began to feel very warm, and sweat started to roll into her eyes. Frances swept a lace handkerchief over her brow and kept going. She felt the minutes racing by. How long would it take for the servant to leave a note at the master's club before proceeding to whatever plans he had?

She almost cried out in relief when she found the right papers. "The Battle of the Sapphire River, by Maj. Daniel Colcombe (ret.)"

"My lady—he's back!" cried out Mallow. "He's just paying off a hansom."

Oh God. But all was not lost. She fought to stay focused.

"Bring me one of the boxes." Mallow ran in. *I've never seen Mallow run*, realized Frances. Well-trained servants never ran unless it was a matter of life or limb. Like now.

Frances slipped off the string and put the manuscript inside. Mallow started to tie it up again.

"Wait," said Frances. "Just sit in the same chair with the other box." Mallow obeyed instantly, and Frances followed her out of the bedroom, closing the door behind her. This was a tight corner, but the situation was not impossible. She opened the desk drawer, grabbed the revolver, and tossed it into the box before quickly tying it up again.

When the colonel entered his flat, he saw both women sitting in chairs. Frances had one box, and Mallow had two. He didn't seem surprised, because his servant had no doubt left him a message.

"Lady Frances, I was left word that a nonexistent cousin was visiting. You must have a reason." He flashed a smile, but it didn't reach his eyes.

"I didn't want to advertise my presence and knew you would come around. I simply wanted to see you once more before I left London, as you suggested in your note. We bought a few items for a trip and planned to leave this afternoon, but I wanted to make sure you had no further details."

The colonel stayed by the door, where he could keep an eye on both women. His eyes swept over Frances and Mallow and their boxes.

"Nothing at all, I'm sorry to say, but at least there have been no further incidents."

"I'm glad for that as well. I just wanted to make sure there were no further dangers to look out for. We'll leave now, for an extended stay with my aunt and uncle." She smiled at the colonel, but he didn't smile back. His eyes were hard and didn't leave her as she rose.

"Lady Frances," he said. His voice was silky and menacing. "Before you go, please unwrap that box and give me back the manuscript."

"I beg your pardon," she said, forcing injured innocence into her voice.

"I don't have the patience for this, my lady. Your little plan was well executed and might've worked if you had been just a little faster or if it had taken me just a few more minutes to find a hansom. But now, I want you to sit back down, open that box, and give it back to me. I give you my word that you can then go on your way and I'll forget this ever happened. Do it now or undergo the indignity of my taking it from you by force."

Gone was the paternal look. Colonel Mountjoy was angry. There would be no talking her way through this.

"Oh, very well," she said a little petulantly. "But you are very wrong, Colonel. These papers belong to the Colcombe family, and you haven't heard the last of this." He said nothing as she undid the string, trying to keep her hands from trembling. *I'm really doing this*, she thought.

She slid off the top of the box and reached in. But instead of pulling out the manuscript, she emerged with the colonel's service revolver. Frances had hoped it wouldn't come to this, but she was not leaving without the Colcombe manuscript.

She heard Mallow gasp and cry out incoherently. The Colonel bit his lip and just stared at the revolver in her little hands.

Frances willed her voice not to shake. "We are walking out of here, my maid and I, with the manuscript. And I swear, Colonel, if you try to stop us, I will shoot you."

No one spoke or moved for several long moments. Then Mountjoy started to move toward Frances, but he was able to take only one step.

"Not one inch closer. I mean it. I know how to use this." With her thumb, she pulled back the hammer.

"Another benefit of your much-prized college education?" he taunted.

"I do know that this is a Webley. It is a top-breaking six-shot revolver. It is fully loaded. I never claimed to be a great marksman, but I can get off four shots before you reach me, and at least two will hit you."

The colonel decided to take her at her word and tried another tack. "Lady Frances, do you realize what you're doing? Do you know how serious a crime it is to hold a man at gunpoint? I renew my offer—put the gun down, leave me the manuscript, and on my word of honor, I will forget this entire incident."

"I'm not leaving without it."

"If you kill me, how could you possibly explain it?"

But Frances had worked that out. "I'll tell the constables you tried to have your way with me when I made a friendly call. Mallow will bear witness. I grabbed the gun and shot you in panic. You'll get an unmarked grave. I'll probably get a medal."

"Have you lost all reason? One thing you can say for the Seaforths is that they were all men of reason."

Frances just smiled. It was as if she was in some sort of dream. But despite the air of unreality, she felt in control. The colonel was helpless.

"I'm a woman. And aren't all women completely unreasonable and incapable of logical thought?" she asked rhetorically. "But I found this manuscript, didn't I? And now I'm thinking of the Sapphire River, the men who died there, and mostly of Danny Colcombe, who lived but was never the same—to the day he was murdered. This manuscript is for them."

Now the colonel looked nervous, and Frances took some satisfaction in that.

"Whatever you think I did, I committed no murder."

"Maybe not directly. But men died because of this manuscript, and you must accept some blame. And you're a thief and blackmailer." The gun was heavy in her hands, even balanced on the box, and it was hard to hold as her hands started to sweat. "We'll discuss your sins another time. I want to leave. Step away from the door, Colonel. Mallow and I are going home."

She was wondering if the colonel would rush her, but instead he twisted around and, before she could react, turned the key in the lock and pocketed it. Then he gave her a nasty smile.

"Lady Frances, I do believe if I attacked you that you would shoot me dead. But you won't shoot in cold blood. The only way to leave this house is by killing me right where I stand and removing the key from my corpse. And not even you would do that."

They just stared at each other for a few moments, Frances with a look of determination, the colonel with a slight smile.

"It seems we are at an impasse," said Frances. She had not expected the locked door trick, but she still had a card to play. She still held the ace of trumps.

"A suggestion, Lady Frances. You claim ownership of the manuscript. So do I. You gambled that whoever removed the manuscript from the Colcombe house would keep it for the power it has, and you were right. This would seem to be a matter for the courts to decide. We'll call a constable. He'll take charge of the manuscript, and his superiors will hold onto it until a judge can decide. If you believe you are right, you will win. What can be fairer than that?"

That would suit you so well, thought Frances, *having a kindly old bobby come in, take the revolver away, and take the manuscript away. "No need for any fuss, just give the papers back to the nice colonel. He won't even press charges." An agreement that she was just a little overwrought, that's all; nothing a few weeks in the country won't cure. What can you expect from a woman? They're so emotional . . .*

Frances was furious. But she remained cool. *Very well then— send for a bobby.*

"I agree, Colonel," said Frances. "A fair solution. As your telephone is outside of this suite, and your man is out, may I suggest we send my maid Mallow to fetch a bobby?"

Mountjoy's eyes narrowed. "Why should I trust your maid?"

"For heaven's sake, she's a *maid*. Surely you grew up with them. They do what they're told, and that's all. If I tell her to get a bobby, she'll get a bobby, not board the *HMS Dreadnought* and take charge of a company of Royal Marines."

Colonel Mountjoy mulled over that. "Very well. I will open the door and let your maid out and lock it again. And you will try not to shoot me. Do we have an agreement?"

"Mallow—" She looked right into her maid's eyes. "—you heard what the colonel said, didn't you? Fetch a constable."

"Yes, my lady." Her voice was steady as she stood and met her ladyship's eye.

"There's usually a constable just around the corner," said Mountjoy. Mallow ignored him. *My goodness*, thought Frances. *I've never seen Mallow actually snub someone. Good for you.*

"She knows what to do," said Frances. "Mallow, take my purse."

"Why should she need money?" asked a suspicious Mountjoy.

"Do use your head, Colonel. A young maid tries to convince a constable that the daughter of a marquess is holding a British army officer at gunpoint. We'll be lucky if he doesn't send her to Bedlam. He may want to consult his superiors at his station, and I'll want Mallow to take him there by hansom, for speed."

"Very well," said Mountjoy cautiously. Mallow picked up Frances's bag.

Meanwhile, Mountjoy produced the key and Mallow took a step to the door.

"Colonel, lay one hand on her and I will shoot you."

"And I thought servant-mistress loyalty died with the old Queen," he said. He quickly opened the door just wide enough for Mallow to slip out and then closed and locked it behind her.

Mallow's heart was pounding, and she felt she could hardly breathe. Walking as fast as she could, she headed along the street, where, as the colonel said, there was a bobby at the corner. She paused for a moment, then continued past him to the next street, where she found a hansom. She realized that this was the first time she had ever ridden in one by herself.

"Scotland Yard," she said. "And I'll pay extra if you can get there in under ten minutes."

The driver laughed and snapped his whip. Mallow leaned back in her seat. There was one police officer that her ladyship really seemed to respect, and Mallow prayed she was making the right decision.

Despite some near-accidents, the driver earned his extra fee, and Mallow walked quickly into police headquarters. At first, it seemed simple. Just fetch the inspector. However, once in the reception area at Scotland Yard, she was overwhelmed. It wasn't like when they visited Superintendent Maples. Everyone seemed so busy, and the constables behind the tall counter looked large and imposing. How could she possibly get their attention? She wished she had Miss Garritty with her. No one intimidated her. Or better yet, Miss Pritchard, the maid to the old marchioness, Lady Frances's mother. There was a reason the junior maids called her the "Tigress." She had once given a tongue-lashing to a lazy railroad porter that had become the stuff of legend.

Well, thought Mallow, *I too am a lady's maid, just like them, only somewhat younger. I too serve a lady. And I too don't have to put up with insolence.*

She took a breath and headed to where a constable was filing papers.

"Excuse me, Constable, but I have urgent business with Inspector Benjamin Eastley of Special Branch. Kindly direct me to his office."

He looked at her with some amusement, taking in her plain dress and working-class accent—no doubt someone's maid to report a lost toasting fork or something like that.

"Perhaps you could just tell me, darling, and I'll see what I can do." He gave her a grin.

Something popped. Lady Frances wouldn't stand for treatment like that. Neither would Miss Garritty or the Tigress.

"What you will do, Constable, is stop being impertinent and point me in the direction of Inspector Eastley."

She hadn't realized how loud she was. Several other bobbies turned, and the smile quickly vanished from her constable's face.

An older man, with sergeant's stripes on his sleeve, stood up from a desk toward the back and joined them.

"Now what seems to be the trouble?" he asked. The sergeant was not from London but had a soft, gentle accent from the West Country. Mallow wanted to cry, but she knew all hope of being taken seriously would be gone if she did.

"I am here at the request of my mistress, Lady Frances Ffolkes. Her brother is the Marquess of Seaforth. It is extremely important I speak with Inspector Eastley. And only Inspector Eastley."

"But miss—"

"Sergeant, am I going to have to speak with your superior?"

As her ladyship liked to say, in for a penny, in for a pound.

The sergeant hesitated a moment. "What is your name?"

"Miss June Mallow."

Everyone stared as the sergeant picked up the telephone and spoke for about a minute. Mallow held her breath, wondering if she was going to be sent to the inspector—or be arrested.

He hung up and turned to the constable. "Please escort her to Inspector Eastley's office."

My goodness, thought Mallow. *My goodness.* She looked at the sergeant as she followed the constable. What was on his face? Surprise? Anger? With a rush, she fancied it was respect.

But then nervousness returned. She still had to meet with the inspector, and as she gathered from her ladyship, he was an important man.

The constable smiled again as they walked.

"So, June, you work for some real toffs. That must be exciting. Why do you want to speak to an inspector anyway?"

"We don't call them 'toffs.' We call them 'my lord' and 'my lady.' What it's about is none of your business. And when you address me, you will call me 'Miss Mallow.'"

For the second time, Mallow had wiped the smile off the constable's face. He shook his head. When walking a beat, stealing kisses from pretty housemaids had been a perk of the job. But he wasn't going try on this one, even if she did have a sweet face.

Down another hallway, they found themselves in an open room where several constables were working, some in uniform and some not. Mallow's escort led her to a private office and introduced her to Inspector Eastley. He left quickly, shutting the door behind him. These Special Branch boys were a serious lot—a private lot—and there was nothing to be gained by mixing with them.

The inspector invited Mallow to sit, and she did, on the edge of her chair.

"So your mistress is so busy she now sends her maid to harangue me?" He seemed to think that funny. Mallow didn't know what "harangue" meant, but it didn't matter.

"Not at all, Inspector." Mallow had rehearsed what she needed to say in the hansom. "Lady Frances has found the manuscript in the home of a man named Colonel Mountjoy. He surprised us, and her ladyship is holding him at gunpoint. She sent me to fetch a bobby. And I decided to call on you, sir. I don't know how long she can hold him off, so you will have to come quickly."

Well, thought Mallow, *everyone keeps smiling at me and I keep upsetting them. Just like Lady Frances.*

"This isn't some sort of joke, Miss Mallow? Your mistress has an uncertain humor."

"Do you think, sir, I'd come all the way here to tell a joke?"

"The desk sergeant said you created quite a scene downstairs."

She continued to hold her voice steady. "My apologies, sir. But her ladyship's situation is serious."

They were silent for a few moments, as if Eastley was considering Mallow's account and the implications. Then he jumped up quickly, startling Mallow. He jerked open his door. "Smith, call for a coach then grab a couple of the lads, steady ones. We're on the road in five minutes. Miss Mallow, come with us. Let's see if we can stop this before your lady gets hurt. Or rather, before she actually hurts someone else." He found that funny too.

Before she knew it, Mallow was bundled into a carriage with the constables. *I did it*, she thought, *I really did it. My goodness.* Miss Garritty and Miss Pritchard may have more experience than she had serving their ladies, but one thing was certain— they never had to fetch a Scotland Yard inspector.

<hr />

Colonel Mountjoy seemed very pleased with the way things were playing out. His eyes followed Mallow until she was out of site, and then he smiled. "Now all we have to do is wait," he said grandly.

"Why don't you sit?" said Frances. "I hate looking up."

"Excellent idea." He made himself comfortable and stretched out his legs. "I really want you to know I killed no one. I know there have been deaths surrounding this—Major Colcombe and an Australian private in Rotherhithe. And other . . . incidents. But not my doing. I don't even know who did these things."

"I do," said Frances.

"Indeed?" He smiled.

"Don't mock me. I do know."

"Will you share your information?"

"Why don't I wait? I can explain it to the police at the same time."

The colonel bowed. Now he really was mocking her.

"I don't suppose that if I gave you my word I wouldn't assault you, you would put that revolver down?"

"No," she said. She gripped it tighter. It was so heavy. She had never held a gun for more than a few minutes. Frances felt her fingers cramp, but fortunately, the Colonel didn't seem to notice or care that she was in distress. *Please hurry, Mallow. Please do the right thing.* She glanced at the clock.

They lapsed into silence. Then Frances's ears picked up a hoofbeat. There was very little traffic in the cul de sac. Was it the police? Or just her imagination? No, that was definitely a pair of horses and a carriage of some kind. The colonel heard it now—he cocked his head, and they both heard it stop outside of the house.

"It appears as if it's not just a constable, but a wagon full of officers. Well, why shouldn't the daughter of a marquess, armed with a revolver, merit the full treatment?" He was practically jovial. "With your permission, dear lady, I will stand up and view their arrival."

"Of course," said Frances. Sweat was beginning to run down her brow again, and her fingers were in such pain, she doubted she could even pull the trigger now.

Frances couldn't see the window, but she could see the colonel watching with a triumphant smile—but it was wiped off in a second. His face grew very red, and then he turned on her. She didn't think that she had ever seen anyone as angry as he was now. Despite the gun, she almost thought he'd attack her anyway. But it didn't matter—Frances almost wept with relief. Mallow had come through.

"You—you—imbecile. You fool. You stupid little girl, interfering in men's business for your silly sentimental ends. Do you know what you've done? The mess you made—a silly, stupid child with not enough to keep her busy. By God, you'll regret this."

And there his rant ended, because Inspector Eastley, Constable Smith, and Mallow were at the door. Frances heard the rapping. The colonel ignored it, as if he had other options. The rapping became a pounding. "Colonel Mountjoy, this is Inspector Eastley of the Metropolitan Police. Open the door or I'll have my constables break it down."

With a final look of hatred at Frances, Mountjoy produced the key and opened the door. There was quite a crowd outside: the inspector, Smith, and two uniformed constables. One of the uniformed men Frances instantly recognized as the helpful constable when she was attacked in the mews—the one who wouldn't give his name. She smiled. So she was right about that, too.

And Mallow was strutting like a peacock. Well, she should. She met her mistress's eyes, and Frances nodded. *You did beautifully, dear girl.*

Also looking pleased with himself was Inspector Eastley. "Oh my, what a scene. Lady Frances, your maid here told us what was happening, but we thought it a gross exaggeration. I see she was completely right. I compliment you on a most excellent servant, a woman of great spirit. They'll be talking in admiration about her for months back at the Yard." He chuckled.

"I am glad to hear it, Inspector, but would you mind taking charge? This pistol is getting very heavy."

He laughed again. "Of course. You may turn it over to Constable Smith." Frances expertly uncocked the gun and handed it to the constable. It felt so good to be relieved of the weight, and she massaged her fingers. Smith then picked up the revolver and stuck it in his belt, like a pirate.

"Nicely done, my lady," said Eastley. "You continually surprise me."

Mountjoy, who was sulking throughout these proceedings, found his voice. "Inspector, you and your men saw this woman holding a gun on me. She was also stealing my property—"

"All in good time," said Eastley. He turned to the two uniformed constables. "You two can leave now. Tell the driver to wait at the corner and remain with him until we're done here." They saluted and left. "We're a little less crowded now. So Colonel Mountjoy, you were saying about Lady Frances?"

"I want her arrested right now."

"You will not!" shouted Mallow. The girl really was full of spirit today. "Her brother is the seventh Marquess of Seaforth." For Mallow, that said it all. Frances smiled.

"Thank you, Mallow, but that's not necessary. I won't be arrested today. The colonel would have to press charges. I do have that correct, don't I, Inspector? And he isn't going to." The inspector looked curious.

"Why won't I?" asked the colonel.

"Oh, it would be embarrassing for me to be arrested. My brother would be furious at me. Still, it would be just another day in the life of mad Lady Frances. But you, Colonel. The papers would be full of news about a distinguished officer like yourself being held off by the diminutive daughter of a marquess. I can't imagine what that would be like. But maybe you have a bigger appetite for humiliation than I expect."

The inspector laughed again. "She has you there, Colonel. I take it, then, there will be no charges? I'll assume that's a no."

"She still has my property," said the Colonel.

"This manuscript?" Frances pulled it out of the box. "It has Daniel Colcombe's name on it. Inspector, you may use the telephone in the hall to call the Colcombes, and they will confirm I am an agent on their behalf."

"Yes, I could, but I don't think that will be necessary. I'll take you at your word. Now, you, Colonel, do you want to make a complaint? I didn't think so." He clapped his hands together and rubbed them in satisfaction. "I think we're done here."

"May I have my revolver back, at least?" said the Colonel.

"Tempers are still a little high, so we'll hold it for now. Wait a few days and call for it at my office. Lady Frances, the constable and I will be pleased to escort you and Miss Mallow home. Colonel, I wish you good day."

The colonel was still furious but had mastered himself and had even put a smile on his face, although Frances could tell it was fake. As the two women headed to the door, he said, "You won today, Lady Frances. But you still have no idea what you've done, the people you thwarted. You made a lot of enemies."

"I already have plenty. A few more won't hurt."

"You were lucky, my lady. Next time you won't be. Next time I won't underestimate a Seaforth."

Frances spun around in the doorway to face the colonel. Mallow recognized the bright red spots on her ladyship's cheeks. "Underestimate a Seaforth? Don't flatter yourself, Colonel. Your mistake was underestimating a woman." Her eyes flashed to Mallow. "Let me change that. You underestimated two women. You'll think twice before making assumptions about ladies. Or maids. Good day, sir." And with that, they left.

It felt wonderful to be outside. The sky was overcast now, and it looked like rain any minute, but Frances didn't care. Just being out of that flat and holding the manuscript was enough.

"Smith, why don't you and Miss Mallow walk to the corner and return with the police carriage. I want a few moments with Lady Frances."

The two made a comical pair as they headed off: Smith was about ten inches taller than Mallow and twice her weight. But

Mallow looked on him with something close to favor. A police constable had actually become acceptable in her eyes.

"I got your message and informed the local police," said Eastley, "but the man has fled, and that would seem to indicate guilt. He was a lifelong soldier who had no doubt been in a lot of tight spots during his career, and he'll be very good at hiding and evading capture. But he's getting on in years and has a bad leg—we'll find him. Your reasoning was tight and clever, I must say."

"Thank you, Inspector. I take that as a high compliment. If you open the ranks to women constables, I shall apply and request you as my commanding officer. I am not mocking you; I am serious."

"I know. That's what frightens me. But ask your maid what she did at Scotland Yard. I'd be inclined to make her, not you, the first female constable." If he thought that would upset Frances, he was wrong.

"She's bright and brave and would always follow orders, which is more than you could say for me."

He laughed. "But to the matter at hand, you and Miss Mallow took a huge risk trusting me, but in the end, you decided I was on your side. So why didn't you come to me about Mountjoy earlier?"

"And if I told you I knew Mountjoy had the manuscript? There would be requests for warrants and all kinds of delays—meanwhile, he'd be alerted, and we'd never get it."

"Fair enough," he said, nodding. "But tell me why you trusted me at all."

"I knew you'd ask that. You were generally unhelpful and rude, but you never warned me off. You never fussed about my safety. You didn't really mind what I was doing. You wanted me to investigate this so I knew we were on the same side. You weren't encouraging about my theories, knowing I'd work all the harder to prove myself right. I was your silent partner."

He bestowed the smile of a teacher to a particularly good student. "Yes, you're right. I took a tremendous risk as well, allowing you so much free rein. I shouldn't have done it, but I needed someone who could go where I could not, ask questions I wasn't allowed to. Still, you surprised me tremendously—you were a lot bolder than I expected."

"Oh, but you were protecting me all along. I figured that out eventually. It was Constable Smith and others. I recognized the young constable you brought along today. He escorted me home after the attack in the mews." Frances explained how she figured out the whole thing—that a constable was watching over her and didn't want Frances to trace him back to Inspector Eastley, so he refused to give his name. Inspector Eastley and Special Branch had been protecting her.

"It was Tredwell who stalked me in the mews, looking for the manuscript. I had spoken with Audendale that morning. He no doubt spoke with Tredwell about it—the men were close. Tredwell instantly jumped on a train to track me down, feeling I had the manuscript. Your constable protected me in the mews— but Tredwell got away. And the man who insulted me in the Australian bar? Smith or one of your other minions struck him down too for using threatening language with me at the tavern. And I know it was Smith, his face hidden by a scarf, who intercepted me when I was in a carriage with Mr. Bramwell and who made sure that man will think twice about assaulting a young lady in his company."

"Nicely said," replied Eastley. "All Smith knew was that you were trying to escape the carriage and a rescue was in order. Your run into the night was unfortunate, if understandable. Just know this, my lady: it was an enormous gamble. We couldn't protect you completely, and I don't mind saying it again—you surprised me repeatedly. We protected you as best we could, but we couldn't direct you. You were the one who found out Tredwell was the murderer and Mountjoy was thief—I hadn't suspected either one. Mountjoy was always a slippery sort, but I wouldn't have thought this of him. Good show! In the end, you were smart, Lady Frances, and we were lucky. I shan't tempt the fates by doing that again."

Frances gave the inspector a delicious pout. "I'm disappointed. I would so like to work with you again, Inspector, but I fear we never will."

"My feelings are exactly opposite. I hope never to work with you again, but I'm afraid we will."

Frances was feeling good about finding the manuscript and the inspector's compliments, so she merely said, "If I thought you were serious, I would be deeply insulted. But I know you're not." And Eastley just shook his head.

The police carriage was approaching, which was good because it had gotten very dark and a few drops were already falling. The inspector helped her into the police coach as the sky opened to release a good English downpour. Frances took a rear-facing seat next to Mallow. The poor girl—Frances had put her through a lot. Some time off and a present were in order. The coach traveled to the end of the street where there was room enough to turn and slowly headed back to the main road.

Frances could see the houses as they rolled along. A man exited the little park. Probably he had been enjoying the warm weather, but now he was in for a soaking. He walked slowly and carefully. Why didn't he just run? He'd be drenched. Frances hoped his house was close by. Then she saw him ascend the steps to Mountjoy's building.

Oh God.

"Stop the coach—at once."

"Lady Frances, are you quite all right?" asked Eastley. Mallow was alarmed too.

"It's him—he's here. Stop now." Inspector Eastley didn't waste a moment. He stuck his head out of the window and ordered the driver to stop.

"You two stay here. Smith, come with me."

The two men stepped out of the coach into the rain, and although Frances remained inside, she leaned out of the window. The man at the top of the steps had used the door knocker, and now the door was opening. Colonel Mountjoy was standing there, and then the man pulled something out of his coat.

"Police! Drop your weapon and put up your hands," shouted Eastley. Everything actually happened fast, but to Frances, at the time, it seemed very slow. The man turned to Eastley, then back to Mountjoy. His arm went up slowly; his hand held a gun, and then Frances heard a crack.

It was Smith. He had pulled the colonel's gun from his belt and fired. The man tumbled down the steps, with Mountjoy staring stupidly after him. Frances thrust the box with the manuscript into Mallow's arms and raced into the pouring rain. With Mountjoy, Eastley, and Smith, she stood over the dead body of Sergeant Tredwell.

But there was little time to ponder that. The two constables on the corner came running, and Eastley had one of them remove Frances and Mallow in the police coach immediately. This was not an East End murder; it was a crime in a fashionable and expensive neighborhood. It would get a lot of attention quickly, and the daughter of a marquess could not be found at the scene.

The coach stopped at a hansom stand a few blocks away, where Frances and Mallow caught a cab: one couldn't pull up at a respectable residence in a police vehicle. Mallow started to give the order to go to Miss Plimsoll's, but Frances said no, they'd be going to the Seaforth house, the safest place for the manuscript.

She felt a little numb. The nerves, excitement, and that final bit of deadly violence had overwhelmed her. But better he should die with a bullet than with a rope. He had killed Danny and Private Barnstable, but Frances couldn't find it in her to hate him.

Leaning against the side of the hansom, she closed her eyes and listened to the rain. It felt as if her body was crashing.

"Inspector Eastley said you were quite impressive at Scotland Yard," said Frances.

"It wasn't that difficult, my lady. If I may be so bold, the inspector may have exaggerated in what he told you."

"I see. Well, you will tell me the whole story someday. I had of course hoped you would fetch Inspector Eastley, the one man we could trust. What made you decide to get him and not the nearest bobby?"

"You had spoken well of him in the past, my lady. And besides, I could not fetch a mere constable. It wouldn't be proper for the daughter of a marquess to have dealings with anyone ranked lower than an inspector."

Frances just stared at her. There was no trace of a smile on her maid's face. Did Mallow really believe what she had said? Or was she making a joke? She leaned back in her seat.

"One more thing, my lady," said Mallow a little tentatively, because her ladyship seemed so tired.

"Hmm?"

"I know it's not my place to say so—but oh, you were magnificent. You were just . . . magnificent."

Frances worked up a smile. "Thank you. But it would've been for nothing if you hadn't brought the inspector back so quickly. In a few days, we're going shopping, and I'll buy you as many skeins of wool as we both can carry. But right now, I do need you to tell the driver to stop."

"But my lady, we're not yet at the Seaforth house."

"I know, Mallow, I know. But the magnificent Lady Frances Ffolkes is about to be sick, and better in the street than the cab."

CHAPTER 18

"It was two crimes revolving around the same manuscript. That was the confusion. Once I sorted that out, everything fell into place," said Frances.

It was two weeks later, and Frances's appetite had returned. She was back in the cozy library at Hal's house, and Hal was looking admiringly at her over the remains of their dinner. She had started to tell it to Hal in bits and pieces, the story of how she had tracked down the manuscript and revealed a murderer, until he advised her to think like a lawyer and order her thoughts.

"You sound just like one of my college professors, and you're absolutely right. With multiple motives and unrelated culprits, it's still hard to make sense of it. But everything goes back to Danny Colcombe's manuscript.

"The rumors of the manuscript permeated London's military community thanks to comments Danny had made both to other officers and to enlisted men who had served under him." Colonel Mountjoy, she explained, wanted to use the manuscript, and the rumors surrounding it, for political ends, to blackmail for power. Even before he had his hands on the manuscript, Mountjoy visited the general to see if maybe Colcombe had shared portions of it with him.

"But I thought the general was an innocent party here?" said Hal.

"Oh, he was. But he felt very guilty that he had been forced to yield to his superiors in London and send the Empire Light Horse into a battle they couldn't win. He knew some of the rank and file hated him for that. He saw the publication of Colcombe's book as an act of atonement, so he supported it. Mountjoy probably told him he'd like to help the book get published, as a fellow officer."

"And that's when Tredwell entered the picture?" asked Hal.

"Yes. Tredwell had spent his entire life serving the general. Mountjoy's visit, plus rumors he had heard from other soldiers he had served with, made him obsessed with the idea of quashing the manuscript and protecting the general's reputation.

"Mountjoy hadn't counted on Tredwell visiting Danny to see if he could stop its publication. And Danny probably kept odd hours and invited anyone in. Tredwell showed up, an argument ensued, and no one heard the gunshot in that part of the house. Tredwell staged it to look like a suicide or accident. But he was illiterate. Danny had dozens of manuscripts, and Tredwell couldn't tell which one to take. He had to leave without it. Then the adaptable Mountjoy took advantage of the chaos following his death by paying a call, picking the lock, and stealing it, free to proceed with his blackmail plans."

Franny continued. "But for the short term, at least, Mountjoy didn't want any attention focused on him. He was a member of the Secret Service. He dropped a quiet word to Mr. Bramwell and the Heathcote circle that he heard I had the manuscript. It was rather clever, actually. I was known to be in the Colcombe house, and the families were friends. It wasn't too hard to believe."

"While Tredwell was still looking for it."

"Yes. He hadn't given up. He heard Barnstable was making a fuss about the manuscript, so he killed him, too. It was easy.

No one would expect a retired, crippled soldier to commit two murders, no matter how upset he seemed. Enter Inspector Eastley of Special Branch, called in to solve a possible murder with political repercussions, thanks to the missing manuscript. The inspector knew that because of my place in Society, my connections, I could uncover things and ask questions the police could not. But he was watching over me."

"I don't know if I approve of him using you that way," said Hal, frowning. Frances should've bristled at his protectiveness, but it came out rather endearing.

"But don't you see? He trusted me; he depended on me. He had few people he could trust. Colonel Mountjoy was in the Secret Service, also under the authority of the Home Office, and was privy to certain Home Office information. Eastley didn't know who else in the Home Office might be loyal to Mountjoy rather than to the Metropolitan Police."

"He chose well," said Hal gallantly. "But how on earth did you discover Mountjoy was with the Secret Service?"

"Men can be very careless around women. It can be advantageous to be thought silly and stupid." That had been another clue. Colcombe had joked about the men who rode by night, a similar image to the Shadow Boys—a nickname Colcombe would've known. At some point, he told Barnstable to beware of men who worked in the dark. The Secret Service and the Boers both worked in the dark.

"And Mountjoy made another mistake. He assumed I'd trust him because he was one of us, because he belonged to my brother's club. But I fancy myself a judge of character, and Eastley seemed to be an honest man, working class or not."

"And Lord Gareth Blaine? What was his role?" He pretended to be casual, but she saw him watch her closely.

"What makes you think he was involved?"

"You know I act for his family as I do for yours. I know whom he associates with. The Heathcotes thought you had the manuscript, thanks to the colonel. Lord Gareth was assigned to make a deal with you."

"Yes. They truly believed I had the manuscript. It was worth the effort they put into it if they thought there was a chance to obtain it."

She tried not to show the hurt. But she still felt Hal's eyes on her. He was an amiable man, but he hadn't become one of the most respected solicitors in London without being able to read people.

She was lost in thought for a moment, and Hal used the break to reach for a copy of the *Times* from the sideboard.

"I assume you've seen this article? The commissioner of the Metropolitan Police has issued letters of commendation for Inspector Eastley and Constable Smith for stopping a 'dangerous madman' from assassinating Colonel Mountjoy. They left out your role, dear Franny."

She suppressed a shudder. "Can you imagine if Charles had found out about my involvement with that? Or what would've happened to Eastley if his superiors learned he had formed a partnership with the daughter of a marquess? I'm delighted he and Smith were honored and pleased I didn't come into it."

"Ah, but you left out the key part. How did you get Mountjoy to give up the manuscript?"

Yes, that was the tricky part. Charles had asked her the same thing—how exactly had the manuscript come into her possession? She had been deliberately vague with him—and was now vague with Hal.

"I used my strong persuasive skills to convince him of the error of his ways," she said.

"Franny, I'm trained in the law. Do you really think you can get a lie by me?"

"Oh, very well. If you want the truth—I seized the manuscript at gunpoint." She looked him full in the eye, and Hal turned serious.

"Others would think that was a joke. But I actually believe you," he said.

"You flatter me," said Frances—and changed the subject. "The *Times* had one thing right—Tredwell was a dangerous madman by that point, obsessed with protecting the general's honor and killing everyone with a connection to the manuscript. It was no coincidence he was there that day—I think he followed me hoping I'd lead him to Mountjoy, who didn't give out his home address readily, only his club address. I think Tredwell had concluded by that point that Mountjoy had the manuscript, perhaps because I was clearly still looking for it."

"And at some point, General Audendale realized what his old sergeant was doing, didn't he?"

"Yes. They had been together a long time, and eventually, Audendale realized just how disturbed the man had become, trying to protect his master's reputation without any sense of reason. Tredwell may have been very vocal in his defense—some of the Empire Light horsemen blamed Audendale, which would've enraged Tredwell. He probably began by suspecting Tredwell in Colcombe's death. And with Barnstable's death, he became certain. That's what broke him—murders committed by a man he had trusted above all others and on his behalf."

"Men with the highest motives. And the lowest."

"It was honor run amok, Hal. Tredwell, who should've been enjoying a quiet retirement in the local pub, was out murdering for the general's reputation, which Audendale himself didn't even care about. Private Barnstable, who should've been tending to flocks of sheep in Australia, died trying to honor the wishes of an officer he served under. And Danny Colcombe died trying to restore honor to the Empire Light Horse. The whole thing was revolting."

All of them should be alive instead of trying to settle a past, trying to bring some sort of end to a pointless war that everyone just wanted to forget. Dear Danny—it hit her in the heart—Danny, finally hopeful again for the future.

"You miss him terribly, don't you?" asked Hal. She saw sympathy and understanding in his eyes, not the sort of amused condescension most men used for women's outbursts.

She started to cry, but Hal was there for her, and he knew not to say anything for a while.

"I'm a fool," she said. "A sentimental fool." Frances dried her eyes and looked at Hal. Was that amusement in his eyes? No, just sympathy.

"What you felt, you felt deeply, and that was the source of your courage and strength. The only foolish thing would be to feel shame for those feelings."

Hal really did always know the right thing to say.

Frances gave one last sniff. "That was kind of you. But nothing can excuse dragging my poor maid Mallow through this."

"I daresay the girl enjoyed the adventure," said Hal with a wry smile.

"You may be right. She has some hidden depths. The next day, I apologized and thanked her profusely. And do you know what she said? 'That's quite all right, my lady. Working for you has its compensations.'"

Hal laughed. "Quite a pair of adventuresses you two are! However, I don't think your brother will be so easy to soothe."

At that, Frances frowned. "No, he said he knew I was more involved than I was willing to admit and was going to ask around until he found the truth. Meanwhile, he told me he had showed some portions of the manuscript around Whitehall, and there has already been talk of change and modernization. He said he had Mrs. Colcombe's permission to arrange for full publication, and Danny was going to get a posthumous Victoria Cross for heroism. That's all good, but I was wondering what happened to those involved. I can hardly ask Charles."

"I can help you there," said Hal. "I'm not without contacts myself." True enough. A Society solicitor would have as many connections as a marquess. "First, you will be glad to hear that the Conservative Party has decided to cut ties with Mr. Bramwell. You'll be reading in the next few days that he will be 'resigning for reasons of health' and leaving London. He'll never serve in office again and will live in well-deserved obscurity in the country."

"And Colonel Mountjoy?"

Hal sighed. "I'd like to see him prosecuted for theft, but it would be a hard case to make—he could claim Colcombe gave him the manuscript, and Mrs. and Miss Colcombe would need to testify, which they'd hate to do. But it's not all a loss. His masters in the Home Office are furious with him, and he was exiled. He was sent to New Zealand, as far away from the seats of power as possible, with some vague military attaché title. His career is also over."

"New Zealand is very appropriate, actually. I hope the colonel thinks of me every election day—women have the vote there, and it amuses me to imagine him watching women line up at the polls."

Hal laughed.

"One more thing," said Frances. "I am planning to write to Dorothy. I think it's time she introduced her son to his family."

"Franny—" He fixed her a look.

"What?" Frances was wide-eyed innocence. "Of course I will keep her secret. But I can use my powers of persuasion to explain how delighted the Colcombe ladies would be with a grandchild and nephew. As well-bred women, they'd happily ignore the circumstances of conception."

"You may be right," he said, cautiously.

"I know I am."

Hal nodded, and Frances watched him think. The subject of romance had come up.

"Franny, I know I have no right to ask. But nevertheless, I want to know if I am wasting my time. Where do we stand? In short, may I continue to court you?"

Frances put her hand on his. "Yes, Hal. You can court me, and you're not wasting your time. You and I will continue to be friends—special friends," said Frances. "And we shall see how our . . . friendship grows over time. But as I said before, there are things I want to do before I get married. I am not ready yet, and I hope you can accept that." Frances peered at him closely and watched him think of a response. She had deep feelings for Hal, but she couldn't get married yet, couldn't settle down to worry about hiring scullery maids and presiding over tea with the vicar.

"If I can continue to spend time with you, then I will be satisfied, dear Franny." And smiling like a little boy, he leaned over the table and gave her a gentle kiss. *He wants to know why I chose him over Lord Gareth*, Franny thought. But she wasn't going to tell him, at least not yet. It had been a somewhat awkward meeting with Gareth yesterday. She'd told him that she forgave him but that they were not well suited to each other.

She was indeed an adventuress, she thought with a certain pride, and she would be better matched with a man who complemented her rather than one who was similar to her. Gareth had seemed upset, but he would recover, rather more quickly than he realized, she thought ruefully. The point was that Hal was kind. And kindness seemed a lot more important than it had several weeks ago.

"I do so love you, Franny." And Hal kissed her again even more warmly—just as a maid walked in carrying a silver salver. Hal instantly pulled back, and Frances watched the maid: her face was composed, but there was amusement in her eyes.

"I do beg your pardon, sir. But you have a visitor, and he says it's most urgent."

Hal glared and took a card from the tray. He smiled wryly. "It seems that your brother has decided to pay me a visit."

"At this hour?" asked Frances. No one made calls this late unless it was very urgent indeed.

"I showed him into your study, sir," said the maid. Hal muttered a thanks and told her to tell Lord Seaforth he'd be there momentarily. When she was gone, Hal passed the card to Frances, who read the brief note on the back.

"Mr. Wheaton—may we discuss my sister?" So Charles wasn't just teasing anymore. He was concerned about Hal's intentions. Or maybe his researches had paid off and he really wanted to find out if Hal knew she was brandishing firearms at members of His Majesty's Secret Service. Or partnering with Special Branch.

Or all of the above.

Hal took back the card and patted her hand. "I'll go see him. Stay here and have some dessert. There's no need for him to know you're here at this moment."

"I'm coming with you," she said crisply. "This is really quite ridiculous of him. He's becoming more like our father every day, and it's time I had strong words with him." She had red spots on her cheeks.

"Franny, as your suitor, and for that matter, as your solicitor, I suggest you let me handle this."

"Now you're being ridiculous, too. You two men will probably do something stupid like get into a duel over me."

"Hardly. We'll discuss this like rational men. And dueling went out of fashion in your grandfather's day. It's the twentieth century."

"I don't need a reminder of what century this is." It was going to be *her* century. "Now if I know my brother, he's pacing back and forth, and if we don't see him soon, he'll wear a hole in your carpet."

And without further comment, she stood and began walking toward the study so briskly that Hal had to scramble to catch up.